CARCONNE MOUNTAINS
KARRATHAR
MORTISIAN
BASE
To Lorn

YARRICK

IMPERIAL CREED

By the same author

YARRICK: CHAINS OF GOLGOTHA
A Commissar Yarrick novella

THE DEATH OF ANTAGONIS
A Space Marine Battles novel

Short fiction by David Annandale appears in:

SPACE MARINES
Edited by Christian Dunn, Nick Kyme and Lindsey Priestley

THERE IS ONLY WAR
Edited by Christian Dunn, Nick Kyme and Lindsey Priestley

DEATHWATCH: XENOS HUNTERS
Edited by Christian Dunn

More Imperial Guard from Black Library

HONOUR IMPERIALIS
(Contains the novels *Cadian Blood, Dead Men Walking* and *Redemption Corps*)
Aaron Dembski-Bowden, Steve Lyons and Rob Sanders
(Coming 2014)

FIRE CASTE
Peter Fehervari

COMMISSAR
Andy Hoare

GAUNT'S GHOSTS: THE FOUNDING
(Contains books 1-3 in the series: *First and Only, Ghostmaker* and *Necropolis*)
Dan Abnett

CIAPHAS CAIN: HERO OF THE IMPERIUM
(Contains books 1-3 in the series: *For the Emperor, Caves of Ice* and *The Traitor's Hand*)
Sandy Mitchell

A WARHAMMER 40,000 NOVEL

YARRICK

IMPERIAL CREED

DAVID ANNANDALE

BLACK LIBRARY

For Margaux, with thoughts of our snowbank.

A BLACK LIBRARY PUBLICATION

First published in Great Britain in 2013 by
Black Library,
Games Workshop Ltd.,
Willow Road,
Nottingham, NG7 2WS, UK.

10 9 8 7 6 5 4 3 2 1

Cover illustration by Phroilan Gardner.
Maps by Adrian Wood.

A CIP record for this book is available from the British Library.

ISBN: 978 1 84970 602 5

Printed and bound by CPI Group (UK) Ltd, Croydon, CR0 4YY

It is the 41st millennium. For more than a hundred centuries the Emperor has sat immobile on the Golden Throne of Earth. He is the Master of Mankind by the will of the gods, and master of a million worlds by the might of his inexhaustible armies. He is a rotting carcass writhing invisibly with power from the Dark Age of Technology. He is the Carrion Lord of the Imperium for whom a thousand souls are sacrificed every day, so that he may never truly die.

Yet even in his deathless state, the Emperor continues his eternal vigilance. Mighty battlefleets cross the daemon-infested miasma of the warp, the only route between distant stars, their way lit by the Astronomican, the psychic manifestation of the Emperor's will. Vast armies give battle in His name on uncounted worlds. Greatest amongst His soldiers are the Adeptus Astartes, the Space Marines, bio-engineered super-warriors. Their comrades in arms are legion: the Imperial Guard and countless planetary defence forces, the ever-vigilant Inquisition and the tech-priests of the Adeptus Mechanicus to name only a few. But for all their multitudes, they are barely enough to hold off the ever-present threat from aliens, heretics, mutants – and worse.

To be a man in such times is to be one amongst untold billions. It is to live in the cruellest and most bloody regime imaginable. These are the tales of those times. Forget the power of technology and science, for so much has been forgotten, never to be re-learned. Forget the promise of progress and understanding, for in the grim dark future there is only war. There is no peace amongst the stars, only an eternity of carnage and slaughter, and the laughter of thirsting gods.

PROLOGUE

The doom began with Mistral. It would reach far beyond that system, and there are those of us who feel its effects to this day. But it began with Mistral. It began ten years before the arrival of a freshly minted commissar named Sebastian Yarrick.

Throne, was I ever that young?

The vector of the doom was Preacher Guilhem. Called to the Ecclesiarchy from birth, he had ministered to the manufactorum workers of Mistral for more than a century and a half, moving from one baronial holding to another. Only rarely did he preach in the chapels of the homes belonging to the great families. In all those decades, he had never sought advancement, and it had most certainly never been offered. He was one of the anonymous millions of low-level servants of the Adeptus Ministorum, those priests whose lives are a single, unending sacrifice to the glory of our God-Emperor. This did not make him a saint. I never met him, but Rasp would come to hear much about the man. He was a vicious old bastard. Defending the faith against the heretic and the xenos demands an indomitable rigidity, but Guilhem had reached a point in his life where holy dogmatism had become little more than bitterness and a generalized resentment towards anyone whose behaviour rubbed him the wrong way. Which, by now, had come to mean everyone. The men and women who worked the weapon forges of Mistral were drones, so exhausted by the end of their shifts that their demonstrations of faith, however honest, lacked the fire Guilhem demanded, and any shred of intellectual engagement. He responded with sermons whose spiritual worth had, over the years, been eroded a grain at a time until they had been reduced to a core of hectoring abuse. He had lost his calling, but he did not know it yet.

On the day Guilhem took the first steps that would lead to the deaths of millions, he spent twelve hours preaching to rotating shifts of workers in the chapel of Vahnsinn Manufactorum 17, on the edges of Hive Arral. It took the full twelve hours for him to remind every worker of that forge of the duties of faith and the unworthiness of the individual. Twelve hours of sermons, of projecting his voice to the back of the nave without the aid of a vox-speaker. It was deep night when, his responsibilities to Vahnsinn 17 discharged for the week, he set off on the long hike from the chapel to the hab complex where he would sleep for a few hours before heading off to the next manufactorum, there to begin the cycle again.

The paved route to the habs was circuitous, winding between several open-pit mines and immense materiel warehouses. Guilhem took a shortcut instead. He scrambled over slag heaps and wandered through a wasteland of dark red rock and eternal, corrosive wind. About a kilometre from the chapel he was walking over a flat, scoured plain, squinting against the incessant sting of dust. He'd taken this route before. The area wasn't a well-frequented one – the seams had proved unpromising. Because little work had been done here, he had no reason to believe the ground was unstable.

On this day, it was. The rock beneath his feet vanished, leaving only air. He dropped down a narrow chute. The walls battered him from side to side as he fell. He heard cracks that he would not know until afterwards were his left arm being smashed like porcelain. His head took so many blows, coherent thought was so much broken glass when he hit the bottom.

He lay where he had fallen for a long time, writhing. His lungs were flattened, and it was half a minute before his screams had any sound. Then they bounced off the rock, distortions of his pain coming back in his face. Hours passed, perhaps even a day, and the truths sank in one by one. No one would find him. Death would not be quick, but it *would* come, and it *would* be painful.

If he had not taken that shortcut, if he had walked two paces to the right over the plain, if he had broken his fool neck on the way down... So many *ifs*, so many moments that could have prevented the damnation to come. But of course he took that path. Of course he fell. Nothing was avoidable. Everything was preordained.

I've seen too much to have any real faith in chance.

I don't know how long it was before he heard the whispers. He must have been down there for a considerable span, lying broken in the endless night. I know something of what he went through. I have weathered my own such fall. What

I don't have for him is sympathy. He was the voice of the Imperial Creed in that small corner of the Imperium on that particular day, and his responsibility to remain true to it was no less than that of the Ecclesiarch himself. He failed in his duty.

Dereliction disgusts me. There is only one answer for it. And every fool who resents the role of the Commissariat should look to the example of Preacher Guilhem. He was one man. He was insignificant. Yet his failure had an incalculable cost.

His failure was not that he heard the whispers, but that he *listened* to them. Perhaps they had always been present on Mistral, waiting for a receptive ear. Perhaps they were called by the desperation of a weak man. What I know, and what matters, is that they offered Guilhem a bargain, and he took it. The man who had blustered and browbeaten all within earshot gave up everything he was sworn to uphold when faced with his own death. He was rotten, hollow, and his will snapped as easily as his bones.

He was also a fool. He gained nothing in the bargain. When he emerged from the pit, his body renewed, he had bought himself very little more time. He would be one of the first to die in the name of his new mission. And with every step he took towards the hab complex, the doom came marching for us.

CHAPTER 1

OBSERVE AND LEARN

1. Yarrick

I watched the deployment embarkation as if seeing one for the first time. There was a strong element of truth to that impression. During my years as a storm trooper I had taken part in many mobilizations, many invasions, but I had always been in the midst of the troop formations – one cog among thousands of others, marching into the drop-ships. Now, briefly, I stood apart from the great mass of the troops. I was on a balcony overlooking the loading bay of the *Scythe of Terra*. For the first time I saw the full spectacle of a regiment about to enforce the Emperor's will. The perspective drove home the magnificence of the engine of war that was the Imperial Guard. Below me was the 77th Mortisian Infantry Regiment. The sons and daughters of the dying hive-world of Aighe Mortis stood at attention in phalanxes of geometric perfection. They were no longer individuals. They were a collective entity, a massive fist as clockwork and unwavering in its precision as the limb of any Titan. I saw and understood how right and proper was the anonymity I had known before. I had been completely replaceable. I was still, only now I was required to understand *why*.

This was what I was learning from my new vantage point, in my new identity, in my new uniform. The peaked cap and the greatcoat with its epaulettes creating an imposing silhouette, the colours of authority and discipline embodied in the dress black and the crimson collar: this apparel obliterated the identity of its wearer as surely as had my storm trooper armour, or the khaki fatigues of the Mortisians. But where the troop uniforms merged the self into a force-multiplying whole, my garb stood out. Visibility was vital to the commissar. He had to be seen in order to inspire courage and fear. The clothes were the symbols of authority, of righteousness, of discipline. They were what bore the meaning of the rank. The actions that were carried out when they were worn had to be worthy of them, and were crucial to maintaining their power and honour. The actual individual under the cap was irrelevant.

So I thought.

I was not alone on the balcony. I was there with Dominic Seroff. Together we had been the terror of our dorms at the schola progenium. Smiling fate had seen us in the same platoon, inflicting terror of a different sort on the heretic and the xenos. Now, as I answered the calling I had felt for as long as I can remember, Seroff too had donned the black coat. I on the right, Seroff on the left, we flanked a legend. Lord Commissar Simeon Rasp had summoned us to witness the final minutes before embarkation. On a grand podium opposite the hull doors, Colonel Georg Granach held forth to the soldiers of the regiment, praising their faith and zeal, and prophesying martial glory.

'Tell me what you see,' Rasp said.

I glanced away from the troops, and caught Seroff looking my way. Each of us was inviting the other to speak first and get it wrong. The set of Seroff's mouth told me he was willing to let the silence stretch to embarrassing lengths. I knew his canniness. He knew my eagerness. I had already lost. It was simply a matter of recognizing that fact.

Seroff looked too young to be a commissar. He had somehow made it through our dozens of battle zones without picking up a single scar. He still had the face of a joker. With his blond curls struggling to push his cap off his head, I wondered how seriously troopers would take him as a commissar. I sometimes wondered how seriously he took his role himself. The contrast with Rasp bordered on the grotesque. The lord commissar waited, impassive, for one of us to answer. His eyes did not move from the floor of the bay, but I knew he was watching us both. His hair, now invisible under his cap, was a close-cropped and dirty white. His angular features had a youthful strength thanks to juvenat treatments, but they had also been sharpened by long experience. He did have scars. The most noticeable was a harsh 'V' that ran the length of his cheekbones, coming to the point just below his nose. It was a souvenir of an encounter with the eldar. The xenos who had branded him had not survived.

I took a breath, bowed to the inevitable, and answered. 'I see what I did not fully understand before now,' I said. 'In the Guard, the individual is irrelevant. It is the mass–'

Rasp raised a finger, cutting me off. 'No,' he said. His voice was quiet but drew attention with as much force as if it were drowning out the colonel's vox-amplified speech. 'If that were true,' Rasp said, 'there would be very little need for commissars.' He pulled his bolt pistol out of his holster. Holding the barrel in his left hand, he placed the stock in his right, keeping his fingers open. 'Not one of my fingers is strong enough, on its own, to hold this pistol and fire it.' He closed his fist, lifted the pistol one-handed. 'With all of them working as one, I am lethal.'

Seroff frowned. 'Isn't that what Yarrick said?'

Rasp shook his head. 'You are both missing an essential element. If I were to lose even one of my fingers, I could still fire the weapon but my accuracy and my speed would be compromised. Lose the thumb or the forefinger and I will be hard-pressed to do more than simply hold the gun.' His eyes, a cold blue so pale they were almost white, flicked over each of us in turn, judging whether his instruction was sinking in. 'Am I making myself clear?'

'The collective strength is created by that of individuals,' Seroff said.

'Ignore the importance of specific positions at your peril,' I added.

Rasp returned the pistol to his belt. 'Quite so,' he said. 'It falls to us, to *you*, to preserve the health of the whole by ensuring the proper functioning of the part. And should the finger be gangrenous...'

'Sever it,' I said, 'and take its place.'

Rasp gave a single nod. The lesson was over.

We listened to the rest of Granach's speech. He had moved on from broad considerations of regimental honour to the specifics of the mission. Or at least, he had pretended to do so. What he said was little different from any number of commanding officer exhortations I had heard, back when I had been one of the thousands on the embarkation deck. Granach struck me as working from a script, one he had trotted out many times before. He spoke with energy and enthusiasm, but his delivery was over-rehearsed. The more I watched him, the more I saw a man discharging a difficult but necessary duty, one he would be happy to see over and done.

Rasp grunted. 'Gentlemen,' he said, 'I hope you're noting the colonel's oratory. I have the greatest respect for his tactical prowess, but he is no rhetorician. What, in your estimation, is the problem here?'

'Too familiar,' I said.

A thin smile from the lord commissar. 'Precisely. How many times have you both heard the same vague thoughts, assembled with very similar words?'

Seroff shrugged. 'Isn't it all an inevitable but necessary ritual?'

A single shake of the head, as precise and emphatic as the one nod earlier. 'Is it necessary that the troops be addressed? Yes. But the address should never be ritualized. Its truth becomes robbed of urgency. It fails to inspire. Have you read the *Legomenon Victoriae* of Lord Commander Solar Macharius?'

I had. Seroff hadn't. He tried to bluff by looking very focused and interested, as if he were comparing a Macharian address to Granach's current effort and would come up with a cogent answer in another few moments.

Rasp wasn't fooled. 'Correct that lacuna, Commissar Seroff. You will see the true art of the military speech. Read but one address and you will be already well launched on a new crusade. When you stand before warriors, you must inspire them.' He made a sweeping arm gesture towards the deck. 'I know, as do you, that too many of those soldiers are, whether they know it themselves or not, politely waiting for Colonel Granach to finish so they can get on with it. That is not how it should be.' He favoured first Seroff and then me with a hard look. 'That is how it must never be when you speak. Your authority will inspire fear in the troops who fall under your eye. This is right and necessary, but it is *not* enough. The mere sight of you must grant them fire. And when they hear you, they must be happy to give up their lives.' He paused. 'At great cost to the enemy, of course.'

'Of course,' I agreed.

Rasp listened to Granach a few moments more, then grimaced. 'Word for word,' he muttered under his breath. 'These generalities are death,' he told us. 'Except in cases of necessary secrecy, tell these loyal servants of the Emperor why they are about to kill and die. Let them know the stakes. Give them a sense of purpose. Tell them why we are here. You heard General Rallam's address to the commanding officers. His style is rather too clipped, but he was precise.

'Commissar Yarrick. Tell *me* why we are here.'

'We have come, at the request of Cardinal Wangenheim, to suppress a heretical uprising led by Baron Bartholomew Lom of Mistral.'

A snort. 'True, but rather bluntly put. If you were speaking to your charges, you would find more of the poetry of war in your soul, I trust. I once heard you when I visited the schola progenium, Yarrick. I know what you are capable of. But yes. We have come to quell the turbulent Baron Lom.'

Rasp looked up, away from the assembly. His gaze drifted to the outer hull doors. He seemed to be staring through them, as if he could see Mistral turning below.

'Lord commissar?' Seroff asked.

No answer at first. There was a faint tightening of his jaw, the only sign of an internal debate. Finally, he said, 'You are political officers. You know this, but I wonder if you have grasped the full implications of that fact. Your duties are to guard against deviation. The realities will mean rather more. Necessity will drive you to swim in murky waters.'

He fell silent. He hadn't disclosed anything truly revelatory. He had articulated that which was never said, but understood by all but the most naïve. There was something else he was on the verge of saying. I hesitated before speaking, but as the seconds mounted in silence, I realized that the moment was slipping away. I decided to be direct.

No, that's a lie. I didn't decide. I have always been direct. That is my special curse. It is also, I know, why I have been seen as a curse myself. That's a thought to keep me warm at night.

'Are the waters of Mistral murky?' I asked.

Rasp made a noise in his throat, a stillborn laugh. 'So the local expression would have it. It's been years since I last set foot on its surface. But I would be surprised if matters have changed for the better since then.'

'They can't have,' Seroff said. 'Otherwise we wouldn't be here.'

'True. And yet...' Rasp frowned. He thought for a moment, and then his expression cleared. He had come down on one side of a hard deliberation, and was now at peace with his conscience. 'Gentlemen,' he said, 'this mission appears to be very straightforward – an insurgency that is beyond the abilities of local forces to contain, but that is nevertheless limited in scope. Our rapid triumph is a certain conclusion, and is therefore not to be trusted. When matters are at their most cut-and-dried is when you must be most wary.'

'On Mistral?' Seroff asked.

'Anywhere,' Rasp answered. 'Everywhere. But today, yes, on Mistral.'

I ran through questions in my mind, examined angles. I applied the lessons of my mentor. Assume the hand of political manoeuvrings, even and especially where none seemed present. What was the context lurking behind the rebellion? Why would Rasp be uneasy? He had been here before. That was an interesting piece of data. What did that tell me, then? A possibility dawned. 'Is Baron Lom known to you?' I asked.

The corner of Rasp's mouth twitched. He was pleased. Not just with his student, I think, but also with the opportunity to speak further. 'I have met him twice, and then only briefly,' the lord commissar said. 'But I was impressed. The family has a storied history of service in the Imperial Guard. I believe that certain off-shoots have even produced some inquisitors.' He had continued to stare at the far wall as he spoke, but now he finally faced us. And there was the hard, unflinching, evaluating gaze. It was perhaps the most visible expression of the qualities that had made him pre-eminent among commissars. Nothing escaped those eyes. Nothing was beyond their judgement. When I was pinned by that gaze, I knew to listen to his next words as though my soul depended on them.

'Heresy has no respect for reputation or family,' he said. 'I have seen it take root in the heart of individuals who had, until that very moment, been so free of taint as to be saints. No one is beyond its reach except the Emperor Himself. No one. So I do not suggest *for a second* that Baron Lom is somehow above suspicion. But…' The finger held up again, emphatic as an enforcer's power maul. '*But*... the fact remains that Lom's profile is not the usual one for a heretic. And the political waters of Mistral are of the very murkiest.' He clasped his hands behind his back. 'So, fellow commissars, my final command before we head into battle – eyes open. Always.'

Down below, Granach had finished his address to the regiment. The phalanxes turned and began to march into the drop-ships. It was time to go.

2. Saultern

He never liked the descents. Buckled into his seat, held in place by the impact frame, he was just another egg among a hundred others, waiting to be smashed if the landing went wrong. And every drop felt like it was going wrong. There were no viewing blocks in the passenger hold of the drop-ship, no way to tell when the ground was coming up or what was happening outside. The journey from low orbit to ground was a prolonged violent shaking in a metal box. All of that was bad. The worst, though, was the helplessness. He understood that the immobility was necessary to prevent a broken spine or worse, but his instinctual reaction was to revolt against the perceived imprisonment. For the length of the descent, he had no agency. His life was in the hands of forces beyond his control, beyond even his knowledge, and he wasn't even granted the illusion of having a say in his survival or fall.

Logan Saultern, Captain of Third Company, 77th Mortisian Infantry Regiment, liked this descent even less than the dozen other drops he had taken. That was because he was seated opposite a commissar. The man's name was Yarrick, and the fact that he was young as political officers went was no comfort to Saultern. He had those commissar eyes. If anything, he was worse than the usual watchdog. His stare was direct, unwavering, unblinking, and did not move until he had seen whatever it was he wished to see. Yarrick didn't look at Saultern for long. One glance, not much more than a second, and that was it. Saultern watched the commissar eye every other trooper visible from his seat. Yarrick favoured a number of them with an evaluation at least twice as long as Saultern's.

He was so caught up in parsing what that might mean that, for once, Saultern barely noticed that the drop had begun. He withdrew into a sty of bitter self-loathing. *That's how much I'm worth*, he thought. *A quick oh-it's-you and then we move on*. He had no illusions about his ability to command, just as he had no illusions about how he came to be a captain. The last of the great mercantile families had long since fled the decaying, played-out Aighe Mortis, but the children of some of the more clandestine relationships remained.

Occasionally, a flare-up of paternal guilt or some other sudden excess of sentiment would lead to random acts of largesse and the bestowing of favours. That had been Saultern's luck. Swept up by the last founding, his training had mysteriously been redirected to the officer class. He didn't even know what faction of old Mortisian money had ties with him. He didn't care. What mattered was that he had no business being an officer. He had survived the streets of Aighe Mortis by being as nondescript as possible, and he resented having that camouflage stripped away. The men he commanded made him uneasy. The sergeants terrified him. One, Katarina Schranker, was a veteran sergeant. Covered in the tattoos and scars of dozens of battlefields, her grey hair shorn to stubble, she made him feel like his actions were being watched by a compact tank. He had muddled through his missions until now, but he had been part of rear-line reserves in minor engagements. This time, he and his company were being sent out in the first wave. Intimations of mortality fluttered in his chest. Yarrick's lack of interest was further confirmation of his approaching demise. *He knows I won't be around long enough to matter*, Saultern thought.

The landing was a violent jar. The captain's teeth slammed together, and he bit through his lip. Blood poured down his chin in a humiliating rivulet. The bow of the drop-ship opened, becoming a ramp the width of the hull, while the impact harnesses retracted. Cursed, kicked and howled at by sergeants, men and women leapt up from their seats, grabbed their packs and pounded down the ramp into the early morning light of Mistral. Yarrick was among them. Saultern had no idea how the commissar had moved so fast. One moment he was sitting there, impassive, then Saultern glanced down to wrestle with unbuckling his straps, and when he looked up Yarrick was gone.

Saultern hurried to catch up. He wasn't the last out of the drop-ship, but was still far enough back from the main body of soldiers for his uniform to feel like a costume, not a mark of rank. Then, as he descended the ramp, he encountered Mistral's weather, and for a few moments all thoughts of shame and inability were swept away.

Mistral's rotation was very rapid. Saultern knew this. He also knew that the planet's days were only eighteen hours long. He hadn't realized what one of the other consequences of the rotation would be. He hadn't counted on the wind. It rushed at him from the west as he left the shelter of the drop-ship. It almost knocked him over. Close to a gale force, it threw him off balance, pushed and kept pushing. Its howl was a mournful white noise. There were very few gusts, just a constant battering, a stealing of breath and of sound. Everything else was muffled. Even the Leman Russ tanks rolling out of the next ship to the right had lost the intimidating power of their engines' roar. Saultern's vision was reduced, too. He had to squint to keep his eyes from watering. Each step was a struggle to move forwards in a straight line, and not stumble sideways. *How do I command in this?* Saultern thought. *Throne, never mind that. How do I* fight *in this?* It felt as if the wind were blowing through his head, rattling concentration. He clutched his cap, as if to keep what sense he could make inside his skull. He reached the bottom of the ramp and looked around.

The regiment was disembarking on a wide plain that extended south and west to the horizon. Its tall grasses bent and whispered eternal obedience to the wind. To the east, the land rose until it became a mountain chain whose peaks had been weathered into distorted columns and agonized claws. To the north were low, rolling hills. Into those hills was where the regiment was headed. That was where he was supposed to lead.

Waiting at the base of the hills were the locals: small contingents sent by the loyal barons. Altogether, they didn't appear to Saultern to add up to much more than a company. There were enough family liveries and colours to make the Mordian Iron Guard look drab. These men were parade soldiers, Saultern thought. They were nothing but plumage. They looked as ridiculous as he knew he was.

He saw Yarrick standing at the head of his company. For a moment, Saultern thought the commissar had already deemed him unfit and removed him from command. But the commissar was not charging into the hills. He was standing still, waiting. Saultern felt the man's eyes bore into his soul from hundreds of metres away. Still clutching his cap, he ran forward, shoving his way through lines of mustering soldiers, until he reached Yarrick.

'Captain Saultern,' Yarrick said. The greeting was clipped, formal, as iron-spined as the man who spoke. He saluted.

'Commissar.' Saultern returned the salute.

'Are you ready?'

Saultern wasn't sure, at first, that Yarrick had spoken. The words were so soft; how could he have heard them over this wind? But the commissar was watching him, waiting for a response. He was horrified to hear himself answer honestly. 'No.' He waited for the bolt shell that would terminate his command.

Yarrick did not move. His expression, such impassive stone for a young man, did not alter. He spoke again, still quietly, projecting his words over the wind to Saultern's ears alone. 'Are you willing?'

'Yes.' To Saultern's surprise that was the truth.

'Then lead.'

The two words were an absolute imperative. Saultern could no more disobey them than arrest Mistral's rotation. When his full consciousness caught up to his actions, he was marching up the slope of the first hill, his company behind him, Chimeras on either side, the tanks of Colonel Benneger's 110th Armoured Regiment chewing up the terrain ahead. The wind battered him from the left, while a stronger wind, given a shape in cap and coat, stalked at his shoulder and held him to his course.

3. *Yarrick*

It was easy to despise Captain Saultern. It would have been too easy to dismiss him. I hadn't expected the strength of my office to be needed so soon. Shoring up a quailing officer before the first shot had been fired was a bit much. The first shot could easily have been my own, putting down a coward. I'm not sure what made me pause long enough to think and look clearly. It might have been Saultern's absurdity. I do know that what saved him in the end was his honesty. Whether he intended to speak as he did or not, he did not dissemble, and to speak that one word, *no*, to a commissar, took courage, even if it was of an unconscious kind.

Rasp wanted me to keep my eyes open at all times. To be a good political officer meant having a deep understanding of actions and consequences. So he taught, and so I believed. His views were not shared by all the members of our order. There were plenty whose approach began and ended with merciless disciplinarianism. Rasp, however, was a lord commissar. Achieving that exalted rank meant being more than a blunt instrument. Seroff and I were privileged to receive his wisdom. We were learning that being a commissar meant reading currents.

It meant seeing what was really before me, not what I expected to see.

So Saultern was still drawing breath, and, for the moment, behaving like a captain of the Imperial Guard. Was sparing him wise? I still had my doubts. He was convinced that he was unfit to lead. If he was correct, was I condemning troopers to a needless death by leaving them in the command of an incompetent? I was trusting my instinct, which was telling me that a man with so few illusions about himself was less likely to act stupidly than an officer with delusions of superiority or, Emperor save us, a belief in his own immortality.

I had made the decision. I would accept the responsibility

for it and for its consequences. I would learn from what followed. That was the only way, Rasp said, to fulfil one's duty, to become a commissar in the truest sense possible. Observe and learn. Observe and learn. The mantra spun through my head, a resolution and a comfort.

Observe and learn.

We crested the hill. Beyond it, the land dropped sharply until it was well below the level of the plain. We descended into a valley only a few kilometres wide. The two linked Vales of Lom were an oasis in Mistral's desert of wind. Here, in these deep, sheltered declivities, the topsoil was not blown high into the atmosphere at the first hint of cultivation. Better still, rich nutrients carried on the winds for thousands of kilometres ran into the wall of the Carconne Mountains, and accumulated on the valley slopes. The vineyards had first been planted there twenty centuries ago, and the amasec they produced was the finest in the subsector. It was at least as big a factor in the Lom fortune as the family's industrial holdings.

The wind diminished as we moved lower down, but suddenly became shrill. It keened. Then I realized I wasn't hearing wind. Two of the tanks exploded ahead of me. The grey air was stained with the black teardrops of incoming heavy mortar shells.

My mantra changed.

Fight or die.

CHAPTER 2
THE GOLDEN VALES OF LOM

1. Rallam

War, General Allek Rallam had opined more than once, did not have to be complicated. Stripped of all distracting inessentials, it was no more than a simple exercise in arithmetic. 'Whatever force the enemy throws at you,' he explained whenever and to whomever he could, 'hit him back with that plus more. That's all you need. Don't come babbling to me about fancy-named gambits. Bunch of sad old tinsel covering up the fact that you don't know what you're doing, or don't have the salt to get it done. The plus-more is all you need. Nail the bastards with your plus-more.'

Today's assault was a perfect example, one that he looked forward to shoving into the face of that overthinking book-worm General Medar the next time they met. Medar would have to appreciate the conditions: the heretics confined to a clearly delineated geographical location, nothing coming in from the outside to add any variables to the demonstration. The territory of Lom consisted of two long, narrow valleys bounded by hills to the west and south, and to the east and north by the Carconne mountain range. There was only one practical route in, and that was from the south, driving the spear tip of his plus-more over the lower hills, down into the first of the valleys.

Inside his Salamander Command, behind the rear lines of the advance, Rallam leaned over the hololith table. Black icons of his forces were updated in real time as they moved over the three-dimensional representation of the topography. The enemy's positions were still speculative, appearing as translucent red. Rallam considered his opposition: one deluded aristocrat and the forces he could muster to his aid, backed into valleys with no easy retreat. Laughable. Barely worth the expense of the fleet's travel to this system. His regiments would roll over Lom and his heretics, crushing them like ants beneath the blade of a land crawler, scraping the ground free of their filth. And then he would have a tale with which to beat Medar over the head.

Two Leman Russ icons vanished. The vox chatter erupted. Rallam looked up. The noise leaking from the vox-operator's headphones sounded like screeching static. Lieutenant Jakob Kael, Rallam's adjutant, spoke briefly to the operator, then joined Rallam at the table.

'Well?' Rallam demanded.

'Mortar fire, general. Griffon shells, from the sounds of it.'

So the enemy had some heavy ordnance vehicles. Well, now. Rallam thought about that for a minute. Really, he couldn't say that he was surprised. Mistral did produce artillery vehicles along with infantry for the Guard, after all. To be expected that the heretics would find a way to get their clutches onto some choice equipment. It didn't change a thing. Not one. Too late to make any modifications to the main thrust of his strategy, anyway. His forces were committed.

He had a sudden mental picture of Medar laughing. He could hear the man's supercilious, more-educated-than-thou chuckle, saw him tapping the side of his nose the way he did when he really wanted to grind someone's gears. Rallam shoved the image away. 'The advance continues,' he told Kael, then addressed the vox-operator. 'Get me some Lightnings over those Griffons. I want those hills levelled if that's what it takes, but the advance does not stop.'

2. Yarrick

Every battlefield becomes an outpost of hell. Between the churning of tank treads, the trampling of boots and the cratering of artillery, the longer conflicts last, the more their landscapes come to resemble each other. But they do not all begin as devastated grey. It can be easy for soldiers to forget this, as they move from zone to zone, seeing nothing but eternal struggle, ruined cities, and ravaged, bleeding earth. They are reminded, though, on those occasions when they are present for the birth of war, when they are in the vanguard and arrive on the field of battle that, for a few precious moments, is still only a field.

I saw that on Mistral. I don't know if I can call it a privilege. I saw the Vales of Lom before they were destroyed. I saw the vineyards. The vines were huge, their grapes hanging several metres from the ground. They were planted in rows so regular and groomed they resembled oil paint brushstrokes. Their leaves were a deep yellow so rich that it graced the eye in the same way the amasec of the grapes would bless the tongue.

I can imagine standing on the floor of the valley, looking up at slopes that had been transformed into art. I imagine the pleasure it would have been to take in this sight, and how restorative the memory of such an experience could be. I can imagine these things, but I don't know them. I never experienced them. I was among the last to see Lom's beauty, but there would be no recollection in tranquillity of those images for me. When we witness the destruction of beauty, it is the destruction that we remember, that will forever remain the defining impression of a location. The beauty that came before becomes nothing more than the prologue to horror.

The shells walked the line of our forces. Geysers of earth and bodies shot skyward. Smoke rose from the slopes on either side as the Griffon mobile mortar platforms fired from camouflaged positions. A terrible hail fell, rocking the ground with concussion and flame. There was no shelter. There was no hiding from the mortar barrage. There was only speed and retaliation.

Fight or die.

The tank companies turned east and west. They brought their guns to bear on the Griffons while creating an avenue through which the more lightly armoured Chimeras and the infantry could flow. The cannons opened fire. They blanketed the slopes with shells. Fire raced down the vineyard rows. Smoke roiled, turning day into a twilight lit by the muzzle flare of great weapons.

I ran forward with Third Company. There was nothing for us to fight yet. The only strategy open to us was to get clear of the ambush's kill zone as quickly as possible. So we turned Lom's strategy against him. We were rushing towards him even faster than before. I glanced at Saultern. He was running hard, face set with the tunnel vision that comes with pushing through blind terror in the name of duty. He was being a Guardsman, but not a captain.

There was a slashing roar overhead. A squadron of Lightning fighters screamed past, the streaks of Hellstrike anti-tank missiles lancing the air. I saw a Griffon explode as it tried to evade its fate. It rolled down the slope, a burning metal ruin. The Leman Russ counter-barrage added to the toll. The mortar fire tapered off.

But not all at once. A shell hit close. The blast threw me off my feet. I landed face-first on broken ground. Wet things rained down around me. I was splattered by the life of the men in the centre of the blast. Skull ringing, cheeks scraped open, I pushed myself up. Saultern was nearby, sprawled flat. I hauled him up by the collar while Sergeant Schranker led a squad forward. Chimeras roared past us on either side. The air was thick with dust, smoke and exhaust. It was hard to see, hard to hear, hard to think. None of that mattered. The troops around us were staggering, trying to shake off the effect of the explosion.

'*Lead,*' I hissed at Saultern.

He blinked at me. I wasn't sure if he understood. Then he pulled his pistol from its holster and held it high. 'Third Company,' he yelled. 'To me!' He did well. His voice was loud. He was heard. He gave me the look of a man desperate to prove himself, to *me*, if to no one else, and he headed off, weapon still raised. The company reformed in his wake and followed.

I realized, at that moment, that Rasp's injunction to observe and learn extended also to myself. I had to know the nature of my own power in order to use it, and use it well.

The tanks caught up and passed us again as we reached the

valley floor. The Griffons had fallen silent. The slopes had become an inferno. Fire had spread from vine to vine along stalks as dry as kindling. There was a new roar in the valley now, and a new wind. They were the progeny of the growing firestorm. It was its own force, and raced ahead of us, devouring centuries of the vintner's art, exulting in its release by the genius of war.

Lom had drawn first blood. We had not been slowed, we had hit back, and his fiefdom was being consumed. As we approached the upward slope that would take us out of the first valley and to the yet-narrower pass that led to the second, we finally had our first sight of the main body of the enemy forces. They waited on the high ground, line upon line of infantry backed by tanks and APCs. The soldiers' uniforms bore the livery of the Lom family: a deep vineyard-red, marked by a diagonal slash in yellow and green. They carried the Lom banner: yellow sceptre and blade crossed over a field of green. It was, I knew from the background data, the same standard that had flown over the family's estate for millennia. Even from a distance, the numbers looked higher and the heavy support more substantial than we had expected. Lom was strong.

He wasn't nearly strong enough.

A taste flooded my mouth when I saw the traitors. It was sour, bitter-ugly and lip-curling. It was the taste of hatred. I felt a rush of energy, brought on by the need to bring the enemies of our God-Emperor to heel. It gave me the breath I needed to call out as I ran. 'Third Company!' I shouted, zeal sending my words soaring over the promethium growl of engines and the hollow, crackling voice of the fire. 'There stands the heretic in all his arrogance! Will you let that stand?'

'No!' cried the men and women of Third. The heretics' flamboyance was a contrast to the drab khaki of the Mortisians, but the nondescript nature of that uniform was misleading. Simply to survive the hives of Aighe Mortis was a victory. To leave their filth, corruption and poverty, and fight across the galaxy with discipline was an honour beyond compare. The Mortisians regarded any sartorial display of pride to be meaningless vanity, and beneath contempt.

In this instance, they were certainly correct.

'Will you let even a single soul among them draw one more breath?' I asked.

'No!'

'Then drive them from this place! Drive them from existence! *Drive them from the memory of man!'*

I knew that my voice only reached so far. But as we surged forward, tearing up the hill as if we were the fire itself, I felt like a ferocious electrical charge had seized the entire company, and beyond it the regiment, and even farther beyond it, the armoured brigades. It was as if the tanks themselves understood what was being asked of them, and leapt forward with ravening eagerness. It had to have been an illusion, my own crusader ecstasy finding itself reflected in everything and everyone around me. And yet, even as I abandoned myself to the fury, there was an analytical sliver of my mind that took note of the events, and was satisfied with my work.

Tanks exchanged fire. We had the greater number, but the narrowness of the valley here meant that we could have no more abreast than did the foe. For the moment, the degree of high-explosive devastation was equally shared. We took what cover we could behind the Leman Russ chassis. There was a deafening boom, and the tank before me halted. I threw myself back just before it exploded. The heat burned my face. Three soldiers didn't move fast enough. They were shredded by massive pieces of shrapnel. But there were always more of us, and we moved on, manoeuvring around the wreckage. The losses kept coming, and so did we.

Halfway up the slope, the charge came. Infantry from both sides poured out from the shelter of the tanks. The battle was primeval. Though we butchered each other from a distance with las-fire and tank shell, we ran for our foe as though we were armed with clubs. The tactic was war at its most basic and brutal. It was barely a tactic at all. It was a clash of animals, of insects, the pure collision of two forces. In the slaughter that followed, the only thing that mattered was simple physics. The Lom forces had the advantage of high ground. It gave them speed, and they hit us with greater force. But we had the numbers.

'Now!' I roared to the troops within earshot. 'We are the Hammer of the Emperor, and there is no resisting the force of our blow.'

They slammed into our wall, and we smashed their advance. We kept pushing and pushing and pushing forwards, our thousands and thousands giving us a momentum that could not flag.

Off to the side I saw Seroff urging on Seventh Company. And then I found myself in a hell of struggling bodies. I fired my bolt pistol point-blank into enemy faces, saw their heads disintegrate when struck by the mass-reactive shells. The fray became so thick, reloading was impossible. I used my sword. It was a good blade, of strong steel and vicious edge. It killed well. I moved forward through slashed throats and severed limbs. I was drenched in gore. I was barely sentient. I was savage, pure predator. The only reason I existed was to kill. I was making no speeches now. I was using my voice, though. I was venting an inarticulate howl, raging into the faces of my enemies as I tore them apart.

It is easy, in the heat of battle, at the height of righteous frenzy, to feel invulnerable. *What foe,* the warrior thinks, *could stand up to such an unstoppable force as myself? What foe would dare?* The delusion is a necessary one. It keeps us fighting. It makes us throw ourselves into situations where every instinct for self-preservation is crying out in horror. It is also dangerous, and it *will* get us killed if it lasts long enough. Often, it is the duty of the commissar to nurture that delusion in the troops. The soldier convinced of immortality will fight with a furious abandon. Enough such troops will overwhelm the more cautious fighters. And so there is a certain truth to the delusion. The collective is invulnerable. We were the Emperor's Hammer. We battered the enemy. We pushed him back. *We* were invulnerable.

The individual was not.

I was not.

My delusion was punctured when I slashed the throat of a Lom fighter and he fell, revealing another man behind him with lasrifle up and barrel aimed between my eyes. My knees buckled on instinct, and I dropped to an awkward crouch just as the soldier fired. The shot went over my head, killing the man behind me. My balance wavered. If I fell over, I was just as dead as if I had remained standing. My left hand held my empty bolt pistol. I jabbed it into the ground, barrel first, and pushed, giving myself just enough impetus to launch myself forwards and up, sword extended. I plunged the blade into the gut of the heretic. As I stood, I cut him open from stomach to chest. The lasrifle fell from his fingers as he slicked the ground with blood and organs. I yanked the blade free and strode forward over his body.

I was still fighting, but I had been jolted out of my battle trance. Details of the struggle began to register. I saw some similarities of design between the standards of Lom and those carried by the troops sent by the other barons to serve at our sides. The finery made the soldiers look ornamental, but they fought well. As they grappled with the enemy, the collision of colours drove home the fact that this was a clash of kin, and those were never simple affairs. There would be anger, confusion and betrayal beneath the surface of physical violence. And I was struck again by the size of the Mistralian contingent. It was too small to be effective on its own. Why such a tiny mobilization?

Rasp's words came back to me. Murky waters indeed. I had observed, and I would have to learn. There would be more questions to come, and I would seek answers to them all, but not now. There was a wounded Lom trooper before me, pulling out a frag grenade in an attempt to make himself a martyr to his cause. I sliced his hand off at the wrist, grabbed the frag and hurled it back towards the enemy lines. I heard the explosion and screams, but was already hacking at another foe.

We crushed them. The movement was slow, a gradual climb to the top of the pass, but we never took a step back. We crushed them as a glacier crushes the land beneath its weight. As we reached the mouth of the second valley, the inevitable turn of the war came faster. The Lom forces still fought, but they were in retreat. They were down to a handful of tanks. We had the higher ground now, and we pushed them harder, grinding over their bodies with treads and boots. The retreat became a rout.

They fled.

We saw them stream away: a clutch of doomed vehicles, and a large but diminished force of infantry. The sight fed our ferocity. Our cries grew louder yet. They were the roars of carnodons as they took down prey. We descended into the valley, pushed by the winds of judgement. The flanking inferno was those winds given form. We could taste victory. We saw the fire stretch ahead as if to capture our foe in its jaws, and we knew the hand of the Emperor was at our backs.

Before this spectacle my doubts, for the moment, evaporated.

We gave chase, cutting their rearguard down. I saw Rasp, standing in the turret hatch of the Leman Russ *Iron Mercy*. The tank was a Punisher variant, its primary weapon a gatling cannon. It was a vehicle designed to teach a terrible lesson to any infantry who had the temerity to defy the Emperor's will. The cannon's fire was a deep, rapid *chudchudchud* rhythm that scythed the enemy like wheat. Rasp was a statue in black, seemingly forged of the same metal as the tank. His sabre was drawn, and his outstretched arm appeared to be commanding every flesh-destroying round that spat from the cannon's muzzle. I couldn't hear what he shouted as the *Iron Mercy* thundered past. I didn't have to. I could *feel* the exhortation I saw him mouthing. His presence alone was inspiring. I knew all the hard duties that fell to a commissar, but before me was the epitome of what that office meant: to be the living exemplar of the honour of the Imperial Guard.

The upper Vale of Lom had a higher elevation than the first, and ended not in a gradual slope but in a cliff wall as the Carconne range hooked north and west. A waterfall plunged from the ridge a thousand metres up, falling with gossamer delicacy to disappear in an underground river at the base of the cliff. Lom Keep was nestled against the rock palisade. The wall around its grounds was a semi-circle, and the buildings appeared, from a distance, to be carved out of the mountain itself. The front gates of the wall were open, and the Lom forces passed through them. Our Demolisher tanks moved to the fore, their siege cannons already blasting chunks out of the barrier.

We maintained close pursuit of the retreating forces. I could see inside the gates. There was nowhere left for the heretics to run. They turned to make their last stand. This was where they would be exterminated. I expected the gates to swing shut at any moment, sacrificing the Lom stragglers to give the bulk of the troops what shelter the walled grounds could provide. They did not close. They remained wide open. For a moment, I laughed at the incompetence of the rebels. Then I realized that nothing they had done thus far had been stupid. They had, albeit briefly, held our hugely superior numbers at bay. Whatever I was seeing, it was strategic.

The enemy troops had left most of the space before the gate clear. The surface there was not rockcrete. It was metal. For perhaps five seconds there was a pause. Then the rumble began. It was a sound of the earth, lower, more profound than the surface trembling caused by our vehicles. Inside the wall of Lom Keep, vast blast doors, large enough for a hangar, rose from the ground on hydraulic lifts. They parted on either side, opening the way for the thing below to emerge.

A few seconds later, our tanks began to die.

CHAPTER 3
THE CRY

1. Rallam

He had come to watch the conclusion of the exercise. At this stage of an operation, when the inevitable was occurring, and everything was moving towards the foregone conclusion, a certain space opened up that Rallam was loathe to miss. For a few minutes, he barely needed to issue any commands. All the gears had been engaged. The machinery was running. Everyone, from regimental colonel down to squad trooper, had an assigned role and was carrying it out. And when the enemy was on the run, then there was nothing to interfere with the performance of Rallam's war machine. He could then allow himself the luxury of enjoying the spectacle of victory.

The Salamander Command vehicle had followed the infantry and heavy armour through the Vales of Lom. He rode outside the hatch, taking in the roar, smoke and fire of the conflict. He knew what Medar would say: he would go on and on about the artistry of war. Rallam found the man's intellectual disquisitions tiring, but in these moments, these special moments, as ephemeral as they were exquisite, he had to admit Medar had a point.

Midway along the downslope of the second valley, Rallam ordered a stop. They were a few thousand metres from the keep. From this distance and height, the general had a commanding view of the endgame. Rallam climbed out of the hatch and stood on the roof of the chassis. 'Lieutenant Kael,' he called. 'Join me, will you.' When Kael clambered up beside him, Rallam spread his arms wide and said, 'Well?'

'Very–' the adjutant began, then stopped. 'What's that?' he asked, pointing at the grounds of the keep.

'Throne of Terra,' Rallam muttered. He said nothing else, and he did nothing. The seconds marched by. He and Kael stood in silence. Rallam had had the sickening sensation of being witness to another rare moment, one so rare he would not live to see the like again. And there were no orders to give. There was no action to be taken. The machine was running.

Something was lumbering out of the ground. It was a good twenty metres high. Rallam did not know what it might be called. It had a vague kinship to a Titan, but it was no more one of the god-machines than were the ork grotesqueries Rallam had witnessed hauling their destructive bulk over the more nightmarish battlefields of his experience. It was, he thought, a madman's dream of a Titan. Mistral had heavy industries, but it was not a forge-world. The thing that rose before the Mortisian forces was precisely the kind of abomination the Adeptus Mechanicus's monopoly over technology was designed to prevent. It was what could happen if the attempt was made to construct a Titan without the proper resources, without the necessary components, without the knowledge, blessings and rituals of the Mechanicus.

The thing was not a Titan. It was a gargoyle.

It walked on four legs, jointed like those of a reptile. The legs supported a massive trunk. It had no head, though the top was rounded, suggesting the stump of a neck emerging from broad, monumental shoulders. Anti-air turrets surrounded the stump. Massive exhaust pipes festooned the torso like quills. There were four arms, one extending from each quadrant of the symmetrical main body. Its hands were weapons, and even from this distance, Rallam could make out that one set of fingers had the familiar silhouette of an Earthshaker cannon. The beast was at least partly forged out of the pieces of other vehicles. Rallam could almost understand how the *idea* of the monster could come into being. But the Mechanicus would never allow such a patchwork nightmare to be built. Yet there it was, real, functional, deadly. If the Mechanicus was not involved, how had this thing been born?

The speculation and the horror ran through his mind in the time it took for the walker, with ponderous, macabre majesty, to emerge from the ground. The seconds were sluggish. The event seemed to last far longer than it did. But when Rallam blinked his way out of the trance, barely anything else had moved other than the monster before them.

'Your orders, general?' Kael whispered. There was desperation in his tone, but no hope.

'Kill it,' Rallam said, almost as softly.

The walker's torso spun on a vertical axis. The hand with the single, massive cannon pointed uphill.

'Earthshaker,' Rallam said sadly. It seemed to him, even at this distance, that he was gazing straight down the barrel.

The gun fired. A piston movement of the walker's arm absorbed the recoil. Rallam saw the flash of the muzzle. He heard the scream of the shell. For a fraction of a second, he felt the explosion that killed him and his vehicle.

That was a rare moment, too.

2. Yarrick

The monster walked out of the estate. The gate wasn't wide enough for it, and it took a section of the wall down on either side. It spun again, bringing a different arm to bear. This one had six fingers, and each finger was a Leman Russ battle cannon. It fired two at a time. The sound was the beat of a giant's war drum: *buh-boom, buh-boom, buh-boom*. There were double hits on three of our tanks. Two of them died smoking and crumpled, the shells coming in diagonally on their weaker upper armour, punching in and killing the vehicles with internal blasts. But the third tank was a Hellhound. Its chassis disintegrated in the explosion. The inferno cannon spun end over end over the field, a crushing baton. Flaming promethium splashed wide. It was a fountain of agony, and the area for a dozen metres around became a hell of fire and screams.

I heard a new rhythm, a faster one. The anti-air cannons on the monster's shoulders had roared to life, sending up a cloud of flak at the Lightning squadron as it made its attack run. One fighter caught a round in the engine. It was blown to the left as it disintegrated, and cut its wingman in half. The others reached their target. The sacrifice was useless. The fighters had exhausted their Hellstrikes on the Griffons. The fire of their wing lascannons and fuselage autocannons glanced off the walker's upper armour as if they had been shooting a hill.

Another spin, and another arm. This one was upraised.

It fired a single rocket. As the missile shot skyward with no apparent target, I had a moment of incomprehension. I'm not sure if I really didn't understand what I was seeing, or if a horrified subconscious blocked the knowledge for mercy's sake. But then I realized what was going to happen next, and why the rest of the Lom troops had not emerged from the cover of the estate walls, and how few seconds stood between us and annihilation.

'With me!' I yelled, and raced for the walker. The gambit was desperate, perhaps lunatic, but there was nothing else to try. There would be no other chance, no cover, no escape from what was coming. I had never run faster. In the corner of my eye I saw Saultern sprinting beside me. Good. Both of us moving meant the rest of Third Company reacted instantly.

Eyeblinks after the launch of the rocket, troopers were converging towards the heretic machine. The movement was rapid. I wished I could hope that it was quick enough. In the sky, the rocket arced down and split into multiple warheads. It was a Manticore's Storm Eagle, an infantry-killer. If we were caught in the open, that would be an end to us.

The cluster-bomb payloads hit just as I was passing beneath the main body of the walker. There was a series of blasts in such close succession it sounded like a stubber the size of a mountain being fired. The world was filled with fire and wind. The kill was huge. It extended for hundreds of metres back up the slope. For a moment, the vineyard inferno seemed to stretch across the breadth of the valley, its two halves meeting to become a single gigantic conflagration. Then the flare of the explosions was succeeded by the shock wave and the choking cloud of debris. When the echoes faded, entire companies were turned into meat.

In less than a minute, our triumph had collapsed. Our lines were a butcher's leavings. Still behind the walls, waiting to follow the walker, the Lom soldiers resumed fire. What would have been a threat a few minutes before was little more than a distraction compared to the menace of the great machine.

I didn't think about the cost. I didn't think about where we stood. I thought only about what had to be done now. I fired upward with my bolt pistol, straight into the belly of the beast. Every soldier there with me started shooting, too.

Seroff had made it to our doubtful cover, and he shouldered his way to my side. 'Do you have a plan, Sebastian?' he asked. 'Because this feels like spitting at the sun.' He kept firing, though.

Of course we couldn't do any damage to the walker. I was taking another gamble. Whatever team was piloting the monster could not possibly have prior battlefield experience with its operation. Mistakes would be easy to make. Mistakes I hoped to trigger. 'The sun can't be distracted,' I answered. 'This can be.' There were no leg turrets. The walker's only weapons were the heavy guns and rockets of its arms. It had no standard anti-personnel measures. The mind behind its design had been thinking of large-scale attacks on distant armies, and had given no thought to close quarters. The machine was invulnerable to our small arms, but if we attacked as if it weren't, we might infect the humans inside with doubt.

Saultern, a few metres away, shouted, 'Betzner, light up one of the leg joints!'

'Sir!' the hulking trooper acknowledged. He shouldered his missile launcher, aimed, and let fly. The rocket streaked to the leg and exploded on the inside of the knee. I saw no damage, but there was a pause in the walker's actions. It hadn't fired since we had begun our attack.

Deklan Betzner waited while his loader readied another rocket for him. His eyes were flicking across the bulk of the walker, hunting weaknesses. Betzner's focus had an almost feverish intensity, as if the mere existence of the machine were causing him pain.

'Captain,' I called to Saultern. I gave him a quick nod of approval, then pointed at a new target.

He grinned. To Betzner, he said, 'The hand next, trooper. Take out the battle cannons.'

The Leman Russ survivors were firing at the walker now, and Betzner fired his other missile just as the monster's cannons opened up once more against our tanks. The rocket hit. It destroyed one cannon, and damaged the others. They fired anyway. My jaw dropped at the foolishness of the walker's crew. In the next second, the monster held a massive fireball at the end of its arm. The light felt like the Emperor's blessing.

The monster made a noise. I tried to tell myself I was hearing horns, sirens, some kind of mechanical alarm warning of damage. This was not one of the holy god-machines of the Legio Titanicus. There was no sacred machine-spirit to anger or wound. This was a heretical mechanical construct, gigantic in size and power but also deprived of the Emperor's blessing, gigantic in flaws. I knew all this. But the sound belonged to a wounded animal. It was a screech that resounded over the valley, drowning the din of the guns and firestorm. The obscenity started walking again, and its movements, too, were those of a frantic beast. The steps were unpredictable, their jerkiness clear even in a creation this size. We had to run to avoid being trampled, but we weren't being targeted. The walker was turning to flee.

It stumbled back through the gates, collapsing still more

of the wall as its arms waved in panic. The wailing continued, sounding more and more like a voice. The guns of the 110th Mortisian Armoured Regiment battered the monster. Our tankers had its measure now, and were exacting their vengeance. I heard the deep-throated note of the Demolisher cannon. Its blow smashed a great hole in the walker's armour, dead through the centre of its torso. The creature stopped cold, just inside the gate. Smoke and flame shot out of the rent and exhaust pipes. The monster's scream rose in pitch, and I couldn't pretend I was hearing anything other than true agony. My being thrummed with religious horror. There was a moral instinct to cover my ears. Many of the troops around me were doing so, and there was no shame in that action. There was, rather, a shunning of the unclean. I resisted the urge to block out the sound, sensing a greater duty to bear witness.

Observe and learn.

To serve the Imperium and its Creed, I had to know the enemy.

But when the thing came that was worse than the scream, we all heard it. It was so loud. It was so big. We heard the monster speak. The voice was broken, distorted, dying, and it was human. But what it shouted was not human at all. It came from a place of madness. It was language twisted against itself, words that tore the very idea of meaning asunder. To speak the words was worse than a crime, and to hear them was to experience a danger worse than anything else on this day.

The ripples of the words were so immense that the metallic groan of the walker's collapse and the explosion of its core seemed insignificant. Those events, though, did have meaning for the Lom troops. Many were crushed as the monster fell forward. Still more were immolated in the grounds-filling blast. My eyes were dazzled as if I had been staring at the sun. But I didn't notice.

I was rooted to the spot. The echoes of that cry seemed to grow louder by the heartbeat as my soul filled with holy dread.

CHAPTER 4

THE DISCOMFORT OF QUESTIONS

1. Yarrick

And when we broke from the paralysis into which that hideous prayer had plunged us, we slaughtered them. The final minutes of that war were a crushing victory, but we would never celebrate them. We might have toasted the actions that brought down the walker, if even they hadn't been tainted by the machine's death cry. But there was nothing song-worthy in the extermination that took place on the grounds of the keep. It was necessary, deeply so, on a number of levels. There was the strategic concern: the enemy had to be destroyed. There was the moral imperative: the heretic cannot be suffered to live. But in the burning intensity of the moments after the cry, we were, all of us, to the last soul, driven by something far more primal. Horror, disgust, revulsion, terror – they were all at play. Our deepest selves had been raked open by syllables beyond our comprehension. We had heard something we could not face, yet would always remember. Those words cast mountainous shadows over our psyches. They pushed us to seek salvation through annihilation. Perhaps, in the venting of our fear and rage upon the final defenders of Lom, we would calm the mounting spiritual storm.

I say 'we'. I say it with confidence. I saw my own terrified rage reflected on the face of every trooper and officer. I saw it on Seroff's. I even saw it on Rasp's as his tank roared through the gates. There are some passions that no amount of discipline can conceal. Though we killed with brutal ferocity, it would be wrong to say that we were like animals. No matter how frenzied the savagery of beasts, it pales before a killing motivated by religious fear. That is the special province of the human. I wonder if even the Adeptus Astartes know what it is to fight like we did during those terrible minutes. I have served for more than two centuries, and I know them capable of unspeakable carnage. I have seen the Blood Angels in combat. I have seen the aftermath of the Flesh Tearers' massacre at Gaius Point. But they do not know fear. We humans, we pitiful, weak mortals, we know fear. We know it intimately, in all its richness of texture and nuance. And we knew it that day. It gave our assault a quality of desperation. We weren't desperate to win. We were desperate to kill as brutally as possible, as if we could drown the memory of that awful cry into the blood beneath our boots.

We couldn't, of course. The cry would be with us forever. But we tried. We surely tried.

I barely used my bolt pistol. When I had relied on my sword earlier, it had been because of the near-impossibility of reloading in the worst of the close quarters fighting. Now was different. I could use the pistol. I could reload. The Lom forces were resisting, but the death of the walker had decimated them. The combat was not difficult, yet I chose to use my sword. I made the battle more of a struggle so I could exhaust myself with the killing of my foe. I had to feel the impact of blade against bone, the splash of traitor's blood in my face. I had to strike my horror down with hacking slashes. I saw many troopers using bayonets instead of las-fire. We finished the Battle of Lom in the ugliest way possible, yet I would never look back on that terrible hour with shame. It is not one that I look back at willingly, but what happened was necessary. We cleansed the land of the heretics. Then, in the calm that followed, there was space for us to find our centre again before we confronted the next shock. And we knew there would be a next one.

Smoke covered the aftermath of the struggle. It came from burning engines of war, and from the conflagration of the vineyards. It hovered over the valley, turning sky and air a grey-brown. It filled each breath, but stopped short of becoming choking. Our forces took the time to re-forge organizational units, tend to the casualties, and get a sense of where we stood. Granach, the most senior of the colonels, replaced Rallam as mission commander. And once we had found our footing, it was time to face what we had defeated.

The enginseers were the first to move forward again. The walker, though an insult to their creed, was also an irresistible temptation to their curiosity. They swarmed over its carcass, forcing it to reveal its secrets. Rasp stood with Granach near one of the legs. The lord commissar had his hands clasped behind his back. His left hand opened and closed twice. It was a signal for the benefit of Seroff and myself: *Come close enough to overhear, but do not intrude.* Once again, our mentor wanted us to observe and learn.

Seroff and I advanced to within a few metres of the two men. We faced away from them, looking towards the keep, and shared a tabac while we listened.

'A decisive outcome,' Granach was saying.

'You don't really believe that, colonel, do you?'

There was a moment's silence. Then Granach sighed. When he spoke again, I heard no trace of the rote, mechanical orator from the *Scythe of Terra*. He had been given the freedom to speak his mind by one of the Imperium's most feared political officers, and so he did. 'I wish I could,' he said. 'We have completed the mission assigned to us. We have crushed the Lom rebellion. Is it wrong to want that to be the end of the matter?'

'No,' Rasp said. 'Not wrong. Human. But this is Mistral.'

Granach cursed. 'I know it.'

'The mission was never going to be as simple as winning this battle.'

A mirthless laugh from the colonel. 'Your pardon, lord commissar, but that became clear to me back on the ship, the moment I clapped eyes on you.'

'My presence is not exactly the harbinger of good news, that's true,' Rasp said ruefully. 'A simple mission would be a waste of my time, and for that, colonel, I apologize.'

'I'd rather receive an apology from the bloody-minded old bastard who almost ran us into oblivion.'

I took a quick glance over my shoulder and saw Granach pinching the bridge of his nose, eyes squeezed shut as if warding off a headache. Then he straightened his head, adjusted his cap and squared his shoulders. He had allowed himself a moment of exhaustion and perhaps worse. Now he was ready to lead again.

'What are your orders, colonel?' Rasp asked.

'You're asking me?'

'You are the commander of these forces.'

'Yes, I am. And unlike the late General Rallam, I think I can tell when a simple application of force is not going to be enough to solve the problem.'

'Rallam would say there isn't one,' Seroff whispered to me.

I grunted in agreement. Lom defeated, job done. Time to go. We would already be leaving Mistral, having treated a symptom but not the disease. The existence of the walker meant things were far more complex than a simple rebellion. But Rallam had not been a man fond of complexity. He would not have been able to deny the monstrousness of the construct, but its total annihilation would have been sufficient to declare victory, as long as there were no other signs of something worse. Even though I knew better, I still found myself seeking comfort in the fact that the Lom soldiers had shown no sign of being corrupt beyond the fact of the rebellion itself.

'Your advice, lord commissar, would be most welcome,' Granach said.

'We should learn what we can here,' Rasp said. 'Then... Well, we'll see where that leaves us.'

'Colonel,' a voice called. It was loud, but not because the speaker had shouted. It was amplified electronically, and buzzed with distortion around the edges. I looked to my left and saw Enginseer Bellavis approaching the two men. The tech-priest was a veteran, long in the service of the Mechanicus. Very little of him was still human. His carapace sheathed prostheses, not flesh and bone. Most of his face was metal. His eyes looked like multifaceted jewels, and moved back and forth independently of one another, like those of a fly. The right side of his mouth was a grille, but the left was still flesh, and moved with a disturbing naturalness, though there was no longer a human tongue or teeth behind those lips. His lower jaw, though, was still untouched by bionic augmentation. It was a sinewy, leathered, jutting monument worthy of the most thick-necked, bull-headed sergeant. It occurred to me that if ever there were such a thing as an enginseer who enjoyed a good brawl, Bellavis would be it.

He approached the colonel and Rasp, the hum of servo-motors accompanying his metronome-regular stride.

'What is it, enginseer?' Granach asked.

'We have gained access to the control node,' Bellavis answered, pointing up at the hump on the body of the walker.

'And?'

'I believe you and the lord commissar should see what we found there.' His manner of speech was human enough, at least when it came to his diction. But there was the same mechanical precision to his enunciation as his gait, and there was no inflection. He sounded like a machine imitating a man.

The colonel nodded. He and Rasp followed Bellavis. As they started off, Rasp called to us as if just noticing that we were nearby. 'Commissars,' he said. 'Join us, if you please.'

Bellavis took us to the far end of the walker. There, when the monster had collapsed, a leg had ended up stretched forwards. It created a gradual slope up to the top of the machine. It was climbable. Bellavis's servo-arm gripped a ridge that ran the length of the leg. Thus secured, he ascended as easily as if he were walking level. He looked back at the rest of us. We had to scramble, and even where there were metal spurs or pockmarks of damage to act as handholds, it was hard going. With a short burst of binary static, Bellavis said, 'Apologies.

The interior of the device is very badly damaged. The routes its crew would have used to move around are no longer viable.'

'That's all right, enginseer,' Granach said. 'We'll manage. Just show us what you've found.'

He led us to the structure in the centre of the trunk. From a distance, the hump had appeared featureless. Up close, the welding seams on the metal were clearly visible. A strip of tinted crystalflex ran all the way around, providing a view of the outside world to the occupants. The quality of work was impressive, in a distressing way, in that such a thing had been created. But it was also slipshod in comparison to the magnificence that emerged from the forges of the Mechanicus.

One side of the raised structure had been ripped open by the enginseers. Bellavis led us inside. There we found a throne. Or what passed for one, at any rate. It held the position of a throne, but was more like a black metal plinth about two metres high and one wide. A tangle of cables linked it to the panels and control surfaces. Emerging from the top of the plinth were a human head and shoulders. They were all that remained of the man's body. The rest had been replaced with the mechanisms of the throne. The effect was so bizarre, I thought for a moment that I was looking at a flesh-coloured bust sitting atop the throne. Mechadendrites ran from the man's head to the plinth and the walls of the command centre. There was so little of the human being, the creature might almost have been a servitor, but the agonized rictus on his face told us otherwise. He had died in great pain, and it was clear that the anguish had been more than physical. I was looking at the frozen moment of a soul in final torment.

'Colonel,' Rasp said. 'Commissars. Allow me to introduce Baron Bartholomew Lom.'

Granach stared back and forth between the head and the lord commissar. '*That* is Lom?'

'None other.'

'But what...' The colonel flailed for his question.

'An involved procedure,' Bellavis said, interpreting Granach's sputtering as a request for information. 'He has been made into the equivalent of a princeps for this machine. The work is substandard.' I thought I detected a hint of emotion in the enginseer's words, as if he were disgusted by the slipshod craftsmanship on display. 'It is effective nonetheless, and was done beyond the aegis of the Mechanicus. It is an affront to the Omnissiah, and will be destroyed in due course.'

'Did he undergo this voluntarily?' I asked.

'An important question,' said Rasp.

'I cannot say,' Bellavis answered. 'However, the only signs of violence are the trauma inflicted during the battle.'

'He was lord of this region,' Seroff put in. 'He commanded the rebellion. Who could force him to do this?'

'Or persuade him,' I said. That one of the nobility of the planet could be made to spend the rest of his life as the governing intelligence of this monstrous device was a disturbing prospect. But the implications were worse yet if he had *chosen* to do this blasphemous thing.

'This is Mistral,' Rasp reminded us. 'The waters will be murky.'

I saw more clearly what Rasp meant. We were confronted with irrefutable evidence that the roots of the rebellion ran deeper than the Vales of Lom. That the abomination before us was the idea of the dead baron, and him alone, was impossible to believe.

'There is this, too,' Bellavis said, and moved behind the plinth.

We followed him. There, in a vertical line down the centre of the plinth, were runes. They began at the base of the throne, engravings running all the way to Lom's neck. They continued up to his shaven skull in the form of tattoos. They were unpleasant to look at. There was something inhuman about their shapes, something more and worse than xenos. If I gazed at them too long, it felt as if something were squeezing my eyes. If I did not look elsewhere, my eyes would be crushed.

'There is our heresy,' Seroff said. He stepped around the side of the plinth, so he wouldn't have to see the runes.

'Further proof of its existence, yes,' said Rasp. 'But as to its full reach, and whether we have extinguished it or not, and why we find Baron Lom like this, this tells us nothing.'

'We should see the keep,' I suggested.

Rasp nodded. 'My thoughts exactly. There is no more to be learned here.'

Granach turned to Bellavis. 'When you're done here...' he began.

'We shall destroy everything,' the enginseer reassured him.

We left the walker and made our way to the keep. The main door had been blasted open by a stray rocket during the fighting. We entered in the company of a squad led by Captain Saultern. The troopers swept each room ahead of use. They found no hold-outs. The fortress was deserted.

Though it presented an aggressive exterior, its walls high and forbidding, its turrets plentiful, Lom Keep's interior was that of a home rather than a redoubt. This was the first time war had come to the vales in many centuries. The Lom family had lived as merchants, not warriors. This was the residence of wealthy landowners and flourishing vintners. Though the murder holes of the walls admitted very little daylight, plentiful lumen strips and glow-globes kept the atmosphere cheerful. Thick, hand-crafted carpets covered the stone floors. In the great hall, tapestries hung on the walls. Some dated back centuries, others were far more recent, but no less exquisite in their artistry. The repeated theme was the light of the Emperor shining down on the bountiful production of amasec.

Between the tapestries were portraits of the barons of Lom, going back dozens of generations. The family resemblance was striking: proud, narrow features that would have seemed haughty but for the kind, searching eyes. Most of the full-length paintings portrayed their subjects in the uniform of officers in either Mistral's militia or its regiment of the Imperial Guard: the Mistralian Windborne. As Rasp had suggested, there was one figure clad in the robes of Inquisitorial office.

The furniture, too, was extraordinary. Each piece was as meticulously wrought as any of the tapestries. Great hall, library, smoking room, bedrooms: they held a record of generations and centuries of refinement, with each new acquisition chosen for the grace of its relationship with the pieces that came before.

'Where's the corruption?' Seroff said softly.

'Well hidden,' I answered, more confidently than I felt. I was having trouble reconciling this home with the terrible thing in the grounds.

We examined the books in the library. We found historical treatises, family biographies and devotional works. There was nothing heretical in the spiritual texts. I had read a few of them myself. I held up a *Life of St Cecilia* to Rasp and raised my eyebrows in a question. 'I know,' he said. 'I know. We keep looking.'

On the ground floor, at the opposite end of the keep from the main entrance, we found the chapel. Its doors were closed. Seroff and I waved Saultern and his men away and moved forwards to grasp the ornate brass handles. The rank and file had seen much of the ground floor, but it was better, from this point on, that we restrict whatever remained to be discovered to a select few eyes. I exchanged a look with Seroff, and we hesitated a moment before pulling. I wasn't sure what concerned me more: that we would encounter monstrous heresy on the other side, or that we wouldn't.

We hauled the heavy doors back and went inside.

The chapel was a large one. There were pews enough to seat hundreds. An entire family and its retinue could worship here, along with a sizeable body of men-at-arms. It was easy to picture an important contingent of the Lom forces worshipping here before heading out to battle. The thought made me squirm. It was the iconography that bothered me. I had expected more runes like those we saw in the walker. I had expected desecration, sacrilege, the unholy spoor of heresy. Instead, a gigantic, magnificently crafted gold aquila rose above the altar. It had not been defaced. There was nothing in the décor of the chapel that was anything less than perfectly orthodox.

I picked up one of the devotional books that sat on the ledges on the back of each pew. I opened it at random. I recognized the hymns. I examined the book's binding. It was old, cracked and creased from decades of use. The pages had the musty smell of age. It had clearly been here long before the rebellion, but why had the heretics not replaced it? Why was everything here entirely devoted to the worship of the God-Emperor? My unease deepened.

'Throne,' said Granach. He whispered, but the acoustics of the chapel picked up his words and amplified them. 'What have we done?'

'Our duty,' Rasp snapped. 'Whatever we see here, remember what the lord of this house became. Remember that. Things are not what they seem.' His voice was strong, but I didn't believe he wasn't feeling some of the same disquiet. Between what lay outside the keep and what we saw inside, a gulf yawned. It was so wide that we were finding it impossible to draw the two together. But there was no ignoring the unholy runes on that plinth and on Lom's skull. There had to be a way of explaining the paradox, even if everything we had seen thus far only deepened it.

'There is nothing to be gained by lingering here,' Rasp announced. He turned on his heel and stalked out of the chapel. The energy of his action broke the rest of us from our distressed trance, and we followed him.

'It's the winds,' Rasp said conversationally as we mounted a spiralling marble staircase to the upper floors of the keep. 'They say the winds of Mistral blow the sense out of one's skull. Did you know, colonel, that there is an unusually high incidence of madness on this planet?'

'I'm not surprised,' Granach muttered.

'We would do well to bear that in mind. The winds of Mistral confuse, and the waters are murky. But that doesn't make night into day, or black into white. There is an explanation for what we are seeing.'

I spoke before I realized what I was saying. 'That explanation may be far from reassuring.'

Seroff stared at me as if I had, indeed, surrendered to Mistral's winds.

Rasp didn't reprimand me. He agreed, which was almost worse. 'Very likely so.'

The upper floors of the keep were given over to sleeping quarters. Still we found nothing unusual. Once again, we were confronted with the luxurious quarters of the rich in wealth and taste. The pious rich. It was only when we reached the uppermost chamber of a narrow tower rising above the rest of the fortress that there was any break with the mundane. The room appeared to be a study. It had two windows, one looking south over the expanse of Upper Lom, the other facing north, opening up on the waterfall, which fell so close that the glass dripped with spray. The ceiling was reinforced crystalflex. A telescope stood in the centre of the room. Shelves lined the walls. They were full of astronomical and astrological texts. A massive fireplace, almost large enough for a man to fit inside, dominated the west wall, while a handsome antique desk sat beneath the vale-facing window.

Seroff walked the length of the shelves, his head cocked so he could read the spines of the books. 'Rather esoteric,' he said, 'but nothing heretical. Nothing on any index, as far as I know.'

'There are more indices than are known to us,' I pointed out.

'True,' he admitted. 'Still…'

Rasp blew dust from the telescope's lens. 'This hasn't been used in a long time,' he said. 'I don't think we will find clues to the nature of the baron's heresy in his stargazing hobby.'

I walked over to the desk. Its dark, polished surface was clean. There were no papers, no data-slates, no jottings, nothing. Not even a stylus. I opened its drawers. They were built of a dense wood, but came out smoothly. They were empty. 'This is odd,' I said. As the others joined me, I bent down to look more closely at the top of the desk. There were grooves on the work surface, the scars of centuries of use. I ran my finger through one, came up with a black smudge.

'What is it?' Seroff asked.

'Ash,' I said. 'Something was burned in this room, and there are no personal documents of any kind here.' I looked back at the fireplace. 'The fire was here, at the desk. Not on the hearth.'

'What are you thinking?' Seroff asked. 'Plans for that walker? A heretical manifesto?'

I shrugged. 'Perhaps. I'm more interested in why he chose one spot for his fire over another.' I crossed the room and looked down at the grate. I could see the spotless stone beneath it. The metal of the grate gleamed as if new. I stepped inside the hearth and looked up into the darkness of the chimney. There was no draft. I pulled out my sword and poked upwards. Just at the edge of my reach, my blade scraped against stone. Sealed. 'This fireplace has never been used,' I announced.

'That's a very large ornament,' Seroff said.

'Precisely.' I tugged at the grate. It was bolted to the floor of the hearth. I stepped out of the fireplace and felt along the top of the mantle.

'What are you doing?' Granach asked.

Seroff joined me at the wall. 'Looking for a switch,' he said.

We couldn't find anything. I was sure I was right, though. The artifice was too big, too elaborate to be anything other than camouflage. But the wall was smooth, and none of the fireplace's stones were loose.

'A false fireplace that is a secret door?' Granach protested. 'Seriously?'

'The history of the Loms shows them to be a family with a deep respect for tradition,' said Rasp. 'I would be disappointed if a home of this vintage were lacking that quaint touch.' He strolled over to the desk. He crouched, looking at its massive feet. 'This has been fastened to the floor,' he announced. He straightened, and pulled open the drawers on the left and the right. 'A family of this standing would not have to fumble along a wall.' He reached into the right-hand drawer. There was a click.

Unseen gears engaged with a barely audible hum beneath our feet. The fireplace swung out from the wall. The workmanship was superb. The join between the wall and hearth was seamless. The movement of what was now revealed as a massive stone door was graceful, as if it did not weigh several tons. The opening behind it was the height of a man. Lumen strips lit the way down a spiral flight of stairs.

'The credit for the discovery is yours, Commissar Yarrick,' Rasp told me. 'Lead the way.'

'Please do,' Granach muttered. His invitation was not meant as an honour. He sounded disgusted and dismayed in equal measure by the deepening complexity of the revelations.

I cocked an eyebrow at Seroff, and he grinned at me as we started down the stairs. There was nothing amusing about the situation. Our exchange was a pretence. For all our training, we were also young, and not above the bravado that was sometimes the necessary support to morale. The corrupt thing outside cast its shadow over us once more. Depths, physical and spiritual, awaited us. I did not keep them waiting, and began the descent.

The staircase coiled through the centre of the tower, dropping through the heart of the keep and continuing down through the level of the cellars. The walls and stairs were damp and ancient, pitted by the centuries. But the lumen strips were new. I wondered about that. They suggested that Lom had only started using this region of his home recently.

The smell reached us well before we arrived at the bottom of the stairs.

'Blood,' Granach said.

Yes. The stench wrapped itself around us like miasmal fingers. It grew stronger with every step.

'Finally,' I muttered. There was a dread satisfaction in at last encountering evidence of the corruption of Lom Keep.

The stairs ended at the beginning of a long corridor. There were doors on either side. We glanced inside the rooms as we walked past them. They were empty spaces, long disused to judge from the dust visible within the glow of the lumen strips. These continued straight down the corridor, which ended at a closed iron door.

'What were these rooms used for?' Granach wondered.

'Storage and living space,' Rasp answered. 'The baronial wars of Mistral's past were long, painful ones. The need for a secure, hidden refuge was real.'

'And this?' Seroff asked as we approached the door.

'A place of worship was also necessary,' Rasp said softly.

The smell of blood was overpowering. I didn't hesitate as we had above. I grasped the handle and yanked the door back. It hit the wall hard. The hollow boom echoed up and down the hall like a knell.

As the lord commissar had guessed, the space beyond had once been a chapel. Before me was what I had been expecting since we had first crossed the threshold of the keep. Anticipation did nothing to dull the horror. A faded outline of rust marked where an aquila had once graced the far wall. In its place, daubed in drying blood, was a flowing symbol. It was the curved tear shed by a lunatic eye. I looked away from it, lowering my gaze to the altar. The marble slab had become a butcher's block. Blood, both blackened and fresh, coated it. Streams had run down its sides and pooled on the floor, covering the flagstones as far as the first three rows of pews. Bits of flesh and muscle and fragments of bone stuck out of the coagulated flows. The walls on the left and right were covered in runes. After a quick glance, I kept my eyes on the floor. The traces of blood sacrifice were a sight less harmful than the silent, jagged whispers scratched into the masonry.

'Throne.' Granach's voice cracked.

'We've seen enough,' Rasp declared. 'Shut the door.'

The others stepped back. I hesitated. I stared at the altar. I wasn't satisfied. We had confirmation of dreadful heresy, but how were we any further ahead than we had been in the courtyard? There was something more here. I *would* find it. I would force knowledge from this place, knowledge we could turn against the forces it had come to serve.

Observe and learn.

I could feel dark meaning stretching out from the walls, scratching at the corner of my eyes, seeking purchase on my soul.

'Commissar!' Rasp snapped.

I saw it.

'This sacrilege is recent,' I said.

'What?' Rasp was interested now.

I walked to the altar, wincing at the filth that swirled in the air around me. I tried to narrow my vision to the small detail that had caught my attention. I pointed to a spot on the front of the altar, careful not to come into contact with the defiled stone. 'This blood is old, but not that old. Look at the flesh.' A strip of skin dangled from the lip of the altar. Much, but not all, of it was crusted in gore. There were patches still open to the air.

'What about it?' Seroff asked.

'It hasn't rotted away,' I answered.

'Nicely spotted, commissar,' Rasp said. 'Now kindly remove yourself from there.'

I obeyed. When the door shut behind me, I breathed more easily, even with the stench of blood still thick in my nostrils. We all did.

'So the decomposition is not total,' Granach said as he strode forward, leading the way down the corridor and back up the long spiral. 'How is this useful?'

'It means that the cult activity here is recent,' Rasp told him. 'It means that we might have crushed this heresy in its early stages.'

'Really?' Granach paused and looked back over his shoulder. The light of hope flared in the colonel's eyes. The man was perhaps a more careful thinker than General Rallam, but in the end, he thought like a soldier. He wanted the disturbing elements of this mission swept away so he could leave Mistral and be given another enemy to hammer. 'Then we have ended the threat.'

'I suppose that will be up to the Inquisition to determine,' I said.

Granach glared at me, hope dying as he realized we would not be putting Mistral and its murky waters behind us so soon. He faced forward again and took the stairs two at a time, his anger clear in the very slap of his soles against stone.

'Yes,' Rasp agreed. He laughed. It was a single bark of gallows humour. 'Colonel,' he said. 'Commissars. We have done good work here today.' He paused. 'And all good work on Mistral is met, in the end, by a just and true punishment.'

CHAPTER 5
THE WATERS OF MISTRAL

1. Yarrick

'I hate you,' Seroff said to me. 'I hate you so much, right now.' He spoke out of the corner of his mouth. He kept his eyes straight ahead, his posture at parade attention.

'I hate me too,' I assured him. A little less attention to detail on my part, a little less initiative, and perhaps he and I would not be standing here now. If it had fallen to Rasp to find the site of heretical worship, Seroff and I would not have to receive any honours. We would have been spared what we both knew was just the first of our ordeals in the thick of Mistralian politics.

We were standing in the reviewing line along with the high-ranking officers of the Mortisian strike force. We were arrayed along the magnificent central staircase of the Ecclesiarchal palace in Tolosa, the capital of Mistral. Granach and Benneger, along with Rasp, were at the head of the stairs, the first to be thanked and congratulated by Cardinal Wangenheim on behalf of the people and legal authorities of Mistral. He was followed by a retinue of lesser ecclesiarchs, and then by a contingent of Mistralian nobility.

I call the staircase *magnificent* with a certain degree of irony. Magnificence was certainly the intent of its creators, and was even more so the desire of the mind who commissioned it. But it was so ostentatious that it had pitched into the grotesque. It was thus in keeping with the character of the palace. The staircase appeared to be made of gold. The illusion was so convincing, I half expected to feel the steps give when we mounted them. They did not. They were, I realized, gold-leafed marble. They blazed with the light of chandeliers a dozen metres in diameter. The columns supporting the ornate vault had gold spiralling up their height. There was no gold on the walls, but they were so encrusted with jewels, they seemed to be frozen cataracts of riches. The ceiling was a series of frescoes depicting the Ecclesiarchy bringing the Emperor's truth to the multitudes of Mistral. Unlike the tapestries of Lom, where the light that blessed the figures was clearly a gift from the Emperor Himself, here the illumination came from the figures of the cardinals and bishops, and was rarely a blessing. In almost every case, it was smiting the heretic.

I took in the strident glory around us and felt ill. The refracted light, bouncing off countless facets and reflective surfaces, was trying to make my head pound. More sickening than that, though, was the deeper meaning of the display. Nothing I saw glorified the Emperor. It was all a celebration of the men who lived in this palace, and therefore ruled Mistral. As Wangenheim descended the staircase, coming closer to my position, it was hard not to imagine that he had commissioned every stone of the palace. He hadn't. It had been built centuries earlier. But there appeared to be a tradition of what I could only think of as ecclesiastical corruption here, and Wangenheim showed every sign of maintaining that tradition. The palace was not a shrine to the Emperor. It was a celebration of its inhabitant.

Wangenheim made his way down the staircase closely, pausing on each step to speak to the officer before him. When he reached me, I performed the proper obeisance. I did well in hiding the contempt I felt. Wangenheim wasn't a tall man, but he took up a lot of space. He was obese, and the robes of his office billowed about him like sails. A halo of cherubim fluttered over his head. A soft plainsong chanting emerged from their bionic voice boxes. I couldn't make out the words. I suspected the hymns were in praise of the man, and not the God whose will he was supposed to enact.

Wangenheim's lips were thick and unpleasantly moist. His face was pockmarked and bore the ravages of luxury. There was something of the amphibian about him, and when he took my hand in both of his, my skin crawled as though I'd been given a handful of worms. His grip was dry, though, and powdery. 'I have been told of your actions on the field of battle, commissar,' he said to me. 'And I understand that it is you who discovered the heart of the foul heresy that had been attempting to sink its noisome roots into the sacred soil of Mistral.' His voice was smooth, a baritone syrup. In his youth it might have served him well, but all I could hear was a man enamoured by the sound of his every utterance, a man convinced that he had the instrument to shape language, hearts and minds to his will. 'The Emperor will bless you for your fidelity and devotion to duty.'

'Thank you, your eminence.'

I was young, but I was not entirely stupid. I could see what kind of man stood before me. He was the most powerful authority on Mistral, appointed so by the Adeptus Terra. We had come to this planet to uphold the order that he represented. He was not worthy of his position. A child could have told that at a glance. As a thought experiment, I told myself that perhaps my first impression was wrong, and that this was an able administrator and holy man. I dismissed the idea before it made me laugh. But I knew my duty, and I was bound to honour and protect the office that Wangenheim held. I would not help anything by acting with any disrespect. So I swallowed my distaste. I played the part of the lowly officer in the presence of a great man.

I don't do that any more.

Wangenheim moved one step down, to my right. Out of the corner of my eye, I saw Seroff go through the same charade. I knew how he was keeping himself focused. 'At least there will be amasec later,' he had told me as the ceremony began. 'Good amasec. Lots and lots of very good amasec.'

The bishops blessed us in turn as they made their way down. Many of them appeared to be cut of the same cloth as Wangenheim, but there were others who struck me as more sincerely committed to their calling than to its rewards. The nobles shook our hands. They were less unctuous. They praised and flattered, and while both they and the ecclesiarchs used the stock phrases that were inevitable at events such as this one, I could tell that Wangenheim and his subordinates were genuinely pleased with the battle's outcome. The barons said they were, but there was something rote about their reactions.

As the last of the official party moved down the staircase, Seroff spoke to me again, still without breaking his formal stance. 'I don't think the nobility is all that happy to see us.'

'I noticed,' I whispered back. There was movement in the gallery at the top of the staircase. I caught a glimpse of a man withdrawing into the deeper shadows. I had a brief impression of the swirl of a cloak, and that was all.

'So?' Seroff went on. 'Heretics, every one of them?'

That seemed unlikely. 'Nothing so easy.'

'A split between them and the Ecclesiarchy?'

'Maybe.'

I couldn't tell, staring straight ahead, if Seroff had just winced. The silence made me think he had. 'Throne. I hope you're wrong.'

'So do I.' That possibility raised uncomfortable questions about our mission. Had we been used as pawns in a game that was ultimately an internecine squabble? No, I told myself. A simple political schism would not explain the runes on Lom's skull, or the walker itself.

Too many questions. We had only just arrived in Tolosa, and already I was feeling myself sink beneath those murky waters.

2. *Wangenheim*

He took a few minutes for himself between the ceremony and the reception. He stood in an observation room and looked down unseen on the gathering in the hall below. He waved his hand, and his cherubim ceased their song of praise. The winged servitors were, in almost every sense that mattered, his children. He had provided the genetic material that had been used to grow them in vats. They were an extension of him, his will, his glory. They were not, as far as he was concerned, an indulgence. They were a comfort to him, and a reminder, forceful and constant, of his importance to all who saw him.

The reminders were necessary because there was no rest at the top of the Mistralian power structure. There was no question that the cardinal held supreme authority over the citizens of the planet. But who the cardinal was – that was subject to change by assassination or manufactured downfall. That was how he had reached the pinnacle. He had forged the evidence that had sent his predecessor to the dungeons of the Ordo Hereticus.

Then there was the aristocracy. The secular powers were not without their own strength, and he knew it was their hope to reduce his role to that of a figurehead. He should perhaps be grateful to Baron Lom. His rebellion had given Wangenheim the means of providing an object lesson to Lom's peers. *Do you see? This is what happens when you forget your place.*

Well and good. But had the nobles learned the lesson? That remained to be seen. He would school them further, until he was sure they were properly pacified. Until the last irritant was stamped out, he would keep the Guard on Mistral. The discovery of an actual heretical cult, limited though it seemed to have been, was a gift. There was much he could do with a threat, especially if it had been reduced to a phantom one, to be deployed according to his needs.

There was a subtle clearing of the throat behind him. Wangenheim turned. Vercor, the palace steward, stood in the doorway. She was a tall woman, thin and hard as cable. Her face had all the colour and expression of bone. Her lank dark hair hung down to her neck, and covered her bionic ears. They functioned as directional microphones. She could isolate a conversation from the other side of a crowded room. What was spoken in the palace was heard by Vercor.

'What have you learned?' Wangenheim asked without preamble.

'The barons are surprised by what was found, your eminence.'

'They had not suspected Lom of heresy?'

'It would seem not.'

That was good news. More evidence that the corruption had not had a chance to spread beyond the Vales of Lom. If the cult were not a phantom, it would be much harder for him to use. 'Was there any sympathy expressed?' he asked.

'None. Only disgust.'

That was a shame. On such evidence he could smash a few more families, bring the rest to heel. Still, there was time yet. The fall of Lom had made sure of that. 'All right,' he said. He turned back to the view of the gathering below. 'I should go down. You have listened well. Continue to do so.'

'As you command, your eminence.' Vercor withdrew.

Wangenheim signalled to the cherubim, and they began singing again. Bathed in the exaltation of his power, he prepared to play the good host.

3. *Yarrick*

The reception was held in a ballroom. I had never before heard of a ballroom being present in an Ecclesiarchal palace, but there was no mistaking this hall for anything else. There were more of those huge chandeliers. While not quite as colossal as the ones over the grand staircase, they were big enough. There was more of the omnipresent gold leaf, too. On the walls, this time, in between massive framed mirrors that multiplied the crowd to infinity. The ceiling frescoes here were non-representational.

They featured groups of interlocking swirls. They suggested the movement of dance, without actually depicting it. The materialism of the palace was so ostentatious that I wondered why anyone bothered being coy about the nature of the room.

There was no dancing here tonight, at least not yet, though a chamber orchestra was playing at one end. Servants in what I learned later was the livery of Wangenheim's family moved through the crowd, presenting silver plates loaded with appetizers. Seroff's hoped-for amasec arrived, and we were soon toasting the death of Baron Lom with the product of his own vineyard. I wondered, as I downed a glass, if we were drinking the last that would ever be brewed. The thought was unpleasant, but I let it go as I savoured the drink. It more than lived up to its reputation.

Rasp had Seroff and I stay close. He was teaching us to swim. We watched Wangenheim work the room, stopping first at one group of officers, then another, sharing a joke with nobles whose laughter was just a bit forced. He gradually moved closer to our cluster. With us were Granach and Colonel Benneger. The latter looked like the tanks he commanded. Massive, square of shoulders and head, he had been a faithful disciple of Rallam, and mourned the loss of the general. He was from the same school of the direct application of brute force as Rallam, and would surely be even less happy about the prospect of a prolonged post-victory stay on Mistral than Granach. But the amasec had softened the worst of his edges. He actually seemed to be enjoying himself. He downed another drink, then stared at his crystal goblet as if puzzled to find it empty. A servant appeared at his elbow with a decanter and averted tragedy.

Pleased, Benneger slapped me on the shoulder. 'So,

commissar,' he said, 'you finished this war for us. Well done. Impressive first duty.'

'I beg your pardon, colonel?'

'Found that den of hell, didn't you? We killed them all. This place is sorted.'

'May the Emperor grant that you're right.' Granach's prayer was heartfelt.

I bowed my thanks to Benneger, but said nothing. I was pleased to receive a superior officer's praise, but the memory of the desecrated chapel was a raw one, jagged and bleeding. 'I agree, colonel,' I said to Granach. To Benneger, I said, 'I hope you are right, sir. Nothing would please me more than to be worthy of this praise. I fear, though, that the determination is not ours to make.'

Benneger glanced sideways at Wangenheim. The cardinal was, by stages, making his way towards us. 'If he has his way,' he muttered, 'that holy man will have us here forever.'

I was startled. I saw Rasp's mouth twitch in the momentary trace of a smile. I didn't know which amused him: Benneger's lack of diplomacy, or my surprise at his acumen. Perhaps it was both.

'That may be so,' said a new voice. 'But there are more serious concerns here than political desire. And you are quite correct, commissar. It is not within the purview of the Imperial Guard to determine the level of heretical threat.'

We turned. We had not heard the man approach. He was of average height, but carried himself with an air of haughty command that made him seem to tower over us all. The impression was intensified by his way of holding his head back slightly, so that he appeared to gaze down his nose at whoever stood before him. He was young, close to my age I guessed. His attire was formal, elegant yet severe, with a dark cloak over a waistcoat, trousers and boots whose magnificence made our own ceremonial uniforms look shabby; yet the way he carried himself suggested that this was what he wore onto the field as well. Every thread of his clothes, every swept blond hair on his head, was subject to the same unforgiving discipline. Even if I hadn't seen his pendant, the iron skull-within-the-I, I would have tagged him as Inquisition. I found myself tense up, as if I were an animal reacting to the presence of a rival.

'No one here would imagine, or hope, that the situation were otherwise,' Rasp said smoothly. He bowed. 'Lord Commissar Simeon Rasp, at your service, inquisitor...'

'Hektor Krauss, Ordo Hereticus.' He returned the bow. The movement was a short, quick snap. Somehow, he seemed to be watching us all even in the moment his head was down.

'I'm sure I speak for my colleagues when I say how pleased I am to see the Inquisition has matters in hand,' Rasp continued.

'I am not really interested in formalities or pleasantries, lord commissar,' Krauss answered. 'You will forgive me for being blunt.'

Or else, I thought, and I did so with Seroff's voice in my head. I made sure I did not look at him, but I could sense him bristling.

'Of course.' Rasp's smile was untroubled.

'This event is distasteful,' said Krauss. 'It accomplishes nothing, and is premature in its triumphalism. I would, with all my heart, be elsewhere.' His contempt was genuine, yet his appearance was so perfectly composed that I suspected that, at a level even he did not suspect, Krauss was being less than honest with himself. There was no way that he could lavish such care on his appearance and not be responding, however unconsciously, to a context just as perfectly arranged.

'I'll drink to that,' Benneger said. His grin faded when the inquisitor did not return it. He seemed to wilt beneath the younger man's gaze.

'Has your mission on Mistral been a long one?' I asked, drawing Krauss's attention to me.

'Some months,' he answered. 'Since shortly after the first instances of armed rebellion. Cardinal Wangenheim suspected the presence of a cult from the first.'

'And?' Rasp asked.

'Nothing concrete until your discovery.' If Krauss felt any discomfort over his lack of progress, he hid it well.

'Then perhaps we are done?' Granach ventured.

'I cannot answer that,' said Krauss. 'I must visit Lom Keep. I will be interviewing your men, colonels. Especially those who came into contact with the walker.'

'Of course,' Granach replied. Benneger nodded. One never said anything else to an inquisitor.

Krauss nodded. 'Good.' Wangenheim was drawing near. The inquisitor's lip curled in distaste. He nodded once more, then strode off.

'Manners,' Benneger muttered at his retreating back.

'Oh, shut up,' Granach told him.

And now the cardinal had come among us. 'The Emperor's light shine upon you all,' he said. He gave his words the special emphasis that comes naturally to those who deeply admire their own sincerity. 'Mistral owes all of you a debt of gratitude for your efforts in eradicating a cancerous heresy.'

'Inquisitor Krauss is far from sure that our work is done,' Rasp said.

Wangenheim nodded. 'I share his doubts. The Hammer of the Emperor has done great work for Mistral, but its labours are not yet at an end. There is unrest still, and where there is rebellion, there is heresy.'

No one answered that comment directly. Its self-serving nature was obvious. I saw Benneger fighting to keep from frowning.

'Where will you need us to deploy next?' Granach asked.

'Ah, colonel, I wish matters were so straightforward. We are facing something more amorphous, and far more insidious, than merely an armed rebellion. I called the heresy *cancerous* a moment ago, and a cancer is what it is. It is eating away at all levels of Mistral's society, and, like all beliefs of cowards, does so in the shadows.'

'That is work for the Inquisition, surely,' Rasp probed. 'A hammer is a poor tool for such an operation.' Granach and Benneger brightened at his words.

'There is no doubt that the scourge of the Inquisition shall be used,' Wangenheim said. 'And I have made other arrangements that will, I am sure, guide the weak of our flock back to the true path.' He smiled and winked, very pleased with himself. 'But you must understand, lord commissar, colonels,' he clasped his hands, 'the presence of a large strike force on Mistral is invaluable not only for crushing a rebellion, but for discouraging it from happening in the first place. Do you see?' He smiled and parted his hands, palms up. The gesture made me think of a conjurer's. It was as if we were expected to gasp at the logic suddenly unveiled before our marvelling eyes. 'With you here, we now have time to use other, subtler means to exterminate the heresy.'

'Your eminence,' Benneger said, his voice tight with

frustration, 'that would seem to mean that our stay on Mistral–'

'Will be of indefinite duration. Yes, colonel, that is so.' Wangenheim smiled that moist smile. 'You and your men will be well looked after, have no fear.'

Granach began, 'We should return to the *Scythe of Terra* until–'

The cardinal interrupted him. 'Oh, I think boots on the ground within easy reach of Tolosa will be precisely the deterrent we need. Don't you?'

Granach hesitated. He had authority in tactical matters, but there was no actual conflict at the moment, and he had just been given what amounted to a directive by a high-ranking representative of the Adeptus Terra. He nodded. 'As you say, your eminence.' He sounded like a man condemned to hard labour. I shared his dismay. We were facing the prospect of a prolonged mission with vague parameters, and no clear possibility of a decisive victory. It was a fate no army deserved.

On the other hand, however much I disliked Wangenheim, and could see that we were becoming pawns in his political game, none of this changed what had happened at Lom. There had been a threat far beyond simple rebellion there. There had been a cult. Until we were certain that it had been annihilated, we had a duty here. Coming from the mouth of the cardinal, the truth sounded like lies, but it was still the truth.

Wangenheim brought his hands together again in a delighted clap. 'Splendid! You'll see, colonel. The heretic will soon be purged from our midst. Now, if you'll excuse me...'

His work done, his will enforced, the cardinal moved off. The colonels stared morosely into their amasec goblets. Rasp watched Wangenheim walk away, but then I saw his attention fix on something else in the ballroom. He left the officers to the contemplation of our collective fate, and signalled for Seroff and me to follow. He walked slowly, as if sauntering through the crowd, but there was purpose in his gaze.

In the centre of the room, we were accosted by one of the nobles. During the presentation on the staircase, he had been the first of the nobility in line after the Ecclesiarchy. After a moment I recalled who he was: Rayland, Baron Vahnsinn, chair of the Mistralian Council. He was first among the secular powers. 'Your pardon, lord commissar,' he said.

'Baron Vahnsinn.' Rasp gave him a rigid half-bow.

'I thanked you earlier on behalf of the Council,' Vahnsinn said. 'I would like to offer a more personal thanks to you and your officers,' he nodded to me and Seroff, 'in recognition of your accomplishment on the battlefield.' His politeness was so formal it was moribund. 'I wonder if you would do me the honour of attending a late supper at my Tolosa residence.' He did not sound like we would be honouring him at all. He sounded like he was obliged to ask us to burn his house down. The ice of his manner was underlined by his physical presence. He was tall, trim as wrought iron. His bone-white hair was cut so short it was only one step from having been shaved off altogether. He was clearly a veteran, and of the Imperial Guard, I surmised, rather than of the militia. His face was lined with heavy experience. Scar tissue descended from his right ear, down the side of his neck.

Rasp accepted the invitation with the same grace with which it had been given: none. He nodded once. 'Of course,' he said. 'The honour would be ours.' Now his house was the one being burned to the ground.

'In an hour, then?' Vahnsinn asked, but walked away before Rasp could answer.

There was something about the exchange that struck me as off. It had a rehearsed quality, as if the two men had been partners in this dance of mutual hostility before.

'We're not going, surely?' Seroff said. He was incensed.

'We're going,' Rasp informed him.

House Vahnsinn had properties across Mistral. The family seat was the Karrathar fortress, in the mountains beyond Tolosa. When duty called him to the capital city, he stayed at Grauben Manor. The home was modest in comparison to the Ecclesiarchal palace, but *only* in comparison to that monument. Tolosa was laid out in rough concentric circles around a central hill, retaining much of the street plan that dated back to the fortified city's founding during the Age of Apostasy. The citadel at the peak of the hill had been transformed, expanded and remade as the Ecclesiarchal palace. Other than imposing size, it had long ago lost its original architectural character. But many of the other buildings in Tolosa were reminders of how ancient the city was.

Grauben Manor was one of those reminders. It was in the ring immediately below the summit. We walked there from the palace, Mistral's wind howling through the narrow streets, pushing against us so hard it felt like we were being hit by ocean waves. Grauben's stone walls had turned black with millennia of grime. Its narrow stained glass windows admitted little light, and when we stepped into the entrance hall I was momentarily taken aback to find that the interior illumination was provided by glow-globes, and not by torches. The décor made me think of Lom Keep. In both homes there was a powerful sense of tradition extending back countless generations, a tradition whose preservation was the responsibility of the current baron. A responsibility that was, it seemed clear, regarded as a privilege.

As a valet led us forward, Vahnsinn's voice boomed out of a doorway on our left. 'If there is one thing I cannot abide,' he said, emerging into the hall, 'it is people who accept invitations that are not meant to be accepted.'

'And what I cannot stand,' Rasp retorted, 'are the insufferable twits who issue those invitations.'

Silence as the two men regarded each other, then us. Then they exploded with laughter and embraced. It was the greeting of comrades who had been separated by years and distance, but not in affection. After a moment, they held each other at arm's length.

'Simeon,' Vahnsinn said, still grinning, 'you're a fool to have come to this planet.'

'Rayland,' Rasp replied, 'you *live* here. What does that make you?'

'The biggest fool,' the baron said, and his smile vanished for a moment. Then it was back, and he was ushering us into the room.

It was an intimate space, one used for quiet evenings with friends, rather than for feasting. The table was a square, large enough for four people to stretch out their legs comfortably at their seats. A painting of Karrathar hung over the fireplace, where a fire had been built up. The flames danced and roared as the wind snuck down the chimney to toy with them. The stained glass window rattled in its casing. The panelling on the walls was the same dark wood as Lom's desk. The effect of the room was one of solidarity and comfort, a bulwark against the winds outside. The meal was a rich stew of cubed grox, potatoes and an amasec-based sauce. We sponged it up with peasant bread that was so dense it threatened to sit in the stomach like a lead ball, but was impossible to set aside. It was a deliberately informal repast, and a welcome corrective to the excesses of earlier in the evening.

'How do you come to know each other?' Seroff asked as we took our seats.

'I served as commissar for the Mistralian Guard,' Rasp said. 'I put it down to the inexperience of my youth that I didn't shoot this reprobate in the skull many times over.'

Vahnsinn laughed, and the anecdotes and war stories began. Seroff and I listened and asked occasional questions, the expected ones whose function was to elicit the climax of a tale or the punch line of a joke. As our supper ended and we were moving on to liqueurs, I shifted the ground to more immediate concerns.

'That charade back at the palace,' I said. 'That wasn't only for my and Commissar Seroff's benefit, was it?'

'No, it wasn't,' Rasp replied.

'There are ears everywhere in those halls,' Vahnsinn added. Both men were serious now.

I thought for a moment. 'May I speak frankly?'

'That's why we're here,' Rasp told me.

'It seems, then, that you have both conspired, in however minor a capacity, to deceive the Ecclesiarchy.'

The silence that followed was broken by Seroff's coughs as he choked on his drink.

Vahnsinn said, 'Tell me, Commissar Yarrick, what was your impression of Cardinal Wangenheim?'

'I believe he is self-regarding, power-hungry and a disgrace to the office he holds.'

'You are quick to judge on a brief acquaintance.'

'You disagree with my evaluation?'

'Your judgement is also extremely perceptive. No, I do not disagree. I have known the cardinal far longer, and the only difference between your evaluation and mine is that I would be unable to express myself without resorting to obscenities.'

'So what is really going on here, Rayland?' Rasp asked. 'I know Bartholomew Lom was a good friend of yours, but he was clearly involved with something deeply heretical.'

'What are you hoping to achieve?' Vahnsinn countered rather than answering. 'You know how things work on Mistral. Things only get worse here, never better.'

'I have a duty, and I will follow it. What I want is the information that will allow me to fulfil that duty.'

Vahnsinn nodded. 'That's fair. Well, what we are currently experiencing might be the unfortunate confluence of two events. I do hope I am wrong. One of those events is a divide between the nobility and the Ecclesiarchy. The other is perhaps the heresy.'

'The barons are leading the heretics?'

Vahnsinn grimaced. 'I pray not. Not exactly.'

'Not *exactly*?' Rasp exploded. 'Do you hear what you are saying?'

The baron held up placating hands. 'Let me finish.' He paused for a moment, organizing his thoughts. 'The conflict between my peers and Wangenheim is, at basis, about power, not faith.'

'Go on.'

'The cardinal keeps increasing the tithes. They've become crippling. Wangenheim isn't trying to feather his nest at our expense. He already has more riches at his disposal than he will ever be able to spend. But if he forces us into insolvency, we shall be at his mercy. We will, in the long run, be unable to act in our own interests. Already, half a dozen estates have fallen under direct Ecclesiarchal control. The cardinal will be satisfied by nothing less than absolute rule over Mistral.'

'So the barons are pushing back,' I said.

'As much as possible. But any real resistance will be branded as heresy by Wangenheim. To stand up for yourself means, almost inevitably, going to war.'

'You haven't reached that stage,' Rasp pointed out.

'No. I can still afford to pay the tithe. So can the other major houses. But only just. We're running out of room to manoeuvre. And time.'

'That was why there were so few baronial forces assisting in the fight against Lom,' I said. 'The cardinal doesn't want you to have the opportunity to engage in any large-scale mobilization.'

'Exactly.'

'I'm confused,' Seroff said. 'You make it sound as if there is no real heresy. Resistance to the cardinal's ambition is simply being branded as such. But that makes no sense. What Baron Lom did–'

'Yes, that was true heresy, clearly,' Vahnsinn broke in. 'What is running through the streets, in sympathy with the barons, is a rejection of the cardinal and his works.'

'That is a rejection of the Ecclesiarchy,' Seroff said.

'No,' Vahnsinn corrected, 'of Wangenheim. He would claim that is a distinction without a difference, but I disagree.'

'This is Mistral,' Rasp said quietly.

'Yes,' Vahnsinn agreed. 'It is. Wangenheim is abusing his authority, and bringing disrepute to the Ecclesiarchy.'

'We do not choose our leaders,' I pointed out. 'It is not for us to question what decisions led to his placement here.'

'We don't have to,' Rasp said. 'He has come home.'

'The cardinal is Mistralian?' Seroff asked in surprise.

Vahnsinn nodded. 'He knows how to swim in our waters. That is why I did not take his blustering about a heresy seriously. There were too many other, drearily mundane reasons for unrest, all of his own making.'

'But there is a heresy,' I said.

'Yes.' The baron's eyes were sad. His voice was exhausted. 'But perhaps it is no more.'

'The signs of corruption were recent,' Rasp told him.

'Throne, let that be so.'

'Do you believe we have destroyed it?' I asked.

'I very much want to. I fear for all of Mistral if you have not.'

'I doubt the cardinal is in any hurry to declare the threat extinguished,' Rasp mused. 'Though if the crisis drags on too long, he will appear weak.'

'The threat of heresy will end with resistance to his rule,' I said.

'Very likely,' Rasp agreed.

'And if the cult is still active? If the threat is real?' Seroff asked.

We were silent. The light in the room seemed to dim, as if falling into the shadow of Vahnsinn's fears.

'Tell us what lies ahead politically,' Rasp said to the baron.

'There is a Council meeting at the end of next week. The hope is that the cardinal can be made to see reason.' It was clear from Vahnsinn's tone that the hope was a forlorn one. 'If that happens, I believe that I can ensure the loyalty of the barons.'

'And if not?' I asked.

'Know this, commissar,' Vahnsinn said gently. 'If the cardinal is not amenable to reason, if he pursues his power grab, then heresy or no heresy, the barons will revolt in desperation. There will be nothing I can do to stop it. And we will have civil war.'

The window rattled again. Outside, the wind of Mistral scoured the street. It sounded like Fate, blowing events from the hands of pitiful mortals.

CHAPTER 6
THE PIERCING THORN

1. Yarrick

Wangenheim offered us accommodation in the palace, along with the senior officers. Vahnsinn invited us to stay at Grauben. Rasp thanked both, declined both. He chose a nondescript inn halfway down the slope of Tolosa's hill, and took three rooms for us there. They were comfortable enough, but a far cry from the luxury that could have been ours at either of the other locations. Seroff was clearly disappointed. I appreciated the strategy, but wondered how effective it could be.

'We aren't really safe from spies, here,' I said to Rasp as I wrestled a west-facing window shut that I had made the mistake of opening. As I lowered the window, the wind shrieked its displeasure at being expelled from a room it had barely begun to upend. On the outside wall, the shutters slammed back and forth. I would fight with them later.

'Of course we aren't,' Rasp said. He leaned against my doorway, arms folded, an amused look on his face. 'But it will take them longer to get themselves organized. We've made things a bit more difficult for them. We have also levelled the playing field. If we had accepted either of our invitations, we would have been assured of being watched by only one set of spies. That would hardly be fair. This way, they'll be competing against each other, too.'

'You expected spies at Grauben, too?'

'Of course. The baron would be failing in his responsibilities if he didn't have us watched.'

I wondered if there was a cautious way of asking what I was about to ask. I decided there wasn't, and forged ahead. 'Do you trust Baron Vahnsinn?'

'He is one of my oldest friends. We have saved each other's lives many times over.'

He hadn't answered my question. 'But?' I prompted.

'But he is Mistralian, and must swim the same waters as do all who live on this planet. Indeed, we must, too, though I know you would like to believe otherwise.'

I grimaced. 'I would like to, yes. That does not mean that I do.'

'Good. Then you might survive, and you are learning that to think like a commissar and to act like one are sometimes two different things.'

The shutters banged, insistent.

'You'd better see to those,' said Rasp.

I sighed and raised the window again. The wind whooped triumphantly into the room. I leaned over the sill, reaching for the shutters, and felt like I was going to be sucked out of the room and hurled, end over end, down the length of the street. I seized the shutters and yanked them closed, then lowered the window. Outside, the wind moaned, disappointed. A thought struck me. 'I'm curious,' I said. 'You said that the expression about Mistral's waters was a local one.'

'It is.'

'I would have expected the metaphor to be more...' I gestured at the window. '...wind-based.'

'You haven't looked much outside the walls yet, have you?'

'I saw there was an important waterway system.'

'"Important" hardly does it justice. At any rate, the expression incorporates the two constants of life on Mistral. The full meaning is that if even the winds of Mistral cannot clear the waters of its politics, then they must be murky indeed.'

'I see.' That made a depressing amount of sense.

He left, then. Our conversation came back to me the next day. I was shown that it did not matter whether or not one was native-born to Mistral. Everyone on the surface of the planet struggled not to drown in the currents of its politics. There were no exceptions.

2. *Vercor*

She waited for the cardinal outside the doors to the Ecclesiarchal palace's Chapel Majoris. It dominated the west wing, large as a cathedral in the lesser cities on Mistral. It was more recent than the Chapel Minoris, which nestled at the heart of the palace, a relic of the original citadel. The Minoris was rarely used now. It was completely inadequate for the size and splendour of the services conducted. Over the course of the last few centuries, some cardinals had used it as a more private sanctuary for prayer and meditation. Wangenheim did not. If the Chapel Majoris was suitable for public displays, it was suitable for solitude as well.

He was engaged in such a moment of recollection right now. There was no sound from beyond the massive, closed portal. The cardinal, Vercor knew, would be kneeling before the grand altar. Distance and the thickness of the doors blocked even her hearing from picking up on the whispers of his prayers. That was as it should be. But she heard his footsteps as he walked down the nave, and she signalled the guards. They pulled back the double doors just as Wangenheim reached them.

His robes concealed his feet, and he pulled a long train behind him. He moved slowly, and he reminded Vercor of one of the freight-laden boats that plied the network of rivers that surrounded Tolosa. There was no grace in his step, but there was an unhurried stateliness, and an inexorable momentum. He nodded to her to accompany him, and set off down one of the palace's grand galleries that opened onto the palace's main cloister.

'What news?' the cardinal asked.

'The lord commissar and his two men dined with Baron Vahnsinn last night.'

'What did they discuss?'

'I don't know. There were too many of the baron's forces about for me to get close enough to hear.'

'That is unfortunate.' Wangenheim thought for a moment. 'Vahnsinn was being careful, which suggests he has something to hide. Are they staying at his home?'

'No.'

Wangenheim nodded. 'Good. I would be concerned by signs of any strong ties.'

'There has been no unrest in Baron Vahnsinn's manufactoria,' Vercor pointed out.

The cardinal brushed away her observation with a wave of his fingers. 'I am not interested in his apparent loyalty. Whether he intends to revolt or not is irrelevant. What matters is his inability to act in any way that is contrary to the edicts of the Holy Ecclesiarchy. And we have yet to reach that moment.'

Vercor picked up on the phrasing. Wangenheim was preserving a thin veneer of propriety over his own ambition. She gave a mental shrug. He didn't have to do so for her benefit, but he was being cautious in all things. He was a careful man, and so was a successful one. That was all that mattered. Her family had served his for more generations than could be traced. Historically, the first-born of each generation bore no given name, becoming the incarnation of the family identity, the Vercor that walked the shadows for the Wangenheims. During the last few centuries, the Vercor line had changed in nature. She had borne no children, but her genetic material had been harvested, and her successor grown in a vat, awaiting decanting when her tasks came to an end. Violently, as had ever been the case.

And yet, through the centuries that the Wangenheims had been served by a Vercor, it was never anything as fragile and intangible as loyalty that kept the two families linked. Success was the bond. As the Wangenheims climbed the rungs of the Imperial hierarchies, the Vercors benefitted. The current bearer of the name held no sentimental illusions about honour or tradition. Nor did the cardinal. He knew, as had his ancestors before him, that failure would sever the bonds instantly. This fact kept the Wangenheims honest. If they planned well, and acted wisely, then the shadows at their sides would be invaluable tools.

Vercor flexed her bionic fingers. Servo-motor vibrations ran up her arm. The sensation was a fine one. It was the hum of a strength that could shatter bone. She could do far more than listen. She asked, 'Does your eminence wish action taken?'

Wangenheim took his time answering. They had reached the end of the gallery and turned left into the next before he spoke again. 'No,' he said. 'The Guard is here now. That should be enough to keep order, at least until the Council. The relic arrives today, and the festival will be held the day after the Council. That will be decisive. We'll know then if we need to act, and we will be in a position to do so with finality. It would be better if Vahnsinn and the barons accept the inevitable. Perhaps they shall. If not...' He parted his hands and looked up, as if appealing to the judgement of the Emperor. 'Then we cannot be answerable for the foolishness of the misguided.'

'Very true,' Vercor agreed. Strategically, bringing the barons to heel without violence was preferable. That was a more controllable method of ending the unrest. But a little bit of violence, properly applied, could be of great assistance, too.

She was growing tired of simply listening.

3. Yarrick

Cardinal Wangenheim was true to his word. To a point. Comfortable quarters were provided to the regimental officers. But Tolosa did not have the means to billet the entirety of the expeditionary force. So the colonels resided in the Ecclesiarchal palace, while the captains remained with their companies beyond the city walls. There too, logistical problems arose. There was no room for an encampment in the immediate area.

Tolosa occupied almost the entirety of the island on which it was situated. The dozens of rivers and tributaries that cut across the great Mistralian plains were fed by the Carconne range, rising about a dozen kilometres to the east of the city, but they appeared to radiate from Tolosa itself. They were the original arteries of trade on the planet, and Tolosa was the heart that pumped the flow to the other lands. Though hundreds of ships, from private barges to freighters owned by the great families, anchored at city docks every day, much of the transportation needs were now met by the immense maglev network that cut directly across water and land. The rails met in a junction several kilometres wide just outside the north gates, constructed on the one large spit of land on the island that was not contained within the city walls.

The 77th and 110th could not sleep on maglev tracks. So a bivouac was established in the Carconnes. The land belonged to the Trenqavels, a minor family with distant connections to the Vahnsinns. They were exclusively traders, having no military force of their own, and had been among the first to fall under the thumb of Wangenheim. Rasp declared himself impressed by Granach's choice, and I could see the political logic at work. The Trenqavel land was as close as one could come to neutral territory in Mistral's fraught atmosphere. There were, officially, no sides to be taken. But everyone on the planet knew the situation was more complex than that, and Granach had placed the Mortisians so as to signal the simple fact that the Guard was here to ensure the order of the Imperium was maintained.

The site was a good one in purely military terms as well. It was a shallow valley, wide enough to support the encampment. It provided some shelter from the constant wind, though the tents still shook, their canvas rippling and snapping in the gusts. A maglev line ran through the valley, and there was a station. It was possible to requisition a transport train and have several companies' worth of troops arrive at the city within two hours. There was also an actual road running, via numerous bridges, from the Trenqavel holdings to Tolosa.

An army in limbo presents its own challenges. Tolosa was not at peace, so the 77th and 110th could not head to the next theatre of war. But neither was there any combat to be had here. The unrest was, for the time being, limited to the occasional riot or isolated assaults. These were the purview of the enforcers, and they were managing. So the regiments were held in a state of tedious, indefinite inactivity. Idleness is not the proper state for a soldier. It breeds discontent, lack of discipline, and a lack of readiness. It is a state of false security, and thus high vulnerability. And so, after the first night in Tolosa, Rasp sent Seroff and me back to the troops. He remained in Tolosa. He would monitor the pulse of the intrigues. We would work to inoculate the regiments from the toxins in the waters of Mistral.

By mid-afternoon, I had visited more than a dozen companies. My voice was hoarse from leading calls to vigilance, but I was pleased by what I had seen. Morale was strong. Granach had managed to keep the more disturbing discoveries of Lom Keep from filtering down to the rank and file. The monstrosity of the walker was overshadowed by the triumph over its destruction. The novelty of rest had not yet worn off. I had found very little need for discipline. Still, I was prepared for some challenges as I approached the tents that housed the men and women of Third Company. They were the ones who had been closest to the walker. Theirs had been the full measure of victory, but they had also been the closest witnesses to its horror.

The company's tents, the same khaki as the Mortisian uniform, were in a quadrant on the south-east corner of the encampment. As I approached, I saw a figure pacing back and forth in the wide lane created by the separation between the shelters of Third and 15th Companies. It was Captain Logan Saultern. He hurried over when he saw me. He had been tempered well by the battle, but I saw in his gait and his eyes a return of some of the anxiety that almost cost him his life at the start of the campaign.

'Captain,' I said.

He spoke quickly, sweat on his brow. 'I'm sorry, commissar, I don't know if I should be speaking to you about this, I mean he *is* who he is, and I know I shouldn't question, but these are my men, and–'

'Captain,' I said again, more sharply.

He took a breath, stopped, straightened. 'Commissar.' Another breath, and he remembered once more that he was an officer. 'Your pardon. I'm troubled, and I forgot myself.'

'Do not do so in front of your troops,' I warned. If he made me regret my act of mercy, that would be his last mistake.

'I won't, commissar. But if I spoke badly, it was motivated by concern for my troops. They deserve better treatment.'

'What do you mean?'

'Why are they being interrogated?' he pleaded.

The light dawned. At the same moment, I heard a man's scream come from deeper in the camp. 'How long?' I asked.

'For the last hour. He's had five brought before him so far. He's been with this man for more than twenty minutes and–'

I was already striding past the tents. The scream repeated, and I homed in on its location. It came from the command tent. Saultern had been displaced, his site of command turned into a source of humiliation for him, and of terror for his troops. I brushed through the flaps. I knew I was taking a risk. It was one I believed to be correct. My stride was sure. My vision was crystalline with anger.

Hektor Krauss stood in the centre of the tent. It took me a moment to recognize the soldier slumped on the stool before him. It was Deklan Betzner, the trooper whose missiles had crippled the legs of the walker. The big man looked shrunken before the inquisitor. His face and his left hand were bloody. So were some of the tools on the table beside Krauss.

'I do not appreciate interruptions, Yarrick,' said Krauss. The omission of my rank was a reminder of who held the power in this tent.

'I don't particularly care,' I said.

He was startled, and was unable to hide it. I don't think he had ever been defied before. I believe I did him some good that day. We should all be challenged. Only the God-Emperor is beyond all question.

Krauss turned to face me. Behind him I saw Betzner sag a little more, now with relief at having the inquisitor's attention removed from him. 'What do you think you're doing?' Krauss hissed.

'Interrupting something pointless and counterproductive.' I held his gaze. I knew he had the authority to kill me where I stood. Or worse. Perhaps I had been so disgusted by the need to accept the flagrant abuses of Cardinal Wangenheim that my tolerance had no room for any further misuse of authority. Perhaps my instinctive dislike of Krauss had the better of my judgement. Whatever the reason, I regarded the threat of what he could do to me with disinterested contempt.

The moment was very good practice.

I saw Krauss weigh his options. He could try to browbeat me, but he was not a stupid man. That approach would not work, and would serve only to undermine him before Betzner, setting back what he was trying to accomplish here. He could try to kill me. He might succeed. He would have received training far beyond mine.

But then again, I had already surprised him once.

His face reddened. It was good to see that perfectly groomed sleekness turn ugly. 'Outside,' he said. It must have been hard to speak with his jaw clenched.

Without a word, I took a step back, and held the flap open for him. I waited, watching his complexion shift from crimson to purple. I am not proud that I took a certain pleasure in the moment. But I am not ashamed, either.

He stormed past me, and I followed. We stopped on the other side of the tent. We spoke quietly as we faced each other, both conscious of the importance that our conversation not be overheard.

'You have no authority to interfere in these matters,' Krauss began.

'No, but I have a duty to do so.'

'*Duty?*' Krauss spat the word. 'What perverse conception of duty is this?'

'The same duty you have: to your office. I will preserve the morale of these soldiers, and I will have them fight to the last drop of their blood. So I will fight anything that interferes with *their* duty.'

'The last of their blood might well be shed on this soil if I do not find the truth about the heresy on Mistral.'

'Then seek it. If there is still a cult in existence, you won't find it here.'

'This regiment fought a cult. This company was in direct contact with a heretical device. There is information for me here.'

'Then ask for it!' It was difficult not to shout. 'No one here has anything to hide.'

'Oh?' His voice was so low, I could barely hear it, but that single syllable held a wealth of menace.

I was overreaching. 'No,' I conceded. 'We all have something to hide.' I lowered my voice too. 'Don't we?' Before he could be certain if I had truly threatened an inquisitor, I resumed in a more normal tone. 'But about the battle, there are no secrets. We are happy to tell the Inquisition whatever it wants to know. We know our duty there, too.' I pointed at the tent. 'There is no need for what I saw in there.'

'I am the fit judge of such matters.'

'That man was instrumental in bringing down the enemy machine,' I protested. 'He fired missiles at its legs. That was the sum total of his contact with the walker. Why torture him?'

'He knows something.' Krauss's conviction was absolute.

'Nonsense. He is not an enginseer. He was not in the party that entered the machine, and he didn't set foot in the keep.'

Krauss shrugged. Even that gesture had a contemptuous elegance to it. My words meant nothing. I realized that here was a man impervious to appeal. My role was not a merciful one, but it was pragmatic. There was nothing pragmatic about Krauss. There was only dogma, and in this he took great pride. But perhaps because of this rigidity, he was very good at what he did. 'You disappoint me, commissar,' he said. This time, he used my rank, as if he felt the need to remind me of who I was. 'I know you were trained in matters of Chaos. We have both been formed by the schola progenium. So I know that *you* know that these forces work more insidiously than through simple contact.'

'The walker was made by human hands,' I told him.

'Of course it was. But how?'

'There is no shortage of heavy industry on Mistral.'

'You are being ridiculous. I am not talking about means. I am talking about knowledge. I have seen the hololiths. It is not the product of any Standard Template Construct known to me. Or am I foolishly ignorant? Am I wrong?'

'No,' I admitted. 'You are not.' No STC had ever made such a monster, especially one whose throne was a terrible mockery of the principles that animated Titans.

'So how did Lom acquire the knowledge to construct this weapon?'

'That changes nothing,' I protested. 'This has no bearing on the troops who fought and destroyed the walker.'

'It changes everything. They saw it. More to the point, they *heard* it. I am told it cried out as it fell.'

'Baron Lom did,' I corrected.

That shrug again. 'The two were one at that point. What matters is what it said. Words are potent weapons. The right ones have a great power of corruption.'

'This company is not corrupt,' I insisted.

He looked at me steadily. There was a cold pity in his eyes. 'No,' he said, 'I don't believe it is.'

'Yet you subject its loyal soldiers to torture.'

'You do me an injustice. I am not a cruel man.' I didn't believe a word, though he clearly did. 'I was able to see after a few minutes of unforced questioning that there was nothing to be learned from the first few subjects.'

'But Trooper Betzner is different, is he? He is corrupt?'

'He knows something. One does not imply the other, but certain measures become necessary.'

'And how did he come by a special knowledge that passed over the rest of us?'

'Did I say he was the only one? I have not completed my investigation. But of this much I am sure: he knows something.'

His certainty made me hesitate. I didn't trust his easy recourse to extreme interrogation, but I didn't feel that this was a liar or an incompetent before me. It would have done my pride good to be able to dismiss the inquisitor. But by the grace of the God-Emperor, even as young as I was, I was not that foolish. 'Will you give me a moment alone with him?' I asked.

Now he paused, thrown by my cessation of hostilities. He looked at me closely for several seconds. Then he gave me a single, curt nod.

I returned the gesture, and made my way back inside the tent. Betzner had not moved. 'Look at me,' I told him. My tone was clipped, and I did not crouch before him. He would have seen me as his rescuer when I burst in on the interrogation. It was important now that he understand his fate rested with me, and in the answers he would give. With an effort, Betzner raised his head. One eye was swollen shut, but the other gazed at me first with hope, but then with desperate pleading.

'Inquisitor Krauss has made a serious charge against you,' I said. 'And Inquisitor Krauss is not a man to do so lightly.' That was a lie. I was quite ready to believe that Krauss would condemn a hundred innocents sooner than risk the escape of a single guilty soul. I was no more willing than he was to let the corrupt escape punishment, but there were other means to the same ends. 'The inquisitor is also a man who knows what he is doing,' I went on, and this was a perfect truth. 'Do you understand?'

Betzner had to clear his throat and spit up some blood before he could speak. 'Yes, commissar.'

'He says you know something more than you are saying about the weapon we encountered at Lom.'

'But I don't.' His mouth worked as if he were trying to find the words for an even more emphatic denial, but then he shook his head and was silent. The agony in those three words had been eloquent, though, and he did not avert his gaze.

I looked at him long and hard, evaluating. Betzner's conduct on the battlefield and off spoke volumes for him. My instinct was that he was being truthful. Yet I knew I could not trust my instinct alone. Worlds and more had been lost because of misguided trust. I could not discount Krauss's judgement and experience.

But this battered soldier was not a heretic. He was not corrupt. I was sure of this. And my earlier impulse to spare Saultern had been proven correct. Though that first act of mercy was making me weigh matters very carefully now. These were my first true tests as a commissar. Was I perhaps failing them? Was I giving in to a soft-hearted impulse? Did I have the necessary will to do the hard thing? Could I imagine turning Betzner over to Krauss's tender mercies, or putting a bullet in his head myself? I pictured myself removing my bolt pistol from its holster, placing the barrel against Betzner's forehead, and, with him still looking at me, pulling the trigger.

I experienced no disquiet. I would do my duty, whatever it called upon me to do. I felt a greater clarity, and I left the tent again to rejoin Krauss. He said nothing, waiting for me to speak first. I chose my words carefully, conscious that there were two aspects to this test. One was making a decision about Betzner. The second was dealing with the inquisitor.

Political officer, indeed. A momentary nostalgia for my days of service as a storm trooper washed over me. I dismissed the unworthy sentiment. I had been summoned to act as commissar, and so I would. I embraced the honour of duty.

'I am not saying your judgement is mistaken,' I told Krauss. It was difficult, with that inflexible, superior face before me, to choke back my antipathy. 'But I am convinced that Trooper Betzner has no conscious awareness of the knowledge you believe he has obtained. What use, then, is putting him to the question? You will gain nothing.'

Krauss's eyes focused on a spot just over my shoulder. I could see him thinking. It seemed I had found the correct approach: not to challenge his goals, but to suggest there might be a better way of achieving them.

'I am sure,' I continued, 'that if there is a threat on this planet as serious as...' I caught myself before I said *you think*, 'it appears there is, then we will need our regiments united and strong against it.'

'I never said otherwise,' Krauss answered.

'Then let them fight. Ask what must be asked, but if we sow the idea that there are those among us who have been secretly corrupted, we shall reap a harvest on behalf of Chaos.' *We*, I said, and said it twice. I wasn't sure that he would respond to that ploy, but then he nodded. After all, how could any faithful servant of the Emperor disagree with this inquisitor?

He thought a bit longer. I waited, immobile. At last, he said, 'It is true that my interrogation was not proving fruitful. It is also true that Trooper Betzner did not appear to be holding back. Perhaps you are correct. Perhaps he has no conscious awareness of what he knows.' His eyes grew hard again, his voice challenging. 'But I also am correct. He does know *something.*'

'Then we will watch him, and help him reveal that information to himself as well as to us,' I proposed.

'You understand the responsibility that you are shouldering?' he asked.

'I do.'

'I do not consider you immune to corruption, commissar.'

'You would be derelict in your duties if you did,' I told him.

'I would not hesitate to kill you.'

'Good. As I will not hesitate with Betzner.'

Krauss made his decision. 'Take him out of the tent,' he said. 'I have further interviews to conduct.'

'Coercive ones?'

'I don't expect them to be.'

'Thank you, inquisitor.'

As I walked away, he called out, 'You care for your charges, commissar. That is dangerous.'

'It is necessary,' I replied, though it occurred to me that we might both be right.

In the tent, I lifted Betzner to his feet. 'You have not suffered any injuries to the spine or your legs, so you will walk out of here unaided,' I informed him.

'Yes, commissar.'

'The only value your life has ever had is in service to the Emperor and his Imperium. So it is for us all.'

'Yes, sir.'

'But now, you must justify your continued existence. Do you

understand? Your fidelity must blind us with its truth. At the first hint of a shadow, I will kill you. Do. You. Understand?'

He did, and there was no fear in his damaged face. There was determination. And there was gratitude.

Two hours later, Seroff and I received the summons from Rasp to return to Tolosa. There was an event approaching, one he wanted us to witness.

'Any ideas?' Seroff asked as we boarded the train along with a handful of the more senior captains.

'Only premonitions of doom,' I answered. I was joking, but I was not lying. If what was coming would have an impact on the troops, it seemed unlikely that it would be anything good. Not on Mistral.

'The joys of being a political officer,' Seroff muttered, and I blinked at his echo of my earlier thoughts.

I should not have been surprised. He had heard the same lectures, and the same warnings from Rasp. 'A commissar is a *political* officer,' he had emphasized on more than one occasion. 'Remember that designation. It is specific, in that it names a duty unique among officers in the Imperial Guard. Every solider is a politician to some degree. The higher the rank, the greater the degree. But only the commissar is specifically tasked with those concerns. If you think that your role is simply a guardian of orthodoxy, then you are a fool, and of no use to anyone. The decisions, the prejudices and the clashes of the powerful will resonate down to the lowest trooper. Observe and learn.' A pause. A grim smile of weariness and determination. 'Develop the art of *anticipation*.'

I anticipated nothing good.

In Tolosa, we met Rasp at the Ecclesiarchal palace. He led

us to the Chapel Majoris. 'A service?' Seroff asked.

Rasp shook his head. 'No. A reception of a kind. This time, we are among the spectators, instead of being the spectacle.'

I said, 'You aren't going to tell us who the spectacle is, are you, lord commissar.'

'I have made an educated guess, based on some hints the cardinal has been tossing around, but I have no certainty.'

The chapel was full. Wangenheim's bishops sat in the choir. In the front pews were the two colonels of the Mortisian regiments, guests of honour no doubt because of their great utility to the cardinal. We took our seats just behind them. Next came the barons. I had never seen so many faces held in so studied a neutrality. The very lack of understandable curiosity told me how much hostility and worried suspicion were being kept just barely in check. So the nobility was in the dark, too. Vahnsinn looked straight ahead, not even glancing at us as we passed him. The rest of the seats were pews filled with the lower ranks of the clergy and palace functionaries. I suspected they were here as props. The spectacle, it occurred to me, would be twofold. The cardinal was planning to cow the nobility with the new arrivals, but he evidently wanted to impress whoever this was. There must be no empty seats.

The doors to the chapel closed with a boom. The air grew thick with incense. Wangenheim appeared at a lectern just before the altar, rather than in the pulpit that jutted out from the left-hand pillar at the transept crossing, and that would have had him gazing down at the congregation from six metres on high.

'This is a great day,' the cardinal began. 'I stand humbled before you, grateful merely to be the messenger of the news I bring you.'

I swallowed hard, and mimicked the barons in holding my face in studied blankness. Wangenheim's shameless use of this holy place disgusted me. His humility was as false as his palace was opulent. I had no reason to doubt his faith in the God-Emperor, but his self-interest was obscene. This space should have been given over to the sole purpose of turning our hearts and souls to the praise of the Master of Mankind. Yet it was now a stage for this strutting would-be potentate.

'These are troubled times on Mistral,' Wangenheim said, deep sorrow giving his voice just the right hint of a tremble. 'I know that most of our fellow citizens are steadfast in their allegiance to the Imperial Creed. But none of us can afford to be blind to the toxin of doubt that has infected the land. We have seen a great tragedy enacted in the Vales of Lom. Even as I speak, the enforcers in Tolosa and elsewhere are struggling to quell a heretical unrest. None of us can remain idle in the face of such spiritual jeopardy.' He nodded a few times, as if the barons had just applauded. 'And when our world has a sickness of the soul, it is my responsibility above all to find the cure.

'We need,' he declared, 'a great renewal. And we need a tangible symbol around which to rally. We need it to be known that the God-Emperor protects Mistral. And soon, indeed, all shall know. It is with brimming heart that I can announce that a great relic has come among us. I present to you…' he swept his arms wide, 'the jawbone of Saint Callixtus!'

The rear doors of the chapel opened once more, admitting a procession down the nave. Leading it was Bishop Castelnau. He was a thin man, and shorter than Wangenheim. He had all the presence of a faulty servitor. His voice was reedy and weak, and even my brief conversation with him at the reception had been an agony of tedium. His sermons, I imagined, must have inspired the wrong sort of martyrdom. But for all his physical weakness, he was not without political power. This he wielded with all the special vindictiveness of the true coward. He was Wangenheim's chief cat's-paw, slavish in his loyalty, and rewarded in consequence. He walked down the nave with imagined dignity, a ridiculous figure drowning in his robes. His mitre threatened to slip down over his eyes. It would have been very easy to laugh. It would have been a mistake to do so.

The bishop bore a violet cushion before him. Resting on it was an ornate, cylindrical reliquary of gold and stained glass. Knowing what lay inside drained all humour from the situation. Grotesque as Castelnau was, he carried a piece of a great man, one of the finest cardinals ever to serve the Adeptus Ministorum, a holy man who had been born and raised on Mistral, and gone on to become a great hero during the Redemption Crusades.

The gesture was inspired: the current cardinal was bringing another one home. The naked political calculation was so disgusting, it would have taken a great effort of will to remain quiet. I say *would have* because I had no difficulty biting my tongue. Bishop Castelnau did not walk in alone. With him came the escorts who had seen the relic safely to Mistral. There was nothing ridiculous about them.

Walking behind Castelnau, dwarfing him, was a squad of the Sisters of Battle. The standard borne by the rearmost warrior announced them as belonging to the Order of the Piercing Thorn. On a field of gold, an iron thorn was wrapped with a spiral of crimson that could have been blood or wire. Their power armour reflected the same colour scheme: black with a spiral of red, framed by golden capes. All the members of the squad were tall, but the sister superior who led them was a giant, the equal in height to some of the Adeptus Astartes. She was young, but her face was as unyielding as the standard's emblem.

The clank of armoured boots echoed off the marble of the chapel floor until the doors closed again, and the great organ began playing a majestic processional. The music reached a crescendo as the ten Adepta Sororitas and the bishop arrived at the altar. There, Castelnau placed the cushion and its reliquary. He stepped back, head bowed, then knelt just in front of the pews. The Sisters of Battle stood before the altar. Wangenheim stood beside it, on its dais. Even with the extra height, he was still shorter than the sister superior. He held out his hands, and there was just enough of a pause before he started to speak that I found myself wondering if he had expected the women to kiss his ring of office.

'Sister Superior Setheno,' he said to the leader, 'I welcome the warriors of the Order of the Piercing Thorn to Tolosa, and thank them for ensuring the safe homecoming of Saint Callixtus.' He looked out to the congregation. 'Our Emperor is generous with Mistral. He showers us with good fortune. With this sacred return, we now find ourselves hosts to the hammer of the Imperial Guard, the vigilance of the Inquisition, and the militant faith of the Adepta Sororitas. Our trials are surely at an end. Shall we not celebrate?'

'All praise to the Emperor,' the bishops intoned in unison.

'I said that Mistral needed renewal. It shall have it. We have a great coming together with the planetary Council next week. What more auspicious occasion might there be to rejoice in our brotherhood beneath the eye of the Emperor?'

I saw Seroff's jaw drop. He caught himself, and he closed his mouth with a sharp click of his teeth.

'All praise to the Emperor,' said the bishops.

'And so,' Wangenheim concluded, 'I am declaring that a great Festival of the Emperor's Light shall commence the day after the conclusion of the Council. It shall last a week, and begin with the permanent installation of the holy relic in this chapel, after a procession through Tolosa, that all may see it and draw together in worship.'

'All praise to the Emperor,' said the bishops.

I prayed to the Emperor as well. I prayed that we might all be delivered from the machinations of a madman.

CHAPTER 7
THE ADVENT

1. Yarrick

'He isn't mad,' Rasp said.

Seroff and I were on the streets of Tolosa with Rasp, Granach and Benneger. We were bending into the wind. Conversation was difficult with the words being whipped from our mouths. Listening in would be even harder, given we could barely hear each other. We were walking some of the possible routes that the relic's procession would take, trying to get a better sense of the lie of the land. The colonels needed to know what troop dispositions would be needed to maintain security during the festival. We had every reason to be exploring the field of operations and discussing it with each other. We seized the opportunity to speak with less fear of spies.

Tolosa's character made me think of the ripples in a pond. The palace was the centre of the city's life in every possible sense. It was the splash that determined all else. The larger, more clearly defined ripples close to the palace were made up of the administrative centres and the homes of the aristocracy. The further out one went, the more broken up and ill-defined the ripples became. Power, influence and wealth drained away. Population density, on the other hand, grew enormously. Major avenues and inner defensive walls helped create the overall pattern of concentric rings, but the smaller streets were all part of a tangled maze, and the confusion only got worse in the poorer districts. It was easy to get lost. As long as I could see the palace gleaming at the top of the hill, I had some sense of geography. But whenever we lost sight of it, walking down roads barely wider than a path between the grey stone habs on either side, disorientation set in. Granach frequently consulted a map on his data-slate, and just as frequently cursed its inaccuracy.

The buildings were ancient, like the rest of the city, most no more than four or five storeys high. Their façades were almost completely blank, the windows sparse and narrow. I had seen why back at the inn. The streets rarely ran straight for more than a block, creating windbreaks with the buildings themselves. Even so, the wind found its way through. Sometimes we would walk in relative calm for a hundred metres, only to be met with a ferocious gust and a phantom wail at the next intersection.

We soon found that no one strolled in Tolosa. There were no parks, no sites of outdoor recreation. Everyone on the street was striding with a single purpose: to reach a destination as quickly as possible.

'How can he not be mad?' Granach demanded. 'He is opening the door to civil war. Or have I misread the political situation here that badly?'

'You haven't, colonel,' Rasp assured him. 'The cardinal is taking a huge risk. If he loses, then yes, Mistral descends into war.' He raised his hands as he shrugged with theatrical despair. 'Perhaps that is inevitable no matter what happens next week. War may very well be exactly what Cardinal Wangenheim wants.'

'So he is mad,' Granach insisted. Benneger grunted in agreement.

We paused at another of Tolosa's concentric walls. The road, already narrow, became even more constricted as it passed through the barrier to the next region of the city. There were a dozen such bottlenecks along the circumference of the wall, and the pattern was repeated in each ring of fortifications. They had clear value for controlling the flow of the crowds, but they would also hamper our ability to move across the city quickly.

'With respect, colonel,' I said, 'he may be reckless, but I agree with the lord commissar. The cardinal's decisions are too strategic to be insane. If war is inevitable, it is to his advantage that it comes when the forces of the Imperium are assembled and poised for action.'

'So we do his dirty work for him,' Benneger grumbled.

Rasp gave him a lopsided smile. 'So it would seem.'

Granach was still looking at the wall. Seroff asked, 'Is something troubling you, colonel?'

'The route of the procession,' Granach answered.

'Wangenheim is still working on it,' Benneger told him. 'I asked a few times. Keeps revising.'

'He wants the display to be seen by as many people as possible,' Rasp said.

Granach sighed. 'Will he take *any* of our recommendations, do you think? How are we expected to maintain security for every street in this maze?'

'He will expect us to do nothing more than our duty,' Rasp answered. It was hard, over the howl of the wind, to catch his bitter irony.

2. *Cernay*

It was late, hours past midnight, when Nikolas Cernay left the tavern. He didn't know what time it was. His chronometer had been smashed in a short brawl a good four bottles ago. His head swam with the sick fumes of cheap amasec. He could have afforded better. He could have chosen a more salubrious drinking establishment, too, closer to home. But he liked the Flagellant's Remorse. His family name meant nothing there. No one cared that he headed the Cernay trading concern, or if they did, they were more likely to resent him than play sycophant. As merchants went, he and his family were far from being major players on Mistral. Their grain business was almost entirely limited to Tolosa and its environs. But they lived well, and he had to spend more than enough time at the right occasions, courting the right people. Sometimes it was good to descend a few rings down Tolosa's hill, into the regions where the only wealth that mattered was the weight of a fist.

Two fights tonight. Along with the chronometer, he'd lost a tooth, and won some bloody knuckles. A fine evening.

The wind blasted the worst of the fumes from his head as he stepped out into the street. His gait steadied after the first block. He kept his guard up. There were few exterior lumoglobes in this neighbourhood, and many of those were broken. It would be easy to trip and fall. Easier yet to be jumped. He walked down the middle of the street, buffeted by gusts, avoiding the darkest shadows between buildings. He swung his arms, held his hands open, and struck the cobbles hard with the heels of his boots, announcing his readiness to tackle all comers. If he had to smash another face or two on the walk home, he wouldn't complain. The sound of nose cartilage hitting stone had a charm of its own.

There were other people still out at this hour, but not many, and they kept to themselves. No one approached. Half an hour later he had reached Tolosa's middle ring, where the Cernay residence stood. The more respectable the neighbourhoods became, the more deserted the streets were. There was no reason for people to be outside their homes. All the dining and drinking establishments had been closed for hours. By the time he reached his sector, he was alone.

He was less watchful now. No reason to expect a fight. There was only the eternal struggle with the wind, which always seemed to be blowing against him, no matter what direction he took. There was greater illumination here, but he stayed in the middle of the road. There was no traffic, and he found it easier to walk on the wider surface than on the narrow pavements. He squinted as a particularly powerful gust hit him full in the face, and so he almost didn't see the figure.

He did, though. There was movement to his left, and when he looked, eyes watering, he saw a blur retreat into the darkness of a tiny alley. He frowned, rubbed his eyes and peered at the alley as he went past. No one emerged. He walked on. After another twenty metres he looked back. Was there someone there again? Yes, he thought there was. He had the impression of a robed shape moving in the shadows of the façades.

He walked faster. He could feel his heart beating, and his head was clearing as his mouth dried. He was only five minutes from home. When he spotted a second figure up and to the right, it felt like hours to go.

The other shape stood in a shop doorway, almost hidden in the shadows, but it was not quite hiding, as if it wanted him to notice. He peered at it as he drew level. He couldn't tell if he was looking at a man or a woman. There was only the suggestion of robes and darkness. The figure did not move. But when he had gone past, and he looked over his shoulder, the stillness broke. With a jerk, as if suddenly released into life, the figure began to follow. It flowed from shadow to shadow, a cowled grace. Neither it nor the first hunter seemed to be hurrying. They weren't trying to catch up, but they weren't letting him put any distance between them, either.

He ran. His gaze jerked from side to side. He started seeing movement in every darker pool of the night. The wind raged against him, its idiot roar blocking the sound of pursuing footsteps. It hurled a scrap of parchment his way. He yelped and jumped aside, seeing in the sudden motion the flap of robes, the rush of an assassin.

He ran faster, but already his lungs were protesting. He tried to think who would wish him harm. The Cernays had many competitors. Their hands were not clean. No merchants' were. Violence between the concerns happened. It was also limited. Unrestrained war would profit no one, and would draw the ire of the more powerful forces of Mistral. Shipments were destroyed. Some were stolen. Accidents happened, sometimes fatal ones, sometimes to important figures. But rarely. And there was an art to it. A way of bringing an end about that permitted everyone to maintain the pretence that nothing had happened.

He did not think such an accident awaited him. This was something else. These people wanted to frighten him. They had done so. Would that be enough?

'What do you want?' he gasped. The wind stole his words.

Even he couldn't hear them. He tried again. He didn't slow his pace. His lungs were ragged, and he could only shout a single word with each breath. '*What... do... you... want?*' The effort scraped his throat. *I'm frightened,* he thought. *You've done well. You don't need to do any more.* He took a breath and screamed, 'I'll give you anything you want!'

The effort winded him. He stumbled, lost his footing and crashed to the ground. His nose smacked the paving stones. He heard the music of breaking cartilage after all. Gagging on his own blood, he scrambled to his feet. He looked back, expecting the figures to be upon him. They had stopped. But now there were four, and they were standing in a staggered line across the street. There couldn't be faces inside those hoods, he thought. There was only concentrated darkness. At the moment he started moving again, they advanced once more.

The way was uphill now. He was running again, but it felt like he was trudging through quicksand. The thought came that there was no point to his struggle. If his tormentors wanted him, they could take him at any time. He kept looking back, risking another fall. They were coming still, neither closing nor falling behind. Their robes were long, and he couldn't see their legs. They seemed to float effortlessly up the road. And though they were brazen now, they were still hard to pick out in the darkness, as though the shadows travelled with them.

He called for help, but he couldn't shout any longer. A desperate croak was all he could manage. The wind swallowed it. On either side of him were closed shutters and blank walls. The city had turned its back on him. He was alone.

He whined in terror. Then he was over the top of the hill, and his heart was hammering still harder, now with agonized hope. His door was less than fifty metres away.

A surge of adrenaline gave him a burst of speed. He was going downhill, and the wind's tyranny lost its grip. He had his key in his hand. Another glance back, and the figures had not yet reached the crest. The illusion of having outpaced them gave him the extra strength he needed. He flew over the last few metres and reached the door.

It was iron, set into a featureless wall. Beyond it was a courtyard, and then the house proper. He inserted the key, turned it, and pulled the door open.

Leap over the threshold. Slam the door. Lock it again. The actions were simple, and would have taken less than five seconds. He did not have those seconds. Hands grabbed him. He was hauled away from the door. He struggled. He knew how to fight. He had hurt people very well earlier. But his skills and the ferocity of his fear did him no good. The hands that held him were strong too, and there were too many of them. Two of the figures wrestled him to the ground. They pinned his arms behind his back. He felt rope cinch his wrists, the violent friction burning. A hand gripped his hair and held his head up. He was forced to watch as the other two figures went through the doorway. He didn't hear any screams, but he knew there must have been. The wind keened over the shrieks as his wife, his brother, his parents and his children were dragged, one at a time, out into the street, bound and hooded. His house was emptied. Almost. His aunt, who held a controlling interest in the concern, was not captured. Even through his fear, he wondered why not. Had she hidden? Was she dead? Was she being spared? If so, maybe this was a simple kidnapping. Maybe one ransom later, he would be safely home.

One of the figures closed the door, locked it, then walked over to Cernay and crouched before him. It touched a finger to his lips. It spoke, and its voice killed his hopes. The sound was androgynous, rough and painful, as if the speaker had a mouth lined with barbed wire. Cernay couldn't tell if he was hearing a man or a woman. 'Be silent,' said his captor. 'Save your screams. You will have much use for them later. So will we.'

3. Yarrick

Eight days after our reconnaissance of Tolosa, the High Council of Mistral convened. The chambers of the Council were in the Ecclesiarchal palace. The location was telling. They had once had their own building, still within the central ring of Tolosa, and adjacent to the palace. But the needs of the Ecclesiarchy had grown with its political strength on Mistral, and the Council House had been demolished three centuries ago to make way for the expanding east wing of the palace. The chambers were handsome, spacious, as expensively wrought as every other aspect of the palace. They were also very clearly an annex. Every time the nobility of Mistral gathered, it was reminded of the limits of its political power. Vahnsinn was nominally the Imperial Commander of the planet, but that title had withered in actual importance as the cardinals had asserted their dominance.

Seroff and I met Rasp and the colonels outside the stairs to the public gallery. Though seating was reserved for us, we would be mixing with the good citizens of Tolosa today.

'Well?' Granach asked.

'Ten more abductions last night,' Seroff reported. 'That we know of,' he added.

'If one happened, we know about it,' I said. 'Everyone does.'

The mood on the streets of Tolosa was a tinderbox. Families were vanishing. In every case, one member of the household was left behind to bear witness to the assault. As a result, rumours were spreading like a firestorm. All the stories agreed that the abductors were clad in dark robes. Who they were, and what they wanted, varied according to the prejudices and sympathies of the speaker. But the other point of agreement was the need for justice.

The street was terrified. It wanted blood. If blood was not given, it would be sought.

I dreaded the cardinal's festival.

Granach sighed. 'If only we had arrived here a bit sooner.'

'I don't think so, colonel,' Rasp told him. 'The cult is far more entrenched than we thought. The timing of the attacks, and their visibility, are not the result of a recently improvised plan. There is a systematic project of destabilisation at work.'

'Working very well, too,' Granach spat.

Since the abductions had begun, the colonel had brought in more troops within the city walls and instituted an intensive programme of night patrols. But there were too many streets, too many alleys, too many shadows. The Mortisian effort was proving futile.

'At least the Inquisition is finding that too,' Benneger said.

That was true. If Krauss had been having any success in rooting out the leaders of the cult, he was keeping it to himself. The attacks had also diverted his attention from the troops for the time being.

Granach nodded. 'And the Adepta Sororitas haven't involved themselves.'

'Yet,' Rasp amended.

We filed up the staircase. In the public gallery, the lord commissar and the colonels took the front row. Seroff and I sat behind them.

'Are you ready to be edified?' Seroff asked me.

'I already have been,' I said, taking in the architecture of the rectangular hall. The spectators were settled in tiered pews at the rear, overlooking the U-shaped configuration of councillors' seats. Between the horns of the 'U' was a dais two metres high. On it was the cardinal's throne. Behind it, rich violet curtains covered Wangenheim's entrance to the chambers. His route to the meeting was elevated in a literal sense. He would not have to mix with profane powers sitting below.

'And your conclusion?' Seroff said.

'These are very comfortable surroundings in which to declare war.'

'No reason not to mark the event in style. No chance of things turning out otherwise, you think?'

'How could they?' Wangenheim would push. The barons would resist. And there was no more room to manoeuvre. Vahnsinn had told Rasp as much, when they had met the night before. The baron, Rasp had told us, had looked exhausted.

Ten minutes after the last of the barons arrived, Wangenheim graced the assembly with his presence. For the first half-hour, the Council was a turgid dance of formalities, rituals of mutual respect that had become shapes without substance. Then the grievances began.

'Your eminence,' Vahnsinn said. He sat directly below the gallery, in the seat that most centrally faced the throne. 'We must turn once again to the question of tithes. There is a petition before you…' He paused while a page emerged from the curtains to place a scroll on the ornate table before Wangenheim's throne. 'It is signed by the unanimity of this Council. The present demands are unsustainable, and some compromise must be reached for the sake of the continued…

well-ordered... governance of Mistral.' With his hesitation, he signalled that *well-ordered* meant *peaceful*.

Wangenheim did not lean forward to pick up the scroll. He looked down at where it sat on the table as if he were eyeing a dead rat. 'The barons' concern for the wellbeing of our planet is noted,' he said. 'It is also appreciated. That is why I have no doubt that they will understand and support the measures it is incumbent upon us to take.'

'Here we go,' I whispered to Seroff.

A trio of aides entered from the chamber's side doors. They moved to the centre and distributed vellum sheets to each of the barons. I noticed the seals affixed to each sheet. 'Those are not proposals,' I said. 'They're proclamations.'

'So he's not even pretending to have a debate. Is he trying to provoke them?'

'I'm sure he is.'

'We are,' Wangenheim said, 'in a time of crisis.'

'What is this?' Baron Eichen interrupted. He looked up from the vellum to glare at the cardinal. His hands were shaking. He was a big man. His collar was too tight, and dug into his fleshy neck. His face had been flushed from the moment he had entered the chamber and settled himself with a wheezing, groaning sigh in his seat. Now he was a violet almost as deep as the curtains.

'It is,' the cardinal began, 'what the situation calls for. It is–'

'It is a lien!' Baroness Elleta Gotho exploded. 'A lien on all land, property and holdings! You are trying to destroy us!'

Wangenheim pressed his lips together. He looked like a displeased amphibian. But his body, I noticed, was relaxed as he held up a hand to silence Gotho. His anger was a show. The truth, I guessed, was that he was very satisfied with the way the meeting was going. 'I am doing no such thing,' he said. 'I am acting as a defender of the Sacred Imperial Creed. It is under attack, as I *hope* my friends before me have noticed.'

'Of course,' Vahnsinn said. I heard now the exhaustion Rasp had mentioned. This was a man who knew how the game was going to be played, had no taste for it, and had no choice but to assume his allotted role. So he made his futile gesture towards keeping the peace. 'We are of one mind with the Holy Ecclesiarchy in rejecting the heretical crimes that have been committed.'

'I am relieved to hear that.' The corners of Wangenheim's lips turned upwards. The effect was even more batrachian. 'Then there can be no objection.'

I winced. Seroff put a hand to his forehead. The chamber erupted as the barons shouted over one another. Baron Maurus, who was a placid-looking man, more clerk than aristocrat, had the loudest voice of them all. His cry of 'Thief!' cut through the hall. The silence before a storm descended.

'You will wish, of course, to reconsider that outburst,' Wangenheim said. He spoke quietly. The air filled with ice.

Maurus hesitated. I watched him glance around the chamber at his peers. His fury was reflected a hundred times over. He turned back to the cardinal. 'I will not. If we accept these terms, we will no longer have any independence of action. We will be entirely dependent upon the pleasure of the Ecclesiarchy.'

'Quite so,' Wangenheim answered with a calm perfectly calibrated to infuriate. 'We have indisputable evidence now that the heresy infecting Mistral was not limited to Baron Lom. Drastic measures are required.'

'You accuse us of collusion with heretics?' Vahnsinn asked. He spoke not with anger, but a profound sorrow.

Wangenheim said, 'Is there any other conclusion available to me?' He performed his own sorrow well. I didn't believe in it. I saw and heard the actions and words of a man whose blood was cold. He should have been sunning his bloated carcass on a rock, not draping it in the finery of his holy office. 'I am charged with the protection of the Creed. I perceive the threat. I have no choice but to place this world under the direct, unwavering protection of the Adeptus Ministorum.'

'You mean under your personal control,' Eichen barked. He had turned a still-darker shade. I wondered if his heart would survive the session.

Wangenheim shrugged. 'You cannot refuse,' he told the barons.

Vahnsinn stood up. 'But we do.' He had shed the fatigue and the sorrow. His three words were determination itself. The man who spoke was a leader. He would not lack adherents to his cause, now that he had declared it.

I checked my chronometer.

'What are you doing?' Seroff whispered.

'Noting the moment that Mistral went to war,' I said.

Wangenheim gazed at Vahnsinn for a long time before speaking again. He seemed to be taking the full measure of his opponent. When he spoke, it was with a chilling honesty. 'I will make you comply,' he said. He might have said, *You will be made to comply*, and preserved the illusion of being the reluctant enforcer of laws that had nothing to do with his own agenda. But he didn't say that. 'I will,' he emphasized. *I*. Not *we*. The actions, the desires, the will, the threat – they were all his.

'He doesn't care who knows what he's about, does he?' Seroff said, full of wonder at the cardinal's colossal audacity.

I looked behind me, at the gallery full of gaping spectators. To a soul, they understood the import of what they were witnessing. I saw many faces, but not the ones I sought. I faced forward again. 'The Sisters of Battle are not here,' I told Seroff. 'Perhaps he cares just a little bit.'

'Smart man.'

Down below, Vahnsinn was nodding. 'You are welcome to try,' he said to Wangenheim. He turned around, and looked up to the gallery. 'Citizens of Tolosa,' he said. 'People of Mistral. You see what corruption has wrought. Ask yourselves where the true heresy lies.' Then he strode out of the chamber, the other barons close behind.

The gallery was in an uproar now. I could barely hear Seroff's slow whistle. 'That was smartly played,' he said.

Rasp twisted around on his pew and faced us. 'Quite right,' he said. 'Have you ever seen such grand theatre?'

'I wish we hadn't,' I said.

Wangenheim stood up suddenly. 'Indeed!' he shouted, silencing the crowd. 'Indeed,' he repeated, far more softly. 'Ask yourselves that question. Where does the heresy lie? You should always be asking yourselves that question. Our vigilance against corruption must never falter. Ask yourselves the question again tomorrow, when our great celebration begins, and you turn to face the Emperor's light anew.'

And then it was dusk on the eve of the festival, and I walked the streets of Tolosa, accompanying Logan Saultern as he inspected Third Company's security preparations. The captain's troops had responsibility for the southern quadrant of the central ring, beginning just beyond the great square before the palace. They were out in force. Over a third of the regiment now patrolled Tolosa, coordinating with the muscle of the Adeptus Arbites. We could have had every Mortisian on the planet in the city, with the logistical nightmare that feeding and billeting such a number entailed, and we would have been no better off, accomplishing little more than diluting our strength among Tolosa's millions.

We could not protect every street and home. I knew there would be further abductions in the night to come. The cult was growing bold, and with good reason. There had been no apprehensions, and there was no safety. No one walked the streets at night any longer, but that made no difference. The citizens cowered in their houses when darkness fell, clinging to the comforting illusion of refuge, even though all the victims had been dragged from these very homes. Whether they were poor, rich, serf, or minor nobility made no difference. The cult had use for them all, it seemed. The more troops Granach committed to secure the streets, the more futile the effort appeared. The only effect was the growing resentment of the Tolosans. The soldiers who could not ensure their safety became instead the objects of their wrath.

Wangenheim had, at least, settled on a procession route. It snaked through almost every neighbourhood on his quest for maximum exposure. The only positive thing that could be said about it, from a security standpoint, was that it was no longer subject to change. Maintaining complete overwatch along the entire length of the route was impossible. Instead, Granach had established a multitude of checkpoints. Some were at street-level. Others were on the roofs. All of them had been manned continuously since the cardinal had finalized the plans two days ago. Vehicular traffic was now banned along the entire route. During the procession itself, a large escort would travel both with the relic and in parallel. The great square and its environs, meanwhile, would be under heavy protection. This was where the crowds would be at their largest, and where relic and dignitaries would remain in one place. It would be the most inviting target of all.

The warriors of the Order of the Piercing Thorn claimed for themselves the responsibility of protecting the relic itself during the procession, and of the platform during the ceremony. The rest fell to us, though I knew very well that Krauss or his agents would be present too, travelling a web of shadows according to his own particular agenda.

The Sisters of Battle. The Inquisition. The Adeptus Arbites. The Imperial Guard. Each force with its own agenda. The territorial responsibilities overlapping. I wondered if Wangenheim had truly thought through all the consequences.

Saultern and I moved from station to station. Each had at least two troopers. The area was as locked down as it was possible to be, as far as I could tell. 'Has one of the colonels been by?' I asked.

'Yes, commissar. Colonel Benneger. He said he was pleased.'

'Good. Where did you pick up these strategic skills, Captain Saultern?'

He smiled with a pleased modesty. 'I cannot take credit for what you see, sir. I spoke to my sergeants and followed their advice.'

'You did well, in that case.' A commander who wasn't afraid to listen to subordinates with more knowledge than he had. I congratulated myself on sparing the man's life.

'My one hope is to do well tomorrow.'

'That is true of every member of the companies assigned to this action, captain,' I told him. 'I know we shall do well.'

That was an easy sort of confidence, and a truth that was so partial as to be almost a lie. Of course the men and women of Aighe Mortis would do their duty. But I said nothing about their odds of preventing the procession and the ceremony from being disrupted. The more I thought about it, the more I was reconsidering Rasp's claim that Wangenheim was not mad. Staging such an event in the immediate wake of pushing the barons to the brink was beyond reckless. Even if he expected an attack of some kind, even if he *wanted* such an eventuality, if he thought he could control everything that would follow he was a fool. The mood of the citizenry was too volatile. The cardinal was letting his ambition take him into the realm of lethal hubris.

We approached a scene that confirmed my suspicions.

'Not again,' Saultern said.

Ahead of us, as we walked towards the west, the block ended at a wide intersection. The street we were on, one of the major arteries that circumnavigated the ring, crossed the even wider boulevard that led to the great square. Guard posts protected by prefab plasteel barricades had been established at all four corners of the intersection. Crowds of men were gathering around each of the posts. Most of the men were young, the same age as the uniformed warriors who stared back at them. There were a few older faces in the mix, displaying the thuggish pettiness of the frustrated leader. All the expressions were hard, eager for any excuse to engage in violence. What surprised and alarmed me was the range in clothing. I saw labourers, merchants' sons and even a few aristocrats. They had come from all regions of the city, from all the strata of its society. They were united by resentment, I guessed, and also fear. But there was desire there too. They were looking for someone to hit, and so ease their own terror.

'How much of this have you encountered?' I asked.

'More and more,' he said. 'But no one has done more than stare or yell from a distance. This is new.'

I walked faster. There was no danger of the troopers coming to harm. They were armed, the crowd was not, but a slaughter would not help anything.

I was still a dozen metres from the intersection when a towering figure arrived from the direction of the square. Setheno said nothing as she approached the nearest group. Deklan Betzner was one of the troopers in the guard post, and even he seemed small next to her. She stood before the civilians, face impassive. The men backed away. She took a step towards them. They stumbled into the centre of the intersection. The other groups noticed what was going on. They all moved to the centre. Setheno now faced a single large group. Still she said nothing. Her silence stilled all conversation.

I slowed down, watching. I held up a hand, but Saultern had already stopped walking. He understood. The scene needed no disruption from us.

The force of her presence was formidable. It was due to much more than just her height and her power armour. I had heard of venerable prioresses whose mere glances could strike entire companies with the sense of their unworthiness, but Setheno was no ancient. She must have been a veteran of some experience to be a sister superior, though she was young enough that I guessed her ascension to that rank was recent. She had, certainly, the air of sanctity, of an utterly impermeable faith, that was common to all the Adepta Sororitas. There was something else, though. She radiated an aura of extreme threat.

If the crowd had attacked the Mortisians or Setheno, the

result would have been the same. I think the troops seemed like closer kin, more human, and so the mob could imagine attacking them. The Sisters of Battle had not been transformed into something beyond mortals like the Adeptus Astartes, but they were still profoundly *other*, and the fact that they were still unenhanced humans made their difference from the common woman or man even more stark. The people resented the Imperial Guard, but they feared Setheno.

Still not a word. She stood motionless as the crowd became more compact. Swaggering bravado and free-floating anger evaporated. In their place came the need to stand close to one another. Setheno's hands were at her sides, relaxed. Her stance was neutral. Her white hair and pallor only made her seem like a marble statue clad in crimson night. But she was a statue that could burst to violent life. The wind tossed her hair and cloak as if trying to goad her to war. I was suddenly very aware of the pommel of her sword.

She took another step towards the crowd. I heard the faint jingle of the icon chains that hung from her breastplate. The men backed up in perfect unison. This was a dance now, its steps preordained. Setheno cocked her head. Perhaps the men did not flee at that moment, though my memory may be far too charitable. They did leave. Quickly. Within seconds, the intersection was clear of civilians.

I walked forward again. 'That was an impressive demonstration of herding, sister superior,' I said.

She turned to me. This was the first time I had been close enough to see her eyes. They were unusual: an almost translucent grey flecked with gold.

She still had visible pupils then. And the man speaking with her still had two arms.

'Thank you, commissar,' she said. 'Though it would have been preferable if my intervention had not been necessary.'

I bristled. 'These soldiers do not require your protection.' Behind me, I heard Saultern's intake of breath. I think he expected me to be bisected where I stood.

'Not my protection, no.' She looked away from me and swept her gaze over the streets. 'I was referring to their ability to maintain security.'

'We know our duty, sister superior, and we know how to perform it.'

'Really.'

'Yes,' I said simply, biting off a host of retorts.

Several seconds passed. She appeared to be taking the measure of the Mortisians and the territory it was their mission to hold. 'We shall see tomorrow, won't we?' she said, walking back towards the square.

'Would you have preferred a massacre?' I called after her. 'On the eve of the festival? Would that have improved security?'

'You speak as if a massacre were avoidable,' she said without looking back.

When her figure had dwindled sufficiently, Saultern asked, 'What did she mean?'

I wasn't sure. Was she presuming the Imperial Guard's incompetence? Or was she commenting on Wangenheim's folly? Both? 'I don't know,' I admitted. I faced Saultern, but I spoke so to all the troops at this station. 'What of it?' I asked. 'Does the opinion of the Adepta Sororitas matter so much to the warriors of Aighe Mortis? Will you accept the judgement of others? Or will you impose the truth of your worth through glorious action?'

The roars that greeted my questions were gratifying. Good.

The Mortisians had something to prove. They would need to do so tomorrow.

Saultern and I continued on past the intersection. There was one more post at the end of the next block, and one more beyond that. The procession would not pass this way, but this close to the square, Granach wanted the security cordon to have a wide margin.

A hundred metres from the position, I heard running footsteps behind me. I whirled.

Betzner was sprinting towards me. He flew down the narrow pavement faster than a man half his size. Saultern gaped. I saw the urgency on Betzner's face. I realized he was responding to a threat. There was no cover where we stood. 'Run!' I yelled at Saultern, and we pounded towards the guard post.

Betzner ran faster yet. As though carried by the wind, he caught up to us. A massive weight hit me, and I went flying. In the same instance I heard the energy burn of a las-shot. I struck the ground. My lungs were flattened, but I rolled and rose to my knees, ready to act even as I struggled to draw breath. The pavement where I had been a moment before was scorched from the las-strike. Betzner was standing just past the burn, firing his rifle at the rooftop of the apartments opposite us. Seconds later, the troopers at the posts at both ends of the block followed his example. I could see no one up there, knew that I been in the sights of a sniper. The enemy let off a couple of shots in response to the storm assaulting him, but they were wild.

The firing continued until rockets rose from two directions. A fireball engulfed the roof. The top of the building collapsed onto the floors below. The wind spread the smoke and dust over the city to the south. Whoever had been up there was dead now.

I stood up. 'I am in your debt, Trooper Betzner,' I told him.

'No, commissar, I am in yours.'

'You just saved my life.'

Betzner waved his hand at the demolished roof. 'From a sniper. You saved me from the Inquisition. No contest, sir.'

I squinted at the building, then looked back at Betzner. 'Your eyesight is remarkable,' I said. 'Someone was evidently up there, but I never saw him.'

The big man looked uncomfortable. 'I didn't *see* him, exactly,' he began.

'Then how did you know he was trying to shoot me?'

'I... I'm not sure.' Betzner went from uncomfortable to anxious.

'But you knew.' Krauss's insistence on Betzner's uncanny knowledge rang in my ears.

The trooper nodded.

'Perhaps you saw the flash of the scope,' I suggested, offering him thc bait of a plausible lie.

He did not take it. 'No, commissar.'

Betzner would bear watching, then, as I had pledged to Krauss. But he had not given me any reason to question his loyalty. To the contrary. 'All right,' I told him. 'Resume your duties, trooper.'

There was a cascading series of cracks. Stonework gave way, and more of the apartment collapsed. It had lost half its original height. The fires started by the initial explosions were now burning out of control. At least the buildings that lined this street had been cleared of inhabitants. No one was permitted inside any structure that overlooked the procession or the square. At this moment, that felt like a small mercy.

I doubted that I had been personally targeted. I was an

officer, and so my death would have served to send a message. The enemy was growing brazen. We should dread the events of the next day.

Message received.

CHAPTER 8
THE FESTIVAL OF THE EMPEROR'S LIGHT

1. Rasp

In the hour before dawn, Rasp went to Grauben. It was a gamble. He wasn't sure the baron would still be in the city. As he walked he saw no one, but he was sure eyes followed him. Reports of his walk would reach the ears of the barons and the Ecclesiarchy, no doubt. Perhaps he could just as well have made the visit in broad daylight, but there was no need to make the job easy on the spies. He took from them the cover of crowds. Let them hide on deserted streets. Let them run afoul of each other. Those thoughts amused him, and there was so very little amusement to be had as Mistral toppled into civil war.

Rasp took his small joys where he could find them. The galaxy refused to offer him anything more. And it was important, he believed, that he not neglect them. If he did, it would be easy to drown in the darkness of endless war. His life was a mosaic of battlefields. He had no idea how many thousands of soldiers he had come to know and seen die. If he was to be equal to his calling and to his duty to the Emperor, his morale had to be a model for the troops and officers he would inspire. A finely developed appreciation for the absurd had served him at least as well as his pistol. Of his two protégés, Seroff was the one with the more vigorous sense of humour. If he shaped it properly, it might sustain him through the long hells of war. Yarrick was a harder read. He was too intelligent not to see the absurd when he encountered it, but his response seemed to be to focus with even greater ferocity on the duty before him. Rasp had seen the man smile, but not often. The young commissar's intensity would be, Rasp thought, either his making or his damnation.

There were no lights visible through the shutters of Grauben. The house was asleep. Rasp pulled the chain that hung to the right of the iron door. The bell that rang inside the house had a deep resonance. When the door opened, Rasp was surprised to see Vahnsinn himself.

'Have your serfs deserted you?' he asked.

'I was expecting you,' the baron said, shutting the door behind Rasp.

'You were so sure I'd come here?'

Vahnsinn shrugged. 'I was hoping, then.'

Rasp looked at his tired eyes. 'You haven't slept.'

'No.' Vahnsinn led the way to his study. The room was larger than the one where they had dined with Yarrick and Seroff. It had much of the same warmth and intimacy, though. It was more library than den. Bookshelves were floor-to-ceiling. Many were free-standing, occupying most of the study, leaving just enough room for a desk and, facing the fireplace, two armchairs. Vahnsinn touched a decanter on the desk. 'Will you drink?'

'Thank you, no. Why didn't you sleep? Are you expecting something to happen today?'

'Aren't you?' Vahnsinn tapped a finger on the desk, then sat heavily in the left-hand armchair.

Rasp took the one on the right. The chairs were angled towards each other. Rasp watched his friend. The baron studied the flames. Rasp said, 'I expect that I will be surprised unpleasantly many times today.'

'That is wise.' He clasped his hands. 'So, Simeon. Why are you here? What have you come to ask of me?'

'I want your help.' Vahnsinn winced, but Rasp carried on. 'How large a contingent of your forces do you have in the city?'

'A small one. The token permitted by Wangenheim.'

'Even a small one can be very useful.'

'To what end?' Vahnsinn sounded reluctant even to ask the question.

'To help keep the peace. And to restore it, when the need arises.'

'In other words, to make war against my fellow nobles.'

'They are on the brink of treasonous rebellion,' Rasp reminded him.

'Are they? Has the Ecclesiarchy been officially recognized as the sovereign authority over Mistral?' Vahnsinn did not hide his bitterness. 'I am the Imperial Commander. Does that count for nothing?'

'Of course it matters.'

Vahnsinn did not appear to hear. 'I answer to the Administratum, and ultimately to the Adeptus Terra, *not* to the Adeptus Ministorum.'

'Rayland,' Rasp said. 'No one has said otherwise.'

'Haven't they? You saw what happened at the Council. You saw what Wangenheim did. You *know* he's in the wrong. And now you come here, asking that I help suppress the righteous anger of my fellows.'

'That's right. I am.'

'Why? By the Throne, *why*? Is the Ecclesiarchy above all sin?' He pointed to a bookcase past Rasp's shoulder. 'You know I've always loved history. The books behind you have a great deal to say about the Age of Apostasy. I think Wangenheim might be a fellow student of the past. I think he might be taking more than a bit of inspiration from Goge Vandire.'

'Careful,' Rasp warned. Vahnsinn was close to crossing a very dangerous line. The baron reined himself in. Rasp sighed. 'There is nothing just about the situation,' he said. 'But there I have no choice in the matter, and neither do you, really.'

'Of course I do.'

'No. I feel nothing but disgust for what the cardinal has orchestrated, but I have to acknowledge its success. He has placed you in the wrong. Especially now – he is the protector of the Imperial Creed, and if the nobles revolt against him, what does that make them?' When Vahnsinn kept silent, Rasp continued. 'And this cult, not only is it a real threat, one that must be dealt with, but its heresy has been directly linked with the nobility. Your position is untenable, and that's putting it in the best light possible.'

Vahnsinn glowered at him. 'So my choice is to be a heretic or a powerless figurehead. Shall I hand over the keys to Grauben and Karrathar to the cardinal at the ceremony this evening?'

'I'm not suggesting that,' Rasp protested.

'Oh? You have something to offer me?'

Rasp nodded. 'It isn't perfect. But it's better than nothing, I think. If you help us–'

'If I betray my friends, my conscience and my interests, you mean.'

'If you take the one action open to a loyal subject of the Emperor,' Rasp corrected, merciless, 'you will be well-placed when the conflict comes to its only possible conclusion. What do you think is going to happen? We will crush the barons' rebellion as it draws its first breath. If your colleagues feel hard done by now, afterwards they will be destroyed, their homes burned, their families destitute if they are not imprisoned or worse. Do you think that even Wangenheim would have no room in the new state of things for the nobles who proved themselves true defenders of the Creed?'

'Are you making a guarantee?'

'You know I'm not. I'm speaking as your friend, and your friend is apparently able to see the realities here a bit more clearly than you can. If you stand with Wangenheim, do you think that, politically, he would be able to discard you afterwards?'

'Politically, he will be able to do whatever his heart desires,' Vahnsinn muttered, but he looked thoughtful.

'There are no guarantees,' Rasp said, more gently now. 'But there are good possibilities, and terrible certainties. Also, you know what is right.'

Vahnsinn made a face. 'Negotiating with a friend isn't fair play.'

'I do what I must.'

'I'm sure you do, lord commissar.' But now Vahnsinn wore a smile, a small one. His face became serious again as he studied the fire for a minute more. Then he looked at Rasp directly. 'If something happens today…'

'You mean "when". We do each other no favours pretending otherwise.'

The baron nodded. 'When something happens, I will be ready. I won't be at the ceremony. I won't toady to Wangenheim. I can't. But I will assign a detail of my guard to work with your troops. And when the need arises, come here. Let the request come from you, please, Simeon. Not from that reptile.'

2. Krauss

He could hear the tumult of the crowd gathered for the procession. It would be passing along a boulevard a few streets over from where Krauss stood before the outer door to the Cernay residence. He hammered against the iron, and waited.

He had already spoken to Louiza Cernay. He had already gone through the house. He had learned and found nothing. That had been the case at the scene of every one of the abductions. The single survivors of each household did not know why they had been attacked. It was clear that they were hiding nothing. Krauss had never encountered people so happy to see an inquisitor, so desperate to tell him everything that came to their minds. They would have been happy for any explanation he could give. Even the darkest rationale would be a foundation upon which they could recreate some order in their lives, some sense and meaning in the world. Anything was better than the purely random. There was no protection against that.

No one uttered the word 'Chaos'. The victims lacked the knowledge that would take them to that conclusion. Krauss did not enlighten them, but he could see its corrupting touch sinking deeper and deeper into the fabric of Tolosa. The attacks, lacking any clear purpose, could mean anything, and happen to anyone. If their only purpose was to generate fear, their goal was more than accomplished.

Krauss refused to accept that there was no deeper goal. The heretics were still human, and there were, he believed, limits to human beings' willingness to engage in the purely gratuitous act, especially one that involved many people, careful planning and precise execution. The success of the attacks pointed to a level of organization. There was order here, and where there was order, even of the most toxic kind, there was an endgame.

It was possible that the targets were chosen by sheer chance. The spread of terror might be the actual tool, and so the vectors of its creation were unimportant. But Krauss had hit a dead end. He was no closer to rooting out the heresy now that it was boldly announcing its presence than when it had concealed itself behind political divisions. So he was going to revisit ground he had already covered. He would talk to Louiza Cernay again. He would seek a reason why this house, and not the ones next to it, had been attacked.

No one came to the door. He knocked again. Five minutes passed. Nothing. The silence beyond gathered force. Krauss snorted. He removed a thin cylinder from his belt. He tapped one end and it began to hum. When he inserted it into the lock, the micro-force field that the master-key generated conformed itself to the shape of the tumblers. He opened the door and strode through to the courtyard.

It was evening, but no lights shone through the slits in the shutters. The courtyard was sheltered from the wind, and the ground-floor windows were unshuttered. They, too, were dark. Krauss didn't bother knocking on the house's door. He unlocked it, and let himself inside.

The interior had the stillness of absence. But there was also the stench of spoiled presence. Breathing through his mouth, knowing what he would find, he climbed the stairs. At the top he found a corridor whose walls bore portraits, going back generations, of the patriarchs of a comfortable merchant dynasty. Doors to the left and right opened into bedrooms. Krauss headed for the end, barely glancing in the rooms he passed. He stopped in the far left doorway. The space beyond was furnished with a bed, cabinet and dresser that were old enough to have been purchased at the time of the house's construction. They were still in fine condition. No doubt the contents of the jewel box on the dresser was of similar vintage and quality. Krauss didn't have to look inside the case to know that every gem, ring and bracelet would still be present. Theft had not come to this home. Murder had.

Murder and corruption.

Despite her grief for her family, her terror for her own safety, and her anxiety about speaking to the Inquisition, Louiza Cernay had greeted Krauss upon his first visit with a resilient dignity. She was an old woman, reaching the outer limits of what juvenat treatments on Mistral could accomplish. Her gait was stiff, her hands held by arthritis in a permanent curve. She moved with an elegance of care.

There was no dignity now, but there were the inscriptions of pain and fear. She lay in her bed, her throat cut, her eyes gone. Her hands were raised, clenched into sharp claws. The walls were painted in her blood, patterns forming words that Krauss could not, and would not, read, but that spoke of revels and torture and blasphemy. The blood on the wall had dried, but the smell of death was moist. The crime was quite recent. The display, Krauss thought, was for the benefit of the killers themselves. They did not expect anyone to see this.

The last detail Krauss registered before he turned from the scene was Louiza Cernay's eyes. They were not missing. They were simply not in her skull any longer. They had been cleaned and placed on the dresser beside a hand mirror. They had been orientated to stare at the ceiling. Krauss did not look at the rune up there again. Once was enough. When he had glanced at it, he had begun to hear a sound at his back. It had been both laughter and the snapping of bone.

He had his confirmation. The attack on the Cernay house was not random. The cultists had returned. There must be a reason to finish off the last of the Cernays in secret. Krauss made his way back down the corridor, paying more attention now to the other rooms. He saw nothing out of place. Dust was already settling in the unused spaces. On the ground floor, more of the same: the everyday had been suspended, but not disrupted.

The house was clean, its larder well stocked. In the dining area, the table had been set for a breakfast for one. Krauss ran a finger over the silverware, wondering who had laid it out. There were serfs' quarters at the back of the house, but they were empty.

He found his answer in the wine cellar. The household staff were stacked against the wall, hacked apart by the blows of heavy blades. Krauss pulled his needle pistol from its holster. He stalked between the ceiling-high racks of amasec, his footsteps silent. He didn't think he had living company. He did not rule out the possibility. There were more blood runes on the walls, and there was another smell here: a warm harshness to the nose and the back of the throat, as if the air had recently been filled with powdered stone and sawdust.

In the middle of the cellar, the racks had been destroyed, the bottles smashed. Krauss eyed the pile of smashed wood. There didn't seem to be enough of it. He tried to equate the theft with the murders, came up with mere absurdity. The pile sloped upwards towards the centre. He stepped forward to see if it concealed something.

The wreckage gave way beneath his weight. He fell into darkness, striking his head with an echoing *crack* against the lip of the cellar floor. Stunned, he was dead weight when he hit the ground three metres down. The blow knocked the air from his lungs and the pistol from his grasp. Consciousness dimmed. The world grew ragged at the periphery. Someone very distant from him, who nonetheless bore his name, had fallen into an underground tunnel. He wanted this person to get up. He tried to shout a warning, but he was too far away. The dark behind his eyes melded with the darkness without. He struggled against the fall of night. He managed to raise his head. But then he was no longer alone. He was surrounded by figures, and they kicked him into oblivion.

3. Yarrick

The procession was a triumph of Wangenheim's aesthetic, and his taste reflected the traditions of the Mistralian cardinals going back centuries. The gaudy Ecclesiarchal palace seemed to have sprung into being at the behest of its current occupant, but the accumulation and shaping of such excesses took generations. Now that aesthetic walked the streets of Tolosa. The reliquary containing the jawbone of Saint Callixtus was housed inside a huge chest. It appeared to be of solid gold, and encrusted with diamonds the size of my fist. The chest was mounted on a wagon pulled by grox draped in ceremonial rugs that resembled waterfalls of silver. The wagon was covered by a crystalflex cube of near-perfect transparency. The corners of the cube were ornamented by yet more diamonds. A thousand preachers, representing every region of Mistral, marched in parallel lines with the wagon at their centre. They carried metal poles three metres long, at the end of which multi-coloured lumoglobes dangled from short chains. The globes rocked back and forth with the gait of the clerics. The entire spectrum of light waved, shifted and danced over the diamonds of the cube and the chest.

The effect was impressive, if vulgar. The announced goal was to invoke the name of the festival. In this, the procession was a failure. What it really did was remind all who gazed upon the parade who it was who had brought the relic back to Mistral, who it was who had willed this spectacle into existence. The sun that shone upon the city that evening was the munificence of Cardinal Wangenheim.

I walked with the mobile troops, moving on a parallel course with the procession. The people of Tolosa lined the streets ten deep. We marched behind them, watching at ground level for anyone paying attention to something other than what was passing by. A full platoon on either side of the road was going from rooftop to rooftop, securing that possible ambush site.

The procession had begun at Tolosa's southernmost gate, just as dusk had begun to fall. Three hours later we were, by my estimation, about two-thirds of the way back to the palace and its great square. All the time, wind had raged against the display. It tried to yank the lumoglobes from their chains. It howled at the spectators, and snatched their hymns from their lips. Its efforts were in vain. The crowds wept and cheered as they watched the chest go by. For a few moments, the people forgot the nightly abductions and the political turmoil.

Setheno and one other Sister from the Order of the Piercing Thorn walked on either side of the chest. I wondered what they thought of their duty today. Did they appreciate the way the art of the reliquary had been submerged in the crude and the grandiose? Did they feel they were performing a useful service? Or did they feel manipulated? I did. So did Seroff and Rasp. So did the colonels. They had all said as much. So had some of the braver troopers, though I had shut those conversations down whenever I had encountered them. The sentiment was present, though, and I had no doubt that it ran throughout the regiment. We were being used by a man who turned all offices and all duties, holy and secular, to his personal use.

We approached the square, and the procession had been almost without incident. There had been a few arrests, but the detained were drunks, not cultists. Mobile duties complete, I joined Rasp on the officers' viewing stands that had been constructed to the left of the main platform. Seroff arrived shortly after.

'Anything?' I asked him.

'No.'

'Almost enough to make one feel optimistic, isn't it?' Rasp said.

'Should we be?' Seroff asked.

'What do you think?' Rasp sounded grim.

The question was rhetorical, but I answered all the same. 'I think someone is trying to lull us into a false sense of security.'

'Commissar Yarrick,' Rasp said, 'you are a cynic.'

'I prefer to think of myself as a realist, sir,' I told him.

He gave his short, mirthless bark of laughter. 'Very laudable, Sebastian. Now behold the spectacle presented for our edification. Tell me, are we in the realm of realism here?'

'Yes,' I said without hesitation. 'Without a doubt.'

'Well done,' Rasp said. 'Well done indeed. How very clear-sighted of you. A necessary quality. You may have a long life ahead of you.'

'But it isn't the only necessary element,' Seroff put in.

'What's another?'

'Knowing how to act realistically.'

Rasp looked surprised. 'That is a rationale for corruption, Commissar Seroff.' His use of Seroff's rank at that moment sounded like a rebuke.

'I misspoke,' Seroff said. He was not abashed. 'Knowing *when* and how to be realistic,' he amended.

I would have sworn that Rasp winced at that moment. 'True,' he said. He began to say something else, but he was drowned out by a sudden, deafening hymn.

The magnificat of the relic had begun.

When I had told Rasp that what I saw before us was realism, I was being honest. But not irreverent. I had seen enough of Wangenheim's machinations now that, though I did not doubt his faith, I was convinced that it was surpassed in intensity by his ambition and self-regard. But even if he was using a sacred display for his own political purposes, the sacred was still present, and it awed. The Ecclesiarchal palace, looming in the background, was a folly of vulgarity within its walls, a testament to the vanity of its inhabitants. Its exterior, however, was majestic. Soaring hundreds of metres into the sky, it imposed awe through size alone. It dwarfed all who gazed upon it, reminded us of our insignificance compared to the Father of Mankind. The palace was squat in its construction, and the newer wings made it even more massive. It spread out for more than a kilometre in either direction, embracing all vision. Despite its horizontal reach, the palace sent the eyes and heart skyward, thanks to the fluting that marked its entire façade. Thousands of lumoglobes illuminated the exterior, bathing it in a warm, orange light. As night fell, the colossal building detached itself from the dark. It was the strength of faith given form in stone.

In the square, the platform picked up on the multi-coloured play of lights of the procession, and intensified the effect. There were more lanterns, more powerful. Their wind-driven dance created colliding pools of light. The platform shimmered in an excited aura. Its banners flapped, crackling. Wangenheim stood in the centre, resplendent in robes so heavy they resisted the wind. The platform was covered in material that was the same white-violet-gold colour scheme as the cardinal's robes. The filigree seemed to flow from Wangenheim to spread across the entire surface of the platform. The intended implication seemed to be that he was the centre and source of everything on Mistral. My outrage at the hubris was tempered by the fact that the design also made him look like a spider in its web. His display spoke the truth in defiance of his will.

The Sisters of the Order of the Piercing Thorn lined up in front of the platform, and faced the crowd. The square was filled with tens of thousands of worshippers. The Adepta Sororitas squad numbered ten. The crowd appeared to take a collective step backwards, leaving just a bit more space between the unwashed and the holy warriors.

The wagon stopped a few metres short of the platform. Wangenheim raised his arms, and the crystalflex cube over the golden chest opened and folded itself back. Six preachers to a side climbed into the wagon and grasped the chest by its handles. It must have been equipped with an anti-grav field for it to be possible for those old men to move that mass. They did not so much carry it as guide its floating journey off the wagon and up the fifteen steps of the platform.

All the while, vox-casters had picked up the hymns of the clergy, and broadcast the chants over the square and to the city beyond. In the pause of each verse, I could hear echoes in the streets behind us. The amplified praise overcame the wind.

Wangenheim lowered his arms. He kept them outstretched as the chest was brought up to him. The preachers dropped to their knees. Whoever it was – an enginseer I imagined – who had sent the signal for the crystalflex shield to disassemble, and for the anti-grav to trigger, now conjured another theatrical miracle. The chest's lid, sarcophagus-massive, opened and fell back. Wangenheim took a step forward, leaned over and reached into the chest. Then he straightened, and raised the reliquary high above his head.

'Saint Callixtus!' the cardinal shouted. The vox-casters made his voice the father of thunder. 'You have come home at last. Will you honour us this day with your blessing?'

An answer came. For a frozen, irrational moment, I thought that the light that burst from where he had been standing a few moments before was a piece of Wangenheim's spectacle.

The concussion of the blast proved me wrong.

CHAPTER 9
UNDERMINED

1. Yarrick

The central portion of the platform blew skywards. Wood and metal and rock debris showered down over the square. Wangenheim went flying forwards. Setheno caught him before he hit the paving stones. One of her Sisters snatched the reliquary as it tumbled through the air. The grox lowed and turned violently from the stage. It overturned the wagon, crushing Bishop Castelnau. The roar of panic rose from the crowd, thick and loud enough to be a physical sensation pressing against my ears. Then the second bomb went off.

The explosion happened at the main entrance to the square. It wasn't huge. It sounded muffled, as if it were punching through a thick obstacle. It was still bad enough. It scattered bodies, and pieces of bodies. Blood splashed into the square. The worst damage was the psychological effect. With blasts going off both in front and behind, the crowd became frenzied. The roar became a great shriek. People ran from the platform, and they ran from the entrance. They collided. They clashed. They tore at each other. The trampling began.

And then, to the north and south, where secondary streets met the square, more blasts. Just big enough to seal the fate of every soul in this space.

On the viewing stands, we were standing on rocks surrounded by frothing rapids. We were helpless. I had seen routs on the battlefield, but before me was the total absence of any form of discipline. Fear turned human beings into blind, mad animals. We drew our pistols and shot anyone who tried to climb the stand. It was that or be dragged into the maelstrom of panicked flesh. There was nothing to save here except the command structure of the regiment.

By the wreckage of the platform, the Adepta Sororitas had formed a circle with the cardinal at the centre. They presented an impregnable ceramite barrier. They began to force their way towards the palace gates. By sword and gun, they cut down threats to the safety of Wangenheim and the relic.

The riot of panic forced the hand of the Imperial Guard. The largest concentration of the Tolosa-based Mortisians had been gathered around the square as the procession had completed its route. The troopers' mission was to maintain the security of the area. Now, as the soldiers already present in the square were joined by the reinforcements pouring in from the adjoining streets, that mission forced them to kill the people they had thought to protect.

There was no choice. There was no reason left in the civilians. They trampled and clawed and killed each other as they fled in all directions and none. Order could be restored only through the peace of the dead. Even so, the Mortisians did fire one great warning volley into the air. It was not heeded. The herd was too far gone. So the lasrifles were lowered, and the culling began. I grimaced. We were trapped in an ugly business. There was no glory, and precious little honour to be had, in the deaths of civilians. There was only brute necessity. The Hammer of the Emperor had the unalterable duty to smash His enemies. To find the ones responsible for the madness unleashed in the square, we had to survive it. And so the Hammer was called upon to sacrifice some of the Emperor's faithful.

This would not be the last time I was party to such a merciless calculus. Neither would it be the worst.

The Mortisians moved in from the perimeter of the square. The squads linked up with each other, forming a lethal cordon. They marched forwards. The killing was methodical. The Guard advanced, paused, fired, and advanced again. The beats of the march were the pauses during which the civilians had the chance to rein in their panic.

They never took it. What followed was not a slaughter. It did not have that intent. We would have stopped shooting at the first opportunity. No, I will not call what happened a slaughter. It was a massacre. It left me with indelible memories of its every detail. It does not haunt my dreams, though. We acted as was necessary. And its shadow has been swallowed by the darkness of events so much more terrible that any attempt at comparison is an obscenity.

Gradually, the numbers of shrieking, clawing civilians around the viewing stand thinned. At length, they stopped trying to climb up. The killing ended with a few hundred survivors, traumatized into catatonic silence, gathered in shivering groups in the centre of the square. The site of the festival's great climax was carpeted by bodies frozen in contortions of agony and terror.

'Get me a vox!' Granach ordered. His rage barely masked his horrified disgust. He and Benneger descended from the viewing stand. Rasp, however, climbed to the top row of seats. 'Soldiers of Aighe Mortis!' he called. His voice rang over the square. I saw thousands of faces turn his way. 'I salute your commitment to duty!' he shouted. 'I salute your actions, which shall yet prove to be the salvation of Mistral! You have preserved the discipline and integrity of your regiment!' He understood that the action had come at a cost to morale. This had not been combat. It had been the hard labour of executioners. 'Thanks to you,' Rasp continued, 'the enemy's attempt to topple Tolosa into disorder has failed! His blow has fallen short, but ours shall not. Forward now to vengeance!'

I listened to Rasp turn the massacre into fuel for victory, and I learned.

Seroff and I moved among the troops, reinforcing Rasp's message. The faces of the troopers around us were tight, their eyes narrowed against the grim demands of the night. I passed Saultern and clapped him on the shoulder. He gave me a quick look of gratitude, then turned with rapt attention back to the lord commissar's speech. The rhetoric soared, and my own blood responded to its strength and truth.

I saw Granach and Benneger conferring at the nearest blast site. I approached, and looking at the small crater, I understood how the security sweeps had missed the bomb. It had somehow been planted beneath the street itself. That was why the sound had been muffled. The force of the blast had had to punch up through the cobbles. The pit had collapsed in on itself, destroying the evidence of how the saboteurs had achieved this feat.

Then, even as Rasp was still speaking, I heard more explosions in the distance. They came from every direction. There were so many, it was hard to distinguish the blasts from their echoes. And when those echoes faded, in their wake came the rising clamour of riot.

2. Setheno

'Is that what they call maintaining security?' Sister Cabiria asked.

'I doubt they call it that at all,' Setheno answered. They had, at his insistence, escorted Wangenheim back to his private quarters. He had been jumpy even after they had reached the safety of the palace, not relaxing until they had reached his doorway, where he was greeted by the palace steward. Vercor had bowed to the Sisters of the Piercing Thorn, showing due respect, while making it clear that her obeisance was a question of etiquette, rather than an acknowledgement of superiority. The steward was a weapon in the clothing of servitude. Setheno had given her a curt nod. She had no doubt the woman was skilled, but she was a killer, not a warrior. Setheno had restrained an outward show of her distaste. Just.

Now she was standing on a balcony at the other end of the hall from the cardinal's chambers. He was still sequestered in there with Vercor. Setheno gazed down at the great square. The Mortisians had left, and the enforcers were doing what they could to restore a semblance of order after the massacre. This sector of Tolosa now had something like calm. But beyond, Setheno could hear the rumble of rising madness and conflict. She tapped a finger against the balcony's stone balustrade.

'You think we should be out there, sister superior?' Cabiria asked.

'We are where we should be,' she answered.

'But you wish otherwise.'

Setheno could have rebuked her for insubordination. She did not. She did not think she would be honouring her newly acquired command by disciplining the truth. Nor would she be honouring their friendship. They had entered the Order of the Piercing Thorn within a few months of each other. Cabiria knew her too well for Setheno to pretend she was not chafing against the limits of their mission. Inaction did not suit her. She accepted that she and her Sisters were not here for riot control. They were to protect the relic, and combat any threats to the Emperor's Church. So they had done, rescuing both relic and cardinal. Their duty was to remain on site. But Setheno did not like the sense of being *useful* to the cardinal. The man was a politician, not a theologian, and his politics were grubby. And Setheno could not shake the intuition that the conflict spreading through the city's streets had an acute spiritual dimension.

She looked at the shattered platform again. It looked as if a Titan had stepped on it. She wondered how the enemy had managed to place a bomb underneath. She had no faith in the Mortisians, but even they did not seem to be *that* incompetent. As she watched, the wreckage stirred. Robed figures emerged. They were fast. They were firing lasrifles at the Arbites within seconds of appearing. More and more of the enemy poured out from under the platform like a stream of shadows. A large group made directly for the palace entrance.

'Sister superior?'

'Yes, Cabiria. To war.' She turned from the balcony and ran

down the hall, joined by her Sisters. They passed the cowering bishops, and headed for the staircase to ground level. Setheno did not smile. She did feel satisfaction. She was rushing to righteous combat. She would clean her blade of civilian blood by washing it in the vitae of heretics.

As the squad approached the main doors, they shuddered with the impact of a heavy blow.

3. *Wangenheim*

The *boom* reverberated through the palace. The floors remained firm. The walls did not vibrate. But the sound carried, and it also carried meaning. It felt like a hammer striking Wangenheim's bones. He froze, his words to Vercor forgotten. 'What was that?' he gasped. The words had the shape of idiocy in his mouth. His mind was filled with the vision of an iron battering ram smashing against the palace door. His reason knew such a tactic was futile. But his reason was a slave to his panicked imagination in this moment.

'A rocket, I think,' Vercor answered.

That was not reassuring. 'Will that work?'

'If they have more than one.'

A second explosion resounded.

Wangenheim looked around frantically. He didn't know what he was seeking.

'There is a squad of the Adepta Sororitas protecting you, your eminence,' Vercor reminded him. 'No one is crossing the threshold of this palace.'

That was reassuring. He choked down the instinct to flee. *This conflict is what you wanted,* he told himself. *It is here, the situation is volatile, but the conclusion is preordained.* The forces he had gathered in his corner were overwhelming. The barons would be crushed. The cult was so easy to tie to the nobility, to use as another club against them, and it too would be exterminated. It could not have the strength to oppose him. It had not had time to sink roots into the soil of Mistral. The evidence at Lom was proof of its recent emergence.

Only Baron Lom *had* used a corrupt machine of tremendous power.

And the growing mayhem in Tolosa looked like much more than a terrorist attack. It looked like war. Worse: it looked like control slipping from his grasp. No, he corrected. It was not slipping away. It was being taken. He had an enemy. A strong one.

'Do you have orders, your eminence?' Vercor prompted him.

He looked at his steward. Her stance was hungry. Very well. She would be fed. 'Can you leave without alerting the Adepta Sororitas?'

Vercor didn't answer. She was clearly offended by the question.

Wangenheim cleared his throat. 'Do so,' he said. He tried to put the iron of authority back in his voice. He had been weakened on all fronts this evening. 'Go to Vahnsinn's home.'

'You believe he is working against us?'

'I don't know. But someone is coordinating these attacks. If he is the enemy, kill him.'

4. Rasp

He was back at Grauben. He had hoped not to return so soon after his last visit. He was not surprised to be disappointed.

As Rasp waited outside the mansion's door, he heard another wave of explosions, a *crump crump crump* of concussions that came so close together, they could have passed for artillery fire if they had not been so spread out geographically. The blasts were hitting every few minutes all over the city, turning Tolosa into a cauldron of blind, instinctual terror.

The door opened, this time by one of Vahnsinn's serfs. He gave Rasp a precise bow. 'The baron expects you,' he said.

'I imagine he does.'

The serf led the way up the stairs, past the mansion's upper floors to the roof. There was no shelter there, only crenellations about a metre high. The wind was ferocious. Vahnsinn stood by the southern edge, looking down the slope of Tolosa. It was a good vantage point from which to witness the city's torment.

The serf waited halfway out of the trap door while Rasp joined Vahnsinn. There was a pulsing glow in the distance. The baron nodded towards it. 'A fire,' he said. 'It spread quickly. The wind, you know.' He had to raise his voice to be heard, but it still sounded flat to Rasp. It was the voice of a man who had moved beyond despair and into exhausted apathy.

'There is more than one kind of fire out there,' Rasp said. 'We need to put all of them out. We need your help.'

Vahnsinn shrugged. 'I said you would have it, and it is yours. I don't see what good it will do.'

'Your troops are familiar to the populace. That will help restore calm.'

'I admire your conviction,' Vahnsinn said, but he turned around. 'Our entire contingent is to be placed at the disposal of the Imperial Guard commanders,' he called to the serf. The other man nodded, then closed the trap door behind him.

'Are you keeping a reserve to protect your home?' Rasp asked. 'The situation is ugly. It will get worse before we can contain it.'

Vahnsinn shook his head. 'I'm leaving Tolosa.'

'Abandoning ship?' Rasp was disappointed.

'Leaving Wangenheim to his games. I will be found at Karrathar when sanity is restored.'

'That will not happen without your help.'

More explosions in the distance. The glow of the fire flared.

'Will it be worth it,' Rasp asked, 'for sanity to reign over ash?'

5. Vercor

The wind and the sporadic percussion of bombs did her no favours, but Vahnsinn and the lord commissar were speaking in the open air. Standing in the shadowed entrance to an alley between two mansions across the boulevard from Grauben, Vercor fine-tuned her hearing. She caught the gist of the conversation between the two men. She weighed options. Vahnsinn had made his opposition to the cardinal clear at the Council, but he had done nothing more. She did not doubt that he would jockey for more power, but he was saying nothing to suggest he was going to move against Wangenheim. His apparent neutrality could lead to him being even more dangerous once the current spasm of violence subsided, if the people saw him as an orthodox counter to the Ecclesiarch's rule. There might be some value in his unexpected death during the confusion of this night.

Only Wangenheim had not authorized such drastic action. Not unless Vahnsinn presented an immediate threat.

Threat. There was one. Not the baron. Coming up behind her. Soft leather muffling footsteps, sound hidden by the constant moan of the wind. Hidden to all but one with her hearing. She did not turn. She waited, letting the hunter draw closer. She held her hands loose at her sides, revelling in the subcutaneous hum of the servo-motors preparing for action.

Two more steps. One.

Now.

She whirled, arms outstretched, palms flat as blades. She caught her robed attacker in mid leap. Her blow struck him in the sternum. She heard the crunch of bone. She created movement where none should be. The man flew off to the right side and smashed into a blank stone wall. He slid to the ground, jerking as if electrocuted. His hands clawed at his chest, but only for a few seconds. His bones had punctured his heart. While he twitched his last, Vercor picked up the blade he had dropped. It curved twice. In the faint light that reached the alley from the street, she saw a hint of runes on the metal. She curled her lip. The weapon was unclean, and she hurled it away into the night. She turned her attentions to the corpse and pulled back the man's hood. His hair was patchy, his skin a network of tattoos, scars and scabs. His mouth was hanging open, and Vercor saw that all his teeth had been removed. His gums had been sheathed in metal that came to a razored edge. His tongue was scored with deep cuts.

Vercor stood up from the corpse. The extent of the heretic's corruption was worrying. It had not happened overnight. The abductions had left no doubt that the cult was still active, but if it had been so for longer than suspected, the roots might run very deep. Wangenheim's game with the barons suddenly looked less like a calculated risk. For the first time in her decades of service, Vercor suspected the cardinal of recklessness.

More stealthy footsteps. More than one person this time. Moving past the mouth of the alley, but not heading her way. She advanced to the edge of the shadows to watch the street.

It took her a few moments to see them. Even then, she wasn't sure she had spotted them all. Hooded figures, men and women, emerging from the shadows as if born from them. At least a dozen. They converged on Grauben.

Vercor hesitated. Her instructions were only to observe. But what she saw closing in on the baron's mansion was an enemy who transcended factionalism.

She emerged from the alleyway at a full run. She hit the nearest cultist and knocked him to the ground. She stomped once on his skull, hard, then turned to the next. As she killed him, she spotted more robed figures approaching the mansion. There were far more than a dozen.

6. Yarrick

We fanned out across the city. No one was easy with the division of the forces, but the attacks were too numerous to be dealt with one at a time. The reports that Granach was able to piece together suggested small commando raids. He responded in kind. He wanted speed, and that was what we gave him. I travelled with Saultern's company to the southern end of Tolosa. We rushed towards the glow of the flames. The night sky was flickering, becoming tainted by the fires below. The burn was a big one.

As we reached the gates to the ring, we were joined by a hundred of Vahnsinn's guard. So Rasp had been successful. Knowing that these forces too were being shared among the Mortisian contingents, I was surprised that their numbers were as high as they were. Vahnsinn had somehow managed to hold a greater force within the city walls than I would have guessed.

We moved quickly despite the growing riots. We ploughed

through panic and anger. People fled destruction and turned on scapegoats. Most retained enough presence of mind to flee the path of armed soldiers.

Most, but not all, and that was regrettable.

Much of the lowest ring's southern quadrant was aflame. The buildings were packed together, huddling close in their poverty. The construction here was mostly wood. Old, dry timbers had needed little excuse to combust. A firestorm was forming. Unchecked, its embrace could encompass the entire ring, surrounding Tolosa with a wall of fire.

Saultern stood as if mesmerised by the towering blaze before us. The heat from the engulfed buildings baked our exposed skin. I saw the hesitation of his inexperience again. There was no visible enemy to fight, and he was paralysed. 'Captain,' I snapped. 'Firebreaks.'

He blinked at me. There was a second of incomprehension. Then his face cleared. He sent the Vahnsinn guards west, while he took his company east. 'Find the limits of the fire,' he said. 'Bring down the buildings there. Smother the flames' advance.' He glanced at me for confirmation. I did not undermine his command by nodding. Instead, I moved off with the troopers, leading the charge to comply with his orders while burning cinders fell from the sky and smoke choked the streets.

About five hundred metres on, past flame so intense it was forming whirlwinds, we found the storm's edge. A narrow street ran between the conflagration and the tenements it was just beginning to lick. No lights shone from the broken windows. The block looked as if it had been abandoned by even the most desperate some time ago. It would take little to knock it down. Saultern sent a demolition team in. They worked quickly. Five minutes later, while the block still resisted the flames, the charges went off. The walls blew in, and the structure collapsed in on itself. The wind caught the billow of dust and hurled it into our eyes. When we could see again, we had our firebreak.

Something about the way the tenement block died bothered me. The rubble was too sunken, as if the ground had tried to suck the buildings down. I walked towards the collapse. I clambered over the shattered beams and masonry. The destruction sloped towards the centre. This was too much like a crater for my liking.

'Commissar Yarrick?' Saultern called.

'I need to satisfy my curiosity, captain.' A moment later, I realized someone else had joined me. I glanced to my left and saw Betzner. He was staring towards the centre of the collapse, frowning. 'Do you see something, trooper?' I asked.

'No, commissar. Yes. I mean, I'm not sure.' He pointed.

I saw nothing but the play of shadows in the wavering light of the flames. We moved further down. Midway to the centre I saw what Betzner must have been indicating: the shadows under leaning slabs of floor were too dark, too deep. Betzner could not possibly have seen them from the top of the slope. He was right, though. 'Get your captain,' I said softly. 'Tell him what we see.'

Betzner scrambled away. He returned with Saultern and the bulk of the company. I didn't have to say anything. Saultern needed no prompting. He sent a dozen troopers forward while the rest trained their weapons on the shadows. The soldiers pulled, dug and hauled at the wreckage until the truth of the shadows was revealed.

Tunnels.

* * *

7. *Seroff*

Captain Monfor saved Seroff's life. He did so in the simplest way possible: he was a full head taller, and the las-fire hit him first. It came from two angles. It burned his skull apart. Seroff dropped flat. There was no cover. The company was caught in the open.

The Mortisians had quelled the riot in this south-central quadrant of the city, and had reached one of Tolosa's rare squares. It had once been a market, but had fallen into disuse when a more sheltered one had been constructed to the south. It was a windswept expanse of cobbles that had seen a crowd for the first time in a generation when the procession had passed through. The people had remained after the relic had moved on, celebrating the journey of the saint until the bombs had gone off. The stampede had rushed along the main avenue leading east from the square, smashing all before it, until it had run into the disciplined fist of the Imperial Guard. Monfor had led his company to the source of the blasts. He had taken the square with caution. Roofs were checked for snipers. Troops had moved around the periphery of the square, kicking in doors and smashing open shutters. The buildings had seemed deserted.

And then they had reached the site of the explosion. They had seen the tunnel. Monfor had cursed. And then he had died.

The cultists attacked. Many still wore the uniforms of the baronial houses they served, but Seroff thought the colours and banners looked more degraded than at Lom. Even more of the wretches wore dark robes now. They streamed out of the buildings to the left and right of the crater. Too many to have been hiding when the patrols had checked the ground floors.

The tunnels fed into the cellars, and the Mortisian company was caught in a closing pincer attack. Seroff rose to a crouch, returning fire with his bolt pistol. With no cover, he resorted to quick, unpredictable sprints. He shot and ran, shot and ran.

The unit cohesion of the company was shattered as the casualties mounted. The soldiers who held their ground died where they stood. They took numbers of the enemy with them, but the cultists stayed mobile as they drew the cordon tighter. Seroff couldn't spot a surviving officer. He heard no orders being issued. Had every lieutenant and sergeant been cut down? The answer didn't matter. He knew his duty, and he should have already been exercising it. 'Keep moving!' he shouted. 'Don't let the heretics–'

A frag grenade went off to his left. Others saved his life again. Two troopers disintegrated, sliced into jagged bone and meat. The force of the explosion lifted him off his feet and pitched him over the lip of the crater. His head was ringing before he hit the ground. He smashed into a pile of broken paving stones. His vision blurred. He lay on his back at the bottom of the crater, and his body refused to obey his brain's commands. He couldn't draw a breath. His ears filled with the sounds of defeat as he blacked out.

8. Rasp

'Your home is under attack.' Rasp looked down into the street. He saw a struggle, guessed that one of Vahnsinn's guards was putting up a fight. But many figures were rushing the door to Grauben. It would not withstand the siege for long. He pulled his bolt pistol from its holster.

'Simeon,' the baron said, 'I can't tell you how glad I am to have thrown my lot in with you.'

'Better death than heresy,' Rasp snapped. Vahnsinn's dry levity was misplaced.

Vahnsinn nodded. 'Come with me.' He turned away from the edge of the roof.

'What do you have in mind?'

'Not being cornered on a roof, if it's all the same to you. As heroic as such a last stand might be, I would rather choose a more effective strategy.'

'Agreed.'

Rasp followed him to the trap door. Vahnsinn led the way down to the ground floor, where the halls shook with the battering of the front door. There were only three guards waiting before the entrance.

'They won't hold the enemy back long,' Rasp said.

'They won't have to.' Vahnsinn dragged open a door at the other end of the hall. A stone staircase descended into the cellar. Damp air wafted into the corridor.

'Your alternative to being trapped on the roof is being trapped below ground?'

'Trust me. I'm not an idiot.'

Rasp heard the sound of wood splintering from the mansion's entrance. He shrugged and started down the stairs. He did trust Vahnsinn's tactical judgement. It had been unerring in their years on the battlefield together. Behind him, the baron swung the door closed with a scrape and bang. The steps descended two landings before ending in an empty wine cellar. Rasp looked around in the light of dim lumoglobes. He saw archways leading off the cellar in every direction. 'Which way?' he asked.

'The eight-fold way,' said Vahnsinn at his back, voice sepulchre-dry, and sepulchre-cold.

Rasp turned. Vahnsinn had stopped three steps from the bottom. He held a laspistol trained at Rasp's head. The lord commissar glanced down at his bolt pistol, aimed at the ground. He knew what would happen if he tried to raise it. And now he heard footsteps. Many. A moment later, robed men and women emerged from every one of the vaults. He was surrounded by more than fifty cultists. They were all armed. He knew he couldn't move fast enough to shoot Vahnsinn, but perhaps he could take one or two heretics before they killed him. His death would have that much honour.

'Simeon,' Vahnsinn said. 'Don't be wasteful. Throw the gun away.'

Rasp didn't answer. He spun, firing into the cultists. He couldn't miss. Every pull of the trigger sent another figure to the ground. Between the reports of the pistol, he heard Vahnsinn yell, 'Take him alive!'

The crowd rushed him. He killed three more before he was overwhelmed.

CHAPTER 10
THE GREAT RAIN

1. Yarrick

The cultists started firing almost as soon as we uncovered the tunnel. They had been waiting for us either to find the entrance or move on and leave ourselves open to a rear-attack. Their numbers appeared to be similar to ours. The stream of las-fire that shot out of the tunnel hit us hard, but we answered in kind. The Mortisians had the benefit of discipline. There was a raggedness to the volleys from inside the tunnel. Either the traitors were not a military unit, or they were a patchwork of elements lacking a unified command. Saultern's company spread out, using the rubble for shelter, and fired into the tunnel at all angles. We couldn't see the enemy. There was no need. If our shots went in far enough, they hit a target. The tunnel's walls amplified the screams of our victims. That was a good thing.

'Grenades!' Saultern yelled. Frags bounced into the darkness, lit it up with sudden flashes and painted the air with the shrieks of the wounded.

'Push them back, soldiers of the Emperor,' I called. 'Push them back into their darkness, and exterminate them all.'

We began to tighten the cordon, closing step by step on the bottlenecked heretics, driving them back with fire and explosives. Another few metres and we could deploy the flamers.

'Grenade!' Betzner yelled at my left, and it was a warning. I whirled in time to see the frags arcing through the air towards us, over the rise of the collapse, coming from the direction of the street. I jumped over the slab behind which I crouched, and lay flat, taking my chances with the suppressed, disorganized fire from the tunnel. The explosions kicked up a storm of shrapnel, shredding troops apart. Our assault faltered. The enemy fire from within the tunnel strengthened. And over the rise, having slaughtered our rearguard, came the Vahnsinn forces. I experienced a moment of furious disbelief at the depth of the deception. Then I realized I was on the verge of hurling myself at the traitors as if I could tear them apart with my hands and teeth. I suppressed the instinct, held fast to reason.

We were pinned. The Vahnsinn guards closed with us just as we had with the cultists. The Mortisians were firing as best they could in both directions, to little effect. None of us could do more than stay flat on jagged rubble, and shoot blind. The jaws of the trap closed on us. The Vahnsinn troops would overrun our position in minutes.

I scanned the terrain for a better position. Nothing that would stand up to more than a few seconds of concentrated fire. Then I noticed a depression about ten metres beyond Betzner, a bit further downslope from us. Another tunnel entrance, I hoped. 'Betzner,' I yelled. 'Drop a frag there.'

I pointed. He understood. Still lying flat, he pulled a grenade from his belt and tossed it. The throw was awkward, but accurate enough. I shielded my face from the explosion. When I looked up, I saw the opening of a shaft. It was narrower than the one we had been assaulting, less than two metres across. Perhaps the cultists were not watching the secondary egress points. Perhaps they did not have the numbers to do so. Perhaps I was living in futile hope.

It was the only hope we had.

No way to signal except through example. No way to be the example except through risk.

My duty to the Emperor.

'To me!' I roared. I rose to my feet and pounded towards the shaft. The wind was at my back. I leapt over wreckage, sprinting with no thought to falls or broken limbs. Las streaked the night around me. I ran a web of death. I snarled my defiance. I *would* reach the target. Duty would permit no failure. I would show the way and run through my own death in the name of that duty.

The Emperor protected. It cannot be luck that preserved me in those few moments. I am not so proud as to believe that my own speed was sufficient to throw off the aim of our foe. The Emperor sent the dark, the confusion and the surprise to be my shields. I made a last leap and dropped down the shaft. I banged my shoulder on the way down, and landed awkwardly. The fall was less than two metres. There was just enough illumination from the burning city that I could see crude handholds carved into one side of the shaft. I climbed back up, bolt pistol in one hand. I popped my head up and provided what covering fire I could as Betzner made his run. Behind him, the rest of the company was rising up and charging this way.

We lost many, but we saved more. The last of the Mortisians to reach the shaft did so only a few seconds ahead of the Vahnsinn force. We had lost close to half our strength, but what we had was enough to hold the enemy at bay for the moment. Saultern ordered lumen tubes triggered, and we saw that we were in a tunnel that sloped downward for twenty metres before hitting a T-junction. We moved down quickly, Saultern and myself in the lead. We were just arriving at the intersection when our own tactics were used against us again. A pair of frag grenades tumbled down the shaft. The concussion of the blast knocked the air from my lungs. The entrance to the tunnel collapsed, burying another three troopers.

'We won't be going back that way,' Saultern said, sounding worried.

'Nor should we,' I told him. I raised my voice. 'The only way forward is through the blood of traitors and heretics.' I found that the rhetoric of victory came easily to me. I hadn't thought of myself as any kind of preacher while I had been a storm trooper, but my training for my new post had shaped me more completely than I had guessed. The words were there for me to weave my exhortation. More important yet, I believe, was the strength of my faith. Thanks to it, I articulated my duty with fervour. I began to grasp the idea of rhetoric as a blade of tempered steel plunged into the guts of the enemy. Speaking just to Saultern again, I said, 'They've done us a favour. There will be no further attacks from that direction.'

He nodded. Then he gave me a look that was very close to pleading. 'Commissar,' he said, for my ears alone, 'I would welcome the insight of your experience.'

I looked at him. The captain was only a year or two younger than I was, but an unbridgeable gap of the lived lay between us. He was doing himself credit as an officer, but he had the haunted look of a man seeing the horrors of the battlefield for the first time. Each atrocity we encountered was new to him. His system was taking sudden, repeated shocks. If he survived the initiation, he would, I thought, do well. But his inexperience was real. At least he had the humility to admit he wasn't in any position to replace a general, even if he was ordered to do so.

I thought for a minute, but decided not to relieve him of command. He was giving me cause to do so. He was indicating a reluctance to lead. But he was being honest with me about reaching the limit of what he was capable of as an officer. 'We're going to use the tunnels against the enemy,' I told him. 'We find the cultists, kill them, then return to the surface for Baron Vahnsinn's guards. Clear?'

He nodded.

'Announce our strategy,' I told him.

He hesitated.

'Announce it,' I insisted. 'Proclaim it as if it were your own.'

'But–'

The Emperor protect me from honest fools, I thought. 'Do it,' I said.

He did, and we moved on, taking the left-hand branch of the intersection. A few dozen metres further on, we hit another junction, this one with four branches. And then another. I paused. I exchanged a look with Saultern. He didn't need prompting. 'Anyone with mining experience?' he called out.

'I do, captain.' The man who shouldered his way forward was Sergeant Kortner. 'My family is from the Deeps.'

The Deeps. The played-out mines of Aighe Mortis that had become habs plunging as far into the crust of the planet as the hives above-ground reached for the sky. Entire generations never saw the light of day. Kortner had the fish-belly skin tone of that segment of Mortisian society. He had always struck me as having a perpetual squint, but now that we were in tunnels, he seemed more relaxed, his eyes open to take in the minimal lighting.

'Can you take us to the enemy's position?' I asked.

He grinned. 'Watch me.'

Without hesitation, he took the second passage to the left. At each intersection, he listened closely, but when he made his choices, he was definite. As we marched down the tunnels, I saw him examining the walls. He ran his hands over the stone.

'What do you notice, sergeant?' I asked.

'These aren't cellar tunnels. They can't be. And they weren't constructed by our enemies. Or very few of them were, at least.'

'Oh?'

He shook his head. 'The system is too big. There are too many branches and side tunnels. I think it goes on for hundreds of kilometres. It can't have been dug simply for a military campaign.'

'Impossible to keep work on this scale hidden,' I said.

'Exactly, commissar. And look.' He aimed his light at the wall. 'This was a mine. The excavation was done centuries ago. Some of the connecting tunnels are new.'

'The enemy just modified the existing network.'

'I believe so.'

Kortner's conclusions were cause for both dread and hope. If such a vast warren existed under Tolosa, then the enemy could reach any point in the city undetected. Cutting off this avenue of attack might well be impossible. On the other hand, it would be no more feasible for the enemy to control the entire network. Our foe was as vulnerable to ambush as we were.

'Why weren't we told about this?' Saultern asked.

Because the cardinal is a political strategist, not a military one, I thought. *Because it never occurred to him that the threats he was exploiting to his own ends were real and dangerous.* What I said was, 'Attacks on this scale using sewer systems are beyond unusual. And we don't think about what lies beneath our feet unless we are forcibly reminded of it.' That was all true enough. But only partly. In my head, I cursed Wangenheim.

'How well can you navigate?' I asked Kortner.

'Well enough.'

I waited for Saultern. He started thinking like an officer again. 'Bring us to them,' he said. 'Then, find an exit to the street and we'll take the Vahnsinn force.' He couldn't keep his eyes from flickering in my direction. I kept my nod almost imperceptible.

'Yes, captain,' Kortner replied. He took point, an alpha predator in his element. The further we went, the more speed he picked up, as if the scent of the enemy's blood were calling him. He never hesitated for more than a second at each junction. I tried but failed to spot the cues he used, but the nuances of direction, slope and currents of air were too subtle for me. After several minutes he slowed, his steps growing quiet. A moment later, the rest of us could hear the echoes of marching feet. The sound was confusing as it bounced and multiplied. I had no idea how close we were, or whether or not the foe was approaching. Saultern held up a hand and signalled silence.

Kortner stopped a few metres from the next junction. A

larger tunnel ran from left to right ahead of us. He looked back at us and nodded, then crouched and raised his rifle. The troops at the front of the advance followed his example. The next in line remained standing. We were three abreast in this tunnel. We waited to reveal the Emperor's anger.

The enemy marched past along the major passageway, oblivious to the danger in the side tunnel. Saultern held the company back. I felt the energy build around me. There was a collective need for vengeance, and the prospect of imminent satisfaction took the shape of a vibrating, silently snarling joy. It coursed through my own blood. At the same time, I concentrated on what I was seeing. We had the chance to see the enemy.

Observe and learn.

The fighters who passed us were a disparate group. Many, but by no means all, wore robes. I saw the livery of all the baronial houses of Mistral represented. The parade of heresy revealed just how wide and deep the treachery ran. Some of the uniforms were still in parade-worthy condition. Others were just visible beneath the robes. Still others were ragged, defaced by twisted runes. I saw, in this patchwork army, the full extent of Wangenheim's folly. For all his megalomania, I did not doubt his faith. I could not blame him for the arrival of the cult on Mistral. But his political machinations had pushed the barons to the point that legitimate grievance had found common cause with darkest heresy. He had wanted a war. That was clear. Well, he had one. And like every other fool who thinks he can make flames dance to his will, he had lit a fire that might burn everything down.

We would extinguish those flames, I vowed. And we would begin by extinguishing the wretches before us.

As the last of the heretics passed through the junction, Saultern chopped his arm forwards. We opened fire. The quarters were close, the range short. The slaughter was great. We cut down the rear elements in seconds, filling the dank underground air with the stench of scorched flesh. Confusion spread through the enemy ranks. The lack of a unified command made itself felt. I heard calls to attack, and others to retreat. For a few seconds, the cultists did nothing but collide with each other. That was long enough for us to hurl grenades around the corner into their midst. We backed away, and still felt the explosions in our bones. The blasts were murderous in the confined space. They sounded muffled, surrounded by all those bodies.

We charged, bringing our wrath down on a stunned enemy. We ran through a swamp of blood and shredded flesh. The remaining elements tried to muster a defence. We smashed it with contempt. We overran them with the same disregard for weapons fire as when we had run for the shaft. But now we weren't individual warriors evading death. Now we were death itself. The butchery was total. An errant shot burned across my right epaulette. We lost two other troopers. But the enemy lost everything. The heretics were reduced to writhing, dying worms.

Drenched in the blood of the foe, we paused. I looked at Saultern. There was a wild glint in his eye. He was being shaped by war, its blows and cruelty pounding out the son of weakness. With every hit that did not break him, he was forged a little more surely into an officer of the Imperial Guard. I watched him closely. He blinked a few times, and tried to wipe the worst of the blood from his face. He looked strained, but rational. He turned to Kortner. 'Sergeant,' he said, 'lead us to our next battle.'

He grinned, the old hand deciding that this inexperienced captain might have some mettle after all.

We moved off. As before, Kortner chose the tunnels as if he had known them all his life. We were fast, rushing to complete our act of justice. We ran past at least two sets of handholds leading upwards to street or cellar. Kortner ignored them. He found a slope. Even I could tell it was a new dig. He was leading us up one of the enemy's points of rapid exit.

The slope became a ramp that took us into a warehouse. The building was empty, a mere shell. Its function now was to conceal attackers until the moment they burst from its doorways and struck. My mouth filled with the iron taste of anticipation.

But as we reached the doors, a new sound began. Huge. Terrible. I recognized it. I knew what it meant. It meant disaster.

2. Vercor

The battle did not end in victory or her death. Instead, it melted away before her. She grappled with another cultist, a man who relied on his size and strength to compensate for his lack of combat skill. He rushed her, striking like a battering ram, knocked her back into the alley and against a wall. She punished him for his stupidity by reaching up and snapping his neck. She looked past his toppling corpse for the next foe. There was no one. Startled, she padded out of the alley. The street beyond was deserted. The door to Vahnsinn's manor was damaged, but still stood.

Vercor had the dizzying sensation of walking an abandoned stage. Everything about the last few minutes rang false. She shook her head. She had been deceived, but the contours and the reasons for the deception escaped her. She felt a professional shame.

She examined the façade of Grauben. The great house was silent. No light filtered out from between the shutters. She knew it was as empty as the street. Perhaps, she thought, the theatre she had witnessed had not been mounted for her benefit. She might even have advanced the object of the spectacle by taking part in the combat.

She had been a pawn, a superfluous one at that, not even important enough to remove from the board once the round of the game was complete. Now the game had moved on, and she was forgotten. The insult was humbling. The implications were worse, as the scale of the cardinal's miscalculation was revealed. She felt her confidence in the power of her patron waver further. At the abstract level, she had known that no family was forever, that falls came in time to all but the Emperor. But she had never contemplated the possibility that the Wangenheims might stumble during the term of her existence.

For the first time in centuries of service, a Vercor began to re-examine the calculus of loyalty.

The street vibrated. Something mechanical, something under power, passed by beneath her feet.

Then came the great noise.

3. Setheno

The heretics did not enter the palace. The Sisters of the Order of the Piercing Thorn burst through the great door, throwing back the startled besiegers. 'The way is clear!' Setheno taunted the heretics. 'Is this not what you wanted? Why do you not claim your prize?'

The cultists tried. They hesitated before the holy rage of the Adepta Sororitas, but then they attacked. Some kept their distance and fired their rifles. They wore recognizable uniforms, ones that marked them only more clearly as traitors. Others risked being cut down by their own comrades and charged. These were the most degenerate of the heretics. Their robes were tattered, and so was their flesh. They pulled their hoods back, revelling in the blasphemy of their faces. They had mutilated themselves in the grip of a dark ecstasy. Sigils spiralled from cheek to eye, leaving trails of dried blood. Bisected tongues tasted the air like serpents'. Howling a hatred that had moved beyond articulation, they ran at the Sisters, brandishing blades. Setheno noted the weapons. They were twisted, fantastical creations, many of them multi-foliate. They had been forged with a perverse care. The cult that was now showing its hand had had time to prepare its weapons and to degrade many of its converts to subhuman levels. The noxious weed had deep roots. Uprooting it would be a great task.

It was past time to begin.

Setheno ignored the las striking her armour. She and her Sisters strode forward, and the cultists hesitated as punishment came to meet them. Then the clash came. Setheno swung her sword in from the side. She struck a heretic in the gut. The force of her blow cut all the way through to his spine. His mouth dropped open in shocked pain. His lips moved as if he would utter a curse. With a jerk and a lift, she severed his backbone, splitting his body in two. She completed the movement, raising her blade high as the corpse fell apart. Another cultist came at her, howling. She brought the sword down. She felt the crunch of his skull shattering. There was a satisfaction in the brutality of the execution. She drew her blade out, smearing its length with the man's brain.

The enemy's charge faltered. It was nothing more than a race to the slaughter. To Setheno's right, Sister Liberata sang the Hymn of the Eternal Purge, her voice a crystalline razor slicing through the bayings of the foe. The squad moved down the length of the porch, and nothing that approached them survived. Heretic blood spread over the marble and cascaded down the steps. The unholy would not defile the Ecclesiarchal palace on this night. Setheno matched the rhythm of her kills to the beats of Liberata's song. She performed the liturgy of murder.

Within its first few minutes, the result of the engagement was inevitable. Setheno saw the enemy's rearguard falter. Those soldiers, more sane than their brothers, had realized the futility of their effort. Vitae was pooling across the square, and none of it had come from the Sisters of Battle. The traitors tried to retreat. As one, Setheno and her squad sheathed their blades and raised their bolt pistols. The square rang with precise, merciless fire, until the ten women were the only living beings within its confines.

Bloodied silence fell over the square. The distant reports of combat in the rest of the city were audible once again. There was the long rumble of a collapsing building. It sounded quite close, likely no more than a thousand metres to the south. Removing her helmet, Sister Genebra cocked her head in the direction of the collapse, then looked at Setheno. 'What are your orders, sister superior?' she asked. It was clear she hoped to engage further with the enemy.

Setheno listened to the sounds of the convulsing city. She still wore her helm, and so she was able to conceal her grimace of frustration from Genebra. She had the nagging sense of revelation hiding just over the horizon. She knew there was a game being played. She knew she and her Sisters had been placed on the board by Wangenheim. But the cardinal had an opponent at least as subtle. The game had slipped from his control. Setheno could not see its contours. She saw only the limits of her own position. She knew just enough to be conscious of her own blindness. What good, she wondered, was insight, when all it revealed was its failure?

The desire to see beyond limits was dangerous, and she suppressed it. Still, she could not erase the residue of frustration it left behind.

Because she was deprived of clarity, she had no choice. 'We are a single squad, Sister,' she told Genebra. She was aware of the others listening. 'We cannot be everywhere in this city.'

'We could be,' Cabiria put in. 'Just add one of us to each company of the Imperial Guard.'

The idea had appeal. It would mean taking the strength of faith beyond the confines of this square. But it would also mean submitting the squad to the same dilution of force that was afflicting the Mortisians. It would mean, she suspected, being the good pawn for one of the players of this game.

So much she did not know. But she did know what her vows dictated.

'No,' she said. 'We could be leaving the sacred relic unprotected.' She gestured at the Ecclesiarchal palace. 'This is the redoubt of the Adeptus Ministorum. This is what we guard. Not the city.' Even as she spoke, she heard the short-sightedness of the pronouncement.

'If Tolosa falls…' Cabiria began.

'It hasn't.'

Then the air itself denied her words. It trembled. It was filled with a vast percussion. The beats of this rhythm dwarfed anything that had come before. This was not the sound of individual explosives and of street-by-street combat. It was the thunder of bombardment. It was gigantic. It was a city's doom.

4. Vahnsinn

He was proud of the maglev. All of the modifications of the tunnels beneath Tolosa had taken time, and keeping the work secret had required an effort whose challenge had been equalled only by its expense. But the track was his signature. It was a monumental excess. It was not necessary. He could have made do with a tunnel leading from Grauben to the exterior of the city's walls. But the risk of doing too much had been irresistible. And now he sped beneath Tolosa, undetected, unstoppable. Perhaps he would reach the surface before the great spectacle had begun. It would be a shame to miss it.

The train had almost reached the limits of Tolosa. He knew this because, as a further gesture of excess, he had ordered the caves that marked the limits of the walls painted red. He would be at the surface very soon. Then Vahnsinn heard the destruction begin. So he would miss the opening bars of the symphony he had devised. He almost closed his eyes so that he might visualize the event with greater clarity. But he knew each moment of the song by heart. He smiled at Rasp. The lord commissar sat, arms and legs manacled, on the bench opposite him. 'Do you know what that is?' he asked. He felt the vibrations from the explosions as a hum in the metal floor of the train.

'Enlighten me,' Rasp conveyed contempt and disinterest very well for a man who had only just regained consciousness.

Vahnsinn leaned forward. 'I will,' he said. 'That is the sound of education. Cardinal Wangenheim is learning what it means to make an enemy of my House.' He smiled. 'Your troops are receiving instruction too, I'm afraid. They are answering for the colonel's mistakes. Yours too.'

'Answering for our loyalty, you mean.'

The irony struck Vahnsinn with such force that he wanted to dance. Could he laugh with his entire body? Yes, he did believe he could. The faith revealed to him by Preacher Guilhem was a perpetual unfolding of wonders. He laughed again as he thought about how many more wonders and transformations awaited. 'No,' he said to Rasp, calming himself. 'That is, in this instance, the least of your mistakes.' Anger replaced laughter with an abruptness that caused him physical pain. 'You underestimated us,' he said. 'How could you have so little respect for our strength? You know what our forges are worth. You have used their issue often enough.' Rasp said nothing. 'How many Basilisks do you think fire at my command? How many Griffons?'

'I never questioned your strength,' Rasp said quietly. 'I never questioned your loyalty, either, and I should have. *That* is the crime for which I will seek penance. After I see what is left of you once the Inquisition has done its duty.'

Vahnsinn snorted. 'You're a bore, Simeon.'

The train slowed.

'Good,' Vahnsinn said. 'We'll be at the surface soon. Then you can see. You *will* be enlightened.'

5. Bellavis

It was the way in which Veteran Sergeant Katarina Schranker was standing that drew his attention. As he had given up more and more of the flesh and its reflexes, Enginseer Bellavis had found himself becoming more interested, in a detached fashion, in the intricacies of human body language. About a hundred metres from the rows of Leman Russ tanks, she was looking at the command tent. Schranker was the sort of soldier who appeared to be rolling from one battle into another, even when none was around, and pleased to be doing so. At this moment, she was still, her focus intense, as if in actual combat.

Bellavis walked over to her. 'Something?' he asked.

She nodded at the command tent, fifty metres away. 'The captains just went in there. All of them.'

'War,' Bellavis said.

'War,' Schranker agreed. She hailed another sergeant who had just emerged from between the ranks of tents on the right. 'Strauss,' she called. 'Better start stirring bodies. Something's coming.'

And then the night made her words true. Bellavis heard the bombardment start up. His bionic ears parsed the sound of the distant storm. He calculated how many hundreds of artillery units were firing. He distinguished the voice of the Earthshaker cannon of the Basilisk from the Griffon's heavy mortar. He determined how far the units were. The Griffons were much closer than the Basilisks. They had been moved into position on top of the ridges overlooking the Trenqavel land. From that height, the Mortisian encampment was well within range.

All of this took less than a second. For another fraction of a second, Enginseer Bellavis assessed the information with academic interest. He discerned trajectories, whether the barrage was aimed at one target or several. And then, faster than calling to the tent, he was contacting Captain Ledinek over the vox-unit embedded in his throat. He reported to the commanding officer of the base that the entire area was about to be blanketed by shells and heavy mortars.

He spoke automatically. His mind had already formulated what he had to say, and had moved on. He had reacted quickly to the reality of threat, but could do nothing to neutralize it. What remained was to seek cover.

Before he had finished speaking, sirens began to wail, drowning out the endless howl of the wind. The men and women of the 77th and 110th regiments would not die in ignorance, then. That much, he had accomplished.

Schranker was racing for the tanks, yelling that they be started up and spread out. Bellavis had spoken so she could hear him, and so she knew as well as he did that there was no time to take any meaningful action. But the attempt needed to be made.

Bellavis had made his. He finished his survey of the camp. There was no cover. There was nothing to be done in the final seconds except wait. A vestigial instinct, a trace of the man of flesh and emotion he had once been, reacted with the ghost of anger. The impassive consciousness that was the greatest part of his identity regarded the response with distant interest, and made a note to consider the phenomenon at greater length, should he survive the next few minutes.

Then came the whistling. The sky was torn by tears of iron. Bellavis dropped to the ground. He tucked his servo-arm against his body. He covered his head with his arms. The camp exploded. The barrage was massive and sustained. The ground erupted as if a volcano beneath it were waking from a nightmare. Earth erupted skyward in huge fountains. Tents and soldiers disintegrated with every strike. Vehicles turned into flying scrap metal. On the landing pad, the Lightnings blew up, their munitions adding to the destruction. The noise was an overwhelming staccato thunder, and Bellavis's bionic hearing shut down to protect him from the noise. A shell hit a few metres to his left. The explosion lifted him into the air. He came back down hard. Beside him now was a crater. He rolled into the depression. The cover was symbolic. He was seeking shelter in probabilities. It was all he had.

He lay curled and motionless while the world around him tore itself apart.

6. Yarrick

We pieced together the larger picture afterwards. At the time, none of us knew more than our tiny portion of the destruction. The disaster was heralded by the illusion of victory: the cultists vanished. In some cases, they were annihilated by Imperial forces. In others, they melted into the night. The Vahnsinn guards were among those who slipped through our fingers. I knew even then that they must have taken the tunnel network. The warren was so extensive, two armies could cross paths, ignorant of each other's presence. Of course there had been a signal. Of course the heretics had known what was coming. To this day, I am not sure if the signal had been sent by the forces in the city, calling in the bombardment because we were beating them, or if the artillery strike had always been inevitable. Though I have no proof, I am convinced of the latter case. Vahnsinn divided our strength by forcing us to respond on multiple fronts. He eroded our smaller units. He even destroyed some of them. But we had the numerical superiority inside Tolosa, and when the tide turned, as it must, he withdrew and punished the city.

I curse the day the traitor was born. The consequences of his crimes were, I am sure, beyond his most fervid dreams. His memory should be expunged from the galaxy, but I will never forget him. He taught me as surely as did Rasp. He taught me that treachery and tactical genius could co-exist. He taught me the danger of underestimating a foe. I have no doubt that he always planned to rain hell upon Tolosa, but he held off until his artillery would have the greatest impact.

The forges of Mistral had been labouring towards this day for years. Many loyal citizens had worked unknowingly on the weapons that would be put to monstrous use. And now the guns roared. The barrage was divided between two targets: the regiment's encampment and Tolosa itself. The blow that fell on the more concentrated space of the Trenqavel valley was like a meteor strike. What hit Tolosa was closer to a hail, one where each stone was an explosive shell designed to shatter fortifications.

The shells came down on us. There was no point in seeking shelter. The shells gutted every building they struck, the explosions blasting stone across the streets. There was no shelter at all. The warehouse was hit seconds after we emerged from the doors. It blew apart, knocking us down like leaves. Blood pouring from my ears, covered in powdered mortar, I forced myself to my feet. I could barely think. Two needs forced me on: preserve unit integrity, and defy Vahnsinn's devastating move in any way I could.

I wavered for a moment as my head spun. What did I think I could do? Another shell landed fifty metres away, blowing a deep crater in the street and shattering the façade of a group of abandoned shops. The earth lurched. I staggered, but my duty and my hate grew in tandem. What did I think I could do? I could stand. And in standing, perhaps I could share some of the strength of purpose I felt with the company.

Become a symbol, I thought. *Become a symbol.*

I spat out dust and shouted, 'Stand fast, Third Company! Stand with me! Stand with each other! Stand with the Emperor!' I don't know if a single soldier heard me. I couldn't hear myself over the shattering booms of the shells and the ringing in my ears. But they could see me. Saultern was their captain, but it fell to me to be a symbol. I was a political officer, and I had seen enough of politics to know how easily the image became the reality. Mistral was awash with toxic images, rotted by false loyalties and opportunistic uses of our most sacred Creed. Enough.

I strode to the rubble of the warehouse and climbed the heap until I was a few metres above street level. I disdained useless shelter. If a second shell fell on this spot, it would kill me whether I stood defiant or crouched, cowering. I chose to stand. My personal survival was unimportant. The individual commissar meant nothing. There was exhilarating freedom in the fact that it was the office itself that mattered, and the role it fulfilled. I pointed at the sky and channelled all my hatred in a throat-tearing laugh. 'Is that the best our enemy can do? Does he think this will make us bend our knee?'

And then, by the Throne, this happened: a shell dropped where I pointed. I reacted without thinking, and brought my arm down as if directing the fall of the high explosive. It landed on the other side of the street, directly across from me. In the fraction of a second before the blast, I had time to think, *stand fast.* I knew how important it was that I not fall. My exhortation became a roar, as if I were shouting down the explosion. I was struck by a wall of heat and wind. Stone shrapnel tore my face, shredded my coat. I stood in a gale of war. Below me, the troops were bowled over. Somehow, I stood. The true defence of the Imperial Creed demanded that I stand, and so I did.

The wind and the fire abated. I could feel blood flowing down my face. Its warmth soaked my neck and chest beneath my uniform. I ignored it. For the moment, the shells were hitting further upslope from our position. The shrieks of their descent were just distant enough that I could make myself heard. I must not waste this window. 'You see?' I called to the Mortisians. 'The heretics can do nothing against us! Shielded by our faith, we are invincible!' I faced south. 'It is from there that the enemy attacks with artillery. When he is done, and the heroes of Aighe Mortis still hold Tolosa, what will he do? He will hurl himself against the walls. And what will he find there? Death!'

'*Death!*' came the cheer.

'We should thank our foe for this gift!' I gestured behind me at the explosions and smoke. 'Because now we know where we must meet him, and give him his reckoning!'

'To the wall!' Saultern shouted. He stood directly below me now. He, too, was becoming what he needed to be.

'To the wall!' I repeated. I strode down the rubble. I could not hear the shouts of the troopers, because the shells were falling close again, and the world was shaking once more. But we were a unit consumed with purpose and righteous fury, and the devastation only spurred us on. We moved off at high speed, heading further downhill, towards the outer fortifications of Tolosa. We ran as if to meet the shells.

The artillery did not let up. The shells hammered down on the city. I began to think of them as the blows of a monstrous, petulant infant. There was no consistent pattern to the devastation. This was not a walking barrage. Its only goal was destruction. It had a strategic value: the damage to the city would hurt our efforts to counter-attack. But with his forces withdrawn, Vahnsinn had no way of pinpointing the Mortisian emplacements. He was throwing a massive expenditure of ordnance at the city to uncertain effect. There was more than a military goal here. There was more even than punishment. The act was excessive, and that, I realized, must be its value for Vahnsinn and his allies. I stored the insight away. I felt that I had come to understand something important about our foe. Perhaps we might use it against him. The excess was irrational, and that was fertile ground for mistakes.

Less than a thousand metres separated our position from the city's battlements. We seemed to be making no progress. The journey was an endless race through the shrieks and thunder of shells, and the explosions of buildings and roads. The civilians of Tolosa cowered in their rooms, and they died as surely in their homes as they did outside them. The streets were strewn with corpses. We passed fallen buildings from which issued cries of pain and moans of desperation. Still the hail fell, punching new, bleeding wounds in the city. The night shattered. It became a mosaic of jagged shards. And through it all, we moved with purpose. We were what remained of order in this region of Tolosa, and we would be enough. There was no alternative.

We reached the battlements. They had taken some direct hits, but had weathered them well. The wall was rockcrete, fifty metres high and thirty metres thick. Some portions were slumped, but there were no outright breaches yet, at least in this quadrant. We climbed the nearest staircase. Atop the wall, we looked south.

The sky was greying with dawn. Before the gates of Tolosa

lay the great maglev junction. It was intact. As far as I could see, not a single shell had fallen here. There was still strategy behind the mad excess of the heretic bombardment. Vahnsinn wanted the use of the rail network. He would need it. The bridges and roads that were the other land-based approaches to the city were too eccentric in their advance, and too narrow, to allow the rapid deployment of an army.

Near the horizon, I could just make out the muzzle flashes of the great Basilisk guns. Ahead of them, a stain as dark as treachery spread over the land. The contagion travelled over road and track and waterway. Siege was coming to Tolosa.

CHAPTER 11
MOVE AND COUNTER-MOVE

1. Yarrick

Saultern stared at the junction. Its implications had seized his attention more forcefully than the gigantic array of forces in the distance. As it should. When he turned to look at me, his face was an agony of uncertainty. He was showing more and more promise as a captain, but he was now faced with a decision far beyond the authority of his rank. 'Should we destroy it?' he asked me.

Who did he think I was? What magical prerogatives did he think I had? I doubted we had the means to destroy the transportation hub – the wall's turret cannons would have to be lowered below the horizontal to fire at such close range, and it seemed clear that the defences had been designed with the express purpose of preventing that form of self-inflicted wound. Even if we could manage it, that action was no more mine to order than it was his. Yet, even as I acknowledged these truths, I found myself thinking beyond my immediate duties, and about the sheer imperatives of war. If I could see a way to ruin the tracks, would I? Yes, I would. Without hesitation. Damn the consequences that might befall me.

The individual is unimportant. The symbol is what matters.

None of what flashed through my mind was of any use to Saultern, though. He needed to be decisive, and to be taking action. He needed my help. 'No,' I told him. I was not expressing a belief. I was reminding him of simple realities. Did he think we could wreak any meaningful destruction with the few rockets and grenades we had left? 'We need to reach Colonel Granach and inform him of the situation. Get our vox working, captain. Nothing else matters now.'

Behind us, the shells continued to fall upon Tolosa as if the enemy would flatten the city and spare himself the need to take it. The deafening rhythm made it difficult to speak. I looked back up the hill of the city while Saultern and Trooper Guevion, the vox-operator, struggled to establish communication. We didn't know who was still alive. I imagined the worst as I watched Tolosa burn and fall, the awful light of its martyrdom even now brilliant against the strengthening dawn. If the colonels were dead, I wondered, if we were all that remained, what then?

Then we would descend to the wall and take the junction, and when the heretics arrived, we would do terrible things to them.

The dome of the Ecclesiarchal palace was a proud silhouette against the sky. It was shrouded in smoke, but its symmetry was unharmed. It was riding out the bombardment. Either all shells had missed, or it had shrugged off their impact. Its massive shape dominated the city, and called us all to duty and belief. My heart swelled. The building was more important than the venal fool who dwelt in it and believed it to be his home. It was our faith given architectural form. It was the unwavering will and vigilance of the Emperor. It could not fall, and so neither could we.

'I have someone!' Guevion shouted. She clamped the earpiece to the side of her head.

'Colonel Granach?' Saultern asked.

'No, sir,' Guevion said after a moment. She looked up, uncertain. 'Sister Basilissa, speaking for Sister Superior Setheno.'

'How can we possibly be reaching them?'

'They have set up a listening post at the top of the dome. Less interference.'

'Better equipment too,' Kortner said without bitterness.

'Can they reach our other units?' Saultern asked.

'I think so, sir.'

Saultern nodded, and gave Guevion a short sitrep to relay. Neither hesitated, but I saw a flicker in their faces. I knew what it was, because I felt it too: swallowed pride. It was an unwarranted luxury, but it was real all the same. It was an article of faith that the Adepta Sororitas and the Adeptus Astartes looked down on the humble soldiers of the Imperial Guard. The ferocious sanctity of the Sisters of Battle and the genhanced physiology of the Space Marines raised these warriors beyond the realm of the merely human. Setheno and her squad had done nothing to dispel this impression. Now we had to confirm their judgement that the Guard could not be trusted to complete its mission without the help of its superiors.

The wound of shame passed over the company, a shared wince. Perhaps there was an anticipation of humiliation to come, once the war was won. I will affirm that, at that point, there was still no question in any of our hearts about the inevitability of our victory. We had been hit hard. The barons had the initiative. None of that mattered. The simple fact was that we would defeat the traitors. The alternative was unimaginable.

We didn't know everything, then. There were things that we couldn't imagine, but they awaited us all the same.

Step by step, we re-established communication with our scattered forces. Step by step, the coordination of our strength returned. Step by step, we discovered silences. There was no word from Seroff.

And step by step, something worse than a siege approached.

2. Rasp

He saw enough from the windows of the maglev train. Vahnsinn made sure of that. There was no secrecy, no concealing of tactics. Vahnsinn was proud of his war, and he appeared certain that Rasp would never be in a position to act against him. The train's route took it first across the great alluvial plain, racing towards the bulk of the baronial forces. For the first few hours Vahnsinn kept them in the rear car, where panoramic windows and ceiling revealed the full spectacle of the savaging of Tolosa.

'I'm glad you could see some of this while it was still dark,' the baron commented. He gestured at the late-morning sky. 'We lose many of the best colours in the day.'

It was a taunt, of course. Rasp didn't want to give Vahnsinn the satisfaction of responding to it, but he had to understand what had happened to his friend. The better he knew the type of man Vahnsinn had become, the better his chance of fighting back. As much as his anger demanded answers, though, so did his grief. It wanted an accounting. It wanted to know how the soldier he had counted as his comrade on dozens of battlefields had transformed into a man who judged the aesthetic value of the deaths of thousands. A man who had managed to wear the mask of what he had once been so convincingly. So Rasp said, 'Why?'

Vahnsinn turned from the burning city. He cocked his head. 'Why? Have I been that unclear?'

'I know why you're at war with Wangenheim.' Though he wondered if that were really true. He suspected that the politics of Mistral had provided the means, and not the cause, for the conflict. 'But what you just said…' He paused, more for effect than out of genuine puzzlement. 'A few days ago, you made a plausible case for a rebellion that would still be faithful to the Emperor Himself. I see and hear nothing but obscenity now.'

Vahnsinn regarded him steadily, his smile growing broader until it seemed his skull itself was showing through his flesh. 'What do you call that, Simeon?' he asked. 'Was that supposed to be subtle? Were you trying to anger me? Or trick me into a revelation?' He approached, then leaned forward until his face was inches from Rasp's. He continued to speak through the dreadful grin. 'I don't have to defend my reasons,' he snarled. 'I'm proud of them. And there will be no secrets between us, old friend. No need for tricks. Not any more. You want a revelation? I'm going to share many with you.' He straightened, and moved back to the window. He looked out over the rushing landscape. 'We're coming very close to the time for the first,' he said. He glanced over his shoulder at Rasp. 'Aren't you curious about what it is?'

'You've made it clear you're going to tell me.'

'And so I will.' He went to the door leading to the next car and rapped on it once. It opened, admitting two guards. They wore the livery of House Vahnsinn. Rasp examined it closely as they unshackled his legs. Though the two men were not wearing cultist robes, there was still something disturbing about their uniforms. It took Rasp a few moments to realize what it was. They bore the Vahnsinn coat of arms on their chests: three vertical spears before a mountain background. The spears drew Rasp's eye. The design of the shafts had been altered. The work was detailed, precise, and from a distance, invisible except for the unease it created. Up close, Rasp could see that the shafts were no longer simple, bold lines. A spiral moved up their lengths. They were twisted. They were, Rasp thought, the perfect symbol of what Vahnsinn had become: a mask of loyalty and faith concealing deep, terminal corruption.

Once he could see the alteration, it seemed to Rasp that the threads were spreading out from the spear shafts, as if the rot were reaching further and further. The shadow that had fallen over Vahnsinn and the other barons was progressive, he realised. Perhaps some of the men who fought under these banners still believed themselves to be faithful servants of the Emperor. Others had fallen far from His light. The insidiousness of the symbolism disturbed Rasp. Vahnsinn might stylize himself the leader of the barons' war, but Rasp doubted he had instigated the process of rebellion. There was another force at work here. It had taken Vahnsinn. It was using him, as surely as he was using those beneath him.

The guards hauled Rasp to his feet. His legs were numb from being seated in the same position for hours, and he almost fell. His arms still chained before him, he was taken through half a dozen cars, all loaded with men-at-arms and cultists, towards the front of the train. Vahnsinn led the way, accepting the salutes and bows as his due. The lead car was nearly the same as the rear one. It was prepared for the comfortable seating of the baron, and the shackling of his prisoner. The upper half of the car was clear plasteel. The only difference was the discreet steering console. Another guard stood before it, facing forward. He was so motionless, his presence faded from existence.

Rasp's escorts fastened him to his seat, and now he was looking towards the army. Vahnsinn spread his arms to embrace the perspective of his might. 'And this,' he said, 'is the harvest that fool cardinal has reaped.'

It was on the tip of Rasp's tongue to call Vahnsinn a liar, but there was, to his surprise, a ring of truth to the baron's words. Perhaps, Rasp thought, Vahnsinn had fooled him so completely because he had said a great deal that wasn't a lie at all. Perhaps Wangenheim's power play had pushed Vahnsinn to rebellion and heresy, or at the very least weakened his resistance.

Whatever the cause, the train was passing over the result. The army advanced towards Tolosa. It was coming not from the mountains, where most of the baronial redoubts stood, but from the direction of the great manufactorum hives. The massive industrial output of Mistral had been turned against its political and spiritual centre. Hundreds of artillery guns were spread across the plain. They advanced over the fertile land, their treads scarring the soil, leaving it ruined mud in their wake. Troops in the thousands beyond counting marched between the Basilisks. Rasp saw little discipline. There were no formations. As the train sped overhead, he saw a blur of banners, and a motley collection of uniforms and robes. He was looking at a mob, not an army. But the mob had a single goal, and its collective being marched with grim purpose.

Rasp reached for his contempt. 'Do you call that an army?'

Vahnsinn was untroubled by the insult. 'No,' he said. 'I call it a tide. The Imperial forces on Mistral are going to drown.'

And there he'd said it: *the Imperial forces*. The perspective was telling. He saw the Imperium as Other. Rasp found the clarity helpful. His enemy was defining himself. 'I think we will surprise you,' he said, making the *we* a declaration.

Vahnsinn cocked an eyebrow, amused. He gestured at the ranks of Basilisks. 'I grant that our manufactoria are limited to the production of artillery. Our few tanks have been difficult to acquire. But I have destroyed your base. *Your* tanks are gone. So is your air support. You have nothing but infantry left, if that. Your defiance is engaging, and I would expect nothing less from you, but really, do try harder. The Imperium has lost, and you know it.' He spoke with no trace of boasting, but with the patience of an instructor dealing with an ignorant pupil.

'Oh? And if you take Tolosa, what then? Is that an end of it? Mistral is yours?'

'It already is.'

Rasp had no doubt that, on one level, this was true. Though the Ecclesiarchy had extensive land holdings, they were given over to agricultural and mining concerns. There were no settlements on them. Mistral's population lived in baronial territory. Rasp did not want to believe that the entire civilian population had been corrupted, but the dominant authority in the lives of the average Mistralian was the nobility. The hand of the Ecclesiarchy was felt at a distance, and its effective power would vanish quickly if the nerve centre of Tolosa was neutralized. Its spiritual influence had already been weakened, thanks to Wangenheim himself, and would wither further without enforcement. Rasp did not trust the faith of the masses.

But none of that mattered. Mistral could not remove itself from the Imperium without consequences. 'How long do you think that you will reign here?' Rasp said. 'How long before skies are dark with landing craft and drop pods? What you have begun this day will not end here.'

'Of course it won't.' For the first time, Vahnsinn spoke with fervour. His eyes shone with a believer's fire. 'This *is* just the start. There is truth on Mistral, old friend, but it must not remain here. Whoever the Imperium sends here will spread the truth across the galaxy.'

'What truth?'

'You'll see it. In due course.' Vahnsinn turned to the guard before the steering console. 'The next junction,' he said, and the guard nodded. Vahnsinn looked back at Rasp. 'We have to continue your education.'

The guard pushed some levers to the right. The train rocked as it took a sharp bend. Now it was travelling west, and then north-west. It was heading back into the mountains.

'Where are we going?'

'Home,' Vahnsinn answered. 'To Karrathar. There is so much truth to show you.'

3. *Yarrick*

'No,' Granach said, 'we don't blow the junction. We might need it ourselves.' He pointed at the stain that was creeping towards us over the horizon. 'Besides, the enemy isn't using it.'

True. The infantry was advancing on foot, keeping pace and providing escort to the creeping artillery guns.

'We don't know if that's the totality of their forces,' Benneger pointed out.

'No,' Granach agreed, 'we don't. But if it isn't, sending an advance force by maglev isn't going to be of much tactical use.'

'What about their supply lines?' I asked. I understood Granach's desire to preserve the hub. It could be very useful for mounting a counter-attack. We still had not been able to make contact with the base. We didn't know the status of the bulk of our forces, but if we still had some capabilities there, the means to quickly link up would be invaluable. And yet I couldn't help but see that eventuality as a distant hypothetical, an expression of hope rather than a strategic possibility. The reality was that a siege was almost upon us, and the besiegers had a massive network of rail lines to keep them reinforced with troops and materiel. 'Colonel, none of the shells are falling close to the walls. The enemy clearly does not want to risk accidentally damaging the rails. This hub is of great importance to the barons.'

'It's a risk,' Granach admitted. 'One we'll take.'

'I disagree, colonel.' Setheno's voice came from the vox. We were standing around the transmitter to include the Sisters of Battle in the decisions being made regarding the city's defence. Most of the city's contingent of the regiment had now gathered at the wall. There was still no word from Seroff. No one had seen anything of Inquisitor Krauss since before the procession. The Sisters of Battle remained at the palace. Duty to the relic, the sanctity of the location and its strategic importance dictated that necessity. I could hear

Setheno's frustration. It was only in part because of Granach's decision. She had no wish to be behind the front lines.

'I'm sorry that my decision does not meet with your approval, sister superior,' the colonel said. I was astonished by how close he came to outright sarcasm. 'But this is my determination.' He received silence in response. He cleared his throat. 'Meanwhile, we have another problem.'

'The tunnels,' said Benneger.

'Precisely. The heretics left by that method. They can come back the same way.'

The tank commander drummed his fingers against his thigh. His body language was tense. Deprived of his vehicles, he was adrift. 'What do you propose?' he asked Granach. 'Go underground and wait for them there?'

I said, 'With respect, colonel, that would be impossible. There are hundreds of kilometres of tunnels. They cannot be held.'

'Then we're wasting our time,' Benneger declared. 'There is no keeping the enemy out, so let him in.'

'Abandon the city?' Granach was horrified.

'A tactical withdrawal.' Benneger looked restless, ready to leave on the instant. The big man was vibrating with nervous energy. 'There is no sense in trying to defend what is already lost. We leave the city, make for the base, regroup, and bring the wrath to these vermin.'

'We have no way of knowing the base still exists,' Granach reminded him.

'The city will not be abandoned,' said Setheno. 'Do as you will, soldier.' It was clear she was speaking to Benneger, stripping him of rank and pride. 'But be prepared to answer for your actions, either through shame in this life, or in judgement after its end.'

Benneger kept his reaction down to a twitch of his fingers.

'We will keep the city,' Granach told him, speaking as softly as he could over the constant drumming of the artillery.

'How?' Benneger demanded.

'Seal the tunnels,' I suggested.

'Oh?' Benneger rounded on me. 'Do you know the locations of all the entrances, commissar? No? I'm sorry. For a moment, I thought you'd said something useful.'

'He's right,' said Setheno.

'Thank you, Sister,' Benneger began.

'Not you,' she corrected.

While Benneger sputtered, Granach said, 'I don't see what choice we have. Tolosa is the only thing like a defensible position we have. But we can't have the enemy coming at us from beneath our feet.'

'These won't be small incursions,' I said. 'The enemy forces won't be engaged in sabotage. This is an invasion. They need to get large numbers of troops into position quickly. The smaller tunnels won't be of any use to them.'

'At least initially,' Granach agreed. He turned to Benneger. 'Take three companies. Search every likely basement. Move up the slope. And spread the word in the civilian population. They'll be taking shelter in the lower levels of the buildings anyway. Maybe we can find the underground routes in time.'

'A search during a bombardment.' Benneger gave him a sick smile. 'You're a bastard, you know that?'

'I'm a bastard with seniority.'

'And so am I.' Benneger jabbed a finger at my chest. 'You're with me, Yarrick,' he said. 'Come and reap the rewards of your bright ideas.'

* * *

4. *Seroff*

When he came to, he was surrounded by thunder. A giant was hammering the ground. The blows vibrated in his bones. Seroff opened his eyes, blinking against the sunlight, and got to his feet. He winced at every shell impact. They were coming frequently, and in a cluster nearby. He started climbing out of the crater. The fighting here was done. He was alone. Corpses lay scattered over the terrain. He had almost reached street level when he looked back and noticed that the rear wall of the crater was vertical. He was looking at the remnants of the building that had stood here before the cultists had blown it up. There was an opening in the wall. Giving in to his hunch, Seroff worked his way back down over the rubble and walked across the crater floor to the opening. It sloped steeply down into the earth. At first, Seroff thought it was perfectly black. He had nothing to light his way, and was about to turn to go, but then his dazzled eyes adjusted to the darkness, and he saw that there was a faint light coming from the interior.

He had no unit and no orders, but there was something here that called to his curiosity. So he followed it.

He made his way down by measured steps, right hand on the wall of the tunnel. After a minute, his eyes began to adjust. After a few metres, the passage opened into a much wider tunnel, one with multiple branches leading back to the surface. This, he realized, was how the cultists had hit the Mortisians from so many angles at once. Ahead, the main tunnel curved to the right. The light came from around the bend.

Seroff made his way forward. Walking was easy. The surface was level, cleared of obstructions. It would be possible for a large contingent to move fast down this route. Past the curve, the light came from a single lumen strip on the roof of the tunnel. It provided just enough illumination to show the way ahead. In the distance, he saw the glow of another strip.

Something else began here, too. There was luminescence on the walls, so weak that he could only see it in his peripheral vision. He picked up impressions of lines, runes, serpents, the ghost of movement. They made his head hurt, and they chilled his blood. The construction in secret of this passage was disturbing in itself. That the time and effort had been taken to apply ritualistic markings to the walls was even worse.

There was no point going further. He had to link up with the regiment again, and sound a warning. He stopped walking, and was about to turn around when he heard a gasp. The sound echoed down the tunnel, pain hollowed out by repetition. Seroff waited. After several seconds, the gap between two very slow and laboured breaths, the sound was repeated. It came from a darker patch on the left-hand wall. Seroff approached. There was another side passage. He peered inside. The light from the lumen strip barely leaked in. He was staring at a world of deep grey, but at last he made out a room. There was a man's body on the floor.

Seroff thought for a moment, then crouched. He found the figure's shoulders, and dragged the man into the main tunnel. His arms and legs were bound. His clothes and reflective armour were in tatters, and the face was such a confusion of blood and bruises that it took Seroff several seconds to recognize Krauss.

The inquisitor was barely conscious. Seroff undid the rope, hoisted Krauss over his own shoulders, and staggered back towards the light of day. By the time they reached the surface, Krauss was beginning to function again.

'Put me down,' he said.

Seroff did. Krauss clutched a slab of broken rockcrete to steady himself. He was a far cry from the figure he had presented at Wangenheim's reception for the Mortisian regiments. His nose was broken. His left eyelid was so swollen, Seroff wasn't sure there was still an orb beneath it. He spat out some blood, and a tooth bounced off the ground. He looked as if he had been worked over with a power fist. But when he straightened, the arrogance of his bearing was undiminished. His right eye blazed.

A shell shrieked in and blew out the façade of a building half a block down. Seroff winced. Krauss took in the ongoing devastation of the war as if it were a personal slight on his honour. 'Tell me what is happening,' he said.

You're welcome, Seroff thought. 'I've been unconscious,' he said. 'We were fighting small-scale insurgencies before I was struck.'

'Where is the rest of your unit?'

Seroff gestured at the corpses. 'Everywhere.' He looked back at the tunnel entrance. 'Where does that lead?'

'I don't know. Though its purpose is clear.' Krauss paused as the bombardment hit another crescendo in the near vicinity. 'No vox, I suppose.'

Seroff shook his head. 'And I have no idea where the rest of the regiment is.'

Krauss limped back towards the tunnel. 'Then we have little choice. Come.'

The inquisitor's presumption of command was repulsive. Seroff bit his tongue as he followed. Krauss was right. The tunnel was big. They had to know the nature of the threat, and neutralize it if they could.

Back inside, they paused to let their eyes adjust. 'You resent me,' Krauss said.

Seroff knew better than to lie. 'I don't see the relevance.'

'Anything I wish to know is relevant to me.' He started walking again. 'You did not answer my question.'

It wasn't a question. 'Forgive me, inquisitor,' he said, 'but I can't imagine that this is a novel experience for you.'

'I don't expect to be liked. I do expect to be feared. I am not pleased, but not entirely surprised, when an individual who imagines himself in authority resists me, such as your comrade Yarrick. I sense something else from you. You will tell me what it is.' He kept his voice barely above a whisper.

'I shouldn't be resentful,' Seroff answered, surprised by his own willingness to indulge in sarcasm with this man. 'After all, what I am, I owe to the Inquisition.'

They reached the bend and moved towards the first lumen strip. The runes were waiting.

'I don't understand,' Krauss said.

'I was privileged among my fellows at the schola progenium. I had clear memories of both my parents. I was six when they died…'

'I still don't–'

'… in the prisons of the Inquisition.' They were moving past the room where Krauss had been left. The markings on the walls, pulsing grey at the edges of Seroff's vision, were sinuous, stretching without interruption into the gloom ahead. He felt like he was walking into an embrace. He looked straight ahead, rejecting the contamination that sought to erode his soul. His distaste for Krauss gave him a focus around which to consolidate and shield his identity.

'I'm surprised you were admitted to the schola,' said Krauss.

'I find it hard to imagine a place would be found for the offspring of heretics.'

'None was. My parents were not heretics. This was confirmed after their deaths.'

'Are you saying their arrest was an error?' For Krauss, that implication seemed to be the true outrage.

'Not at all. I have too much respect for the Inquisition's skills. I'm saying that they ran afoul of the wrong political faction at the wrong time.'

Krauss grunted. 'You have never exercised the special sanctions of your rank, have you?'

'No. This is my first posting. And what does that have to do with anything?'

'I wonder if you are capable of doing so. You are predisposed to seeing innocence instead of guilt.'

I have no difficulty finding you guilty of arrogance and fanaticism, Seroff thought. 'I know my duty and my oaths,' he muttered.

They passed under the second lumen strip. The designs on the walls were no longer an embrace. They were a tangle. Seroff's shoulders tensed. It was as if the lines were closing up the way back behind them.

Krauss held up a hand. Seroff froze. After a moment, he heard it too: an echo reaching them of the sound of marching boots. Many of them.

And something else.

'Is that an engine?' Seroff asked.

CHAPTER 12
THE EXERCISE OF AUTHORITY

1. Yarrick

Back into the city we went, back under the worst of the shells. The walls would receive their measure of hell, I knew, once the enemy was close enough to target them with accuracy. For now, they were protected by their proximity to the maglev junction. But the iron rain continued to smash Tolosa. With Benneger in command, we began our search. We tried to move quickly, but we had to be systematic, or the mission was futile. And so we advanced, a phalange of order hammered from above by an agent of Chaos in the form of destructive chance.

Beneath our feet, the ground's vibration was continuous, whether the faint thrum of the most distant strikes, or the violent shake of the nearby impact. As we moved building by building, street by street, the city eroded around us. Homes, businesses and chapels exploded and collapsed. History was being pounded to dust. Sometimes, a structure we had just searched was reduced to rubble moments after we left it. At least the wasted effort was balanced by the buildings that were destroyed before we could enter them. The waste that was not balanced was the lives lost when shells hit mid-search.

We found small entrances to the underground network, and we sealed them with grenades and mines. After the first two hours of the search, there was still no sign of a major access point. I could feel time slipping through our fingers like water. Every minute, the enemy drew closer. Every minute, the division of our forces presented a greater danger. And we had no choice.

I felt more than just time was being stolen from us. So was morale. We were at war, reeling under the blows of our foe, and unable to hit back. When we had left the wall, the infantry was still just a spreading, corrupt stain near the horizon. It had not yet resolved into soldiers we could kill. And there was no retaliation against the shells that fell, and fell, and fell. They were the new reality of Tolosa. After hours of bombardment, it seemed that they had *always* been the reality of Tolosa.

I moved from squad to squad. I was fighting two intangible battles. I took part in the searches, forever prepared for an absent target. And I fought the despair that ate at the purpose of the troops. *Be the symbol,* I thought. *Be their anger. Be the image of the fight.* 'We are at war with cowards,' I said, and because no more than a handful of soldiers could hear me at any one time, I repeated myself until I was hoarse, and when it felt like I could no longer speak, I made myself shout all the louder, because that was what duty demanded of me. 'They do not dare depend on meeting us in open combat,' I said. 'They assail us from a distance, because they know what will happen when we are face to face. They compound their crimes, adding cowardice to heresy, and murder to cowardice. They massacre the citizens of this city, and to what end? Are we killed? No. Are we less resolute? No. Have they stoked the fires of our righteous vengeance? Yes. Oh, yes, comrades, in that they have surpassed themselves!'

The words came easily. Soon I was barely aware of speaking them. The content of the individual sentences became less important than the belief and the determination they conveyed. I had to incarnate the rage of the Imperial Guard. I had to be purpose made flesh. If there were enemies before us, our anger would have a target. But we were commanding human beings to go against every instinct for self-preservation and expose themselves to manifest danger for an end that was nebulous.

We were searching a vast area for something whose existence we could only surmise. We were dying for a hypothesis.

Tolosa's concentric rings were losing definition. The walls were coming down. These older barriers could no more withstand the direct hit of Earthshaker ordnance than the houses they protected. When the invasion came, it would be stopped at the outer wall, or it would not be stopped at all. We approached a gateway between the first and second rings up from the base of the city's hill. The passage had collapsed. It was impassable, but there were massive breaches on either side. There was nothing but low mounds of rubble to impede passage. As we passed over the wall, the perversity of war struck. A shell fell on the wall again, only a few metres from the damage. It was, in effect and horror, what every soldier must hold to be impossible, for the sake of sanity: a second strike to the same spot.

I had already crossed the wall, and rejoined Benneger. At our backs, the world shattered. Wind, sound and force fused together. A battering ram the size of the war itself smashed into us. I was walking, and then I was flying. I heard only the blast, saw only the blur of stone and fire. I slammed into the façade of a building on the other side of the street. I fell to the ground, gasping. My mind registered that I felt like a sack full of shattered bottles. I forced the realization down before it swamped my consciousness. There was duty before all else. If I fell unconscious, I was failing in it. The roar of the explosion had not yet started to fade and I was rising to my feet. If my legs were broken, I would fall, but if I did not fall, then I had no excuse not to act.

I was yelling something. I don't know what it was. I couldn't hear myself. No one could. My thoughts weren't coherent. I was little more than pain and the drive to do what I must. I suspect that what came from my throat was nonsense, a shout that was an end in itself, my anger hurled back at the explosion. The smoke was whipped away by the Mistralian wind, whose cry was even more eternal than the bombardment, and whose breath was pushing us all ever deeper into the terminal maelstrom of battle. The ruins of the wall were splashed with blood. I saw troopers burned by the blast, torn to pieces, crushed by stone and rockcrete. Everywhere were the walking wounded, military and civilian. Most of our force had already crossed when the shell hit, but there had still been the best part of a company either still going over the wall or in its close vicinity. The losses were terrible.

The sound faded. The wind blew the dust into my eyes and mouth. I coughed, choking mid-yell. I doubled over, spat out a wad of thick, bloody phlegm, then straightened. 'For the

Emperor!' I tried to call. I heard only a hoarse croak. But I was still standing, and my fist was raised in defiance. Men and women were staggering to their feet, and they were looking at me. I doubt most of them knew who I was. I was caked in dust, and I gradually realized that the warmth I was feeling on my nose and cheeks was blood streaming from a re-opened gash in my forehead. I would have been barely recognizable to those to whom I was most familiar, and many of these squads had been under Rasp's supervision. Perhaps my uniform was still clear enough. Perhaps even that didn't matter. I was standing. I was fighting. The effort to be the symbol was killing. Each step sent the shards of broken glass clattering up and down my spine and legs. But move I must, and so I did, and I began to cut through the stunned fog that surrounded us.

I say that the effort to be a symbol was killing. There was a blessing, though, in the fact that the symbol swallowed the man. My own weaknesses were irrelevant, harmless as long as I could keep the shape of the symbol animated. Sebastian Yarrick could bleed, and he could wince, and he could wish for – though not succumb to – oblivion. But the commissar walked, and exhorted, and challenged, and was unbowed.

Being a symbol is nothing. Being a legend… I accept the burden laid upon my shoulders by the will of the Emperor, and it is an honour that I am deemed worthy to carry it. But I will shed no tears when he declares my duty done, and calls me to the Golden Throne.

I looked for Benneger. We needed the symbolism of my role, but we also needed leadership. We needed to move forward, and do so quickly, before a fatal inertia set in. I spotted him a few metres up the road. He'd been thrown at a different angle from me, as if we had been struck by a hand as capricious as it was violent. He was sitting with his legs out before him. As I approached, he was giving his head a single, convulsive shake every few seconds.

I was careful to crouch before I came too close. It was important that no one be seen to loom over the commanding officer. 'Colonel?' I said. I wasn't shouting, but my voice was still a rough, painful whisper.

There was no answer. Just another shake of the head, hard enough to make his shoulders twitch.

'Colonel?' I tried again.

He turned his head towards me. He blinked. His eyes didn't want to focus. He seemed to be looking in two directions at once. I don't think he entirely knew who he was.

Once more, more quietly, for his ears alone, but with the crack of a whip. 'Colonel Benneger. *Sir*.'

His eyes cleared. He frowned. 'Yarrick,' he said. 'What...'

'A shell, sir. Are you injured?' I could see that he wasn't. He wasn't even bleeding. But I wanted him to realize that for himself.

He lifted his hands, appeared to recognize them as belonging to him. 'No,' he said.

'What are your orders, sir?' Another reminder: *Command us*. I couldn't use intimidation on him, as I had with Saultern. But neither could I allow too many more seconds to go by. Captains and sergeants and troopers would be watching. In another few moments, they would also be wondering.

A shell landed three blocks down. The road heaved with the shock. The jolt rocked Benneger to his feet. He brushed himself off, grunting his displeasure. He squared his jaw. It struck me that the colonel must, in his more private thoughts, picture himself as kin to the tanks he commanded. I thought the conceit was ludicrous, but if it gave him some forward momentum, let him have his indulgence.

Benneger cleared his throat. 'Mortisians!' he called. 'We move forward!'

'The search,' I reminded him.

He looked more anxious than displeased. He wanted off this street. I understood the impulse, but we were no safer between the next row of buildings than we were here. We could not allow instinct to govern our strategy, or we would be giving up our lives for nothing. Benneger gave me a brusque nod and called again. 'Forward to discover!' he said. 'I want this street cleared in five minutes!'

It took three times that. We were lucky it wasn't more, as the troops shook off the blow from the explosion. We raced. We looked. We found nothing, and still the shells fell, and still time fled from us. Benneger contacted Granach on the vox as we moved to the next street. The report from the wall was bad. The main body of the enemy was mere hours away. Meanwhile, we were hundreds searching a city of millions, searching for a phantom whose reality could announce our defeat.

Every fall of a shell was now the count of iron time, beating out the moments to disaster.

2. Seroff

They ran back to the entrance. Adrenaline flushed the pain from Seroff's limbs, and he moved fast. So did Krauss, whose injuries were worse. He reached the exit ahead of Seroff, his face contorted by more than bruises, his open eye consumed with an urgent hate. But once they were in the air again, amidst the devastation, the bombardment battering the city near and far, they paused. Seroff felt the same need for action as a moment before, but what action?

'What do we do now?' he asked.

Krauss looked around as if the answer would present itself. He seemed just as stymied. He said nothing.

'We have to contact the regiment,' Seroff insisted.

'Agreed,' Krauss said, his sarcasm etched with acid. 'How?'

Seroff's mind raced. *How much time before the enemy reached the surface?* Impossible to tell, but not long enough. No vox, and no sense of where the rest of the forces were. 'A signal,' he said. 'Some kind of signal. Something that can be seen from a distance.'

'There,' said Krauss. He pointed at the street, at the remains of the slaughter. Many of the dead still had their weapons. Seroff saw the rocket launcher, and ran for it.

'You've used one before?' Krauss asked.

'I have.' He yanked it from the dead man's arms, praying it was undamaged. It was. 'Any others around?' he asked.

'I don't see any.'

Seroff grimaced. 'Just one shot.'

'Lots of rifles.' Krauss grabbed the nearest lasgun and started firing into the air.

Seroff leaned the launcher against a doorway, looked for anything else that could draw attention. Along with more rifles, he found some grenades and demolition charges. Captain Monfor still clutched his bolt pistol in his fist. Seroff tossed it to Krauss, and pulled his own from its holster. The total weaponry at their disposal was pathetic beside the artillery thunder. 'How will we be heard over this?' he wondered.

'Pray for a lull.'

They fired everything they could find. Seroff held off on the rocket, waiting for seconds of calm. He and Krauss staged their own little war. They didn't worry about alerting the approaching foe. If they didn't catch the attention of their own forces, their deaths would be inevitable and meaningless.

Hear us, Seroff prayed. *This is the sound of combat, not artillery. Hear it. Hurry.*

And he did as Krauss said. He prayed for a fragment of silence.

3. Setheno

She stood in the study of Wangenheim's quarters and looked down at the cardinal. 'Would you please repeat that?' she asked. She used no honorific, because she had heard him perfectly well the first time. She simply wanted him to utter those shameful words again. She wanted to see if he had any awareness of what he was doing. She was giving him the chance to repent.

He did not take it. 'We must leave,' he said. 'We cannot have the relic exposed to such risk. We must take it and withdraw to your ship until the situation has stabilized.'

Setheno took her time in replying. The density of absurdity in Wangenheim's demands made it difficult to know which idiocy or crime to address first. The delay gave her the time to master her fury. She had no more illusions about how and why she and her Sisters had been brought to Mistral. If the man before her had not held the rank he did in the Ecclesiarchy, she would have already killed him. But he was who he was, and that stayed her hand. So she took something very like pleasure in her answer. 'What ship?' She bit off each syllable, her jaw tight with cold hate.

Wangenheim's mouth fell open. He could not process her

words. The game had slipped from his grasp. He was good, she thought, at the considered, long-wrought plan. But when contingent events deviated from his schema, he was at a loss. 'I don't understand,' he said. 'Your ship. The ship that brought you here.'

'We are a single squad. What do you imagine? That a cruiser of the Order of the Piercing Thorn has remained on station for our convenience? The order has other duties in this system. The *Laudamus* departed after we debarked from the shuttle.'

'Isn't it coming back?' He was becoming stupid in his fear.

'It is. In time.'

'When?'

'In time,' she repeated.

The cardinal stared at her as if she had begun speaking a xenos tongue. Then he shook his head in a general denial, and stalked towards the study's balcony. It looked south, and offered a fine panorama of the madness he had helped to bring about. He stopped a few paces from the doorway. Setheno could see his body shrink on itself before the spectacle of whistling shells and billowing smoke. There had been three close hits in the great square, but the palace was still unharmed. Setheno could think of no clearer sign of her duty than that. In this, she found the certainty she needed in the midst of Mistral's political winds.

'What do we do, then?' Wangenheim asked.

She knew he was speaking to himself, but she answered anyway. 'What we must. The Imperial Creed is under siege on this planet. We will fight for it until we have shed the last drop of heretic blood.'

'Or our own,' he muttered, miserable.

She fought again with the instinct to strike him down. 'Yes,' she said.

He cocked his head, as if a thought had occurred to him. He looked back at her for a moment, and she thought there was a gleam in his eye, whether of hope or cunning, she wasn't sure. She was coming to accept that in Wangenheim's case, the two were indistinguishable. 'Where is the relic?' he asked, turning away from her again.

'In the crypt. With the icons. It is safe.'

'Is it? Is anyone guarding it?'

She refrained from sighing. 'The palace guard.'

'Not one of you?'

'We are where we can see the flow of the battle, so that we can act as needed.'

'Yes, yes, of course. I wonder if that is the wisest decision in our power.'

'Meaning?' She could sense a web of words and logic being woven, and resented being dragged into its coils.

'The situation is fluid. A crisis could come at any moment, and the relic is an obvious target for the heretics. The symbolic value of its destruction would be immense. I do not doubt the faith or loyalty of the guards, but could they defend against a concerted attack on the crypt?'

'The walls and doors are strong.'

'Strong enough?' He shook his head, still looking away from her. 'And the crypt is the first place they would look. We must do better. The Emperor demands that we do better. The relic should be under your direct observation and protection.'

She said nothing. She knew that self-regard motivated every syllable he uttered, but that didn't make them lies.

'I shall send for it,' he said. Now he turned to face her. 'I shall guard it with my own life.' His smile was beatific and brave. Of course it was. He wasn't arranging to protect the relic. He was arranging for *it* to protect *him*.

'That decision is in your power to make,' she replied. She still withheld the word *cardinal*. She would see him dead before she again granted him the rank he was dishonouring with his every breath.

'Yes,' Wangenheim said, 'it is.' There was the savagery of cold-blooded calculation in his tone. There was triumph in his stance as he straightened, already feeling the shield of the Sisters of Battle extending to his person.

As if shamed by the spectacle, the war fell silent. A shell exploded to the south-east, and then, for a few seconds, there were no other strikes. Setheno saw the streaks of more ordnance rising into the sky, but for a few moments, a bloodied calm fell over the city. From the midst of the false peace, about midway down the hill, a rocket shot upwards. Its flight was vertical. It had no target. It was a waste of ammunition.

Unless it wasn't.

She turned on her heel, and left the cardinal without a word. 'Sister Basilissa,' she spoke into her vox-bead, 'contact Colonel Granach.'

4. *Yarrick*

We didn't see the rocket launch, but at the bombardment's intake of breath, we heard the explosion of grenades. I had just emerged from another fruitless search, this time in a ravaged jeweller's on the north side of the street, with troops from Saultern's company. We looked at each other. All viable units had been accounted for, so who was fighting? A hundred metres to my right was the next major intersection, and Benneger was already starting to lead the march up to the next avenue. I ran to intercept him. The shells were already landing again, and he didn't hear me approach. He looked startled when I stepped in front of him. That worried me. His mind must have been elsewhere. He was not being properly aware of his surroundings.

'Did you hear that, colonel?' I asked.

'Hear what?'

More bad news, but then Guevion came running up with the vox. 'Message from the wall, sir. They think someone has tried to signal us to the north.'

Benneger glanced in that direction. He looked irritated. His reactions were off. He seemed disengaged with the events happening around him. 'Where, exactly?' he asked. When Guevion gave him the coordinates, he said, 'It will be hours before we reach that sector.' He marched on, as if dismissing Guevion's news. Its importance was lost on him. It was something he would re-examine later.

'Colonel?' I walked beside him. I spoke clearly. 'Did you understand? Someone has tried to signal us.'

'I heard. We're not done here, and if we leave now, we'll never remember where we left off.'

I looked back at Guevion. She was still with us, vox mouthpiece in one hand, looking worried and confused. Benneger's responses were clearly not ones she wanted to convey. 'What was the signal?' I asked her.

'The launch of a rocket, commissar.'

'That is urgent,' I said to Benneger.

'Yes,' he said.

There was agreement, at least, but no action, no command to deal with it. 'Get Captain Saultern,' I said to Guevion. 'Tell him we're taking a company to investigate the signal.'

'No,' Benneger said. My oblique attack on his pride woke him up. 'No, we must all go.'

'We must hurry,' I said, picturing the desperation such an act implied.

The colonel nodded, and then he was calling us all to mission. He turned back into the tank commander as the need and the mission sank in. I was worried, though. It should not have been that difficult, and should not have taken that long, to convince him.

The companies moved through the streets. We covered ground quickly. I saw morale shoot up. There was a grim pleasure to the run. We were no less vulnerable to the shells than before, but the psychological effect of the forced march was powerful. We *felt* that we could outrace the doom that rained from the sky. It was an illusion that served us as well as a reality. Even when its falseness was revealed, it lost none of its worth. A line of buildings to our right was hit. Wreckage blew across the street, a storm of brick. I winced, turning my face away from the shrapnel. I winced again when more troopers died, but I did not turn my face away from their sacrifice. Others were wounded, and the ones who could not walk we left behind. We took no pleasure in doing so, but nor did we grieve. There was a goal ahead. There was, we believed, an enemy ahead. So there was retaliation ahead, and it pulled us forward. Its gravitational force was the exhilarating promise of combat. Those who fell along the way weren't unlucky. They simply had not been fast enough.

There was nothing rational about this belief. I knew it was nonsense. I'm sure every soldier around me knew that too. But our bodies believed. The part of our minds that hurl us into battle believed. The conviction of personal immortality is engrained in the human condition. Thanks to it, we commit acts of madness, but also of heroism.

We were less than a thousand metres from our goal when the bombardment stopped. This was no random pause. The sky cleared of shells.

'The tide is turning!' Benneger shouted, triumphant. To me he said, 'A good sign, Yarrick.'

I could still hear the booming of guns. 'The target has changed,' I said. The wall, I realized. The enemy was nearly there, and close enough that the guns could hit it and still preserve the junction. I didn't share my thoughts with Benneger. He had just become even stronger. I didn't want to jeopardize that.

Then I realized something else: if the rest of the city was suddenly being spared, the situation within the walls must also have changed. There must be something that needed preserving.

I didn't have to wonder long. We heard the sounds of gunfire ahead. War had entered Tolosa, and we rushed to welcome it.

There was no time to form a strategy. The only option was the infantry charge. We tore up one more northward street, then west onto a wide avenue. The former market square was ahead of us, now a space of slumped wreckage. The enemy was spilling into it like insects from a nest. The forward elements of the heretics had already reached the entrance of the square and were moving down the avenue. Retreating along the same route, ducking from doorway to doorway, firing all the way, were Seroff and Krauss. They could do nothing to slow the cultists, but they provoked retaliation. They were using the heretics themselves as a signal.

Our advance reached them, and they joined us, charging

back again towards the foe. Funnelled by the width of the street, the two forces collided. They came at us with rabid fervour. The veneer of order that had been present in the Vales of Lom was gone. The corruption of Chaos had had that much longer to do its work. The disguise was gone. These men and women attacked in the name of the cancer in their minds. They embraced death, and did not care whether it was ours or their own that they celebrated. Less than twelve hours before the street had resounded with the cries of worship. It did so again, but a different faith was staining Tolosa with its presence.

Our attack was different. We, too, knew hatred, and ferocity, and the driving compulsion of faith. But we had the added might of righteousness. And yes, we had desperation, which I would hurl against eagerness in any war.

Above all, we had the Emperor. We were His hammer at its most raw and brutal. We smashed into the foe with all the force of His great will. That is a power that nothing in the galaxy can withstand. It falls only to the faithful to have the wisdom to wield it.

I had my pistol and sword drawn. I fired as I rushed forward. The shock of the collision came, and I was in a sea of struggling bodies. Hands grabbed my legs. A cultist already being trampled, already dying, still reached out with his madness to pull me down. I kept firing as I fell backwards. Heads exploded at point-blank range. I was splattered by heretic gore. Still firing, creating a bloody gap in the creatures surrounding me, I slashed with my sword and severed the wrists of my assailant. My feet slipped on blood. My clip emptied, but I found some leverage and shot to my feet. Another second and I would have been buried. I retaliated with renewed fury. I cut faces in half. I spilled intestines to the ground. I slammed forward, never giving the scum another chance to strike at me.

More illusion, of course. But I acted as though it were the truth, and tore through our enemies. My comrades in the hundreds were at my sides. We fought as if there were not enough foes for us all. The vortex of battle devoured us. We were one undifferentiated mass against another. We had but one thing to remember: to advance. As long as we were moving, we were prosecuting the war. Our fury was the greater. And despite Wangenheim's manipulations, our cause was holy. And so we moved forward. Leaving behind a wake of mutilated corpses, the righteous and the heretical alike reduced to ragged slabs of meat, we pushed the cultists back towards the tunnels.

They cut us down. We were as fragile in the face of steel and las as they were. We died by the scores. Nothing kept any of us alive except luck and the special dispensation of the Emperor. But we hit them harder. Within the first minute of the battle, we were advancing over the bodies of their dead, and we were pushing the living backwards.

I began to feel I would be trampling bodies forever. There was another strong surge of cultists, and though I was still advancing, I couldn't see more than a metre ahead. There was nothing but the grasping, clawing, hungry hands.

We reached the square, and the density of the enemy grew worse yet. The bodies were packed in tight as the new arrivals tried to shove their way out of the tunnels. Then I felt heat. I heard flames. I smelt burning bodies, and I was glad. Our troops bearing flamers had managed to move to the front lines, and they brought their weapons to bear. Flaming promethium arced across the cultists. So much flesh incinerating in such close quarters, and I learned something new: the stench of screams.

We fired through the flames and advanced again, pushing harder still, barely waiting for the burn to die down. We threw them back. At last cultists were withdrawing faster than we could kill them. They were retreating.

The roar that went up from the Mortisians filled the world with triumph. 'For the Emperor!' I shouted, and in that glorious moment I was not a symbol. I was not a commissar. I was simply Sebastian Yarrick, a man exulting in his faith and the holy struggle for the Father of Mankind. I did not have to inspire anyone. We were all possessed by the spirit of war. We ran down our foe, chasing him back into his hole.

But then another roar drowned out our own. It came from the tunnel. It sounded like the warning of some beast from the swamp of myths. It was an engine, but it had a rage that went beyond the mechanical. My conscious mind took over again, breaking the trance of combat. I reacted to imminent danger, stopped running forwards and threw myself to the left. I wasn't alone. Our charge split as soldiers sought to evade, racing to either side of the street, while others, caught in their own unstoppable battle momentum, kept going.

The monster exploded out of the tunnel, smashing through the rockcrete of the narrow exit. It was another unholy creation, forged by the same hellish conception as the horror we had fought at Lom. It was constructed around a Basilisk chassis. A battering ram, shaped like a massive spearhead, was mounted on the front. The Earthshaker cannon had been replaced with two turrets, one a flamer, the other a heavy stubber. And the beast had arms. They were attached like sponson turrets to the side of the chassis. They unfolded until they reached across the full width of the square. They were articulated, and ended in gigantic barbed hooks. The battering ram had been engraved with snarling jaws. The machine was black, but streaked with crimson that appeared to flow, as if the chassis were bleeding. And covering the entire monstrosity were runes and sigils. They tortured the mind. They sang a keening, ululating wail heard only inside the skull. They carried the darkness of the tunnel into the brightness of the day. The light seemed to dim around the tank. And for many of the Mortisians of the 77th Infantry Regiment, the light failed completely.

Dozens of our comrades fell under the treads. The arms reached out to either side, flailing with slow, mechanical hunger, scything, crushing and impaling. The flamer and stubber opened up, and completed the rout. Our charge had shattered like glass. We were scattered to either side of the tank. We were running and dying. Soon, we would only be dying.

I ducked low as I ran, and the tank's arms passed just over my head. I barrelled through an open doorway. I took the stairs of the residence two at a time. Behind me, I heard troopers following me, and then the grinding crash of the front wall being ripped open by the tank's arm.

I found a trap door up to the roof, raced to its edge and hunkered down. In the square, the slaughter was terrible, but I saw soldiers gathering on the tops of the buildings to my right and across the way. We weren't out of the fight yet. Las streaked down, punishing the resurgent cultists. The tank ignored the retaliation. It turned to the building opposite me, both its arms flailing at the ground floor until the entire structure collapsed.

I had lost track of Benneger in the melee. I found him again, one roof over from me. I ran across to the next building. The colonel was gesticulating violently. I did not want to believe what he seemed to be signalling. Guevion was crouched over her vox-transmitter before him, looking uncertain.

'Colonel?' I said.

'I'm going to order a retreat. We cannot hold.'

'Hold?' I said, stunned. 'Sir, it is not a question of holding. We must stop them. Destroy them utterly.'

'We cannot hold,' Benneger repeated, as if I had not spoken. He was staring past me, his eyes locked on the machine below. 'We must retreat.'

'If we retreat, the city is lost.'

He shrugged with one shoulder. 'Regroup with the regiment. Consolidate at the base. Get some heavy armour into the field.' He nodded. The gesture was automatic. I don't think he believed what he was saying. I'm not sure he was even aware of his words. 'We cannot hold,' he said again, turning the sentence into an incantation. 'Trooper,' he said to Guevion, 'reach who you can on the vox. Let Colonel Granach know we are pulling back.'

'No,' I said to Guevion. She looked relieved to have her hesitation justified. 'Colonel, your duty is to command this operation, and our mission does not allow for the possibility of retreat.'

Across the square, another building collapsed.

'We have no choice,' Benneger insisted. He never took his gaze away from the tank. He was mesmerized. His eyes were twitching back and forth rapidly, as if they were tracking the convolutions of the runes on the hull.

I stopped in front of him, blocking his view. 'Colonel,' I said, trying once more. We had no time. The Mortisians were fighting desperately, but getting nowhere. Benneger was right: we could not hold. Direction was needed, or we were lost.

'Issue new orders,' I said. 'We cannot retreat. Lead us. Now.' My gut twisted as I realized what was coming. I did not want it. I would not shirk it. Only one of us would fail in his duty on this roof, and that failure was about to end.

Benneger's eyes cleared. He looked directly at me, and I saw a man who had capitulated. He had led armoured divisions with honour and heroism, but in this moment of great need, he crumbled. His orders would only damage the war effort further. I raised my bolt pistol, aimed it between his eyes. 'Colonel Jozef Benneger, I find you derelict in your duties to the 110th Aighe Mortis Armoured Regiment.'

'Don't be silly, commissar,' he said.

I shot him. His head vanished. His final expression had been of arrogant cowardice. He had dishonoured his own record. After this battle, his body would vanish into the anonymity of rubble. It fell to me to give his death meaning. His memory deserved nothing, but the soldiers under his command would sell their lives for victory.

Even as the war between the rooftops and square raged, even as every soldier with a clear line of fire was killing the enemy, a stunned pause fell in my vicinity. Most of the troops around me were part of Saultern's company. They knew me, or thought they did. I was the officer who had saved the life of Betzner. For Saultern, I was the merciful commissar. Now I had just executed a colonel. Saultern had turned white beneath the dust and blood that begrimed us all. No doubt he had a sudden, acute insight into how close to the same fate he had come.

'In accordance with my authority as commissar, and in the furtherance of my sworn duty, I am taking command of this mission.' I swept my eyes around the roof. 'We do not retreat!' I shouted. 'Relay the news,' I told Guevion.

Now I had a tank to kill. Its weapons had exterminated almost all of our forces still on the ground. It was demolishing the entire north side of the avenue, killing the Mortisians with their very shelters, burying them under tonnes of rubble. As it worked with battering ram and arms at yet another building, I saw the streak of a rocket launcher. The missile struck the hull. It did not appear to cause any damage, but the tank reacted like an enraged beast. It brought its stubber to bear, and raked the roof. Rockets would not be enough, but they held the attention of the vehicle's operators.

My path became clear.

'I want a demolition charge,' I said. Three troopers stepped forward. I grabbed the charge from the nearest, then knelt beside Benneger's corpse. 'Make yourself useful one last time,' I said and stripped him of his belt. I called out to Betzner, 'Hit it with a rocket. Let that blasphemy know we are worthy of notice here too.'

He fired before I had finished speaking. The blast engulfed the rear of the tank. I had a delirious hope that Betzner had found a weak spot, but I didn't wait to see. I dropped through the trap door and thundered down the stairs to the second floor. I entered a bedroom whose shattered window overlooked the square. The tank was crossing the pavement. I waited until it had almost reached us before I leapt through the window. I dropped to the roof of the chassis just as the tank slammed into the wall with its ram. Masonry fell on me, knocking me from my feet. Clutching the demolition charge with my left hand, I reached out with my right. I missed the handhold on the hatch. I tumbled from the roof, but grasped the base of the port limb. The yank almost tore my arm from its socket. The mechanism rose to smash the upper floors of the house. It lifted me up, and I let myself fall back onto the tank.

Cultists in the square spotted me and started shooting. The movements of the tank and its arms, and the tumble of wreckage spoiled their aim. I crouched over the hatch, battered again and again by the rain of brick and timber. I tried not to focus on the runes, but I could feel them focus on me. They squirmed beneath me. The metal of the chassis felt like oiled skin. I was atop a beast, one that wanted my corruption even more than it wanted my death. I hissed defiance. I would not let the illusions of toxic art deflect me. I used Benneger's belt to strap the charge to the hatch. Something jagged and heavy hit me in the head, and I swayed, vision blurring. I fought the grey, secured the charge, and triggered it.

Seconds now. I let myself be thrown off as the tank jerked back for another charge at the wall. I tumbled over the front of the chassis, bouncing off the battering ram. The blows were now just more brushstrokes on the canvas of pain. When there was nothing but agony, all I could do was ignore it. I scrambled over a heap of rubble, knowing I was too slow, but knowing too I had already won.

The charge went off. The device wasn't precise. It relied on sheer power to destroy bodies, vehicles and walls. Heat and wind washed over me. It burned and battered, but I lived. The tank did not. The explosion peeled back the top of its armour and incinerated the cultists inside. The engine screamed, sounding even more like an animal, and then died. I crawled away, and another of Betzner's rockets slammed down into the great wound I had opened. The tank rocked with the second explosion, and then again, and again, as promethium and ammunition reserves ignited. The monster's death was not quiet.

Nor was my triumph.

I forced myself up. *Be the symbol.* I charged out from the ruined house, bolt pistol firing. 'Soldiers of the Imperium!' I howled. 'With me!' I cut the nearest cultists down. The response was ragged. The heretics were being slow to deal with the death of the tank, and their frame of reference could not encompass my continued existence. They had thought fear was their special province, theirs to inflict upon us. I had taught them how wrong they were.

I learned something too, though the full lesson would take a lifetime. I am still learning it today: one must be the symbol for the enemy too.

I called the Mortisians to be with me, and they were. The rooftops erupted with renewed fire, while the rest of the troops stormed down from the buildings that were still intact. We were no longer in retreat. We had the initiative, and we had the high ground. The cultists were cornered. They tried to retreat, but the emergence of the tank must have wrecked the other entrances to the tunnel. I saw heretics rush into doorways, then come back out. They had no options left but to fight.

They sold their lives with fury. They made us bleed still more. But they were lost. They knew this, I believe, at every level. There is a special resilience that comes from fighting for a just cause. In the face of certain defeat, it is in the strength to reject that end with such will that sometimes an impossible triumph occurs. There was none of that in our enemies on this day. There could not have been. Their cause was rotten, and so were their spirits. So we broke them. We made them pay for every drop of Imperial blood they spilled.

In the end, the square and the street became a charnel

house. Corpses were piled on top of each other. There was so much blood, it was like walking in a muddy field. In the closing moments of the battle, we were standing on bodies as we fought. And when the heretics were all dead, we rested for the space of one long breath.

But the war did not wait for us. I listened to the deadly call-and-response of duelling artillery guns. There was no time to rest, or to take in the full meaning of what had occurred here. 'Mortisians!' I hailed. 'We have done well. We have saved Tolosa. But our God-Emperor has need of us still on this day. Are you with me still?'

They were. With a shout, and with thunder, we raced for the outer wall.

CHAPTER 13
THE CREST OF THE WAVE

1. Rasp

Lorn was a residence. It had its walls, but it was a home built for commerce and luxury, not war. Karrathar was a fortress. It rose from an isolated, stony, vertical peak in the Carconnes. It was a squat mountaintop, several hundred metres above the valley floor. It looked down upon all approaches by land. To the north, south and west, it presented sheer cliffs. The single road up was a rough, steep series of uneven switchbacks on the eastern face, barely wide enough for a single vehicle. Though the walls themselves were carved from the living rock of the mountain, it had taken the lords of Vahnsinn three generations to haul everything else that had gone into the construction of Karrathar up that roadway. They never improved it, keeping the surface in a state of barely arrested decay. One did not storm Karrathar. One drew near on bended knee, at its sufferance. In three thousand years, it had never been taken.

The only direct access was by maglev. The track hugged the bottom of the valley until just before the mountain, at which point it rose in a dizzying climb to the base of the walls. The rail was supported by a series of slender pillars of ever increasing height. The last was almost five hundred metres tall. The construct was an engineering feat, and a prodigious folly. But every move that had come close to bankrupting the Vahnsinn family had, in the end, preserved it. The stability of their power had kept the Vahnsinns at the top of the Mistralian nobility century after century.

Once inside Karrathar, Rasp had only his faith to sustain him. Vahnsinn blindfolded him before taking him off the train. He was led, stumbling, through the castle. He heard the echoes of stone beneath his boots. He felt a damp chill against his skin. He was in a place of strength and age, not comfort. Then there were stairs. Many, many stairs. The air grew damper, colder. Down, down, down. He tried to measure the descent, but lost the count after the first few hundred steps.

'This would be easier if I could see where I was going,' he said.

'Yes, it would,' Vahnsinn agreed.

The blindfold remained in place. 'What are you risking?' Rasp asked.

The baron sighed. 'I won't insult you by assuming you would not attempt an escape at the first opportunity, so please don't insult me, either.'

'I don't think you'll be giving me much by way of opportunity.'

'Quite.'

They said nothing else. The journey became an abstract

conception, the idea of *descent* with no beginning, and no terminus. Rasp felt as if he were walking through a dark limbo where worlds and meaning had died. But then the descent did end. Now he was in a place of smells. There were currents of heat wafting through the cold. Rasp's face was touched by the foetid warmth of opened bodies. There were sounds, too: the grinding of gears, snaps and tearing that were sickeningly wet. There were screams, there were pleas, and there were noises that no human throat should have been able to utter.

They walked for five minutes more. Then Rasp's guards jerked him to a stop. The blindfold came off. His eyes adjusted slowly. He looked around. He was in a vast hall. Stone pillars rose to rounded vaults. It was a cathedral-like space, lit by torches that smoked with human fat. Rasp stood at the centre. Before him, where the altar would be, was a raised platform that could have been a dais or a stage. On all sides, stretching as far into the gloom as his eyes could penetrate, was the theatre of atrocity. Engines of torture laboured to transform the human frame into the purest expressions of agony. They were tended by robed executioners, who performed their tasks with a care that belonged to religious ceremonies. As they worked they spoke to the small groups of cultists who stood, watched and listened. There were lessons being taught, Rasp saw, to students willing and unwilling.

In the centre of the dais was an iron chair. Shackles hung from it, but it seemed to be an instrument of restraint, not torture. The guards hauled Rasp onto the platform, sat him down, and attached the chains. They stepped back off the dais, leaving its surface to Rasp and Vahnsinn. Other cultists gathered along the periphery. Rasp felt that he had become both audience and spectacle. He glared at Vahnsinn. 'Well? What now?' He let the baron hear only anger in his voice. He set horror and revulsion aside. He would not grant this terrible place any satisfaction.

'Now you will be instructed.'

'I can see what is here, thanks. It has nothing to tell me.'

Vahnsinn's smile was tight-lipped. 'You're wrong, Simeon. You're wrong about so much. I was too, you know.'

Rasp's mouth dried. 'Save yourself the bother. Kill me now. You'll be wasting your time otherwise. You'll never convert me.'

Vahnsinn crouched in front of him, his face serious. He spoke quietly, but with urgency. 'You *will* see the truth.'

'There is no truth here–'

'There's no alternative,' Vahnsinn cut him off. 'You will see what I saw. Then we'll have a different sort of conversation.' He looked almost wistful for a moment. 'Bartholomew Lom and I used to have such wonderful ones. I do miss them.'

'Yet you turned against him.'

Wistfulness shifted towards a snarl. 'Did I?'

'You could have had your rebellion sooner. Instead, your troops helped us put him down. Why?'

'Bartholomew's brilliance with machines of war gave him ideas above his station. I won't tolerate rivals. I really won't.' The snarl faded, replaced by something very like hope. 'I know things will be different with you. We've been friends for much longer.'

'I will not betray my Emperor.'

'Not today you won't. Not today. But we have time.'

'You're going through a great deal of effort,' Rasp told him. 'I'm flattered, but am I really that important?'

Vahnsinn did not answer. He stood up. 'I'll be back later,' he said. 'I have to see to some preparations.' The grin came back. 'I have something special for Tolosa.'

* * *

2. Yarrick

My body had been battered into a single contusion. With no broken bones, it was physically possible for me to keep moving, and so I did. If I stopped, I would fall. But duty kept me going, because we were needed at the wall. And victory kept me running. We had given the enemy his first real defeat. Wangenheim was not calling the beats of this war, but neither was Vahnsinn. The taste of retaliation was delicious. We returned to the wall eager for more.

There, the war was taking on the shape of a prolonged struggle. The city's turrets were at last giving answer to the baronial artillery. Our cannons were not as numerous, but they were just as powerful, and the sheer number of the enemy guns made them easier targets. The advancing infantry carpeted the ground, and were impossible to miss.

The indiscriminate bombardment had stopped. Each time a Basilisk sent a shell our way, it had been aimed with care. The junction had to be preserved. The Earthshakers battered the wall. They damaged it. They did not, however, bring it down. Tolosa's outer defences had been designed with the planet's own military production in mind. The Mistralians knew themselves and their politics well. The waters were murky, and the winds were the threat of inevitable storm. Civil war on Mistral was as certain as the seasons. Provisions had been made. The wall was a good one. So were its cannons. Artillery alone would not overthrow Tolosa.

Neither would it suffice to save the city.

Colonel Granach waited for me at the foot of the wall. He took me aside as the troops I had been leading climbed the steps to the parapets. 'I have fought by Colonel Benneger's side for years,' he said. 'He was a good, sound officer.'

'I don't doubt that he was, colonel. But today he wasn't.'

'I see. His past counted for nothing before you executed him?'

'In that moment, no, it did not. Before you ask me, colonel, I regret the necessity of my action, but not the action itself.'

'I would not presume to question a commissar on these matters.' He spoke more quickly than he had done before. He was, I thought, more than slightly afraid of me. This was not something I had experienced with high-ranking officers. I did not let the novelty give me pause. We all had to act in the best interest of the missions we were given. That was all.

I said, 'I didn't think you were. I do think that it is important for you to know what happened and why, colonel. But what matters most is the result.' I shifted the conversation to the issue that mattered. 'We shut down the enemy strike into the city itself. The heretic losses were total. The tunnel is sealed.'

'Is it the only one, do you think?'

'The only tunnel of any kind? No. It will take us a long time to find all of them. There will be more incursions. But the construction of this one was a major undertaking. They brought a *tank* underground. Commissar Seroff and Inquisitor Krauss told me what they saw down there. I would be surprised if the enemy had the resources to spend on a second such approach.'

He nodded. 'Good. That is something tangible.' He headed for the staircase up the wall. 'Well, Commissar Yarrick, shall we?'

On the parapet, we crouched behind the battlements and watched the next steps of the dance become clear. The artillery duel had reached grinding stalemate. We were punching craters in the infantry, but the cultists were like insects, instantly filling every breach in the advance. The barons' foot soldiers had almost reached the junction. They would be closer than the minimum range of our guns. There would be nothing to prevent them from establishing the base for their siege.

'Are you planning a sortie?' I asked Granach.

'No. We don't have the numbers. They would finish us.'

I grimaced, again wishing he had chosen to destroy the junction. The heretics were about to have a valuable resource at their disposal. 'What do you propose?'

'We need to grind them down. We need them to break against our defences. Their numbers aren't infinite. We just need to withstand the attacks long enough.'

He was going to lay siege to the besiegers. The logic was sound. Our options were limited, especially since we had to assume we had lost the greater portion of the regiments and all our heavy armour. There was a passivity to the strategy that displeased me. We were handing all of the initiative to the enemy, even if that included the privilege of making mistakes first. I doubted, though, that Granach was any happier. For the moment, at least, there were no other choices.

The cultists reached the junction. For the next several hours, the war paused. The guns continued to pound at each other, but our troops waited while theirs consolidated their position. There was an open space between the wall and the transportation hub, interrupted only by the rail lines feeding into the city, and by the road that finally completed its convoluted journey over lakes and rivers of the plain. Before long, it would be filled with enemy forces.

'I would give much for a minefield down there,' I said.

'I would give much to be shut of this planet,' Granach muttered.

Risking snipers, I looked over the battlement at the outer face of the wall. The heretics were not going to have an easy climb. It was sheer, fifty metres high. It was pockmarked with shell damage, but none of the holes went all the way through, or would provide attackers with anything like a useful way up. The poisonous history of Mistralian politics had created a civilization of first-rate fortifications.

'Will it hold?' Seroff had joined us.

'We will make it hold,' Granach said. 'I look forward to our stand together, commissars.' He moved off to inspect the lines.

'Lost your inquisitor friend?' I asked Seroff.

He snorted. 'Headed back into the city. Not enough shadows around here, no doubt.' His face became troubled. 'He saw what happened with Colonel Benneger.'

'Oh?'

'We were on the other side of the square. Too far to make out any details, but I think he realized who had been shot when the tank blew up.'

I shrugged. 'Then he knows I acted with good cause. Not that this falls within his purview.'

'He has a very broad idea of what his purview is, wouldn't you say?'

'He does. He's welcome to his opinions, and he can keep them to himself.'

Seroff raised his eyebrows. 'Strong words.'

'I mean them. I respect his oaths of duty, and his commitment to them. He can do us the same courtesy. Perhaps that would free him up to pursue the real enemy a bit more, instead of persecuting the faithful.'

Seroff nodded, but his attention had already wandered.

'What you did,' he said. 'I don't know that I could have done the same.'

'Of course you could.'

'Maybe. But so quickly.'

'There wasn't time for a debate. There never will be.'

'You don't think he could have redeemed himself?'

'Then and there, no. He was going to lead us to defeat. We would have lost the city. Redemption is fine in the abstract. What the colonel might or might not have done in the future, though, was irrelevant. We had to win. He was in the way.'

'Captain Saultern has redeemed himself,' Seroff pointed out.

'He was lucky. There was opportunity for him to do so.'

He hesitated. 'I'm sorry, Seb, but I have to ask. What if you hadn't killed him? What if you had just gone and destroyed the tank while he was still calling for the retreat?'

His question stopped me cold. It was the one I had felt coiling at the back of my mind since the battle. I had managed to keep it at bay. No longer. I faced it. Before I answered, I prayed to the Emperor that I was being honest with both Seroff and myself. 'There would have been confusion in the ranks. Some would have joined me. Others would have obeyed the colonel. Confusion. Division. The enemy wouldn't have needed the tank to finish us off. That's why our position exists. We preserve the purpose and unity of the regiments.'

'And we judge.'

'If the Emperor wills it.'

'Do you trust your competence in these matters?'

'I have to.' My answer didn't enthuse me, but it was the truth.

'So how are we different from Krauss?'

'We aren't looking for reasons to put a shell through

someone's brain,' I said. 'Now shut up, political officer, or I will have to shoot you.'

I was joking, but his doubts were troubling. They stayed with me as the day slipped towards night and I made the rounds of the wall, exhorting, encouraging, disciplining. I knew I had been right to kill Benneger. Our victory was proof of that. Still, the unease lingered. *Would you shoot him again?* I asked myself.

Yes. Yes, I would.

There would be other Bennegers to come. I would shoot them too. But I would hold onto my doubts. That, I wanted to tell Seroff, was the other thing that distinguished us from Krauss. He had no doubts in himself. I did not think that made him a better servant of the Emperor.

The attack came at nightfall. There was something almost ceremonial about that, as if there were certain observances of war that must be obeyed. We knew the heretics would come then. I don't for an instant believe they thought we would be surprised. The moment the last dregs of sunset bled from the sky, the wind gusted with an exultant blast. There was a roar of thousands of human throats forming words never meant to be spoken, and the enemy charged.

Arc lights speared down from the wall, painting the ground below with a stark, white glare. The road and the grasses of the plain turned the colour of bone. The heretics came on, first a darker shadow spreading out beyond the junction, then outlined as the vermin they were when they hit the light. The enemy Basilisks fell silent. Though I doubted the commanders had the slightest regard for the lives of their troops, shelling them along with the wall would serve no tactical purpose. Our cannons continued to fire, booming into the dark. Our gunners no longer had the barrel flashes to guide their aim, but explosions revealed the silhouettes of the targets, and little by little we exacted a toll.

And now the wall's other turrets spoke in anger. Heavy stubber positions had been built every hundred metres. They opened up, and to the deep, heavy beats of artillery was added rapid, grinding percussion. Bullets ripped cultists apart. The death-white of the ground was stained with the glistening black of spilled vitae. No ammunition was wasted. The enemy came in such numbers that every bullet hit.

The charge did not slow. The cultists ran over the bodies of their fellows, and they reached the base of the wall. They were firing at us the whole time, to little effect. The wall was too high. The occasional lucky shot struck home. We suffered a few casualties. Not many. I strode along the parapet, making myself visible, but moving fast enough to be a difficult target. I rained contempt on the forces below. 'Are you laughing, Mortisians?' I asked. 'You should be. What did they expect? That we would tremble before their show of running and shouting?' The massed shriek of the heretics had been disturbing. The howls continued to be. They were weapons more insidious, and more dangerous, than lasguns were at this moment. We had to respond with faith and resolve. I gave our troops the weapon of ridicule. The cultists wanted us to fear them. We would reject that fear with rage's laughter. The Mortisians responded well. They howled and hooted right back at the cultists.

I knew that there were forces that had to be taken seriously. But that was knowledge harmful to morale, vital to be withheld from the untrained soldier or civilian. I, at least, had been prepared.

So I thought. When I remember that young man, I want to throttle that naïvety from him.

'Let the heretics know what they are up against,' I thundered. 'Teach them what fear really is before you send them to hell.'

Cheers, shouts, warrior laughter. I recognized many faces from the battle in the square. Those soldiers looked at me in a way that implied my words carried special weight with them, and not simply because of my rank. That made me uncomfortable, but if they fought well, the reasons for their resolution were not important.

The battle was one of attrition. As the wind of Mistral eroded home and hill, so the heretics tried to take the wall. Neither they nor we had the weapons to shift the siege from its ancient foundations. They could not go through the wall. Their only way forwards was over it, their only tactic the escalade. The barons knew Tolosa and its defences, and had prepared well. We had shut down their attempt to circumvent the wall. So they came at us with siege ladders. Hundreds of them. We concentrated our fire on the ladders, trying to destroy as many as possible before they were even raised, then blasting apart those that touched the wall. But there were so many. It seemed that there was a ladder for every Mortisian. We couldn't smash them all. A few, perhaps enough, rose against the wall.

The cultists climbed. The suppressive fire of those on the ground became more and more effective. The sheer volume of las and bullets pushed us back from the battlements. Every time we lost stubber gunners, we also lost the precious seconds it took to replace them, and the heretics climbed higher. We had to shoot blindly over the wall. It was impossible to miss, but harder to kill the right enemy.

Granach kept the turrets going, but pulled the rest of us back. We formed a solid, double line, shoulder to shoulder, the forward troops crouched to leave clear shots to those behind. The first of the heretics reached the top of the battlements. They faced a wall of gun barrels. The parapet erupted, the night torn by a storm of las. We sent the enemy flying back into the dark. As the bodies rained onto their comrades, the suppressive fire stuttered. Granach sent us forward again, and we hurled the ladders back.

And then the dance repeated.

Back and forth, back and forth, advance and repulse, over and over as the eternal wind howled. The smoke-deepened night was a limbo of fragmented time. There was no going forward. There was no leaving this present of repeated, endless slaughter. There were minor variations. The heretics began to target the lights. The battlefield became a million still images in the searing, jagged illumination of las. As they neared the top of the ladders, the cultists hurled grenades over the battlements, tearing brief holes in our defence. In this way, some of them actually set foot on the parapet. They died for their temerity, and we hit the bases of the ladders with our own grenades.

Back and forth. We killed far more of them, but they did kill us. And their numbers seemed infinite. The hours wore on, and the steps in the dance became automatic. I fired my pistol with so regular a rhythm, I might have been a servitor employed at a single, mindless task. So many faces shot away, so many skulls exploded by bolter shells, the killing turning into an abstraction. I was no longer reducing humans to pulp. I was taking shapes apart. It was hard to hold back the numbness that would dull my reactions and be my death. When we were pressed hard, I spoke to every trooper within the sound of my voice, calling the men and women of Aighe Mortis to save the soul of Mistral. I don't remember the words I used.

I forgot them as soon as I spoke. But I did feel the fire. It coursed through my blood, and I burned with the strength of the Imperial Creed. Heresy would not stand.

We smashed it down.

Back and forth. The dance wanted us as its slaves forever, but the slaves, Imperial and heretic, were human. I have since come to know what a truly endless war looks like, but the holocaust of Armageddon was centuries distant from me yet. Dawn came, reluctant and ugly, smelling of burned flesh, blood and fyceline. It signalled the end of the dance for now. Exhaustion had come to both armies.

The heretics withdrew to the area around the transport hub. We tended to our wounded and our dead. We had lost some turrets, too. Most were intact, though, or could be repaired. I joined Granach where he stood, just to the left of a functioning turret, watching the enemy.

'A good fight, colonel,' I congratulated him.

'Thank you, Yarrick.' His voice was flat with fatigue, and grim. 'For all the good that does us. We haven't advanced.'

'Every day that the besieged hold out is an advance,' I said.

He snorted. 'Commissar, you don't have to worry about my morale. You can drop the rhetoric.'

I nodded. 'The situation could be worse, colonel. We pushed the traitors back. We will again tonight.'

'True. And the following night, and the night after that. But...'

He didn't have to finish his thought. It had already occurred to me. 'Numbers,' I said.

'Numbers,' he agreed.

And as we stood there, we saw the first of the resupply trains arriving. Everything we had taken from the heretics during the night was being replaced.

'You were right,' Granach said. 'We should have destroyed that hub.'

The shelling of the city resumed. The martyrdom of Tolosa continued.

CHAPTER 14
THE BRITTLE CITY

1. Yarrick

The first incursion happened just after dawn. The cultists came out of the cellar of an icon dealer in the south-east sector of the second ring. A patrol of enforcers was able to kill the invaders before they had gone far. Granach had dispatched one company to keep searching for tunnel entrances, but the enforcers had largely taken over that mission. Krauss had declared all their other duties secondary to this task. No one had questioned his authority to do so.

The military impact was nil. What mattered was what happened afterwards. Krauss arrived on the scene. He investigated the bakery. Its owners had been slaughtered, but that did not, in his eyes, make them victims. It was impossible, he declared, that these citizens had been unaware of the excavation going on beneath their feet. A tunnel to their cellar constructed without their collusion? No, he said. Before the tunnel was sealed, he traced the extent of the new dig running from the pre-existing network. It ran under three habs and a merchants' diversorium. Krauss hauled out everyone who owned or lived in all four. He set the buildings on fire. And when most of the immediate habzone had turned out to see what was happening, even with the occasional shell still landing nearby, he lined his detainees up in the street and shot them.

He then spoke to the spectators. Every citizen of Tolosa had a duty of vigilance, he announced. The word had been given the day before that the tunnels must be sought. If any were not found by the civilians who should have discovered them, those same civilians would be deemed traitors and heretics, and executed.

The story spread from the enforcers to the Mortisians within the hour. An hour after that, I was arriving at the Ecclesiarchal palace. I would be speaking for Granach. 'You've already had your run-in with the inquisitor,' he told me. 'And there will be the cardinal and the Adepta Sororitas to deal with too, I'm sure. This is your domain, Yarrick.'

'Politics,' I muttered.

Granach gave me a pitying, but no less amused, grin. He was finding his humour where he could.

As I left the wall, Seroff called my name. I looked back. He was on the stairs, halfway down. He saluted. 'Better you than me!'

'I hope so,' I returned. 'I wouldn't trust you not to have us all clapped in irons before the end of the day.'

The shelling was more sporadic than it had been the day before. Perhaps we had destroyed enough Basilisks to make a difference. I still had to be careful, ducking into doorways to avoid the worst of explosions in the streets, eyeing the sky every time I heard a shrieking whistle. By the time I reached the palace, there had been another tunnel found, again by the enforcers.

More executions.

I didn't know about the second find until the conference began, but I witnessed its impact. I was one ring to the south of the palace. I rounded a corner and saw a crowd in the street before me. It was furious. The air was filled with shouts and screams. A man, his face streaming blood, burst from the crowd and started to run further up the road. The mob pursued and brought him down.

'It isn't a tunnel,' I heard him scream. 'It's just a storage–' And that was all. The people kicked him to death. A smaller group ran into a house on the right-hand side of the street, a couple of doors down from where I stood. A minute later, they came running out again. There was a small, muffled explosion, shattering the glass of the windows, blowing the shutters wide. Flames licked out from the ground floor.

The arsonists looked at me as they went by. They paused. They were wearing similar uniforms, and bore Administratum name badges. One of them, a middle-aged woman with worried eyes, said, 'It could be a tunnel, couldn't it?' When I didn't answer, she went on. 'We're doing what is expected of us. We aren't being negligent. Please believe me. This street will be sanitized before nightfall. Do you think there will be an inspection?'

The crowd was beginning to thin. The object of its ire was motionless in a deep pool of crimson. With the man's death went the unity of the mob. The people were eyeing each other with caution. They were, I knew, wondering if the man had

had collaborators. Before long, caution would turn to suspicion, then to fear, then to hatred. 'No,' I told the woman. 'I don't think there will be.' I would be surprised if the entire street was not burning before sunset. Perhaps, I thought, a shell might fall here. That would be a mercy. The more limited destruction might disrupt the collective psychosis.

The scene stayed with me the rest of the way to the palace. Once there, I was met by the steward. Vercor's formal livery didn't fool me. The hardness in those eyes was not acquired by supervising serfs. I had seen that look only a few times before. Before ascending to the Commissariat, Seroff and I had fought in a mission to pacify an uprising on the hive-world Turbella. Deep in the underhive, our commanding officers had forged an alliance with the strongest of the gang leaders. The most powerful of them had the same eyes as Vercor: survivors, fighters, mercenaries. The eyes of rats.

'How is it looking?' she asked. She was leading me towards the Council chamber.

'We have thrown the enemy back,' I said. I was not going to offer anything else. If someone deemed this hired gun worthy of detailed military intelligence, that someone could fill her in.

'For now, you mean,' she said.

I didn't answer. I became aware of a faint hum. I glanced down, saw the faint, restless flexing of Vercor's fingers. I had mistaken prosthetics for gloves.

We reached the door to the chamber. Vercor paused before opening it. 'Holding the enemy at the wall won't be enough,' she said.

I know, I thought, but remained silent.

The eyes watched me closely. They were calculating,

evaluating. She was searching for something. I waited. 'You must be a good regicide player,' she said.

I shrugged. 'Indifferent. I don't play it much.'

She grinned. 'Liar. You're playing it now.' She pushed open the door to usher me inside. 'I'm good too.'

I entered the chamber. Vercor had sent me a message. I wasn't sure how to interpret it, though I had my suspicions. I filed the problem away. There was something there that would have to be dealt with, but not now.

Vercor was right that a game was being played. Before me was the table where the barons had sat. There were only three of us in the space now: myself, Krauss and Setheno. Neither the sister superior nor the inquisitor had taken a seat. Krauss was pacing up and down the centre of the chamber, within the 'U' of the table. His face was still a mass of scars and contusions, but he had replaced his clothes, and he had lost none of his imperious, unbending charisma.

Setheno stood behind what had been Vahnsinn's chair. She was still, an armoured impassivity. Though her face was calm, she was looking up at Wangenheim's throne, on my left, with an iron focus. I saw a greater frustration in that gaze than in Krauss's constant movement.

'Welcome, commissar,' said Wangenheim. The cardinal had not been present when I stepped in, but now he arrived, close enough on the heels of my entrance to be startling. He claimed the initiative of the meeting, and settled himself in his throne. He looked down at us as if expecting us to take our seats.

Krauss stopped pacing, but he barely glanced at Wangenheim. 'Good,' he said to me. 'We can begin.' The slight was obvious. Krauss wasn't fighting the cardinal for control of the proceedings. He was simply ignoring Wangenheim altogether. 'What are Colonel Granach's plans?'

'For the moment, to hold the line.'

'Is that all?' Wangenheim asked.

Before I could answer, Setheno said, 'More is needed.'

'We would welcome the Adepta Sororitas at the wall,' I said. *Welcome* was perhaps an exaggeration. But their strength would be an asset.

'No!' Wangenheim snapped. 'I'm sorry, commissar, but the Order of the Piercing Thorn is needed here.'

Krauss gave a half shake of his head, as if shrugging off an annoying insect. 'Your presence will be most useful in the streets of the city,' he said to Setheno. 'I have a patrol route in mind that will maximize the impact of your visibility, it–'

'Inquisitor,' Setheno interrupted, 'you overstep your bounds.'

From Krauss's silence, it was clear that he had never been challenged so directly. Though I had locked horns with him, I had not rejected his authority.

Setheno went on. 'My Sisters and I are not yours to command.' Her outrage was palpable. I wasn't sure if it was Krauss's presumption alone that had incurred her wrath, or if it was the last of a series of insults that had now tried her patience too far.

Krauss glared at her. 'My authority–'

She cut him off again. 'Is no concern of mine. You are, of course, free to attempt to prove me wrong.'

'Precisely,' said Wangenheim. 'The Sisters of Battle are an arm of the Ecclesiarchy, and our first concern must be the preservation of the visible manifestations of the Imperial Creed. Without faith, we are nothing.'

Setheno did not respond. She did not look at Wangenheim.

I thought I saw a finger drum once against the pommel of her sword. I wasn't sure.

'I see,' Krauss said. 'So the forces of the Ecclesiarchy will remain behind the walls of this sanctuary and wait for the struggle in the streets of Tolosa to be won by other means.'

'And what other means are those?' I asked. 'Setting the citizens at each other's throats?'

'We have been brought to this pass by a lack of vigilance,' Krauss told me. 'I am ensuring we will no longer fall victim to this trap.'

'There's a difference between vigilance and madness,' I said. 'What I saw out there was the latter. What do you think you're accomplishing?'

'The people of Tolosa are watching for the enemy.'

'They are doing the enemy's work for him. They are killing each other, not the foe.'

Krauss nodded. 'Yes, they are killing each other. But you're wrong if you think the enemy doesn't already have his agents among them.' He swept his arm, taking in the Council chamber. 'Or perhaps I'm mistaken. Perhaps the Imperial Guard knew and was never fooled by the barons at all.' His threat was clear. 'Are there innocents being killed out there? No. All the citizens of Tolosa are guilty for having let the heretic cancer grow in their midst. The ones who die are reaping the price of their negligence. The ones who live should not consider themselves absolved.'

'Then what are we fighting to save here? Why not cut our losses and let Tolosa burn?'

Krauss cocked his head. 'That is a question,' he said softly.

I gaped. I looked at Setheno. 'Do go on,' she said. 'Both of you. This is most instructive.'

I didn't know what to make of that. Were the common people an irrelevance, their weakness casting them beneath the notice of the Sisters of Battle? Or was she judging the two men before her?

'The question is not a serious one!' Wangenheim protested. He leaned forward in his throne in an effort to project his presence more forcefully into the chamber. He looked petulant and scared. 'The enemy will not cross the boundaries of this city. We will repel him, and then we will crush him.' He spoke as if his words could make his will reality. Just a day ago, that might have been true. No longer. What power he still had was due only to his position, and the authority that granted him over Setheno and her squad. Even there, I suspected his hold was fraying. I noticed now that he had brought a reliquary into the chamber with him. It sat on the right arm of his throne, and he kept his hand on it at all times.

Setheno said, 'Commissar, you haven't told us your evaluation of the front.'

'It's a stalemate for the moment. The enemy can't get past our defences.'

'How long will that state of affairs continue?'

'Not indefinitely. They are being resupplied as we speak.'

'The situation is not tenable?'

'In my opinion, it is not.'

'Then Colonel Granach's strategy is unacceptable,' Wangenheim announced.

'It is, for the moment, the only one open to him.'

'The current configuration of our forces make it so?' Setheno asked.

'Yes.' Beyond the fact that I believed what she said to be true,

I had a sudden intuition of the importance of agreeing with her at that moment.

'Then your colonel is going to have to be a bit more creative,' said Wangenheim. 'I see no change possible in the various deployments. Perhaps the Mortisians could be reinforced with the enforcers–'

'No,' Krauss said.

'Then that is where we are. And it is clear to me that, in the short term, Tolosa will be lost. Commissar, I think it advisable preparations be made for a new base of operations to be established aboard the *Scythe of Terra*.'

To his credit, he kept a straight face throughout his craven speech. His tone was reason itself. He was the adult, explaining the facts of the situation to unruly children. From his position atop the dais, he was able to look down even on Setheno as he sat forward with an air of patronizing concern.

To my credit, I did not shoot him. But I took more pleasure than was seemly when I said, 'That is impossible.'

His face cracked. 'What do you mean?'

'We have no landing craft in the city.'

'There must be some way.' He sounded desperate now, like the coward he was. He turned to Krauss. 'Your lighter is on the palace landing pad. I'm sure that–'

'No,' the inquisitor repeated. He did not even glance at Wangenheim.

The cardinal swallowed. 'Then...' He tried again. 'Then...' There were no words left. Rhetoric had carried him this far. It had given him power, and it had given him his war. Now it abandoned him. It could not save him.

'Then we triumph,' I said, 'or else we die.'

* * *

2. Vercor

She waited outside the cardinal's chambers while he wailed a litany of complaints at the sister superior. Vercor listened with increasing disinterest. Wangenheim had misplayed his hand. He could not see his way through to winning the game any longer. He was, Vercor thought, a sorry product of his line. It was her misfortune that her term of service had fallen under his reign. That service, though, was a contract, not a duty. It was revocable. No Vercor had ever felt the need to abandon a Wangenheim. But no Wangenheim had ever thrown away his political capital on such a folly.

The dialogue in the cardinal's study was one-sided. Vercor didn't hear Setheno say a thing in answer. But there were long silences after some of the cardinal's more lunatic demands, followed by awkward stuttering from Wangenheim. Most of what he said was one fanciful scheme after another to get himself off-planet. When those came to nothing, he said, 'We must have the regiment pull back to the palace. Their forces will be more concentrated here.'

At last, Setheno spoke. 'I'm sure Commissar Yarrick will be happy to relay your thoughts to the colonel.'

'They won't listen. You'll have to force them.'

There was the sound of armoured footsteps walking towards the door of the study.

'Where are you going?' Wangenheim's voice was growing shrill. 'Your duty is to protect me!'

The steps did not pause. 'My duty, cardinal, is to the Ecclesiarchy. You are making the path of this duty clearer, for which I thank you.'

Vercor stepped aside as Setheno exited the study, and closed the door on Wangenheim's shouts. The Sister of Battle gave the steward a long look. Vercor was decades older than the young warrior, but she felt herself diminished by the strength of conviction before her.

'So?' Setheno asked. 'What sort of traitor are you?'

'None. The man in there has betrayed himself. Among others.'

Setheno surprised her by nodding in agreement.

'Changes are necessary if we aren't all going to die stupid deaths,' Vercor said.

'And which ones are you going to make?'

'I'm waiting to see what is called for.'

Setheno's lip curled. 'As opposed to how you are called upon.'

'I lack your fervour, sister superior.'

'Don't wait too long to make your decision, mercenary. You may find–'

An explosion cut Setheno off. It came from deep below. The sound was muffled, but its force vibrated through the stone of the palace's walls and floors. There was something *wrong* about the sound. Vercor suddenly felt sick, as if something vital had torn in a soul she had forgotten she still had.

'Stay here,' Setheno ordered. She drew her pistol as she ran down the corridor.

'Why?' Vercor called after her.

'Protect him. For your own sake, if not for his.'

3. *Yarrick*

I was still arguing with Krauss as we left the palace. 'You've made your point,' I told him. 'The people are terrified. Their vigilance is so high that it has become paranoia. The only tunnels that won't be discovered within the next few hours will be the ones in habzones that have been shelled flat.'

'I don't know what you're asking of me.'

'Continued executions are unnecessary.'

'If there is no enforcement, there is no fear.'

I waited for the echoes of a shell explosion two streets over to pass. 'You've already shown the citizens examples of that enforcement. Word has spread. You know it has. Anything further is unnecessary.'

'Unnecessary? Punishment for treason and heresy is unnecessary?'

'You're putting words into my mouth, inquisitor.' I was offended. '*Every* punishment is necessary for those crimes. But the killing of the ignorant and the innocent is not.'

'Your definitions are not mine,' Krauss said.

As we crossed the square, we were met by Saultern at the head of one of his squads. I was surprised to see them. 'What's happened?' I asked Saultern.

'Nothing, commissar. At least, we hope not.' He glanced uneasily at Krauss. The inquisitor's interest was in Betzner, who kept his gaze on me, afraid of what would happen if he looked to my right.

'Then what...?'

Betzner said, 'The lower levels of the palace. Have they been searched for tunnels?' It was brave of him to speak up. He took a risk in doing so. It did him honour.

'You were the one to think of this?' Krauss asked.

Still looking at me, Betzner said, 'Yes, inquisitor.'

'*Has* the palace been searched?' I asked him.

'It has. There was nothing.'

'You're sure? In a place this size?'

I looked at Betzner. The big man was worried, clearly uneasy to be voicing any opinion whatever in the presence of Krauss.

He was also, I could see, consumed by the urgency of his mission. Betzner's insights worried me. They were becoming unhealthy in their frequency and specificity. What worried me most right now, though, was their accuracy. 'We should look again,' I said.

Krauss nodded. The speed of his acquiescence boded nothing good for Betzner, but that was a concern for later. We went back inside the palace. We descended level after level. I did not put Betzner in the lead, but I took cues from him. Where he looked was where we headed. I half expected to find ourselves in the crypt. Instead, we moved deeper and deeper into storage areas, descending through an archaeology of Mistral's discarded history. Crates upon crates upon crates of paintings and furniture, and documents, records, sermons, edicts. We were heading into rooms whose function was to preserve memory, but had been forgotten themselves.

We didn't need Betzner to tell us when we had arrived at our goal. The atmosphere in this storage chamber was different. The temperature plummeted. My teeth were suddenly on edge. There was nothing to see: just rows and rows of more crates. But a great wrong was at work here.

'How was this missed?' Krauss muttered angrily.

'The threat is new,' I said. 'Can't you feel it?' The toxic sensation was growing worse by the second.

We followed the growing dread. It led us to the far wall, and another stack of crates. Unlike in the rest of the chamber, there was no dust on these.

'Move those,' Krauss ordered.

Saultern's troops stepped forward.

'Wait,' I said. The air was suddenly a riot of ozone, blood and acid. The edges of the crates glowed, outlined by corrosive energy. Reality stretched, thinned, turned brittle and frayed. There was no need to shout a warning, because we all felt the coming rip, and there was no time to retreat because the horror was already here. An iron drum was struck, reverberating throughout the palace. We threw ourselves to the ground as the crates exploded.

Jagged splinters of wood embedded themselves in the stack behind us. Flakes of parchment filled the space, falling and spinning like burning snow. The tunnel entrance stood revealed, its walls and archway covered in runes painted in blood. It sloped steeply off into the darkness. Cultists charged up from its depths. They ran though the dying flames of the explosion, already firing.

We lost two of the Mortisians immediately. We were on the defensive. We were slow in firing back, because we were human. The cultists had the initiative because they surprised us, and because of what arrived with them.

It was tall, larger than a man. It leapt and giggled. Its gait was an uneven, hopping gallop. It was the glistening pink of exposed muscle. It was all strength and flow. There was just enough of a trace of the human frame in its shape to perfect the obscenity. It propelled itself on powerful, clawed legs. Its three arms were half again as long as they should be, reaching out to grab the ground and launch itself into the air every few steps. Its face shifted and travelled, caught in a flux of permanent becoming. The gaping jaw and python tongue were never truly in one spot of its massive frame. The snarl would gape forth from the flank, then be staring straight up, then facing us with eyes the yellow of bad faith. Always there was greed, always hunger, as if there were no deciding which portion of the world to devour first.

Daemon.

I knew there were such things. At the schola progenium I had learned of their existence. I had been taught about Chaos itself, and about the forms it could take. The knowledge was a poor preparation for the reality. I found in this moment that despite my training, I had still, at a deep, instinctual level, believed in the fundamental solidity of the world. My soul could not conceive of the existence of the thing that came at us. Even now, I tried to deny it, to take refuge in the idea of my own madness. On either side of me, soldiers reacted as I wished to. They curled up, shrieking in horror.

This was not a xenos beast. This was a nightmare come to savage them.

It made another leap, and landed with a squelching thud ahead of the heretics. It reached for us. Krauss and I rose as one. His face mirrored my own horror. Our minds wanted to flee into the balm of oblivion, so our training took over, and we attacked. Bolt and plasma pistols fired. I punched a crater into the straining, slithering flesh. He vaporized a chunk of what, at that moment, might have been a skull. Both wounds filled. It jabbered and lashed out. I ducked below the blow. Krauss danced out of the way, and its fists smashed into the crates behind us.

We were fighting. The daemon was fallible. That was enough. The rest of the squad pierced the soul-eating terror and fought back. Las-fire streaked between them and the cultists. The enemy had the numbers and the momentum. The Mortisians had the training. For the moment that made the difference, and the heretics began to die.

Still crouched, I drew my sword and lunged upwards inside the daemon's reach, cutting into the arm where it joined at the trunk. The limb was corded, powerful, and yet there was no bone. My blade sliced through flesh and gristle. The arm fell to the ground, where it dissolved into bubbling ooze. Another arm burst out of the centre of the torso. It hit my chest and sent me flying. I landed in a tangle of smashed wood and torn vellum.

The daemon's third arm snatched to the side and grabbed Trooper Karetzky. Then its jaws were on that side, and they crunched down on the soldier's head and chest. There was a ghastly harmony of snapping bone, spurting blood and a ragged, slashed scream.

Krauss fired again, this time disintegrating the daemon's left leg. The creature fell his way. It used its arms to turn the tumble into a controlled roll. It had already regrown its leg as it reared over him, gaping wide to feast on his blood and soul.

I fired off four shots in quick succession as I got to my feet. I took out both the legs. I bought us nothing but seconds, but the daemon slumped backwards as it regenerated.

Krauss shouted something incoherent. He hit the daemon with another blast of plasma, keeping its attention, and started running. It followed.

More seconds. We used them well. A cultist leapt at me, a sickle in each hand. I straight-armed my sword through his neck. As the weight of the corpse lowered my arm, and the heretic slid down the blade, I fired to my right, and blew a hole the size of a plate through another of the vermin.

Two more troopers went down, killed by las and gutted by blades. Behind us, the stack of crates that ran the length of the room had collapsed, and we pulled back behind the rough shelter, drawing tightly together, focusing our fire, while the cultists continued to charge as if the only thing that mattered was death, ours or theirs, as long as it was ugly. Perhaps they were right.

As we fought, I could hear the crashes of the daemon pursuing Krauss. Though those noises were pulling away from us, the obscenity's laughing, snarling jabbering seemed to be with us still. It was a voice that was just behind my ear, no matter what direction I was facing. The daemon was conversing with itself, with me, with the world, and with something unknowable beyond. The syllables it uttered were words, yet they tore the very concept of language apart. Guttural yet sinuous, they rasped and coughed and coiled. The survival of sanity demanded that they be sounds without meaning. The truth was worse. The words *did* have meaning. It was a meaning that hovered just out of reach, yet distorted the world with the force of its gravity. As I valued my soul, as I had faith in my Emperor, I must never learn what these words said, and my being revolted at the mere idea. But they had teeth, and they ground at my consciousness, they ground at my hope, and they ground at everything that made me human and rational. With every syllable that was uttered, reality became a little bit slicker, as if a coating of slime were accreting over everything around me, and everything inside me.

The heretics had human tongues, not the shifting, twisting, appearing, disappearing thing in the daemon's maw. Yet they were barely more coherent. They were shouting hymns of praise to the dark entities they called gods. Their rants were mixtures of Low Gothic and another language, one that should have been lost to all human memory. The cultists added their dark ecstasy to the babble of the daemon. They exulted in the massacre, in the energy it fed to the forces that had summoned the daemon to the materium. Even if we killed them in battle, we might not defeat them. Every death was a welcome act of worship.

We had no choice. We fought them. We killed them. I tried to drown out the chants with prayers to the Emperor. 'Our Emperor is our strength!' I called to my comrades. 'Hold fast to your faith, and it shall uphold you!'

The others prayed too, and we cut the heretics down with as much dispassion as we could muster. Our defensive posture became a tight circle, with the frenzied traitors hurling themselves at our blades more than they were shooting. They found, I think, insufficient blood in las. There was precision to our combat, and we exterminated the last of the cultists with only one other casualty of our own. That was a young man, Lingen, and it was the daemon's litany that killed him. I hope it was just the madness of the words that was too much for him. I hope that he hadn't begun to understand them. I hope he was granted that small degree of mercy. But he dropped his lasrifle, and shoved his fingers into his ears hard enough to draw blood. A heretic stepped in and gutted him before any of us could help. The heretic, at least, did not have the chance to revel in the death. Kortner decapitated him with his bayonet.

The death of the last heretic was no victory. The daemonic words still spread their poison. The nature of being was becoming worn, fragile. I grabbed a frag grenade from Betzner and ran towards the sounds of the hunt. The daemon was demolishing the stacks by running through them, and in its wake it had left a near-impassable heap of debris. I took the other way around the periphery of the chamber, racing to intercept the chase. The Mortisians were a step behind me.

I was two-thirds of the way towards the other end of the hall and its entrance. Krauss rounded the corner at full tilt. He was no longer firing. Behind him came the daemon. It laughed as it loped and hopped after him. It was toying with him, chasing its prey to exhaustion, and now it bellowed laughter as the game brought it back to us all.

No game for Krauss, but no flight, either. He had bought us the time to kill one enemy. He didn't have the means to destroy the second. I didn't know if any of us did. I ran straight for the daemon. As Krauss and I passed each other, we exchanged a look. His face was grey with more than exhaustion. His training gave him the means to withstand the exposure. His discipline gave him the will. He was human, though. We all break. I picked up the torch for him and charged the pink madness.

The face appeared in front of me. The jaws stretched wide in welcome. The laughter reached into my skull. My vision began to swim with worms. I dropped, sliding forward, and hurled the frag at the maw. My aim was true. The daemon swallowed. Its face actually showed confusion for a moment. I rolled between its legs. The proximity was enough to erode my self. I rose and staggered away, repeating my name in my head, fighting the rot of all I knew.

The grenade went off. The explosion was a muffled, wet concussion. The daemon's central mass burst open. The glistening viscera of Chaos flew in all directions. The monster's knees buckled. It slumped to the ground. Its mouth opened at the top of its trunk. It loosed a scream that spread a network of cracks across the stone floor, walls and ceiling of the chamber. We were all on our knees now, hands pressed to our ears, trying to block out that shriek and the claws that came with it. The daemon writhed. Its torso bubbled and bled. It twisted a full three hundred and sixty degrees, and then kept going. The scream continued, rising and falling in registers impossible for any material throat. The mouth worked, chewing the real, spreading ever wider. And then tearing.

The daemon's muscle-flesh pulsed, its colour darkening as if being flooded with bad blood. It began to split down the centre. The mouth became two. The noise was a scream and snarl at the same time. The voices collided and fought. The colour darkened further. More limbs sprouted. The daemon's flesh changed from the pink of a raw wind to the blue of an angry bruise, and it ripped itself in half.

Now there were two. They were smaller than the original creature, and faster. The diseased humour had vanished. The words were just as toxic before, but now they were howling complaints. The two daemons vented fury and grief at each other, but they lunged at us. One bowled into Saultern and his troops. Arms multiplied, snatching soldiers. The daemon was no larger than a man, but its reach was long, and its strength vicious. It was too greedy to focus on a single victim. It snapped a leg of one, ripped out the spine of another, yanked off the arm of a third. It spread a gospel of agony.

The other daemon had only one target. I knew there was no evading it. It was on me in two leaps. I emptied my bolt pistol into its face. I barely slowed its charge. What passed for its head flowed around the shell holes. I had my sword extended, and it impaled itself as it slammed into me. It knocked me down. The flesh of its trunk held my sword fast. I tried to saw the blade, felt it cutting sinew. The daemon snarled. It leaned down, and all I could see were teeth and darkness. Fangs were already tearing into my soul.

Then the crushing weight on my chest lifted. The daemon was hurled back. The air was filled with a new sound: the clean, metronomic punishment of boltguns. This was so much more than the individual beats of my pistol. This was the music of relentlessness. The shells hit in a directed storm, and they did not stop. The Sisters of the Order of the Piercing Thorn had come, and as I crawled out of the path of fire, I saw the true image of armoured faith.

It was a moment of realization. The contempt that the Adepta Sororitas felt for us sad, weak specimens in the Imperial Guard, and the resentment we returned, were almost articles of unexamined faith in themselves. But now I felt humbled. The ten women had not donned their helms, and their faces were ablaze with something that went so far beyond simple zeal, it should have burned all who gazed upon it. Krauss was dogmatic, and his inflexibility had served him well in this dark place. I would have shot anyone foolish enough to question my own devotion to the Emperor.

But the force that marched towards the daemons crackled with a different order of faith. These warriors were touched with *sanctity*. They hammered the daemons with bolter fire, and they filled the room with a fury as pure as it was limitless. They had no room in their hearts or minds for doubt. They confronted the existence of the daemons with holy rage.

The daemon absorbed the first few shells, but the blows kept coming, and overwhelmed it. With a final gibbering whine at the injustice visited upon it, the being fell apart. Its form vanished. It became a writhing puddle, and then that evaporated back into the void with an echoing moan.

The other daemon had just grabbed Betzner by the throat. The trooper was transfixed by the shape of his death. His arms had fallen limp. But as its twin disincorporated, the daemon dropped Betzner, twisting around in pain and rage. The bolter shells hit it too. It advanced against the onslaught, flowing and leaping, taking the hits but still holding onto its grip on the materium. It closed with the Sisters of Battle. They had to choose their shots carefully while the Mortisians and Krauss moved out of the way. Then the daemon was already there. Setheno was in the lead. She met the thing with her blade, bringing the sword down in an overhead swing that sliced through a third of the daemon's trunk. She immobilized it. Hands with too many fingers grasped her arms. Claws scraped against ceramite. She did not move. The daemon wailed. The rest of the squad surrounded it and shot it into oblivion.

The silence that followed was startling. The voices were gone. Reality reasserted its stability. I joined Saultern's squad. The daemon had killed three, crippled two others. But even those who had escaped physical injury had still been harmed. Saultern was staring at the spot where the second daemon had vanished. His eyes were blank with horror. Betzner was sitting where he had fallen. He was perfectly still. He had withdrawn into himself. I did not think he was exploring anything pleasant. Kortner stood to one side, clutching his lasrifle with whitening knuckles. 'What was that?' he kept repeating. 'What was that? What was that?'

'A xenos obscenity,' I told him. 'The traitors have allied themselves with a degenerate race. The creatures are dangerous, clearly. They can also be killed. Clearly.'

'But,' he began. One hand moved towards his head, then his heart. He was trying to express the spiritual wounds he had received. At some level, he knew he had encountered something far more insidious than a powerful xenos beast. It was necessary, though, that this knowledge remain vague. There were no such things as daemons. To believe otherwise would be harmful to the faith of the untrained individual. To be certain would be even worse.

'What else could it be?' I said.

He looked at me. So did Saultern. So did the rest of the squad. All the survivors except Betzner. 'Nothing else?' Kortner whispered.

'Nothing else.'

I walked over to the Order of the Piercing Thorn squad. Krauss was already there. 'My thanks, sister superior,' I said to Setheno.

She nodded. If fighting the daemon had caused her strain, I couldn't see it, unless it was in the blaze of her eyes. She and her Sisters looked hungry for battle, as if the taint brought onto Imperial land by the incursion would not be expunged until there was a mountain of heretic corpses that reached the sun. She said, 'This changes everything. Our enemies are not just treacherous and heretical. They are witches. They consort with daemons. This is a threat of a very different order.'

Krauss nodded. It was the first time the three of us had agreed on anything, other than our unspoken contempt for Wangenheim. 'We will seal this entry point, but these attacks will not stop.'

'The fight must be brought to the enemy.'

I looked at Setheno. 'I don't think this incident is likely to change the cardinal's mind.'

She holstered her bolt pistol. 'That is no longer my concern. My first duty is always to the faith. The need to stop a daemonic manifestation supersedes any other consideration. We need to break out of the city.'

'To do that, we must lift the siege.' Krauss was pointing out the obvious.

'That falls to the Imperial Guard,' Setheno said, not without sympathy. 'Until there is a way forward, my Sisters and I must protect the palace.'

'That's all right.' I shrugged. 'Meaning no disrespect to your abilities in combat, sister superior, but the addition of your squad would not be sufficient to defeat those numbers beyond the wall.'

'I didn't think we would be.'

Krauss gestured at the wreckage around us. 'A small force, in the right place, can make a difference. This attack was meant to decapitate the leadership of our forces.' He grimaced, frustrated. 'Would that we could do the same.'

He was right. A thought struck me. 'Perhaps we can.'

'How?' Krauss protested. 'Do we even know where Vahnsinn is based?'

'I'm sure the cardinal does,' said Setheno.

'What good will that do when we are besieged?'

'None,' I answered. 'So we break the siege. You were right, inquisitor. A small force can do this. Like a dagger to the heart.'

The idea crystallized, and I was smiling.

CHAPTER 15
THE DAGGER

1. Setheno

Clarity. Setheno had never thought that was too great a hope to have. She did not believe it was hubris. To desire to know how best to serve the Emperor, how could that be a sin? It wasn't. Yet it eluded her like forbidden fruit. She had thought, on the day that she entered the convent of the Order of the Piercing Thorn, that clarity would come to her as a matter of course. How could any Sister of Battle have any doubt as to the correct path of her duty?

She had been very young. That was her only excuse for her naïvety. For not even thinking the word *politics*. She knew better now. She had experience. She still hoped for clarity, though. She hoped that enough experience would allow her to slice through the fog of competing agendas and factionalism within the Ecclesiarchy, and see, always, and beyond any doubt, how she was called upon to serve.

Mistral was not helping in this quest.

As she, Yarrick and Krauss made their way back up through the levels of the palace, they walked a dozen steps ahead of the others. The rest of her squad helped the Mortisians carry the wounded, and she listened to the commissar's proposal. It was a good one. It had a high risk of failure, but it was a good plan. There was clarity in its purpose, and, if it succeeded, clarity in its implications. She approved. She said, 'Do it.'

'Your participation would be helpful.'

She was about to agree when the fog closed in again. Wangenheim would protest with all his might, and the daemonic incursion into the palace, for the moment, strengthened his hand. 'The terms of the conflict have changed,' she said, and then sighed. 'But until we can counter-attack, they only reinforce the need to defend the palace. The siege must be lifted first.'

Yarrick nodded. 'I appreciate your position.'

I wish I did, she thought. For a moment she wondered what it would be like to feel less bound by duty. And in that moment, she was granted a sliver of clarity. The insight was distasteful. It was also unarguable. As they reached the ground floor once again, she said to Yarrick, 'You must speak with the cardinal's steward.'

2. Yarrick

Vercor was still outside Wangenheim's chambers. She grinned when she saw me. It was like seeing a knife smile. 'Are you here to invite me to a game?' she asked.

'No,' I said, and turned around. *Not on those terms,* I thought. *Never on those terms.* I didn't want to work with Vercor. I didn't like the idea of having my back turned on her. I could tell, though, that Vercor had skills useful for what I had in mind. She also knew how Mistral worked. But I would not play the game. I was not Mistralian. The rules of this world had led it to perdition. I'd had enough. I would complete the mission without her.

I walked away, and I was not bargaining.

'Wait,' she called.

I stopped, turned around. I said nothing.

'Tell me what you want,' she said.

'If anything goes wrong, to get us all killed. This isn't an opportunity to hedge your bets, mercenary.'

She thought for a bit, then walked towards me. 'All right,' she said.

'Why?' I asked.

She glanced back once at the closed door. 'Because you're not a fool.'

3. Bellavis

The bombardment had left very little in its wake. As he salvaged who and what he could, Bellavis noted the precision and thoroughness of the work. The enemy's strategy was beyond reproach: canton your foe in a contained, known location, then blanket the area with high explosives. The surprise had been complete. The regiment had been decimated.

Decimated. Not destroyed.

Even as the bombardment was still ongoing, the Mortisians had made for the mountains. There had been no order possible to the evacuation. No companies or squads had been on the run. Only individuals. When the shelling finally stopped, the troops had been scattered over the slopes.

Bellavis had begun the gathering process. He was shielded

by his carapace armour and by the fact that he had long ago shed most of his humanity and its attendant weaknesses. He had recovered quickly. So he had started looking, and gradually, the remains of the regiments had coalesced.

It had taken a day for anything like a fighting force to exist. Over the course of the second day, the Mortisians left the ruined Trenqavel valley and headed in the direction of Tolosa. They stuck to the mountains, moving through narrow passes. They had few vehicles left. The tanks and Chimeras that still functioned travelled along rough parallel routes. Forced to use actual roads, they were more vulnerable to a second attack. At least, with the infantry split off, a new bombardment would not finish everything off.

The Carconnes came to an abrupt end at their western edge. Bellavis stood on a wide ledge high on one of the last peaks. Below him, the chain slumped into foothills, and then, after only a few kilometres, the plains. With the magnification of his ocular lenses on high, he watched Basilisks manoeuvring towards the south, moving ever closer to the walls of Tolosa.

'How long do you think they can hold?' Schranker asked.

Bellavis visualized the battlefield reduced to vectors of force. His calculations were rendered imprecise by the uncertainty of random events. It was one of the great frustrations of his existence that war was an art instead of a science. 'The enemy has lost a large number of guns,' he said. 'Many remain to him, however. Bringing them all in so close will lead to even greater losses. He appears to be gambling that he will be able to ride out those losses, and maintain a concentrated, precise artillery barrage on the wall long enough to bring it down. The gamble has merit.'

'So?'

'Much depends on the inherent strength of the outer wall. The fact that it is still standing speaks well of it. If all of the enemy's resources were already deployed, I would find the outcome, in the short term, difficult to extrapolate.'

'You're about to give me some bad news, aren't you, enginseer?'

Bellavis pointed. 'Do you see the train?' It was many kilometres to the south, on a track that crossed more water than land.

'Yes. It's too far for me to make out any details.'

'Some of its cargo has cannons.'

Schranker sighed. 'They're replacing more than troops, then.'

'So it would seem. I am willing to grant the city another night of successful defence. I say this, sergeant, with more hope than confidence.'

'When a tech-priest starts using words like *hope*, I get worried.'

'I cannot alter the facts before me, though I can wish them otherwise.'

'You still wish?'

'It has been known. I am not a servitor, sergeant.'

'Point taken.' She shielded her eyes with a hand, watching the train. 'Be nice to change those facts around a bit.'

'Agreed. Do you have orders?'

She grimaced when he asked that question. She looked very tired. Her wounds, Bellavis knew, did not make her new responsibilities any easier. She had been burned along her left side when a Hellhound had exploded. She had been running past the tank when the shell had made a direct hit, and the immediate area had suddenly been awash with ignited promethium. The field dressings on her face, neck and arm needed changing, but medical rations were in short supply. So were officers. The command tent had been hit by one of the first shells. None of the captains had escaped. Schranker headed a squad of soldiers who, like her, had survived so many battlefields that their scars had become a form of armour. She was the most senior sergeant still mobile. The leadership of the devastated regiment fell to her. What Bellavis had begun, she had completed, forging a coherent fighting force out of the fragments, and bringing the troops this far.

'The orders are what they've always been,' Schranker said. 'Fight the enemy. Stop him. Kill him.' She grunted. It was her version of a laugh. 'Well, we can fight and we can kill, tech-priest. How would you rate our chances of stopping him?'

Her body language had become harder to read since her injuries. Bellavis wasn't sure what response was required. 'Was your question rhetorical, veteran sergeant?'

'Yes,' she said. 'No.' She shrugged. 'It was irrelevant. The odds don't matter.'

'And if nothing of the regiment survives? The Imperium must learn of the situation here.'

'If we vanish, the Imperium will know soon enough. We aren't heralds. We're soldiers.'

Bellavis bowed his head. 'Merely a question,' he said. 'Not my desire.'

She arched her remaining eyebrow. 'Your desire?'

'To serve the Omnissiah.' He unfolded his right arm and extended the multi-jointed probe that had replaced his index finger. He pointed towards Tolosa. 'And to kill the enemy.'

'Good. I have a plan, then. It may not be good, but it's the only one open to us. And it is simple. An infantry charge.'

'That will be our strategy?'

'You see another option, let me know.'

Bellavis saw none. He kept his silence.

'Delaying the inevitable,' she said, disgusted. 'If that's all we can do, we still have to do it. If Colonel Granach tries any sortie, he'll need our support. Plus I want to see plenty of heretic blood on my boots before it's over.' She turned away from the edge and began making her way down the slope to where the regiment waited. Bellavis followed.

'When they attack, so do we,' Schranker said.

'That will mean crossing a great deal of open land with no shelter.'

'And crossing lots of rivers quickly. I know. Gets better all the time, doesn't it?'

'Just like home.'

That stopped her. She looked back. Her body language was easy to read there. She was startled by what sounded to her like wistfulness. 'Doing what we have to, and never mind hope,' she said. 'Yes. It is like home. You're a surprise, tech-priest.'

'I remember what I was.' He showed her his bionic left hand. 'I lost this flesh long before I entered the Adeptus Mechanicus. It was taken by a rival underhive gang.'

'One that you had to fight, outcome be damned.'

'That is correct.'

Schranker smiled. The expression was a promise of violence, it was pained, and it was eager. 'Yet here you still are,' she said. 'Here we all are, and no regrets. So let's go give these traitorous scum a regret or two.'

4. *Yarrick*

Granach didn't take much convincing. 'I think you're insane, commissar,' he told me. 'I also think nothing less than insanity is called for, at this moment.'

He passed me his magnoculars. I looked through them at the junction. I saw the Basilisks being unloaded from the freight cars. 'Those guns will be inside our minimum range,' I said.

'Exactly. We can take down many of the others, but once they are close enough, they will be able to hit us with impunity. We'll have to attempt a sortie.'

'That will be a massacre.' I handed back the magnoculars.

'There will be a choice of massacres. I prefer the active one. When will you be ready?'

I would have liked another day. If Tolosa could make it through one more night, I would be able to get my team into position under the cover of darkness. We would have the luxury of attacking a target of choice, rather than of opportunity. I would have liked these things. I wished for them, before I answered Granach.

I do not wish for the unattainable any longer. I do not wish I had two arms. I do not wish I had two eyes. I try.

I said to Granach, 'We are ready now.'

There were five of us: Vercor, Krauss, Betzner, Kortner, myself. Seroff wanted in.

'Granach will need you on the wall,' I told him. 'Without the lord commissar…'

He nodded. 'Any word?'

'Nothing.'

'You think Vahnsinn killed him?'

'I don't know.'

'I'm not sure what to hope for,' Seroff admitted, his eyes pained.

'Neither do I.' Our mentor's death or capture filled me with different shades of helpless rage. I kept the emotion at bay by focusing on destroying those responsible.

We turned the enemy's tactics against him and went underground. Vercor took us to a disused sewer access in the north-west of the city, a couple of blocks from the outer wall. Though the enforcers were sealing off every enemy-constructed tunnel they could find, it was impossible to close off the underworld. The town's defence had to rely on the interdicted routes stymieing the cultists by throwing them into the full maze, and on the war being a brief one. If our mission was unsuccessful, the war could well be over come the dawn.

Once into the network, Kortner took the lead. Vercor told him what our heading should be, and he headed off into the tunnels as if born to them. His sense of direction was eerie. There was no direct path, and in the switchbacks, serpentine curves and multiplying junctions, I lost my bearings within the first few minutes. So did Krauss. 'How can he know where we are?' he asked.

'A life in the depths,' I answered. 'We all must learn our environments if we're going to survive.'

We spoke quietly. We had travelled under the defences. We were under the enemy's feet. The journey took close to four hours. It was early evening when we neared our goal. Though the main docks were along the western wall of Tolosa, on the great Garan river, there were other major trade arteries here, with other docks. Flowing almost perpendicular into the Garan was the Tahrn. It ran almost due north for hundreds of kilometres, fed by dozens of tributaries on the plain, and was the route used for almost as many manufactoria as the Garan. A maglev track ran parallel to it.

We were in former mining tunnels for the last leg of the trek, and Kortner took us into a channel that had been used to pump water and waste out of the mines and into the Tahrn. The rusted remains of the hydraulics hung on the walls: massive, flaking brackets, and the fragments of pipes. The channel ran in a straight line for several hundred metres. We saw the exit from a long way off. The light was fading from the sky as we reached it.

The lower portion of the outfall opening was covered by high reeds. I joined Kortner at the front. We waited five minutes, watching. We saw no one. All of us then emerged into the last of the day. We climbed the bank, and stopped at the base of one of the rockcrete pillars that held the maglev track. We were a few kilometres north of the rail junction. The rear elements of the heretic army were a comfortable distance away. They had moved that much closer to the wall.

'Is this far enough?' Krauss asked.

'Not much of a margin,' I said. As if to prove the truth of my words, a train passed overhead. We watched it slow as it arrived at the hub. I timed it with my chronometer. 'Not much at all.' I asked Vercor, 'Was that the sort of train we wanted?'

'No.' She pointed at the cars. 'Those are troop transports.'

'Will you be able to recognize what we want in time?'

'Yes.'

I looked at the pillar. There were rungs for maintenance workers embedded in the rockcrete. I estimated how long it would take us to climb the twenty metres to the track, then looked north. No sign yet of another train. No matter how fast a schedule the barons sought to maintain, there were still limits. Derailments would do them no good.

Nor us, for that matter.

'Forward,' I said. 'Let's get as much distance as we can.'

We moved at a quick march from pillar to pillar, pausing

at each one to watch for an approaching train. The wind's constant roar meant that we would not hear the train until it was almost upon us. An hour passed, and we put another few thousand metres between us and the hub. I felt the Emperor's blessing on our enterprise.

Then another hour ticked by. Twilight dropped towards full dark. I began to worry that there would be no further arrivals until the next day. Behind us, the war began again. Beneath the booming of the guns, I could hear the uproar of human voices. I thought of the squealing of thousands of rodents. My lips pulled back in loathing. I would crush the vermin. I would see them destroyed this night. I would accept nothing less.

I stopped at the next pillar. 'This is far enough,' I said. I grabbed the first of the rungs and started to climb.

'And where is our train?' Krauss asked, sceptical.

'It will come,' I informed him. I would summon one through sheer will, if necessary.

We climbed. At the top there was a narrow steel catwalk running on each side of the track. The hand rails seemed fragile, no thicker than my thumb, no security at all against the violence of the wind gusts. We split up, Betzner and Kortner taking the east side of the rail. We took up our positions, a dozen metres between each of us, crouched low, and waited.

The train would come. I had felt the Emperor's blessing earlier, and I would not doubt it now. The train would come. I repeated that certainty to myself until it became a prophecy and then, after a quarter of an hour, a reality. We saw its headlight pierce the growing gloom. Then the silhouettes of the cars became visible.

'Well?' I asked Vercor.

'Yes.'

'Do it,' I told Betzner.

He took out a canteen filled with promethium, lit the rag that hung from its mouth, and tossed it onto the rail, as far as he could to our rear. Flames spread over the track, a bright flare in the dark. There would be no damage done to the rail, but the effect was impressive. We needed the train slowed, not stopped.

We flattened ourselves on the catwalks. The train rushed towards us, a bullet hundreds of metres long, weighing thousands of tonnes. I kept my head down until the locomotive passed us. When I looked up, the train's speed was bleeding off.

I jumped up. So did the others. The cars slowed further. They stopped being blurs. I glanced at Vercor. I could just make her out beyond Krauss. She was pointing at a car four down from us. It was a cylinder. This was what we wanted. I braced myself.

The car passed Vercor. She grabbed the ladder that ran up the side of the cylinder. She climbed it with the litheness of an insect. Then it was Krauss's turn. Then mine. The train was already starting to speed up again, and the jerk of grabbing the ladder was violent. My legs flailed. I hung by my arms for a moment before I managed to haul myself up.

I climbed the ladder. Betzner and Kortner had come up the other side. When we were all gathered on the top of the tanker car, we took stock. The rear of the train was now just shadows in the night, its configuration impossible to make out, though I could see light shining from the rear car. To the front, there was more light coming from the engine and the first car. Enough for us to manoeuvre.

Betzner rapped a fist against the roof of the tank. 'Promethium,' he said.

I nodded. Good. 'Is the rest of the configuration what you thought?' I asked Vercor.

'Yes. Troop transports front and rear for security. Everything else is cargo. Mostly munitions.'

Perfect. 'Let's go.'

Vercor in the lead now, Krauss and myself just behind. I knew it was killing the inquisitor not to be running the operation. That gave me more satisfaction than it should have. It was also necessary. We were in Vercor's territory now, and our opening shots would be the acts of an assassin, not a judge. At least his pride was not so powerful as to blind him to the demands of the mission.

Kortner and Betzner brought up the rear. They moved slowly, going backwards as much as they could. I warned them whenever we approached the end of a wagon. We reached the last munitions car, then paused before the troop transport. Vercor leapt across the gap between the cars. She landed with feline grace and padded across the roof. She crouched before the locomotive. I squinted, and could just make out the movement when she turned her head to look at us.

Our presence was about to become known. We were ready. I signalled to her with my arm.

She dropped below the roof. Krauss raced after her. I gave him until he reached the far end of the car, and then the rest of us followed. We ran, and I knew our steps were thunderous. I didn't care. We were done with stealth. What mattered now was speed and strength.

The two troopers stopped just before the end of the troop car, got down on one knee, and aimed their rifles forward. I looked at the locomotive. The engine's rear door was open. There was a body just inside, a man's boots sticking out into the night.

There was a ledge between the cars. I lowered myself to it, then crossed into the locomotive. There were three bodies here, and the sounds of a struggle ahead. I drew my sword, unwilling to risk bolt shells in the confined space. I moved down a narrow corridor. There were storage compartments on either side, and small sleeping areas for the crew and security detail. The fighting was up and to the right. It was an armoury. There were three guards, grappling with Vercor and Krauss. Close quarters, no one firing. I grabbed the nearest one by the hair, hauled him back, and thrust the sword into his side. Krauss was wearing spiked gauntlets. With one hand, he knocked the guard's bayonet to the side. He made a fist with the other and punched spikes into the man's eyes. Vercor had her right hand around her opponent's neck. He was turning purple, had dropped his weapons and was clawing weakly at her arms. She squeezed until her fingers met. There was a lot of blood.

The corridor ended at a closed door. I could see, through the armourglass, the control console. There were two men in there. One was at the controls. The other, to my surprise, I recognized. It was Baron Maurus. He looked much less like a clerk now. He wore carapace armour, and carried it well. He had his lasgun trained at the door. His face was dark with rage, and he was shouting something I could not hear through the steel between us.

To the rear, the sounds of combat began. The other troops had been alerted. Another minute or two, and we would all be dead, and the train would have arrived at the hub.

My bolt pistol could shoot through the armourglass, but I didn't dare fire. If the driver hit the brakes, and I damaged the controls, the mission would fail. 'Mercenary,' I said.

Vercor strode up to the door. She cocked a fist. She snapped it forwards and back. The act was a blur, a serpent's strike. The window shattered. Maurus fired. Vercor pulled back, but the shot clipped her shoulder. She grunted, staggering for a step as she ducked below the height of the window. Krauss and I moved to the wall on either side of the door.

'No damage,' I cautioned Krauss.

He nodded, pulling out his gun. He had replaced his plasma pistol with a needle gun. I had a flash of envy for his private arsenal. He held the weapon with both hands, waiting. Maurus kept firing, scoring walls and the far end of the corridor with burns. His every pull of the trigger ate away at precious seconds.

A pause. Krauss rotated and fired a burst through the aperture. Maurus shot again. The las struck Krauss's reflective armour. It knocked him back, his chest smoking, but he still stood. On the other side of the door I heard the thuds of heavy weights hitting the floor.

'Both of them,' Krauss said.

I reached my arm through the window and unlocked the door. 'I'll catch up,' I said.

Without a word, he and Vercor headed off towards the battle at the transport car.

I stepped over the bodies of Maurus and the other heretic. Krauss's needles had struck the baron in the eye, the driver in the back of the neck. Lethal neurotoxin had paralysed their arms, legs, necks and eyes. Their chests. They were still alive, suffocating. That was still more mercy than they deserved.

I approached the controls. There were readouts and adjustments I didn't understand. I didn't have to. There was a throttle, and that was all I cared about. I pushed it to full. I almost put a shell through the brakes, but decided against it. I might trigger a fail-safe.

The train shook as it picked up yet more speed. I looked ahead. The lights of the battle were drawing closer. We had almost won. All we had to do was keep the heretic troops, who must outnumber us five to one, away from the controls a little while longer, and then leap from a speeding train without spreading ourselves across the landscape.

Nothing could be easier, I thought. I gave a short bark of laughter at my own gallows humour as I picked up Maurus's lasgun and ran back down the length of the locomotive. I tossed the rifle to Vercor. She and Krauss were crouched before the rear door. He was shooting into the open door of the transport car. He was choosing his shots well. The return fire was fierce, but his needles were just enough of a threat that the soldiers in the car weren't mounting a charge. Two of their number lay still in the doorway. Vercor opened up with the lasgun. I took a knee and squeezed off shots with my bolt pistol. I aimed with care. I couldn't risk derailment. So I shot straight through the benches. One shell to blast a hole through the thin steel. A second shot through the hole to shatter the flesh on the other side. And then again. At the periphery of my consciousness, I was aware of the struggle happening on the roof of the car. The heretics were going out the rear of the transport, climbing up, and running into the barrage laid down by Kortner and Betzner.

A little bit longer, I thought. *A little bit longer*. The train tore up the track as we fought. Now time worked against the heretics. Every second we held them back brought them closer to their great doom.

I checked my chronometer. Based on where we had boarded

the train, we were only a few seconds away from the victory line. One of the enemy must have realized what we were attempting, and chosen the death of the train and all aboard it over a much greater loss. A frag grenade was hurled from inside the transport car. It sailed through the door, over our heads, and bounced on the floor behind us, rolling into the control compartment.

No, I thought. I threw myself after the grenade. *One, by the Emperor.* I didn't even know how long the explosive had cooked in the foe's hand. I didn't care. If I did not try to counter this threat, all was lost. *Two, by the Emperor.* I picked up the grenade. There was no time to get back to the other end of the locomotive. *Three, by the Emperor.* 'Go!' I shouted at the others as I fired through the locomotive's windshield and threw the grenade forward at the same time. The wind hurled shards of plex-glass into my face. *Four, by the Emp–*

The frag exploded. Flash of fire and shrapnel. The blast and the wind knocked me back. Jaggedness cut my flesh and uniform. The cabin was filled with the sound of injured metal. The control panel shorted. Sparks flew. Smoke billowed at me.

But the train did not slow.

Now. Now, now, now!

I looked back. Vercor and Krauss were gone. Heretic troops were crossing between the cars. No getting out that way. I jumped up onto the burning and steering console, choking on smoke, and pulled myself through the shattered windshield. I was pushing against a hurricane blast. My eyes were stinging, tearing, closed. I had no time. I had no choice. I had only my faith as, with all my strength, I leapt to the right.

It was a good jump. The train did not clip my heels and send me spinning. I plunged, eyes still sealed. Perhaps I was falling into my final darkness.

When I think about this moment, I sometimes believe that I had a shiver of premonition. It seems to me that there are, in my life, currents of call and ever-greater echo. Did that fall whisper to me of Ghazghkull Mag Uruk Thraka dropping me down that infernal well? I don't trust my memory here. It may be distorted by my need to see purpose and patterns. But I have also experienced foreshadowing of an incontrovertible nature. So I do think I was touched by a presentiment of a worse fall to come.

This one was bad enough. I knew nothing but the roar of wind and the speed of flight. I braced for an impact I couldn't anticipate. It came. I hit water. It felt like slamming into steel. It was a steel that gave, and made a fist, and squeezed me as it battered. But it was the pain I had hoped for, and I was ready for it. I rode it out, took the battering and spread my arms, slowing, then arresting my descent. I made it back to the surface, choking and gagging, and relieved to be so. I swam for the shore, where I saw four figures, all moving. Waterlogged, staggering, I didn't stop when I reached land, but climbed up the riverbank. I needed to see what we had wrought. The others followed.

The full length of the train had passed us. It rocketed to the junction. There was nothing that could stop it. The heretics aboard, and those in the junction, would know what was upon them. This pleased me.

It began with the sound of the impact itself, a heavy, grinding, raging clash of metal on metal and rockcrete. Speed and mass turned on each other. The din of war was drowned out by the thunder of the wreck, a thunder that built and built and built. The sheer length of the crescendo inspired awe and fear. I saw the train whiplash off the track like a thing alive. It was a dark miracle. No mass that great should move in this way. And still the sound grew, torturing the night itself, reaching across the plain, crying an agony that must be expressed before the greater thing happened.

Then it came. The promethium ignited first. The tanker car exploded. A liquid sun screamed to life in the junction. Its birth seared the eye. It spread a parabola of fire. As the streams of flame made landfall, the munitions cooked off. The chain of explosions was a second crescendo. It was the great fanfare in a symphony of destruction. Multiple sharp blasts merged into a single *k-k-k-k-krak,* and the finale was so huge it smashed everything. There was light and there was sound, but all contours ceased to exist. I was blinded by my own creation. The shock wave came. It shamed the Mistralian wind, and knocked us flat. The new gale howled. Within it were other shrieks. Things were bending, things were burning. Metal tore. Rockcrete shattered to powder. The world was without form, and void.

And we had done this.

The light and the sound faded. Dazed, half-deaf, I stood up. The landscape was lit by the glow of a hundred fires. There was nothing left of the junction. It was a crater, filled with twisted iron. The tracks leading to Tolosa now ended in contortions like gnarled claws. The enemy guns had vanished. From this distance, I could not tell, through the smoke and fire and wreckage, how many of the enemy infantry had been destroyed, I could but guess.

The sounds of battle had not ceased. The struggle at the wall continued. I heard a distant roar now. It was a human shout.

It was the exhilarated triumph of the besieged descending upon the besiegers.

And then, in the dark behind us, came an answering roar. I had a moment of despair, thinking another massive troop reinforcement had arrived, and we had accomplished nothing except to lure our own troops out to be slaughtered. But then the advancing force became visible. The light from the great burning revealed the standards of Aighe Mortis. Kortner and Betzner started cheering. The surviving rumps of the 77th and 110th regiments were about to join together, crushing the heretics out of existence.

To my right, Vercor chuckled. She clapped her bionic hands together, very slowly. 'Commissar,' she said, 'you do play the game well. Never believe otherwise.'

I didn't answer. She was still wrong. I had not played a game. We had upended the board.

CHAPTER 16
REVERSALS

1. Rasp

There was another level, deeper yet, to hell. It took Rasp hours into his captivity to notice that Vahnsinn, when he visited, did not always leave in the same direction. After Rasp had first been shackled, Vahnsinn headed off to the left to make ready his mysterious threat against Tolosa. But with increasing frequency, he was going right. The beatings, the whippings and worse resumed as soon as the baron turned his back, so it was difficult for Rasp to see where he went. But once, in a well-timed pause as a torturer pulled his arm back for another blow, he saw, deep in the shadows to the right, Vahnsinn begin a descent.

In those moments where the pain dulled enough to let him think, Rasp wondered what was down there. Whatever Vahnsinn was doing, it was having a visible effect on him. His visits were irregularly spaced, but there were many of them.

He wanted to talk. He seemed as shackled to his need to taunt Rasp as the lord commissar was to the chair. He ranted. He mocked. Sometimes, his confidence cracked and strange anger and desperation leaked through. Rasp hoped this meant the war was going against the barons. Even if it was, that didn't account for all that he was seeing in Vahnsinn. Each time he returned from the lower level, he had *decayed*.

Rasp's body was being taken apart, one blow, one cut, one branding, one shock at a time. His nose and cheekbones were broken. He could not see out of his swollen right eye. He had lost the fingernails of his left hand. His ribs moved when he breathed. Most of his joints had been dislocated, reset, and dislocated again. The warmth of the blood covering his face and chest, and running down his limbs, was almost a comfort. He no longer recognized his physical self as an integral whole. It was a collection of autonomous agonies. And still, he could see enough through the haze of pain to be shocked by Vahnsinn's changing appearance.

The disintegration was rapid. The baron was already almost unrecognizable. It was as if the cultured, refined figure of sanity he had presented in the lead-up to the war had been a shell preserved through artificial means. Now the rot, held off too long, was claiming its due. Some of the changes appeared to be self-inflicted. There were cuts on his face, knife slashes as savage as they were complex. He had shaved his head, and the cuts extended over his entire skull. The patterns were runic, yet they were also something greater, and far more toxic. They were beyond a foul language, beyond representation. They did not just hold a dread meaning. They were the result of direct contact with that meaning.

His skin, under the scarification, was changing tone. It was the white of ancient death, mottled with the yellow of bad teeth, the green of festering sins. He had exchanged the uniform of his House for robes. Traces of the Vahnsinn livery were visible on them, as were echoes of all the other noble families of Mistral. They were woven together into a sinew of symbolism that was dominated by repeated images of a sinuous emblem that seemed to be both teardrop and blade.

Every time he reappeared, the robes were altered. They were rotting too, despite the obvious richness of the material. They were not tearing or fraying, but there was something curdled about them. The colours were growing darker, murkier. Sometimes, when Vahnsinn gestured, the sleeves did not ride up his arms as they should, as if the flesh and the cloth were merging.

Vahnsinn hurled insults and curses at Rasp. He blasphemed. He ridiculed the efforts of the Imperial Guard. He was also cajoling, arguing, preaching. He kept pausing after questions, clearly waiting for the moment when at last Rasp would concede, and speak the *yes* of moral surrender.

'Why do you care?' Rasp finally said. It was difficult to speak. Several teeth were missing, and his tongue had been burned and pierced. 'What are you hoping to achieve with me?'

'Hoping?' Vahnsinn asked, genuinely puzzled. 'There is no hope in this place, Simeon. Hope is forbidden. Hope is dead. There is truth, here, though, and you will accept it.'

'Why?'

'Because I did!' The howl exposed an abyss of pain, but no regret.

Rasp gaped. Was Vahnsinn that consumed by his own ego? Did he think he could accept his own damnation if he dragged Rasp down with him? The triviality and expense of the endeavour were astounding. 'Kill me now, you deluded idiot,' Rasp said. 'You're wasting my time and your own.'

Vahnsinn was suddenly transfixed by a point in space above and behind Rasp. 'No,' he said, his voice dull. He cocked his head, still staring. Then he nodded. 'Your destiny,' he said. He kept nodding, agreeing with an invisible interlocutor. 'You have appointments to keep.'

Rasp's blood no longer warmed him. Cold, purposeful and unforgiving, spread from his heart to his fingertips. He didn't understand what Vahnsinn was talking about, but what he heard in that dead voice was not belief or certainty or faith, but simple fact. 'You know nothing of my destiny,' he whispered. Even to his own ears, his denial sounded too much like a plea.

Vahnsinn blinked several times, his eyelids an insect-wing blur. He looked down at Rasp, his eyes clear again. 'What did you say?'

'I won't have you speaking of my destiny.'

Vahnsinn frowned. 'Why would I? It isn't mine to determine.'

Before Rasp could answer, another figure joined them. Baroness Elleta Gotho wore robes similar to Vahnsinn's. Hers, too, were diseased. She, too, had shaved her head. She was one of the most elderly of the nobles, and she walked with a cane. It seemed to grow from her palm. It was a dark fusion of bone and petrified serpent. She mounted the dais, but waited a step away for Vahnsinn to notice her. The other aristocrats, it seemed, had learned from Lom's mistake, and knew their place.

'What is it?' Vahnsinn asked without turning around.

'Tolosa is lost.'

'Good. We can–'

'To us,' she corrected.

Now Vahnsinn faced her. 'This is definitive?'

'Yes. Our forces were exterminated.'

Vahnsinn was surprised, but did not appear enraged. 'How?' he asked, then waved a hand. 'Never mind. It isn't important.'

The absence of rage unnerved Rasp. The ember of triumph that had flared in his chest now flickered.

Vahnsinn turned back to him. 'Unchain him,' he ordered the torturers. He smiled. The deep cuts to his lips made his mouth hang oddly.

The shackles fell away. Rasp was hauled to his feet. He could not stand without help.

Still smiling, Vahnsinn said, 'You think this makes a difference? That something important has happened? You're wrong.' The grin became wider, and more awful. It was the leprosy of joy. 'But something important is about to happen. Come and see.'

They blindfolded him, and he was dragged off the dais. Once more, he was hauled through the clamouring space of Karrathar, up stairs, down corridors, through the stench and cold of corruption. Then a door opened, and he felt the wind against his face.

Vahnsinn removed the blindfold. They were standing on a small balcony jutting out of a turret. Below them was an enclosed courtyard. It was dominated by a single missile and its launch mechanism. 'Do you know what that is?' the baron asked.

Rasp stared. The hope he had been nurturing so carefully was smothered. The rocket was huge, and it did not belong on Mistral. Rasp knew that the planet did not have the Standard Template Construct for this weapon. The missile must have been acquired through theft or black market trade on a scale he did not want to imagine, and whose implications reached far beyond Mistral. The launcher was not, as it should have been, a vehicle. It was clearly improvised, designed for this one location, and for a single target. Cultists swarmed over the machinery. The work was not yet done. The rocket could not launch. But if Vahnsinn was showing him this, the labours below must be almost complete.

Rasp understood Vahnsinn's sanguine reaction to the defeat at Tolosa. Perhaps the baron had always hoped the need to fire the rocket would come. Or perhaps it was not a question of hope or eventualities. Perhaps he had always planned to commit this crime.

'You recognize it,' Vahnsinn insisted.

'Yes.' Rasp barely heard his own voice. It was a broken whisper, whipped away in tatters by the wind.

'Name it.'

Rasp did. He spoke two syllables, and learned the sound of his own despair. He said, 'Deathstrike.'

2. Yarrick

In the streets of Tolosa, in the great square outside the palace, the people were celebrating. They had died in the thousands. Entire habzones had been destroyed. On every street, the scars of the shelling still smoked. There were countless victims still trapped beneath the rubble of collapsed buildings. Even as the rescue parties continued digging, the people danced. The explosion of gratitude was orders of magnitude beyond what Wangenheim had been able to conjure for his festival. If he had managed to orchestrate events so that he appeared responsible for the end of the siege, the people of Tolosa would have been his forever. But he had been invisible during the entire conflict. The citizens had been aware of two forces in their streets: the enforcers, and the Imperial Guard. The Ecclesiarchy had been absent. So now there was celebration, and all gratitude flowed directly towards the Emperor, as it should.

In the Council chamber, the mood was different. We knew the war was not over. We had won a battle, and the chance to take the fight to the enemy. And the configuration had changed. The Sisters of Battle would be at our sides.

That prospect terrified Wangenheim.

'How can you go?' he demanded. He still sat on his raised throne. He still laboured under the illusion that any of us cared about his wailings. We were all free of him, now.

Setheno did him the courtesy of answering. I suspected this would be the last such favour that she would grant him. 'The daemonic influence must be purged from Imperial soil. We now have the opportunity to strike that enemy. Our duty is clear.'

'But–'

'So is my conscience.' And she turned her back on the cardinal.

We ignored him for the rest of the conference. He became nothing more than a background irritant. His time had passed. Tolosa was his to govern as he chose, and as he was able. Our concerns reached beyond the city now. The momentum was ours. But we had to know where to strike.

'The Vahnsinn holdings are extensive,' Krauss said. 'Numerous estates, dozens of manufactorum concerns. There are a few fortified locations, some of them strategically placed in relation to the manufactoria. The–'

'Karrathar,' Vercor said. 'He'll be at Karrathar.'

The steward had, at my suggestion, been invited to attend the Council. 'She seems to know everything about us,' I'd told Granach. 'We might as well learn a few things from her.' He didn't argue the point. I'm sure the cardinal's stuttering outrage at her inclusion helped strengthen my argument.

'Why there?' Granach asked.

'It's within easy reach of the city. More importantly, it's where the Vahnsinns have always gone to ground. Once they are inside, no one has ever been able to make them come out.'

'Then we will make history,' Granach said. 'We'll pry the coward from his hiding place, or we'll bring it down around his ears.'

Vercor nodded, but her expression was amused, sceptical.

Setheno was watching her closely, too. 'With your assistance, of course,' she added.

Some of Vercor's amusement drained away when she faced the sister superior. 'Of course,' she repeated.

An hour later, we mustered outside the walls of Tolosa. The regiment was a fraction of what it had been when we had made planetfall on Mistral. But we were still the Hammer of the Emperor, and we would shatter the enemy. We had dealt him one terrible blow. In that smoke-filled afternoon, standing on the blasted field of battle, not one of us doubted the outcome of the war.

The *conduct* of the war, though, was a bone of contention. The Sisters of Battle were not satisfied with the idea of the campaign being spearheaded by the Mortisians, or led by Granach. Seroff and I stood to one side with Captain Saultern and Veteran Sergeant Schranker, commanded to keep quiet, while Granach confronted Setheno.

'There are dangers ahead, colonel,' she said, 'that you do not have the training to confront. These are matters that go beyond commonplace faith.'

'Are you doubting my faith?' Granach demanded. 'Or that of my troops?'

'That it has the required strength, yes,' she said, as if she were surprised by the question.

I fumed, grinding my teeth in the effort it took to remain still. Seroff whispered, 'Your fault, you know.'

I looked sideways at him, at some level grateful for the distraction. '*What?*'

Seroff shrugged. 'That little operation of yours.'

'What about it?'

'A bit too brilliant, Seb. And she knows it was your idea, not the colonel's.'

'So I've somehow undermined his authority?'

'For those willing to find fault in him, yes.'

I was about to protest the illogic, then thought better of it.

'All politics, even now,' Seroff added.

'No,' I said. 'This isn't just political.' The battle in the depths of the palace rose before my mind's eye. Seroff didn't know. He hadn't seen what I had. For him, the daemonic still existed at an abstract level. 'They really don't think we're strong enough.'

'Aren't we?'

I hesitated. The fact that the Adepta Sororitas had some basis for regarding the Imperial Guard as a collection of weaker vessels did not make their view any easier to accept. 'We'll find out,' I said.

Urgent whispering behind me. I turned around. Kortner had arrived. He was speaking to Saultern, but kept glancing at me. 'What is it?' I asked.

'Trooper Betzner,' he said. 'Something's happening to him.'

Saultern looked confused. 'What do you mean?'

'Where?' I said, seized with premonition.

He led the way at a run. Saultern followed close behind. Deep in the ranks, a circle of witnesses had formed around Betzner. He had collapsed to his hands and knees. He was shaking with such violence that I feared for his spine. His teeth were chattering hard enough to split. He was gasping, and as I pushed my way through the uneasy troops, I thought I heard him trying to form words.

I knelt before him. He clutched at my coat. His grip was unbreakable. His face was grey, sheened with sweat. His mouth worked, struggling. There was an immensity inside him, and it was trying to burst him apart.

'What is it, trooper?' I asked.

'Fire…' he managed. He drew a grinding breath. 'Go…' The word was a plea. His eyes bulging, he said, '*Now*…' That was a plea, too. And consuming terror.

'We will,' I told him, and that shred of reassurance was enough. He collapsed, still shaking, but no longer struggling. He had done his duty, and was now riding out the seizure. I stood and turned to Saultern. I did not have the authority to order him, but I told him what needed to be done. 'We have to leave,' I said. 'Immediately.'

He nodded, and he was already mobilizing his company as I ran back to Granach. He and Setheno were still at loggerheads, though they had paused in their argument, startled by the sound of rapid activity in the troops. 'Colonel,' I said, 'if we don't move out now, we never will.'

'What has happened?' Setheno asked.

'It hasn't, yet.'

I hoped she wouldn't ask more. There were questions surrounding Betzner, questions I could no longer avoid, but now was not the time. Setheno turned away from us and signalled to her Sisters to move out.

That was enough for Granach. He gave me a hard look, but he issued the orders, and the regiments lurched into movement.

2. Wangenheim

He commanded that the doors of the Chapel Majoris be opened to all. The citizens were exuberant, and he should harness that energy. With the most powerful military levers of his power leaving Tolosa, Wangenheim had to leverage the means still at his disposal with care. To be part of the celebration was a first step. To be seen to be leading it was the second, and so he performed the Great Victory Mass.

So many people came, their numbers spilling out of the chapel, through the halls of the palace, and out the main entrance. The scene was too great a gift to be an accident. It was the Emperor's will. The population had come to him after all, and he seized the opportunity.

He conducted the mass in two parts, beginning with what he described as a private benediction to the huge crowd in the Chapel Majoris. Then he moved to the balcony over the palace's main entrance. There he preached his sermon, his voice resounding from vox-casters on the palace walls, retransmitted to speakers across the city. The square still bore the scars and bloodstains of the massacre, but that was nothing in a city that had been so profoundly battered. Below him were the thousands upon thousands, packed even more tightly than the night of the festival, their joy unfettered, their enthusiasm beyond anything he had ever been able to manufacture. They had come to pray, and he was their cardinal, and so the people were now his as they had never been before.

Their rapture became his. The city became his. As he spoke, he revelled in the irony of his triumph. In the end, the barons had played the role he had assigned them, and done so with a hundredfold more force than he had ever dared to hope.

He drew the sermon to an end, and thought about vengeance. The barons would be annihilated shortly. They were no longer his concern. He had never seen them as loyal to begin with. The disloyalty of those he should have been able to trust, though, was a different story, and warranted a different sort of punishment. Vercor had betrayed centuries of tradition. Time she was ended, and her replacement decanted. That was a simple matter. More complex was what to do with Setheno. The Sisters of the Order of the Piercing Thorn had failed him, and by extension the Ecclesiarchy, at a moment of great need. They would all be censured, but the decisions were Setheno's. What was called for, he thought, was a long, slow, painful fall from grace.

The idea made him smile. He let the prospect of retaliation fill him with beatitude as he finished the mass. He spread his arms to embrace the people, his cherubim singing with joy. The people embraced him back with a roar of thanksgiving and triumph. The roar built, louder and louder, wave upon wave. He stood with his arms spread, head back, feeling a new apex of power. He saw a streak of fire piercing the clouds, and for a moment he conceived of it as the physical manifestation of his will.

But then he realized the absurdity of the fantasy. The reality of the fire struck home. And then the terrible seconds began. They were an eternity during which he had all the time he needed to see what was coming, to know that this was a missile from which there would be no running, and no shelter.

Below, the people looked up at him, and no higher. They did not see what was coming. They celebrated, and their happiness was a grating irony in his ears.

All his glory, all his power, and all his plans fell away from him, like water through his hands.

And though the seconds were eternal, still he was not granted the blurring comfort of tears before the fire came.

3. Yarrick

We made for the mountains at forced-march speed. They were our target. I didn't know if they could be our refuge. I didn't know what we were rushing towards, or fleeing from. I don't know if my word alone would have convinced Granach to act as quickly as he did. But Setheno took me seriously, and that was confirmation enough. The regiments moved with purpose and speed. With an urgency that none of us fully understood, we put several kilometres between ourselves and Tolosa.

And then…

The missile was a great howl. I looked up. Its passage was a sword wound in the sky. I knew what it must be. I knew that this was the shape of Betzner's terror. I controlled the impulse to run blindly. My reason knew what the animal within me did not: nothing I did now would make a difference.

Except…

Be the symbol.

My mind flew to this conclusion in a fraction of a second. In the moments that remained, I stopped walking, and turned, standing straight, to face Tolosa. *Unbowed,* I thought. *Unbowed. Unbowed. Unbow–*

The Deathstrike hit. I shut my eyes for the moment of impact. The flash was still blinding. I looked again to see the light of day become a paltry thing before the killing glare of the plasma detonation. The fireball expanded, boiling, furious, to consume all of Tolosa. I forced myself to watch, forced myself to understand the full horror of what I was seeing. The city was in the heart of a star. Down every street, superheated incandescence raced. It devoured everything. Some buildings disintegrated. Others, a little further from the zero of the blast, collapsed. All were destroyed.

Tolosa was scorched from the surface of Mistral.

The fireball continued to expand. It reached beyond the city walls. It was a tide of fire coming for us. Had I been proud of my works when the train had exploded? That event was wretched and puny compared to this.

The shock wave reached us. I could not stand when it hit. I was slammed to the ground. The force swept over the regiments like a scythe through wheat. We were flattened. Setheno managed to remain standing, faith and will refusing to bend the knee before anything except the Emperor. But then she too was lifted into the air and hurled down. Then came the wind, and then the heat, the stages of destruction familiar from the night before, but a thousand times greater.

I forced myself to my feet. I would not stay down before the enemy's blow. I would stand. I leaned into the battering wind. I faced the spectacle of absolute waste. I stared down the fire that reached as high as the clouds.

The great thunder came, and when it passed, the fireball gave way to a cloud of smoke and dust whose mushroom shape triggered an atavistic despair. It was the shape of all things ending. I stared at this too. I made myself understand all the implications of this immensity. This was Vahnsinn's act. He could do this huge thing. This was the measure of our enemy.

We could so easily have been there. Of all the horrors before me, what most disturbed me was the horror that had not occurred. The regiments had survived, and the reasons for their survival smacked of capricious luck. If that fit had not come upon Betzner, if he had been ignored, if he had been killed on the train the night before, if Setheno had not agreed with me, if... if... if...

I wanted to point to a decision that had followed a chain of logic and evidence, and say *here, this moment, right here* was what saved us. But there was only the symptom of a single trooper, a symptom whose only explanation would open the door to another form of darkness. There was no good reason for any of us to be alive. No strategy or perceptiveness had come to our aid. Only chance. Only...

The answer came, as it should have at the start, had I not been weak.

'The Emperor protects!' I shouted, renewed in strength and faith. Only the soldiers in my immediate vicinity could hear me, but I spoke in the certainty that my words would spread to all – not because they were mine, but because they were a simple truth.

To my right, I noticed that Setheno was standing, her presence so emphatic I wondered if I had truly seen her fall. She was watching me. I knew she couldn't make out what I said. I knew that didn't matter. 'Look at what the enemy has done,' I continued. 'Look and feel no fear. Feel hatred. Feel the need for revenge. Fuel the fire with which you will burn the heretic. Tolosa is destroyed. You may think that everything we have fought and bled for these last few days has been lost. This is not so! We do not fight for land, or buildings, or a city, or even the millions of lives therein. No, not even them. We fight for our Emperor. We fight for our Creed! It is greater than any of us, and what more proof do we need of the inevitability of its victory than the fact that we still live? The enemy sought to immolate us with the greatest of his weapons, and he has failed. Let us march on, our purpose forged anew in this furnace. We are the sword point of the Creed, and it is time for the infidel to taste our steel!'

No one cheered, which was as it should be. Vahnsinn had struck us a hard blow. But despite the magnitude of his crime, it was militarily insignificant.

No. That wasn't true. The annihilation of Tolosa had great significance. I saw it in the eyes of the troops after I had finished speaking. We had nothing left to defend on Mistral except for the Imperial Creed itself. Now Vahnsinn would learn how dangerous he had made us.

CHAPTER 17
THE NEED TO KNOW

1. Vahnsinn

In the chapel, Vahnsinn raged. 'How could we *not* know?' he demanded. The other barons said nothing. As he stalked the circle, his robes flapped in odd ways. They were becoming too heavy, as if they were made of leather instead of silk. He had not removed them since his return to Karrathar, and now they tugged and pulled at him. He was finding it difficult to walk as he once did, and that did not help his mood. He rounded on Eichen. 'We should have known! Why didn't we?'

The big man took a step back. His flesh wobbled when he did so. He had grown much heavier over the last few days. His complexion was now permanently the dark red of cardiac arrest. Layers of folded skin like melted wax spilled over the collar of his robe. He was losing form. 'Bad luck...' Eichen began.

Vahnsinn backhanded him. His knuckles were ragged and bony. They tore gouges across Eichen's cheek. The blood was thick, dark, slow. 'What have we been learning? Why have we presented burned offerings? Luck shouldn't hold any mysteries for us any more! If you can speak those words at all, you are unworthy of the revelations we have received.'

Eichen cringed. On his knees, he begged forgiveness. He kept swallowing his words. He sounded like bubbling tar. Perhaps he was the weak link. Perhaps he was why they had not known the Mortisians would leave Tolosa before the Deathstrike arrived. Vahnsinn thought about ripping his head from his shoulders. Instead, he turned away in disgust. The problem was deeper than one fool.

The chapel was directly beneath the torture hall. Sigils were engraved with deep channels into the floor. They were fed by gutters that ran down the walls, drawing blood from the torments above. Around the periphery, remains were stacked. These were the sacrifices used to augment the constant flow of death. They should have been sufficient. The war should be over.

'Get out,' he told the barons. When they had left, some of them shuffling, at least one hopping instead of walking, he turned to the altar. It was a deceptively delicate construction. It was made of wrought iron and the treated bones of Preacher Guilhem, the man who had first spoken the words of truth in Vahnsinn's ear. He had almost turned Guilhem away the day he had first appeared at the door of Grauben Manor. The man had been ragged of clothing and flesh, his eyes filled with madness. But he managed to talk his way past the serf at the door and into Vahnsinn's study, and there begin speaking to the baron. Vahnsinn could no longer remember what

Guilhem had actually said that evening. The words had vanished back into the warp. He remembered only their effect. He had been transfixed by their revelations. He had not left the house for the next three days, doing nothing but listen to the gospel of patterns, of weaving, of change.

Though the truths were now branded on his soul, only one word from his time of conversion remained lodged in his memory; it was a name, and one he had never spoken aloud: *Ghalshannha*. It was a sharp lash of barbed wire across his cortex. Whenever he thought that name, the world seemed to come apart and re-knit itself in ways both surprising and inevitable.

His new faith had taught him about the nature of change. It had taught him to embrace it, to revel in mutability and corruption. And it had taught him the concrete rewards of worship. He had known every one of Wangenheim's steps before the cardinal had even conceived of them. But the rewards had a cost, and the first to pay the price was Guilhem himself. The preacher had done more than accept his fate. He had insisted upon it, even when the skin had been stripped from his skeleton. He had screamed then, but he had also laughed in the ecstasy of a prophecy fulfilled.

Vahnsinn had taken his bones and used them as the heart of the altar. It was a framework whose shape was different depending upon the angle from which it was viewed. From the side, it resembled a box within a box. From the front, it was a long, serpentine coil. It was black with pain and old blood.

Why had the foresight failed him? He had not anticipated the derailing of the munitions train. And he had been just a few hours late with the Deathstrike. Were the gifts not sufficient? 'What more do you want?' he asked the metal and bone.

Silence.

He stalked to the rear of the chapel, where prisoners were held in cages with razored floors. He selected a man and a woman, both former serfs who had refused to convert. He hauled their mewling, bleeding forms to the altar. He chained them to the construct. 'What do you want?' he asked again. He had a long knife with a triple-curved blade at his belt, but he did not draw it. Instead, he went to work on the sacrifices with his hands and with his teeth. When he had done tearing, the floor was awash with vitae. The air was thick with humid stench.

'What do you want?' he cried.

The whispers began at last. The voice at the base of his skull told him what he must do. He nodded. He stepped forward until he was touching the altar. He drew his blade. He began to saw.

He started with his nose.

Shortly after, the voice told him what he needed to know.

2. *Setheno*

The Chimera jounced over huge ruts in the road. It jolted to a halt for a moment as its wheels spun for purchase. They found it, and the vehicle jerked forward again. Inside, its passengers were knocked around the compartment. Setheno kept herself grounded and did not move. She stood over Granach's make-shift command table, studying the hololith of approaches to Karrathar. There were three. The primary one, which still appeared to receive some use, ran in parallel to the maglev track. The other two had once, millennia ago, been caravan routes through the mountains. Granach had sent diversionary forces along the main approach and the more direct of the disused trails. The bulk of the regiments was taking the slowest, most tortuous path. It was in a state of ongoing disintegration, falling apart like fragmented memory. It went much higher than the other two approaches, climbed and dropped abruptly through sharp turns. At times, it seemed to disappear entirely. It was miraculous that the Chimeras were still able to advance.

Granach's strategy made sense, though. Vahnsinn could not interdict all the routes without spreading his forces too thin. So the Imperials would draw his attention on the other routes, giving the true army the chance to get that much closer to Karrathar. It was the next step that didn't satisfy her. The Mortisians were not equipped for a long siege, but Vercor's descriptions of the fortress's emplacement did not suggest any ready alternative.

Except perhaps a small insertion force.

She turned her attention away from the map. Yarrick was speaking quietly to Granach. The commissar had mentioned an insertion earlier. His instincts, she thought, were sound, though he showed signs of excessive tolerance. She had questions about one of the troopers under his jurisdiction. The questions would wait, for the moment, but not much longer.

In the far corner of the compartment, Vercor was leaning against a bulkhead, her face blank. The mercenary had been subdued since the annihilation of Tolosa. She had dropped her posture of amused cynicism, answering the colonel's questions with flat, precise disinterest.

Setheno brushed past the command table and approached Vercor. 'You are troubled,' she said.

'I'm not interested in your sermons,' Vercor answered.

'I do not preach.' She left that to others. 'I chastise.'

A flicker of the amusement returned. 'I can well imagine. With gun and blade.'

Setheno said nothing. She stood before Vercor until the other woman sighed and said, 'I am the end of my family's history.'

'What do you mean?'

'My genetic succession was stored in the Ecclesiarchal palace. The name of Vercor now ends with me.'

This type of concern was mysterious to Setheno. She knew it existed, particularly in aristocratic families. Even the Adeptus Astartes knew a form of it, given the importance of their own genetic continuity. The Sisters of Battle had no issue. The only continuity was in the life of the orders, and in the perpetuation and defence of the Faith. Still, she was curious. The woman was a good fighter. Setheno needed to understand whoever she might be alongside in combat. The mercenary was distasteful, but could not be ignored. She said, 'What does that name mean?'

Now Vercor was silent.

'It meant nothing,' Setheno pursued. 'You have lost nothing. Now you are part of an honourable struggle. You should be giving thanks.'

Still nothing.

The Chimera stopped again, less suddenly. 'The road's out,' the driver called back.

'I'll have a look,' Yarrick said. He dropped the rear loading ramp. He stepped outside.

And then war roared, and the Chimera was turning end over end.

* * *

3. *Yarrick*

They knew. My mind shouted the words as I was hurled to the ground. *They knew where we were. They knew. They knew. They knew.*

It began with another artillery barrage, and it was unnaturally precise. Fired kilometres away, from positions we could not possibly see, the shells came down to punish us for daring to think we could trespass on Vahnsinn territory. The impact was devastating. I was surrounded by flame, explosions, fountains of earth and rock, and the hurtling, shredded death of soldiers. I was thrown down. Before me, like a series of still hololiths breaking into static, I saw the Chimera topple into the crevasse before it. I saw it tipping forwards. I saw it nose down, near vertical. Then it was gone.

We were in a narrow pass. The slopes on either side were steep, but they weren't cliffs. I staggered to my feet, deafened by blasts. Flying rock struck the side of my head. Dazed, I plunged to my right, charging up the mountainside in a lurching, hunch-backed run. At a barely conscious level, I attempted to use the very accuracy of the bombardment to my advantage, reaching for a higher ground that was not the target. And I was right. Though the world-ending sound of the shells still hammered at my skull, the explosions were behind and below me.

They knew. They knew. They knew.

I drew my sword and pistol. I charged at nothing at all, tilting at fate, my throat tearing with a roar I could not hear. I defied the disaster. I denied it. I demanded an enemy I could kill, and the Emperor provided. The shelling ended. The next phase of the ambush began. The heretics burst from camouflaged emplacements on the mountainside. Vahnsinn was not relying on the remote destruction of artillery. He wanted to do far more than smash our advance. He wanted to exterminate us. And now his mad army raced down, towards me, towards our savaged regiments, with ecstatic fury.

I matched their rage. I surpassed it. For all I knew, I was the only one on these slopes, but I ran upwards even faster, though my lungs were ragged with effort and smoke. I fired at the first glimpse of the foe, and the different pain in my chest told me that I laughed as a cultist's head exploded. If I was about to die, I would do so bringing the fight to the enemy, teaching the vermin that though we might be killed, we could never be defeated.

I was not alone. Las-fire streaked past me. I did not look back, but I felt the strength of my fellow troops behind me. We stormed up the slope. The enemy had the higher ground, but he was abandoning it in favour of a massive charge. In the end, that only brought the heretics faster into the teeth of our wrath.

The two forces hit. Combat was awkward on a gradient so steep. It took little to be knocked to the ground, and falling meant never rising again. I grounded myself, planting my blade in the scree when I felt my balance going. I fired shells in quick succession, sweeping my arm in an arc. Every trigger pull sent another cultist to damnation. After the fury of the initial charge, I entered a cold, mechanical detachment. Like a cogitator slaved to a servitor body, I did nothing but pick targets and take them down. The heretics obliged me. Their numbers made them impossible to miss, but the nature of their attack also delivered them to my lethal mercies. I saw fewer and fewer traces of the original uniforms and liveries. As the appearance of the traitors fell deeper into Chaos, so did their tactics. They cared for nothing except to surrender to their bloodlust. After the uncanny precision of the ambush came the tumult of the mob. The cultists were a tide that could sweep us away. So we would have to be rocks.

It was hard to believe these creatures were still human. They were feral. Many of them didn't carry rifles. Some carried no weapons at all, and hurled themselves at me, seeking my eyes with their fingers. When my pistol needed reloading, I switched to two-handed sweeps with my sword. I hunkered down, immovable. I gutted, dismembered, decapitated. A mound of bodies accumulated around me. Blood ran in streams down the mountainside. Soon there were enough corpses to give me cover. The heretic army flowed around me, carried down by its momentum. The worst of the fighting shifted to the gutted road. I cut open another traitor, and I suddenly had a moment of breathing space.

I reloaded my pistol. I took in the full picture of the battle. My instinct was to plunge back into the thick of the slaughter, but I forced myself to think of the mission instead of the immediate moment. We had to reach Karrathar. We could easily bog down here.

The road ahead was gone. The crevasse that had swallowed the Chimera ended on the right-hand side. We could advance by taking the slope. I looked higher. The ridges of the mountains were inviting. We were only a few kilometres from the target. We could make it there on foot. But we had to extricate ourselves from the ambush.

The cultists' numbers were too great. Even if killing them were a simple process, it would take too long. I felt myself grow sick as I realized what I had to do. I had to reverse the equation. We were not being bogged down by the enemy; he was bogged down with us. That meant I had to regard the largest part of the regiments as the means to that end.

Sickening implications unfolded before my mind's eye. I was consumed with self-loathing at the same time that I realized I had no choice, if there was to be any chance of winning the war. I shook the thoughts away. They could paralyse me. I started moving again, committing myself to whatever destiny awaited. The entire decision process had taken only a couple of seconds. That was still too long. I had to move quickly.

The troops who had been the first to follow me up the slope were all from Saultern's company. At the time I put this down to lucky coincidence. I was naïve. I had been putting so much energy in to fulfilling the commissar's symbolic duty, and yet I was too young, too blinkered to understand the consequences. These soldiers didn't just happen to see me. They had been looking for me.

Now they were turning to head back into the fray. With them was Seroff, who had been outside the Chimera.

'Dominic!' I shouted.

He turned and looked back at me. I could see his blood-spattered face clearly in the moonlight. He was puzzled about why I was standing there. I shook my head. If there had been more of us, perhaps a pincer movement would have made sense. It would serve no purpose now. I said, 'We have to try something else.'

He hesitated, but not long. He started back up the slope. I called to Saultern and gestured for him to follow. For the first time in my life, I turned my back on a struggle. I knew Saultern's troops would feel the same reluctance. I prayed I was not leading them to damnation.

In the maelstrom of the conflict below us, there was an

eye of order centred at the crevasse. The Sisters of Battle had assumed a defensive posture along three sides. They were an impregnable wall of ceramite and bolter fire. The crevasse was at the formation's rear. As I drew parallel with their position, I saw that they were protecting the Chimera. The crevasse was deep, but narrow. The command vehicle had fallen about ten metres before becoming wedged between rock walls. Three of the Sisters were finding their way down to help. Setheno was already out and climbing back to the surface, punching rock to create handholds. Krauss was not far behind her. Granach emerged from the upended carrier. He leaned on Vercor.

I called to Setheno. She did not look at me. I tried again. This time she looked up. She saw me. I made no gesture, trusting her to understand. Granach did. He nodded. Setheno didn't respond, and I couldn't afford to wait. From my decision to this moment, less than half a minute had passed, but the roil of combat was moving up the slope again. We would be sucked in, and all would be lost.

I pointed up, at the ridge. 'There!' I said. 'We take that route. We take any route necessary. We make for Karrathar, and we bring this to an end!' I didn't know how we would end the war. But I had the will.

Thirty strong, we made for the ridge, and we were unopposed. The enemy was consumed with the fight on the road. I pushed away the knowledge that I was using my comrades as sacrifices. I focused on the mission. All of us, on the slope or in the fray, had only one true duty in this moment, and I was following it. I looked when we were almost at the top. The Sisters of the Order of the Piercing Thorn were following us. The heretics could no more stop them than they could the rotation of Mistral. I was glad for Granach's understanding.

With the Adepta Sororitas present, the outcome of the struggle in the pass would be assured, but the greater need for the Sisters of Battle was elsewhere. They were coming with us. So, I saw, was Krauss.

Vercor was with them, too. I didn't try to fathom her motivation. But she was useful.

The ridge climbed over a low peak, then went downwards to a pass a hundred metres lower than the one we had left behind, and running east to west. It, in turn, was intersected by a shallow gully that ended at another peak. We were working our way through a maze of geology. There was no direct route. I tried not to think about what time remained to us.

The wind shrieked between the peaks, carrying ragged echoes of the battle. As we advanced, some of the gusts brought us sensory fragments of the hell we sought. There was a stench of bad pain and worse deaths. And though it was impossible, there were sounds, too. Perhaps they were not true sounds. Perhaps they were another thing that slithered into our minds and tricked our ears. The look Seroff gave me told me that he heard the same thing I did. The closer we came to Karrathar, the more we heard its screams.

CHAPTER 18
KARRATHAR

1. Vahnsinn

He collapsed against the altar. The stream of future events slipped from his grasp. His own blood and that of a hundred prisoners had been exhausted. But he had been granted the knowledge he needed, and had acted upon it. He had learned the route that the main force of the Mortisians would take. He had been told where best to set the ambush, and when to launch it. He had learned of the advance of the diversionary forces, and how much of his own strength it would take to counter them. He had learned much. He was drained. It cost him much to be in that state of awareness, to hear the whispers that spoke of unfolding time, of actions yet to be, of destinies and of dooms, and still retain enough of a stake in the here and now to issue commands.

Vahnsinn brought a hand up to his face. He touched the

novel absence where his nose had been. Only hanging scraps of flesh there now, and a jagged point of cartilage. He let his finger explore the edges of the new gap in his face. If he grabbed the flesh and pulled, would he yank the rest away? Would he strip himself of all disguises, and be the exposed skull? He imagined the terror he would inspire, and the pleasure of the image gave him the energy to rise.

He made his way out of the chapel. In the Hall of Truth above, the other barons, his fellow disciples of change, were on the dais, gathered around Rasp. They were hard at work. With blade, with hammer and with bare hands, many of them were taking prisoners apart, making them into object lessons of the slow death. Others were giving Rasp a more direct experience of that promise. They attacked his nerve endings with fire and cold. They bled him. They marked him with hair-thin trails of acid. All the while, Elleta Gotho leaned on her cane and spoke to him. She told him stories. She recounted parables that were all the more potent for being actual events. She was revealing the wonders of Chaos to the lord commissar. She was instructing him on the underlying fabric of the universe: tormenting change.

The barons parted as Vahnsinn approached Rasp. Gotho ceased speaking and stepped back. Vahnsinn stood over his friend. He was hard to recognize, though he was still fortunate. He still had all his limbs. 'So?' Vahnsinn asked. 'Now, do you see?'

Rasp groaned. He said something, but his syllables were bloodied mush. Only the denial came through.

Vahnsinn frowned. He no longer had eyebrows. He felt the puckering of his scarred, scabbed skin. 'Why are you fighting me, Simeon? What point is there in doing so?'

Another answer of soft, wet sounds that once were words. Even so, 'Emperor' came through clearly. Rasp hadn't broken yet.

Vahnsinn grabbed Rasp's hair. He yanked the lord commissar's head to the side. 'You will see,' he said. 'You will kneel.' The urge to start chopping off fingers and legs was strong. A small lapse, and he would kill Rasp. And that was forbidden.

When the voice whispered, there were things it did not tell him. There were lacunae in his understanding of the future. Vahnsinn knew enough to make his plans, but what he did not know troubled him. He didn't know if it was being withheld from him, if there were aspects of destiny so contingent as to be completely unknowable. There were costs to his ignorance. He hadn't been able to wipe out the Imperials along with Tolosa. He was not allowed to kill Rasp, and he did not know why. There was a role being reserved for Rasp. Vahnsinn could see that. He resented the importance it must have. He worried about what his ignorance might portend. But he also knew better than to disobey.

Well. The more Rasp resisted, the greater his suffering. And now Vahnsinn could add to his burden of despair. 'The war is over,' he said. 'Colonel Granach marched for Karrathar, and he has failed. He tried to come at us where we could not see him. That isn't possible. I see everything. Do you understand?' He gave Rasp's head another shake. 'There is nothing left of the regiments. You are alone.'

What was that sound this time? Still a denial, yes, but was it defiant? Or was it the cry of a man whose days now extended into grinding night?

Vahnsinn smiled, enjoying the sensation of loose, shifting lips. 'Don't worry,' he said. 'You aren't lost. You're where you were always meant to be.'

* * *

2. *Yarrick*

The maglev bridge was above us. We had emerged on the valley floor from a cleft in the mountains so narrow that we traversed it in single file. Under the shadow of the bridge, we stood a decent chance of reaching Karrathar's peak undetected. The problem was climbing that peak, and entering the fortress. As we crossed the valley, I worried over my lack of inspiration. To our rear, we heard the sounds of three separate battles. Perhaps our forces might yet punch through, but the best I could hope for was that the bulk of Vahnsinn's army was occupied.

As we neared Karrathar's forbidding rise, Krauss said, 'There is no going up that road without falling to enemy fire. We should have taken the bridge. There is still time.'

'We would be even more exposed there,' I said. We were repeating an argument an hour old.

'Speed,' he said. 'We could move quickly, straight into the heart of the fortress. We would be difficult targets.'

'They wouldn't have to target us,' Setheno told him. 'They could simply blow the bridge. That is their security's obvious weak point. Do you think they would not have it properly defended?'

'And what we are doing, how is it better?' Krauss demanded.

It wasn't. It simply brought us closer. I had no answer. Neither did Setheno. In another few minutes, we would be facing the choice of taking a death-trap road or attempting a vertical climb. I was faced with the possibility that perhaps there were no good choices. Perhaps there was only a selection of defeats.

I turned away from that darkness. I refused to believe it.

We drew closer still, and we were already engaged in a struggle. Karrathar's initial defence was its identity. The fortress's corruption spread over the land, through the air, and into our souls like a slick of oil. The architecture was ancient. Karrathar had seen centuries upon centuries of service, and its masters had been faithful to the Imperial Creed. But now, some subtle alteration must have happened to its form. It was darkness built of stone. Its towers and battlements seemed twisted slightly out of true, so little that we still saw vertical lines, but enough that our spirits recoiled. And the stench was growing stronger, the screams more continuous, more insistent, more sinister. The wind might have been filled with the howls of human pain, but the cries might also be imitations. Mockeries. The Sisters of Battle took point, marching against the toxic miasma. Their faith seemed to conjure a shield that blocked the worst of the despair from infecting the rest of us.

Seroff moved up beside me. 'What are we going to find in there?' he asked, keeping his voice down.

'Nothing good.'

'And rather more than nothing.'

I nodded. 'Yes. I fear so.'

'What you encountered in the Ecclesiarchal palace…'

'It was bad, Dominic.'

'Was our training adequate?'

'For dealing with what I saw? No. For being able to continue to act? Yes.'

'Then I suppose that will do.'

'It must.'

By bringing up that battle with the daemonic, Seroff put an idea in my head. 'Give me a minute,' I said, and worked my way back along the line of troops. I found Betzner. He was looking at Karrathar with loathing. His face had turned grey. We were all feeling the effects of this unholy place, but his suffering was the most pronounced. I knew there was a reckoning coming with Betzner. I did not question his loyalty. I also knew that I could not protect him from his waiting destiny. Aware that I might be making matters worse for him, I said, 'Where is the problem, trooper?'

He blinked at me. 'Commissar?'

'Focus on your distress. I know that everything about what we are approaching is corrupt, but it is not featureless, is it?'

He closed his eyes for a moment. He shook his head.

'Learn from it, Betzner.'

'Yes, commissar.' His voice was a whisper. Something dark was taking a toll on his physical strength as well as his soul. He kept up the pace of the march, though, and his grip on his rocket launcher never wavered. His eyes were open now, but lost focus. He was looking at something that I, thanks be to the Emperor, would never be able to see. After a minute, he gasped in shock. At the same time, I thought I heard, faintly, the sound of running water. 'Oh no,' he groaned.

'What is it?'

'Close. There.' He pointed to a spot at the base of the mountain, several hundred metres to the right of where the road began its zigzag up the slope. It was very close to the last of the valley floor's maglev bridge pillars. 'Commissar,' he said, 'I don't think I can go there.'

'You can and you will, trooper. We will all be asked to make sacrifices before this day is done.'

He did not argue, and fell into a tortured silence. I moved forward to the front lines, and spoke to Setheno. She made for the spot. We drew near, and I heard rushing water again. The sound repeated at irregular intervals. Then we were close enough to see the cause, and I understood Betzner's pain.

Nestled into the cliff face was a sewer outflow. The effluent poured into a narrow canal that drained away to the south along the base. There was another discharge as we arrived. The water was thick with blood and a slurry of human remains.

'Throne,' Seroff muttered.

'What is this?' Vercor asked. For the first time, I heard her express a genuine emotion: horror.

'There are shadows darker than yours, mercenary,' Setheno told her.

The pipe was a couple of metres in diameter. There was a grille over its mouth.

'This is how we get in,' I said.

Enginseer Bellavis came forward. The plasma cutter on his servo-arm sliced through the bars of the grille along the circumference of the pipe. It took him less than a minute to open the way. I approached the noxious opening. Bellavis shone a light into its depths. It sloped upward at a steep angle. Not so steep that we couldn't take it. The air inside was humid, foul, tainted in ways I preferred not to contemplate.

This was my gamble. I climbed in first, before Setheno or Krauss had a chance. Morale was not an issue for the Sisters of Battle. They would be eager to face the horrors that awaited us, and purge them with righteous anger. The men and women of the Imperial Guard were no cowards. Nor did they lack faith. But unlike Krauss, the rank and file were not trained for what was coming. They were, I was sure, going to encounter things they should not even know existed. While Bellavis had been at work, I had seen dread sinking deeper and deeper roots into the faces of all the soldiers around us.

No military force, human or xenos, would give the Mortisians pause. But those who do not worry for the wellbeing of their souls are fools. And there were no fools in our company.

So I made an example of myself. I walked in first, showing my comrades my eagerness for battle, my mockery of the poisoned atmosphere. 'The foulness is only air,' I called out. 'What harm can it do us?' Plenty, of course, but I wished to hold onto an illusion of normalcy for as long as possible.

We climbed, with the Adepta Sororitas in the lead once more. The dark was clammy, moist. Breathing was uncomfortably like chewing. Every few minutes, we had to pause, gripping the walls as best we could as we weathered another flash flood of bloody water. Setheno and her squad were immovable and unmoved, the filth splashing against their armour and sliding off, helpless to besmirch their sanctity. The rest of us were drenched in gore. Setheno looked back at one point, taking in the mere humans who willingly struggled to reach the darkest of battlefields. She wore her helmet, but in the cock of her head, I imagined that I saw a glimmer of sympathy.

Krauss was level with me. About half an hour into our ordeal, he favoured Betzner with a pointed look, then said to me, 'You are playing with fire, commissar.'

'Oh?'

'The means by which you found our way in are dangerously close to witchcraft.'

This is your concern now? I thought. *Here?* I bit back what I wanted to say. 'I disagree,' I said. 'Would you prefer us to have been gunned down on that road? I used the resources of our forces.'

'That is sophistry, and you know it. There is no allowance for expediency in matters of heresy.'

'If Sister Superior Setheno is able to tolerate the help of Trooper Betzner in this operation, inquisitor, I would think that should satisfy you.'

It didn't. In the dark, covered in filth, his inflexible pride shone like a cold beacon. I had no doubt that Krauss was an aristocrat by birth, but he was also an aristocrat of faith. Those beneath him were lesser in all things, including orthodoxy. From an Inquisitorial perspective, that made them criminal.

That he was so unwavering in his duty made him an exemplary inquisitor of his kind. In this moment, his dogmatism made me grind my teeth.

Krauss said, 'There will be a reckoning.'

'I know. And there is another approaching. Would it be all right if we took them in order?'

He didn't bother to answer my retort, which was his equivalent of largesse. 'You cannot protect him any longer.' That was his equivalent of sympathy.

'If you think I would do anything to violate the laws of our Creed, inquisitor, then you still know nothing about me.'

We fell silent.

Up. Deeper into the mountain. The sewer curving, joined by other, smaller pipes. Darkness behind us and before us. We moved in a bubble of our own light, sustained by duty and faith. We knew that we were making progress because the stench grew worse, as did the shrieks. And then, at last, the screams were real sounds. They bounced down the tunnel, hollow pain distorted by distance. They summoned us. We moved closer and closer to the heart of agony.

Then there were new sounds. We heard the clank of chains, snatches of conversation, threads of chanting. We were close. Saultern and I sent hand signals down the line of troops: silence. Another few dozen metres, another curve, and the slope became more gradual. The pipe ended at what appeared to be a metal wall. There were sloshing noises on the other side. After a minute, the wall rose, a shutter, and released another flood. Setheno and Sister Liberata stepped forward and held the shutter up while the rest of us passed through into the space beyond. It was a reservoir of death's leavings. It extended for hundreds of metres, farther than our lights could reach. The ceiling, supported by squat brick pillars, was low enough that we had to duck our heads. Setheno was forced to crouch.

Perhaps, before corruption had come to the Vahnsinns, this had been the means of clearing away the waste of everyday life in a fortress of this size. Now blood and worse trickled in through dozens of grilles set into the low ceiling. Water streamed in from the other side of the chamber. It came, I supposed, from an aquifer. When the levels rose high enough, the shutter was activated, sending the sins of Karrathar down into the valley.

The grilles were irregularly spaced. Dim, flickering, unhealthy light filtered through them. I pictured the reservoir occupying most of the space beneath the lowest levels of the castle. Each room would have its own sluices. We had to pick our point of entry. I spotted a cluster of grates. Perhaps an important chamber lay above them. I waded over to the cluster. I crouched just to one side of the grates, avoiding the fall of blood. It was difficult to see anything, but there were more voices here. I pointed upwards.

Krauss, Saultern, Kortner and Bellavis joined me. While the Sisters of Battle aimed their bolters, Kortner and the enginseer prepared demolition charges and affixed them to two grilles a few metres apart. While they worked, the chanting rose in volume. It gathered definition. It was incomprehensible, but I kept hearing a repeated group of syllables: *Ghalshannha*.

Saultern looked at me with a kind of pleading. I saw the maturing officer feeling himself devolve back into the untested child of privilege. He seemed willing to defer all command decisions to me. That would do none of us any good. I risked a whisper. 'You will be strong enough, captain,' I told him. 'You will do your duty. You did in the Ecclesiarchal palace.'

'That was different.'

'No. This is just more.'

He grimaced. 'Thank you, commissar. I am comforted.' The irony was a good sign. He was steeling himself.

Behind him, Krauss eyed our exchange. His contempt was obvious.

The charges were ready. We backed away. We readied our weapons. I nodded at Bellavis.

The detonation brought down the entire section of the ceiling between the two grilles. It collapsed in a jumble of stone. Some robed figures came with it, killed by the explosion or crushed by the rubble. The Mortisians sent up a suppressive barrage of las-fire as we climbed up the broken slope.

We emerged at one end of a gigantic hall. Though I had led us here, knowing that bringing the fight to the enemy would mean travelling to the heart of hell, I was staggered by the reality. This was where Karrathar's twisting out of true found its source. We were in a place where darkness and torchlight smeared together. The walls and pillars were still stone, but they moved behind one's back, and were on the verge of taking their first breath.

Cultists were here in their hundreds, and they were outnumbered by the victims. Stacked along the walls, beside pillars and next to torture devices were rows of cages. Many of them were empty, but there was still a near-infinite supply of fresh meat for the sacrifices. The prisoners howled and gibbered, their minds already given over to hopeless madness. There would be no rescue for these souls. They were nothing more than fuel for obscenities present in such numbers that they were becoming a single crime so massive that it was dissolving the borders of the materium. We had stepped into a world of blood and screams. That blood was an offering, those screams were a communion, atrocity was worship, and everything was tilting into a maelstrom of endless, horrific change.

Acts of murder and torture blended together around the pillars of the hall. At first, there seemed to be no pattern, just a vast riot of death. But my eyes were drawn with such force towards the centre of the space that I realized I was looking at a spiral. The madness had a shape, and a growing strength.

The heretics close to us were still dazed from the concussion. We started killing them. We brought order to the death in the hall. We also brought purity. We would cleanse this place. We would scour it from the eye of the galaxy, in the name of the Imperial Creed. The Sisters of Battle punched through the cultists like a ceramite fist. We spread out behind them, killing everything that stood, extending the radius of clean, lethal justice as more of our force climbed up from below.

The moment of surprise ended. The cultists retaliated. They rushed at us with a delight ferocious as a welcome, glad we had come, and intimate as hunger. They were making noises that were part shriek, part laughter, part something else. Their tongues had been altered. They gabbled words that sounded like nonsense, but whose awful meaning was eroding reality around us. Their hoods were thrown back. They were proud of what had become of their faces. I could call them human only because that was what they had once been, and there was no name for what they were becoming. They were scarred and mutilated with runes carved all the way down to the bone. They were mutating, too. The skulls of some were sprouting tumours of bone. Others had elongated jaws, teeth that were growing into tusks, skin that hung from their scalps all the way down their backs, eyes that were stretching across their foreheads to meet as one. They came to drag us down into the cauldron of their change.

We cut them down, firing faster than they could close with us. Within seconds, we turned our immediate area into a slaughterhouse. I was aware of a growing desperation in the retaliation of the Mortisians. I understood. The ones who had fought in the depths of the Ecclesiarchal palace had encountered and survived the taint that was reaching for us. They knew its full danger, and did not want to face it again. The others were even more terrified as their understanding of the universe crumbled. They fought to deny, to kill a form of knowledge that was purely and simply damnation.

Yes, I understood. But terror and desperation were fuel for Chaos. 'Hold fast!' I called. 'Be strong in your faith! Purge the heretic with anger, but also with discipline.' I stepped outside of the line, grabbed the first heretic that came near and threw him to the ground. I brought my sword down on his neck, severing it, then strode away from the body in contempt, putting a shell through the next attacker. 'They are less than nothing!' I said, and I knew what I said to be true.

What I did not know was just how dreadful that truth was.

We formed a wide wedge behind the Sisters of Battle. We advanced towards the centre of the great hall of madness. The heretics threw themselves at us, but without firearms, they could not come near. We smashed engines of torture. Two of the troopers had flamers, and they unleashed a cleansing incineration. We were midway to our goal. I couldn't identify any of the figures on the dais. All I could make out in the gloom from this distance was a high level of deformity. The very air was distorting like twisted glass, but we kept moving forward, and all around us the cultists died.

Still they came at us. Still they howled and chanted and raged and... and called. They called. The repeated syllables gathered meaning about them. *Ghalshannha. Ghalshannha. Ghalshannha.* It was a name. It was an invocation. The call was answered. The cultists were less than nothing, just shapes. Empty vessels, waiting to be filled. So now they were. Some of the wretches ran towards each other instead of at us. They collided. They tangled. They fused. They screamed, first in the ecstasy of their dark faith, then in agony. Then their voices were replaced with a single one that merged laughter with mad sermons. The bodily forms melted together and grew, monstrous pink tearing through robes and the degraded remnants of a noble house's livery. The materium wailed as daemons tore through its veil. To our left and right they came, loping and hopping. They were the same species as the daemon in the palace, but they had their own form of fluid identity.

There were four of them.

Their mere existence was the first great blow. It had still been possible, for the average trooper, to cleave to the perception that the heretics were human. Now the order of things had been rent asunder. 'Destroy the xenos filth!' I thundered. My order was a lie, but one hurled against an even greater one. We fought a lie that sought to render everything about the Imperium senseless. And if my lie gave our soldiers a fraction more strength, then it was a worthy one. Perhaps I granted some of them a few more seconds of sanity. Others were beyond saving. They shrieked at what came for them. They stopped marching, dropped their weapons, and stood there, mouths agape, minds gone. They were nothing now but screams made of flesh.

Beside me, Seroff had gone still. He muttered fragments of prayer. Still firing, I grabbed his arm with my left hand. I shook him. 'Commissar Seroff!' I yelled. 'Recall yourself. You are needed.'

His litany became a groan of horror, but he shook himself free and raised his pistol again.

The mad were the first to die. The daemons were upon us in two more leaps. Their cackling sermons intertwined, forging a rope of meaning that tightened its noose around my consciousness. More troopers descended into madness. The daemons scooped up their prey. A doomed soldier in each hand, they took their time, smiling and speaking to their victims with their flowing, shifting mouths before they began to eat. They began with the arms. Blood and horror rained down on the rest of us.

The Mortisians fought back, Saultern leading the attack with such desperation that it was clear that violent action was the only thing keeping him sane. The daemons grumbled in irritation. Not pausing in their meals, they danced away from the las-fire, then rolled back in, sprouting new arms to smash away the resistance. At their feet, the cultists rejoiced. They surged forward with renewed ecstasy. Our defences were shattered. The heretics fell upon us like a wave. We pushed back, firing at both daemons and humans, but the attack was overwhelming. Even as I shot an arm off the nearest daemon, freeing one of the troopers in its grip, another Mortisian to my left was brought down and ripped apart by three heretics. I ran them through with my sword with three quick thrusts. The daemon regenerated its arm, flesh and bone sprouting with a sickening series of liquid cracks, and grabbed itself a new plaything.

The reversal had taken seconds. The retaliation was as quick, and as brutal. The Sisters of Battle ceased their advance. They split into two groups, and came back along our flanks. They hammered the daemons with bolter fire, overwhelming their ability to maintain coherent form in the materium. With their helmets on, the Sisters of the Order of the Piercing Thorn were other than human. They were the strength of faith made manifest. They waded through the heretics, ignoring the assaults. Setheno towered over the other humans as if she were as much a myth as the monsters she fought. She trampled cultists beneath her boots, using the weight of her power armour to snap limbs and crush skulls with every stride. As she passed me, she said, 'Win this war, commissar.'

I was already using the momentum she and her Sisters had returned to us. 'Forward!' I cried. No speeches, then. The only goal was victory, so my only thought was to be the example, to be the symbol. If I fell, it had to be in the act of giving our charge an impulse that could not be arrested.

Reality was collapsing around us. Chaos had found a home in Karrathar, and it was reshaping the very stones of the fortress. Nightmares were ripping us limb from limb. We were only human, but we were the children of the God-Emperor, and we were His hammer, and that was enough. It would forever be enough. We stormed towards the dais. The daemons staggered under the onslaught of the Piercing Thorn. The cultists tried to drag us down. We stabbed and shot as we ran, and they could not slow us. Again I heard the roar of flamers. Their heat was the Emperor's blessing at my back. Their fire was wings, spreading through the enemy and propelling us on.

We were almost at the dais. I somehow recognized the figures on it as the ruling nobility of Mistral. Their robes still bore distorted parodies of their heraldry, just as their faces had just enough of their original appearance to make the transformations all the more monstrous. They were gathered around a bloodied victim shackled to an iron chair. Rasp. He was even harder to identify, not because of any mutation, or even because of the mask of blood concealing his features. It was his slumped, broken posture that turned him into a stranger. If not for the remains of his uniform, I would not have known who the victim was.

I fired as I ran, aiming for the barons to the side. Eichen's head exploded. His massive, bloated corpse collapsed, rolls of fat slapping against the dais like an upended cart of fish. Vahnsinn snarled. He moved away from Rasp, towards the front of the dais. He spread his arms as if to welcome our charge into his embrace. 'To me!' he bellowed. The sound was ghastly, a bubbling, slippery roar emerging from a face that was little more than gaping absences behind torn draperies of flesh. He was a raging skull, his lidless eyes round with unending, furious madness. At his cry, the other barons joined him. They linked hands on either side of him. They took his.

I was only steps away. What happened took three beats of my pounding heart. Yet my memory has chosen to wallow in the dark luxury of the event in its every detail. The electric jerk that ran from Vahnsinn, through the other barons. The flowing of flesh, turning clasped hands into a single limb. Gotho's cane, a muscle-covered bone, becoming a third leg as her body lost definition. The barons *deflated*. Their obeisance to their leader took on its ultimate form. They had acted in accord with a single will since they had sacrificed Lom. They had been one in mind and spirit. Now they were in body. I have wondered since if Gotho and the others understood what they were surrendering to Vahnsinn, if they really knew the terms of their bargain. Had they planned to abandon all identity in the service of the forces they worshipped? I cannot believe that they had, at least at the start.

Of course, at the start, they had likely wanted nothing more than a redress of grievances. They had turned from one turbulent priest to another, and so brought an end to themselves and the world they ruled.

Vahnsinn gasped in triumph. He grew to twice his original height. His arms were monstrous, tongue-coloured tentacles four metres long and ending in grasping talons. From them hung what was left of the other barons: pennants of flesh on which things like faces snarled. He swept his arms together. I saw the spikes of bone protruding from the skin. I ducked and rolled beneath his grasp. I rose to a crouch and shot upward. The shell tore through Vahnsinn's torso and kept going, blasting stone chips from the ceiling. The baron's being, though more stable in form, had some of the same mercurial properties as that of the daemons. His flesh was changing, failing and reforming from one moment to the next. It was both cancer and river, and my shots caused nothing more than ripples.

Behind me, I heard the *chunks* of punctured flesh and shattered bone as some of the other soldiers were not fast enough. Seroff hit the floor beside me with a thud. His scalp hung in a flap down the right side of his skull. Krauss grunted. Vahnsinn lifted him high, the claws of one hand digging through the inquisitor's armour. Krauss fired his needle gun into the arm. Vahnsinn hissed. His arm lost strength. He began to lower Krauss. He pulled back his other fist to the full extent of his reach, then sent the barbed horror smashing into Krauss's face. The puncturing crunch was horrific. Krauss slumped. Vahnsinn jerked his hand free. Krauss's head rolled forwards, pouring blood. Vahnsinn pulled his fist back again. A shadow leapt up and grabbed it. Vercor's bionic grip crushed the baron's fingers together. She shattered the shape of the fist and arrested the movement of the blow.

Snarling, Vahnsinn snapped his arm like a giant whip. He threw Vercor against the ceiling. He caught her in a constrictor coil as she dropped, stunned. He squeezed. And I leapt onto his back and rammed my sword through his skull. At first, his grasp on Vercor didn't weaken. He cursed me, his words still almost human. He jerked his head to the side. I moved with it, keeping the blade through the centre of what had been his brain. I sawed back and forth, twisted the blade. His ranting stuttered. His movement became erratic, jerking. He dropped Vercor. He tried to shake me off. Moment by moment, his flesh shifted, but at every moment, the sword was there, always tearing, always severing. He twitched, then fell to his knees. His spasms were so violent, it was as if he were losing fragments of time, the transition between one position and the next vanishing. At last, his head twisted all the way around. There was nothing that could be called a face there any longer, though there were eyes, and there was a mouth.

The eyes, blood-shot, crazed, focused on me. They seemed to clear. They shifted to a sight beyond the veil of the materium, and they filled with a tragically human understanding. The mouth worked. Through blood and muscle Vahnsinn said, 'Oh. Now I see.' Though the man I had met in Tolosa resurfaced at the last, there was no repentance. There was, instead, a renewed commitment to the cause he had embraced. 'I am yours,' he said to a god false and dark.

His eyes went dull. He was dead, but he did not fall. His body began to tremble. The fabric of reality, already badly frayed, began to rip apart. The wound began inside Vahnsinn. I felt the build-up of energy. The change of Vahnsinn's being did not stop with his death. It accelerated, racing towards revelation. I had just yanked the sword from the baron's skull when the first shock hit. I flew backwards, struck by a coil of unlight that slashed out of Vahnsinn's body like a scorpion's sting. I travelled through alternating frames of the real and the immaterium. Pieces of non-time tried to tear my being apart. I felt the ripple travel through my frame. I had a consciousness of my every bone and cell, and if I did not hang onto each individually, they would be ripped from me. The self that was Sebastian Yarrick came under attack. It would have taken very little to lose it all. It took much to keep it. But I was here for the Emperor, and I would not fail Him. My sense of mission unified my sense of self.

All of this while I was in the air. Time starting and dying. The world existing and squirming. Then I hit one of the support pillars. The pain of the impact was a relief. It was real. I was winded and stunned, and those were conditions of the materium. I knew how to struggle with those. I rose, ready to fight. Krauss and Vercor were unmoving. In my near vicinity, the Mortisians were sending the cultists to oblivion, though the tide of enemy filth had not yet ebbed. There was a demented howl of frustration as one of the daemons disintegrated, its material form hammered to nothing by the Sisters of Battle before it could split into two creatures. There were losses on both sides, yet in this moment, we were the ones clawing towards victory.

But the true enemy still had not arrived on the battlefield.

CHAPTER 19
THE HERALD

1. Yarrick

The dais stormed with corrupted lightning. I could see nothing but a vortex of colours, colours with teeth, colours that devoured each other, colours that were disease itself. The lines between possibility and paradox collapsed. For a moment, we were all breathing blood and bone. I stared at the ecstatic murder of meaning, and I fired at it. I pulled the trigger to affirm my belief in the battle. If I struggled, I declared my faith. I did not rely on my own strength, but on the undying power of the Emperor. I fought for Him, and so I pulled the trigger. The bolt shells evaporated on contact with the vortex. I had known they would. I was defiant. That was enough. And I would kill whatever emerged from that storm.

The sight that tore at my eyes and soul was the storm of thought itself. My mind recoiled as pieces of concepts and snarling abstractions whirled past. Then the gale coalesced. It was no less violent, but it was taken in hand, forced into a coherent form. There was a sudden contraction, and the enemy stood revealed before us. It shone the same toxic pink as the other daemons. Its flesh rippled and flowed as theirs did, but on a frame that was more defined. Where the other daemons were amorphous, their arms too flexible, this one had a frame with the angularity of bone. Two massive horns, almost as long as its torso, jutted from the top of its skull. It was robed. Its finery was far beyond what even the nobles had been wearing. The being had pride.

For a moment, I was reminded of Wangenheim's elaborate Ecclesiarchal attire, and the war in Mistral resolved itself into the struggle between two priests. But Wangenheim, though faithful, in his way, to the Imperial Creed, had only truly been concerned with his own secular power. The garb of the daemon meant something real. It was a much more committed servant of its obscene god than Wangenheim had been to the Emperor, and we were all paying for that difference. The designs on the daemon's robes were also far more intricate than any human could achieve. They were a river of patterns, pulling the viewer's eye from one change to the next. They hinted at great knowledge.

If one could follow the pattern, one would read of changes to come. In one hand, the daemon carried a long staff. It was metal, segmented, and ended in a U-shaped clockwork, with arrows pointing in conflicting directions. Suspended at the centre of the mechanism was the tear-shaped symbol I had seen in Lom's hidden chapel. Some deep, primeval instinct reacted to the sight of that staff, and I knew the device was not for the telling, but the *foretelling*, of time. Another hand held a book. This was a massive tome, ornate, bound in skin. Living skin, for at the centre of the cover was an eye that always looked in the opposite direction of the daemon's gaze. Its third hand was free, and grasping.

The dais, too, had transformed or been replaced. The daemon still stood on a circular platform, but this one was alive. It was a quivering, flattened, slavering thing, bound by metal, surrounded by blades.

All around us, the cultists screamed the daemon's name. *Ghalshannha, Ghalshannha, Ghalshannha*. Those three syllables were the only things they seemed capable of uttering now, as they threw themselves at us with renewed ecstasy. Even the other daemons joined in the chant, and for the first time, I found, to my horror, that I could understand their babblings. *Ghalshannha, Ghalshannha, Ghalshannha.*

The snarling disc rose. Ghalshannha raised its arms high. It spoke. It spoke to every breathing soul in the hall. It spoke to the entire galaxy. Yet it also seemed that it spoke to me, and to me alone. Its voice shook the walls, and it whispered deep inside my ears. 'There is no chance!' it cried and murmured. 'There is only the unfolding of inevitable change. You have walked towards this moment since your birth. You swam a green tide to reach this glory,' it said, and though I did not understand the words, they jabbed at something in my subconscious. 'Accept what is destined. Revel in the ephemeral. The only eternal is transformation.' It looked down at Rasp, still shackled, though the chair was now as much cartilage as it was iron. The daemon wrapped a fist around him.

Still reeling from the double blow of my brush with warp energy and my collision with the pillar, I had been sinking into a morass of slowed time. Rasp's scream shattered the spell. I leapt forward again. The disc caught my chest as it rose. I was lying between the saw-edges of metal teeth as long as my arm. My elbows were on the leathery hide of the monster. The weight of my legs tried to drag me back down. The teeth sliced through my coat and my flesh, cutting towards my ribs. Blood poured down my lower torso. I kept my grip on my pistol and sword, and used my arms to drag myself forward.

Ghalshannha looked down at me as if I were an amusing species of insect. The disc began to spin. The daemon cocked its head in mocking challenge. It tightened its grip on Rasp. The lord commissar's shrieks were no longer human. They were the embodiment of madness itself. The daemon did not appear to be injuring him physically. It was hurting him in some other way, subjecting him to a torture that transcended the body.

The disc spun faster. It made snarling, screeching noises, and I believe that it was laughing at me, at all of us who thought we could defy its master. The battle in the hall whirled past me with increasing speed. I caught glimpses of war and hell. I was shown what was promised to the entire galaxy. I saw the torture garden that the warp would make of the materium, the incandescent insanity that would be added to the nightmare of war. Chaos would come to teach us a new definition of the sublime, and no mind or soul would survive that revelation.

The cultists kept coming at the Mortisians, a flood of rats swarming over angry dogs. Another daemon was overwhelmed by the Sisters of Battle, but not quickly enough, and it split into the lesser blue creatures. One of them opened a mouth over a metre wide. It leapt at Sister Genebra. The disc whirled me away from the tableau. When it flashed the sight before me again, Genebra's decapitated corpse was falling slowly to its knees, while the daemon laughed with its mouth full. Around again, and Setheno was riddling the abomination with bolter shells at point blank range while she hacked at it with her sword.

I dragged myself forwards. The teeth scraped away at my flesh. My centre of gravity tilted towards the disc. My legs were no longer heavy enough to pull me off, so I raised my pistol and fired at the arm that held Rasp. I emptied half the clip. The daemon's tissue was a mixture of warp-stuff and the raw material of Vahnsinn. Ever changing, ever flowing, it was held in shape by a hideous will. Powerful as it was, the will was not strong enough to stand up to the repeated impact of the shells. It parted. Something that pretended to be bone shattered. I severed the limb at the joint. The forearm fell to the disc. It released Rasp and writhed as it evaporated. Rasp hit the edge of the teeth, rolled once, sliced and gouged, and fell to the floor of the hall. He lay still.

Ghalshannha roared. In pain? I don't know. In anger, certainly. I had enraged the daemon, and that was already a victory. My triumph lasted only long enough for me to realize it had happened. The stump of an arm withdrew into the daemon's torso. The book snarled. A new arm burst out of the centre of Ghalshannha's chest. It seized me and lifted me high.

The universe opened up before me, and I knew why Rasp had screamed. To touch the daemon was to touch the skein of time, and now the skein was a noose around my neck, throttling me with ultimate revelation. The course of all that was to come assaulted me. At first, there was only the battering so overwhelming that it numbed. Hit with too much knowledge, my mind rejected all of it, and turned towards the salve of oblivion. But there were no screams to be had there, no delights for my torturer. And so the events acquired focus. They became the history that would make sense to me. I was shown my future, and that of the Imperium.

I was shown, but I did not look. As the visions gathered precision, as the battering became a stiletto, I realised what was coming. I refused it. With all the strength of will and faith, I refused. I denied. I turned my face away. It was like moving a mountain with my bare hands. The weight was beyond measure. The force was a law of the universe. My being wavered. The power was too great. I was only a man. What could I do against change? Who, apart from the immortal Emperor Himself, can resist it?

No one. But what need was there for someone else? The Emperor is without change. He is our bulwark eternally, and He was mine then. I did not ask that He shield me from the knowledge that sought to claw me apart. Nor did He. But He was the reason for my battle. From my earliest memories at the schola progenium to the agonies of Armageddon and beyond, I have devoted every iota of myself to the preservation of the Imperium and to unwavering service to the Emperor. I had come in the name of the absolute truth of the Imperial Creed, and what could this monster's lies matter to me? I found the will. I turned to the Emperor. I embraced the great virtue of ignorance. I shut my eyes to the cancer of knowledge.

I. Will. Not. Look.

Futures possible, impossible and inevitable came at me. They laid siege to my defences. I knew I must fight back or fall.

Fight it. Fight the unholy thing and its visions.

I resisted what would be shown to me, reducing it to slivered, rampaging glimpses. But I could not see the world. I could not see to fight. I could not act. I wasn't strong enough.

What is Will but the strength of Faith? What gives Faith its strength if it is not Will?

Not strength of will, I realized, but strength *in* will.

Become Faith. Become Will.

Yes.

Dimly, I could see the physical world. My body, Ghalshannha, the hall: they were all the ghosts of traces. Still, I could see them. And there was something I could see with greater clarity, something that had a presence in both the world of sequential time, and the hell in which I was held. In the centre of Ghalshannha's forehead, between the horns, an eye had formed. The iris was black, the pupil crimson, and that pupil was an abyss, a vortex of bleeding pasts and martyred futures. It looked into me, and it wished to devour me. If I fell, it would be into that molten centre.

Fight.

Become Will.

Yes.

I.

Will!

I raised my right arm. I tightened my finger on the trigger. I fired into the pupil of that eye. I shot first with desperation, and then, because I had fought, could fight, *did* fight, I shot with exhilaration. I emptied my clip into the accursed gaze. I blasted knowledge to nothing.

Perhaps the shells themselves were able to cause physical damage now that the monster had manifested itself in the materium. Perhaps they were simply symbols of my will. No matter. Dark ichor erupted from the eye. Ghalshannha screamed. *Screamed*. I exulted, and perhaps in doing so, I let my defences down a fractional amount. Something got through to me. My left eye and right arm exploded in agony. Glowing steel in the eye, a monster's jaws on my arm. The pain was ice and fire and lightning and terrible absence. It was, at that moment in my life, the most intense torture I had experienced.

But the pain I had caused the daemon was greater. It threw me to the ground. It shrieked its outraged injury, and through my own wounds I let out a single, harsh bark of laughter. I had forced the daemon to break contact with *me*.

'An end to gifts!' Ghalshannha roared. 'An end to all!' It rose higher. Its anger and pain made the air brittle. The erosion of Karrathar accelerated. The pillars wavered. They began to melt. The ceiling glowed with a spider-web of cracks. Chunks of stone fell. The fragments were wet with deliquescent reality. Still raging with pain, Ghalshannha raised the book and staff high. A wave of force rippled out from the disc. It struck us all. It was wracking change. My skeleton tried to wrench itself free of its shape and fall into endless becoming. I held myself in, growling between gritted teeth. I fought off the mutating blast.

Many of us did. Many didn't. Mortisians and cultists alike fell, their shapes exploding in protoplasmic chaos. Heads became tails. Fingers turned into arms with fingers that turned into arms and so on, until a forest of limbs covered entire sections of the floor before falling to undifferentiated nothingness.

The Sisters of Battle resisted the change, but the blow staggered them, and another, Sister Marica, fell, crushed by the sudden, concerted rush of the two remaining daemons. Betzner dropped to his knees. His mouth was open in an unending, silent scream. His rocket launcher slipped from his shoulder. His hands rose to either side of his head. He clawed at something invisible, hovering a few centimetres from his skull. He was a saint trying to tear away his halo. Then his scream found expression in something other than sound. The halo became real. His head was surrounded by a massive ball of lightning. Energy sparked and crackled. His hands bracketed the lightning. With a reflex action so violent it dislocated his shoulders, his arms shot forward. The lightning followed his gesture and arced from him to Ghalshannha. It struck the daemon's book. Violet flames erupted from the tome. The book screamed as it vanished back into the immaterium. Ghalshannha echoed it with rage, and the disc's movement became erratic. It came closer to the floor.

Betzner collapsed. His body was wracked by micro-tremors.

The hall smeared. The cracks in the ceiling widened. Above the daemon's head, the stone began to twist.

'Feed me!' Ghalshannha commanded. It looked down as it spoke. Where the dais had been was a circular hole several metres in diameter. I realized that some of the chanting that still resounded throughout the hall came from there. I stumbled forward. The daemon was beyond my reach, but there was something important to it below. I stared into the sickly glow of a phosphorescent blood mist. I saw a chapel. I saw an altar that was constructed of barbed-wire thoughts. And I saw heretics sacrificing a line of chained victims. They were not simply butchering the martyrs. There was a ritual of some kind. Runes were being cut into the prisoners until they died.

A stream of pain and dying. Constant sacrifice. Something the daemon needed.

A weakness.

I lurched backwards, reaching for Betzner's rocket launcher. Behind me – and around me, and inside my head – Ghalshannha hissed satisfaction. It was wounded, but it was being fed. I had to starve the obscenity. I was too slow.

Setheno pounded past me, a blur of sanctity and force. The mutating floor shook with her footsteps like a frightened beast. 'Stand fast, abomination!' she shouted. Her sword and pistol were sheathed. The daemon, greedy for the great prize devouring her would be, brought the disc in low and reached out all three arms. It clutched the sister superior in a murderous embrace. She closed her gauntleted hands over two of the daemon's arms. Ghalshannha's growl was triumphant, but when it tried to move, she held its arms still. It reached out with its central one and wrapped its elongated fingers around her gorget. She began to tremble. Her entire frame vibrated. But she did nothing except clutch the daemon in an iron grip.

She was tearing time from the monster's clutches.

I had the launcher. I raced back to the hole. Every movement was a conscious, willed effort. Just as I reached it, a cultist hit me from the side. I fell. He clawed for my eyes. My body had been punished to the point of collapse, but I could not allow it that luxury. I would fight until the war was won or I was dead. Any other option was a defeat and betrayal of my oaths of office. I told my fingers to form a fist. I ordered the fist to swing. It slammed into the bridge of the wretch's nose. He howled and rocked backwards. I hit him in the throat, rendering judgement. He fell, mouth opening and closing like a fish, dragging for air that would never be his again. I left him to die and crawled to the edge of the hole.

Setheno's trembling threatened to send her armour flying apart. She was silent. Ghalshannha was laughing. Snakes of eldritch energy arced from the daemon to the Sister of Battle. I had torn myself from the creature's grasp, refusing its vision, but Setheno's refusal was to release the daemon. A terrible price was being paid a few metres from me.

I raised the rocket launcher to my shoulder. I aimed at the altar, at the greatest cluster of cultists and victims. Reality swam before me. My left eye was watering from the stabbing pain, but the flux was more than my own damaged vision. The stability of the materium was flowing away from Karrathar and into the form of Ghalshannha. Vertigo seized me. I was standing on the edge of a maelstrom. In another moment, it would take all my will just to hang onto the integrity of my being. Movement would be impossible.

But in this moment, movement was imperative. It was duty. I willed it. I thought past the agony of my right arm. I pulled the trigger.

The rocket flashed into the chapel. It struck the base of the altar. The blast concussion rocked the hall, and the floor heaved. A fireball filled the confined space as flames erupted from the opening. Heat and force smashed me to my back. The blossom of fire engulfed the disc; it shrieked and plummeted to the floor, spilling Ghalshannha and Setheno. Raging, burning, the daemon raised Setheno high and hurled her away. Setheno's death grip tore the daemon's right hand from its wrist. She collided with an ornate torture rack, smashing it to bits. Her trembling ceased. She lay still.

Smoke poured from the daemon's body. So did vapours of another sort. Its scars were not healing. Its movements were jerky. I had destroyed its nourishment, and it was losing its hold on its material form. My legs had become a foreign country, but my hands were not so distant that I couldn't still command them. My left hand fumbled at my belt for a fresh clip. My fingers were clumsy, drunk. The clip tried to slip from between them.

Ghalshannha turned its furious gaze from the fallen Setheno to me. Its torn limb did not heal.

I tried to slap the clip home. I missed.

The daemon took a step towards me. Its teeth were bared in rage. But it was also looking at me with something like curiosity. *'You are not his hand,'* it hissed.

The clip went in. *Shoot,* I told my right hand. But the pain was turning into paralysis. The absence was growing. There was nothing below my right elbow.

'You will not be his hand,' the daemon promised.

My teeth clenched with effort, I fought the lie of the paralysis. I *did* have an arm. I raised it. I wrapped my left hand around my right, numbness clutching a phantom. I squeezed. I could not feel the trigger.

Ghalshannha reached out with its chest arm. Its massive claws came at my head. No games now. No dark mysteries to reveal. Only violent death.

I squeezed again. The pistol fired. The shells blew the hand apart. A pink miasma of warp matter shrouded me, crackling. I squeezed again, fired again, and again and again. The daemon stopped, jerked and rocked, its mass real and solid enough to trigger the explosive damage of the shells. I shot away chunks of its body. I injured it.

Be the symbol. Be the example.

'The foe will die!' I shouted. 'Now! All of us, *now!*'

I was heard. As I fired, another stream of bolter shells punched into the daemon's form. Setheno had risen to her knees. Her attack was eerie, as if a mortuary statue had joined the fray. And then my call was answered by every warrior of the Imperium still drawing breath. A barrage of shells and las struck Ghalshannha. The attack was a storm of light and rage and faith. The daemon tried to take another step. It raised its staff as if to call our doom down on our heads. We denied it everything. We did not falter, though we paid for our singleness of purpose. Heretics still attacked. There was still another daemon present, and it pressed its advantage as the Sisters of Battle ignored it in favour of the greatest enemy. Adepta Sororitas and Mortisians died, but they died in a moment of selfless pride. They were martyrs to a victory against a force that had held the fate of an entire planet in its grasp.

Ghalshannha screamed. It burned and shrank. Its staff shattered. Its legs gave out. It collapsed to the ground. For one last time, it glared at me. For one last time, it spoke in my head.

'You are his hand, then. He did not let me see. Do you think you will see, at the end?'

It rocked its head back. I shot away its lower jaw. Its scream changed into something greater, more awful, and final. It became the howl of dreams and reality dying together. A light, dark as rotting blood but bright as agony, grew at its core. It burst out of the daemon. It engulfed its form. With a final cry, Ghalshannha was devoured by its own Chaos, and fell back into the immaterium.

The daemon was gone. The howl was not. It grew. The light reached up to the ceiling. The twist in the rock accelerated. It spun itself into a funnel that reached down into the consuming light. The damage done to Karrathar was irreversible. A storm in the real had formed. The hall began to whirl around the vortex that would swallow the war.

CHAPTER 20
CYCLONE

1. Schranker

The scream hit the battlefield. It struck all the combatants. Veteran Sergeant Schranker knew this because when the claws of ice plunged into her soul, and brought her to her knees, she was not killed by a heretic in the next second. She gasped in pain, helpless for a full second, but in the next she fired her shotgun into the crush of the foe before her. She couldn't see until the second after that, as she struggled to her feet. She hadn't seen her targets, but she had killed them anyway. They were as prostrate as she had been. One no longer had a head. They were not fighting back. They were writhing on the ground, clawing at their own faces. She holstered the shotgun, revved her chainsword, and waded in. There was no resistance to her slaughter. In some faces, she thought she might even have seen a hint of relief as the blade cut through soft tissue and bone to shred vital organs. Around her, the other Mortisians were picking themselves up and washing the slopes of the pass with the blood of the foe.

Until the scream the battle had been a quagmire. Schranker had lost all sense of direction. But now she could see that she had advanced towards the end of the pass. Further ahead, Colonel Granach walked from cluster to cluster of prone wretches, pumping bullets into their skulls. His gait was stiff from his injuries, and he lurched from the dizzying blow of the scream. But he was walking. She decapitated the last of the heretics near her and struggled to his position, negotiating a terrain knee-deep in bodies, most dead, some still squirming. All those she crossed were still after her passing.

A nucleus of organization was forming around Granach when she arrived. There were a few other surviving sergeants. The regiments were shaking off the worst of the scream, and finding that victory had arrived with as much surprise as the ambush.

'Our comrades have completed their mission,' Granach announced.

Schranker looked at the fallen heretics. 'But how–' she began.

Granach cut her off. 'Don't ask.' More quietly, he said, 'By the Throne, sergeant, don't seek answers to this. I promise you they won't be healthy.'

'Yes, colonel.' She rubbed her head. 'I can still hear that... that sound.'

'So can I.'

'Do you think...' She trailed off as a glow in the sky caught her eye. She realized that the echo she heard wasn't in her head.

'Sergeant?' Granach asked.

She pointed, but he had already turned. He saw it too. Everyone did. Over the nearest line of peaks, where Karrathar waited, the clouds were glowing with the reflected light of corruption. Their rotation was already violent. The formation was both storm and wound.

'Well?' Granach called. 'What are you all waiting for? There lies our new battle.' He gave a brief, despairing laugh, and then he said, 'To war, Mortisians! If we're going to die, hadn't we better spit in the enemy's face?'

2. Yarrick

Get up.

I couldn't. I'd had enough. The foe on Mistral was dead. That was enough, wasn't it?

Get up.

The intensity and movement of the light increased. A great wind roared through the hall towards the heart of the wound. The hall was spinning, spinning, spinning, and it was no illusion, no vertigo.

Get up. You are not relieved of duty.

I rolled onto my side, then onto my knees. My eye and arm still throbbed, but the paralysing absence was fading. I had the use of my body again, and I stood. I would not die here. I had not finished my fight for the Emperor. And I was not a lone soldier. I was a commissar. I had charges. I would not let the warp devour them.

Fighting Mistral's darkest wind, I staggered to Rasp's side. I knelt beside him. He was still breathing. I draped one arm over my shoulder. A few metres away, Seroff had found his feet. Blood still coursed freely down his face. I could see bone showing at the top of his skull. His eyes were glazed, but he moved to Rasp's other side. We began to drag him away.

The retreat from the vortex began. The heretics lay everywhere. The psychic feedback of their false god's dissolution had killed them. The nearest bodies began to slide along the floor, caught by the gravity of the storm. But there was still one daemon. It moved to block the exit to the upper levels of the castle. The way we had come was already closed to us. As the floor shifted and flowed, the collapse had become a site of foaming stone. We would be crushed if we went anywhere near that uproar.

The daemon's lunatic babble was inflected with desperate rage. It attacked with the fury of a combatant who knows its war is lost. It would make our victory a bitter one. It rushed forwards. Sister Basilissa was too close. She had barely turned from adding her fire to the banishing of Ghalshannha when the daemon was upon her. She put three bolter shells into the monster before her clip ran dry. She slashed at the daemon with her blade, roaring her defiance, and then it rolled over her. It knocked her down. Its entire lower half turned into jaws that snapped over her power armour. Ceramite and bone crunched. Her fellow Sisters tried to help. The daemon absorbed shells, weathering damage and refusing to release its prey. Then there was the muffled *crump* of an explosion. The daemon and Basilissa were torn apart. She had fought the daemon with the same final ferocity that it had used against her. She had managed to pull the pin on a frag grenade in her belt.

The way was clear, only nothing was clear. Perspective spun and tilted. My centre of gravity shifted with every passing moment, and it was always towards the vortex. Stone was screaming as it was pulled into the maw of unreality. Rock bled. Corpses cracked and crumbled. There had been such extremity of suffering here that it had permeated the walls and floor and ceiling. Karrathar itself was a final, worthy sacrifice to the hunger of the warp. I had to focus on each step to make sure that Seroff and I were moving in the right direction, and not walking back to our dissolution.

The funnel of light and destruction grew in size and power. It wrapped us in the chains of its attraction. It sank hooks deep into us and pulled. I could see the steps up from the dungeons. I knew we were closer, yet they seemed further away, as if Karrathar were stretching out as its interior spun around the grasping wound. The corpses of the heretics tumbled past us. The taint of Chaos was everywhere. We were wading through a surging torrent of the irrational, and it continued to take its toll. More of the dwindling number of Mortisians had their victory stolen from them as their sanity died. They stumbled, and then were dragged wailing to the centre of the end.

Ghalshannha's scream had jerked Vercor and Krauss back to consciousness. They were just ahead of us, able to move on their own, though not much faster than Seroff and I could with our burden. Kortner had Betzner slung over his shoulders. He staggered under his weight, but kept his feet. Setheno was just behind me. She had the mechanical gait of a damaged servitor. She still wore her helmet. I did not know what damage she had suffered from being in extended contact with the daemon, but I was surprised she could walk at all.

We reached the stairs and started up. At first, the narrower confines of the staircase made the world a bit more stable. But as we climbed, the infection spread, the vortex spun, and the steps twisted until we were on a serpent's skeleton. Anyone who fell could bring down the rest behind. As we neared the first landing, the stairs rippled, and two more of the Mortisians lost their footing. They came down like a rockslide. They were dead after the first few bounces, their necks snapped. I shoved Seroff and Rasp towards the wall. The bodies fell past. A leg caught me with a hard blow. My balance crumbled, and I dropped to one knee. I felt the warm pulsing of stone. Our burden slid. I managed to keep my grip on Rasp, found the direction of the wall, and leaned back towards it. Then I could stand again.

We worked our way up from the dungeons to the ground floor of Karrathar. Though we moved further and further away from the heart of the corruption, we did not reach sane ground. By the end, Vahnsinn had turned all of his family seat into a carnival of depravity. The signs of torture dripped from the walls of every room and every corridor. Rituals had carried on even during the battles down below. Furniture had been stacked, smashed and burned. The portraits on the walls had been defaced with sigils that now glowed like phosphorescent bruises. In every large space, there had been gatherings. Mutilated bodies were chained to the floor, arranged around thrones and lecterns. The teachings of Chaos had come through words and actions, and Karrathar had learned them well.

Reality spun faster yet. The storm followed us as it grew. When I risked another look behind us, what I saw was not the interior of a fortress. It was a tornado. The funnel was unlight, the colours of death and shrieking stone. It devoured the blood and latent agonies of the fortress. And we, who still lived, were the most succulent of prey.

In the entrance hall, we encountered two exits. To the left, a bay opened onto the maglev station. Straight ahead, the main doors to the courtyard and the road down the mountainside. Some of the Mortisians were already heading for the door. I looked at the tracks. The train was already rippling. It would be unusable. But the tracks would still get us away from Karrathar faster than the alternative.

At worst, we might fall to our clean deaths.

'Left,' I tried to shout, but my voice was too weak. Setheno heard me. She repeated the command through her helmet's vox-caster. Even allowing for the electronic distortion, her voice was wrong. It was the sound of an empty tomb. Bellavis picked up and amplified the command with rote, near-mindless repetition. His movements and reactions were so mechanical, I didn't know if anything of the human or sentient still functioned inside his bionics.

We struggled through the pitching, spinning real and through the hangar doors. The track was buckling, but we took it. At our backs, the agony of the dying real was the howl of a wounded beast, big as a Titan. I did not look back. I did not dare, but Sister Gema did. What she saw rooted her just long enough for it to seize her.

We tried to run. Seroff and I stumbled faster. My legs were foreign to me again. All my body was. The torn lungs, the beaten frame, the full weakness of flesh pushed too far – none of this belonged to me. It was a vehicle for my will, and it demanded the body keep going.

The track stretched out ahead of us, gradually descending towards the valley floor. It was impossibly thin. It was a ribbon of squirming metal. It would throw us to the void below. We had no choice, and we took it. The roar behind us was deafening. It was eagerness and greed, anger and desire, terror and pain, and the molten fragments of every annihilated future. We were going at a crawl. The coming destruction was a wave. I could feel its shadow towering over us. The next second would be our last.

It wasn't. The next second took us out of the shadow. We were beyond the splashed aura of blood sacrifices. There came the greatest howl yet, and though its echoes still come to me in moments where I make the mistake of imagining myself at peace, it pleases me to think that I heard frustration in that terrible warp-throat.

The maglev track snapped. To the rear, it was whipped into the vortex. Where our party struggled, it coiled over itself. The surface beneath our feet lifted. We fell. I dropped Rasp's arm and tumbled forward. Kortner was thrown sideways. Betzner slipped from his shoulders as he pitched over the edge of the track. I managed to grab Betzner, the strain sending a burst of pain through my right arm again. Kortner was just out of reach. I saw his face in that last moment. He was proud of his fight. I hope that pride stayed with him all the way to the ground.

There was no more running. There was only the reckoning. I looked back. I watched Karrathar's death. The vortex reached from the centre of the mountain to the clouds. The outer walls of the castle bent, melted and flowed into the funnel. A dream of pure Chaos had come to Mistral. The storm spun on itself, a dance of final destruction. The howl was heard across the planet. It was the apotheosis of wind. It was culmination. It was judgement. It was the final consummation of the works of Vahnsinn and Wangenheim.

And it consumed itself. The fuel of sacrifice and unholy martyrdom ended. The materium reasserted its dominion as the cyclone grew thinner, wavered, shrank to a line, and vanished.

We were left with the night, the shattered mountain, and the wind. Always the wind. It pushed against us, an endless war, and it felt nothing at all like victory.

EPILOGUE

I was alone in the chapel tent when Setheno entered. I was sitting in the front pew, staring at the shrine to the Emperor, weighing choices.

We were bivouacked on the great plain, a short distance from the Carconne foothills, and midway between the ruins of Tolosa and the now-silent Vahnsinn manufactoria. The remnants of the 77th and 110th regiments awaited their relief. It was coming in the form of the 252nd regiment of the Armageddon Steel Legion. The cruiser *Scouring Rain* was already in-system. Granach would shortly be handing over military command of the planet. I wondered about his career. There would be little thanks coming his way for a victory such as this.

Nor would all the decisions regarding Mistral be in military hands. The final word would fall to Krauss. Once he had sufficiently recovered, he would evaluate how widespread Vahnsinn's toxin was in the rest of the population. From what I knew of that man, I wouldn't be surprised if he ordered Exterminatus.

I thought about the civilians of Tolosa. Millions of the Emperor's faithful. Not a single one saved. Would our bitter victory now be extended to the entire planet? That was not the choice I had to make, but I felt its shadow all the same. If I held a world's fate in my hands, I wanted to believe that I would not seek its salvation through its annihilation. I wanted to believe that I would find a way to fight on. To fight harder.

Setheno sat beside me. 'A Black Ship is coming,' she said.

'Yes.' I had expected as much. Betzner was a psyker. There was no choice in the matter. 'I'll speak to the trooper myself.'

'He won't resist?'

'He can barely move. But no, I warrant that he won't resist.'

'Very well. I have requested that you be kept informed of his fate, should he survive the scholastica psykana.'

'Thank you.'

'There is another matter.'

I turned my head to meet her gaze.

'You know what you have to do,' she said.

This was the first time we had spoken since the retreat from Karrathar. She had been in isolation, under the care of her surviving Sisters. Her armour had been cleaned, though the damage had yet to be repaired, and I could hear some grinding of servo-motors. Physically, she had recovered strength, but she had not emerged from her struggle with Ghalshannha unscarred. There was a new stillness to her face. She seemed to be denying herself all forms of emotion. The great wound was in her eyes. Her features were still those of the young woman she was, but the eyes were inhumanly ancient. They had once held flecks of gold. Now they were nothing but gold. They were filled with terrible knowledge. 'You looked, didn't you?' I said.

She nodded. 'I did.'

'Why?'

'I have always sought clarity to know how best to serve the Emperor.' She paused, then pronounced a sentence of enormous darkness: 'I have it now.'

I said nothing, but I understood. We had both fought the daemon with supreme exercises of our will. We had simply chosen different paths for the struggle.

'You must have seen some of the futures,' she said.

'Fragments. Much I don't understand.' Mirror shards tumbled before my mind's eye. On many of them was the suggestion of a huge, hulking form. There were no details. It was a blurry shadow. It troubled me with intimations of intelligence and savagery on an unimaginable scale. I flexed my right arm. It was still sore.

'Some you do understand, then.'

I didn't want to answer.

Setheno said, 'Lord Commissar Rasp broke.'

'Did you hear him renounce the Emperor? I didn't.'

She shrugged. 'His fidelity is not the issue.'

'Isn't it?'

'You must kill him.'

'I didn't pull him from Karrathar to put a shell in his brain.'

'Then you made your decision when we were in the keep.'

The flap of the tent parted and Sister Cabiria stepped in. Setheno acknowledged her, saying, 'I'll be with you in a moment, Sister.' She watched Cabiria as she withdrew, and for a moment, her face convulsed into a mask of pain.

'I am sorry about your Sisters,' I said. Less than half her squad remained.

'Thank you,' she said distractedly, and I realized she wasn't thinking about current losses. She rose to leave.

'Free will still counts for something. We are not foredoomed,' I told her.

She said, 'We must act as if we were not, true.'

'I don't believe that you saw only one future. Or all possible ones.'

'Nor do I.' Her face was still again, her voice that of a warrior as determined as she was implacable. 'But we must be certain we can live with the consequences of the ones we help bring about.'

'I am. I will give the lord commissar the same chance I choose for myself.'

'Be well with your choice, Commissar Yarrick,' she said. 'We shall speak again.' She left, walking a path shadowed with the deepest clarity.

I prayed before the shrine a few minutes more, then stepped out of the tent and into the Mistralian twilight. It seemed to me that the wind had a hollow tone. It had nothing but ruins to blow through now. The planet had lost its politics.

I made my way towards the medicae tent. I would spend some time by my mentor's side. As I walked, I saw Saultern speaking to the officers of the watch. The sight of the captain reminded me that I had begun my mission on Mistral with an act of mercy. I would be concluding it with another. I entertained the idea that the symmetry was a hopeful one. I allowed myself this luxury for several seconds before dismissing it, returning to the strength of my prayers, and to the truth that would sustain us all.

The truth was this: the Imperial Creed is a faith of many facets. It is a faith of discipline, of fire, of vengeance. Of will.

It has nothing to do with hope.

Extract from *Corax: Soulforge*
by Gav Thorpe

Three sleek Whispercutter landers skimmed across Atlas, the ten-man craft invisible in the last minutes of darkness. The Whispercutters were little more than winged anti-grav engines, the Raven Guard clinging to their sides exposed to the elements as they soared above the roofs of refineries and worker habitats. Dropped at high altitude from beneath the belly of a Stormbird, the landers were almost undetectable.

'Hard to port,' warned Stanz, shifting his weight.

Agapito clutched the grab rail tighter as the pilot harnessed in the guidance cupola just in front of the commander brought the lead Whispercutter into a tight turn, steering away from the centre of the city. The other two craft split towards their separate destinations, assigned during Agapito's briefing before they had left the *Kamiel*.

Below, Atlas was in turmoil. The headlights of a skitarii column moved along a main avenue towards the Third District, where three fires were burning; arson at empty ruins chosen by Corax to attract attention without putting the populace in needless danger. Here and there, not far from the blazes, the crack of gunfire echoed from the tenements and manufactoria. Las-fire sparkled from several rooftops, targeting one of the abandoned structures.

On the ground, squads of troopers moved from street to street, alley to alley, building to building. Most were normal men, raised under the aegis of the Mechanicum, dedicated to the cult of the Machine-God but otherwise unaugmented. Their squad leaders and officers were boosted, some through cybernetics and augmetics, some through gene-therapy and biological enhancement depending upon the temple and magos to whom they were sworn.

At the forefront of the search for the city's elusive attackers was a small cadre of praetorians. These were the favoured warriors of the Mechanicum, some sporting near-completely artificial bodies. Each was unique, whether sleek and fast or bulky and beweaponed, possessing energy-crackling blades or multiple rocket launchers. Led by lesser tech-priests in the hierarchy of Atlas, the praetorians were as much dedications to the Machine-God as they were flesh and blood fighters.

Looking down, Agapito was glad that Atlas – indeed, Constanix as a whole, as far as the intelligence went – had no herakli. The monstrous, heavily-gunned brutes that had assisted in the fighting against the tech-guild rebels during the latest insurrection on Kiavahr would have been a tough proposition to face. Even so, the enemy had tanks, armoured walkers and transports in abundance, though several companies of infantry were loyal to the magi allying themselves to Lord Corax. It was mainly these divided forces that were currently bearing the brunt of Magokritarch Vangellin's reprisal against the Third District.

Workers had been forced from their homes in the pre-shift hours, filling the streets with dazed, fatigued crowds that hindered both sides. To their credit, the skitarii of Vangellin were as unwilling as those of Loriark and his peers to endanger the non-combatants in the barge-city.

'What is the First Axiom of Victory?' Agapito asked Lieutenant Caderil, who was poised on the side of the Whispercutter behind the commander. A Terran veteran, Caderil would have made company command by now had the Legion not been devastated at the Dropsite Massacre. They exchanged over the vox-net – at this altitude the wind would have required them to shout over their external communicators.

'To be where the enemy desires one not to be,' replied Caderil.

Agapito turned his attention to another of the honour guard he had hand-picked for the mission. 'Harne, what is the First Axiom of Stealth?'

'To be other than where the enemy believes you to be,' came the legionary's sharp reply.

'So what do we do to gain victory by stealth?' the commander continued.

'Attack where the enemy does not want us to be, whilst feigning presence elsewhere,' said Caderil. He pointed towards the centre of the floating city. 'The main temple is our objective, but it is too well defended for direct assault. We have to draw out the enemy force, leaving the temple vulnerable to counter-attack.'

'Just like the Perfect Fortress,' said Harne.

'And Copatia, and Rigus Three, and lots of other places,' said Agapito. 'We don't have the numbers or firepower for a straight feint-and-attack here. Vangellin and his tech-priests won't deplete their defences unless they really need to, so our attack is a second diversionary assault. We have to make the enemy believe we're in much greater strength than we actually are.'

'The lord primarch gets the killing blow,' said Harne with a nod.

'I understand that.'

'It sounds like there's something you don't understand, Harne.'

'If the Word Bearers are on Iapetus, why are we fighting to take over Atlas?'

'Caderil, what is your explanation?' Agapito replied.

'A simple decapitation mission is unlikely to succeed without the element of surprise, and with the defences of the capital against us we lack the time needed to prepare a proper assault. Atlas is only achievable thanks to the presence of Loriark and his dissidents. There is no guarantee we would have any support on Iapetus. We simply don't have the numbers without the aid of the skitarii. Once we control Atlas, we have an established base of operations and also the firepower of a barge-city at our disposal.'

'And any skitarii that survive will likely side with the winners, regardless of who is commanding them at the moment,' added Shorin from the other side of the Whispercutter's narrow fuselage.

'A good assessment,' said Agapito.

'Four hundred metres from drop-point,' warned Stanz. The Whispercutter started dropping groundwards.

'Power up,' ordered Agapito. The whine of jump packs reverberated along the length of the lander as turbines spun into life.

KARRATHAR